the stark beauty

of last things

a novel

CÉLINE KEATING

SHE WRITES PRESS

"It shimmers with the dark radiance—
the stark beauty—of last things."
—EDWARD HIRSH

Published 2023
Printed in the United States of America
Print ISBN: 978-1-64742-577-7
E-ISBN: 978-1-64742-578-4
Library of Congress Control Number: 2023907949

For information, address:
She Writes Press
1569 Solano Ave #546
Berkeley, CA 94707

Interior Design by Tabitha Lahr
Map by Mike Morgenfeld

She Writes Press is a division of SparkPoint Studio, LLC.

Credits
An excerpt, the story "Home," was originally published in *Mount Hope* magazine. The story also won the first place Hackney Award for Fiction.

The first chapter of the novel won the Tucson Festival of Books first-place fiction award.

Epigraph from Edward Hirsch, taken from "A Never-Ending Hospital," a review of *Sloan-Kettering: Poems*, by Abba Kovner, *The New York Times Book Review*, September 22, 2002, used with permission.

*To the Concerned Citizens of Montauk,
and all those dedicated to preserving and
protecting the environment*

Montauk

N

Molly & Billy's
House

Fort
Ba

The
Moorlands

Hither Woods

Napeague Bay

Fresh Pond

Walking
Dunes

Bishops
by the Se
(Julienne & G
bungalow co

Napeague
Harbor

Hither Hills
State Park
(Clancy's after-
party swim)

The
Napeague
Stretch

To New York City

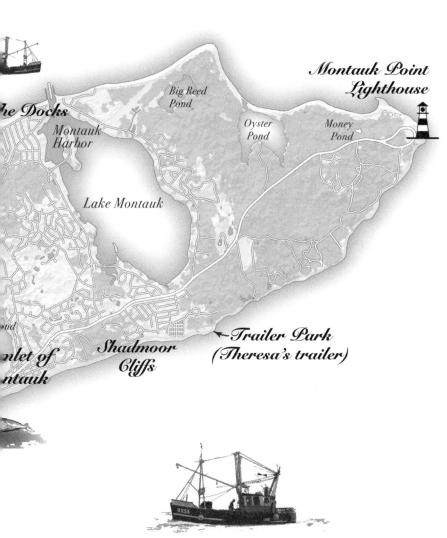

Montauk Point
Lighthouse

Big Reed
Pond

Oyster
Pond

Money
Pond

he Docks

Montauk
Harbor

Lake Montauk

←Trailer Park
(Theresa's trailer)

nd

nlet of
ntauk

Shadmoor
Cliffs

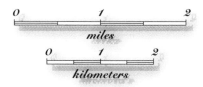

Atlantic Ocean

0   1   2
miles

0   1   2
kilometers

 *Early Autumn*

A NARROW ISTHMUS, a mere thread, connects the Montauk peninsula to the rest of Long Island, formed of piles of rubble left behind as the glaciers retreated eons ago. Here there are pockets of forest, scarred and fluted cliffs. Prairie grass still shimmers on the last acres of downs, and beach sand is streaked with dark-red garnet. Here there is land that has never been built upon, places with an unbroken chain from the time of the glaciers until now. So, when the white froth of ocean rises up and the sun's glow sets fire to the thin strand of cloud that rests like a ribbon along the horizon, it would be easy to believe nothing has changed, that all is as it was and will remain.

The hamlet of Montauk follows the seasons, from cold windswept winters to tourist-laden summers. Though it is now autumn, the sun bakes the earth as in the height of summer, and in the woods, the leaves refuse to turn. Migrating birds and fish linger past their time and whales wash up on shore. There is stillness, an uneasy hush, in the dry heat, the gusts of hot, swirling wind.

CHAPTER 1: Clancy

Clancy Frederics thought he knew everything he needed to know about the Hamptons—mainly that it was not the kind of place where he belonged. But so far, everything was a bit different from what he expected. After two hours of highway sprawl, there was suddenly a sharp bend in the road, an expanse of intense green, a small white church. The light faded from the sky, bronzing a brick post office and glazing a glass-fronted penny candy shop. Pillows of clouds drifted high over a field and caught the reflected light. He passed vineyards and farm stands and swooped around a blue gem of a pond, where a swan dipped to kiss its reflection. After the 100-plus miles of twenty-first century ruin that was Long Island, this oasis seemed false, the world turned upside-down.

As he pulled up at the Sandpiper restaurant on Napeague Bay outside the hamlet of Montauk, a sudden gust whipped off the bay, teasing the carefully coiffed heads of arriving partygoers. The breeze swirled the skirts of the women, who batted them down with one hand while clutching their purses with the other, laughing as they hurried to the door.

Clancy stepped from his car, arrested by the freshness of the air and the sharp briny tang, which teased his memory from long ago. The air was alive with specks of sand dust and pollen. It smelled of salt and something dry—dune grass or perhaps goldenrod. As he headed to the door, his footsteps crunched in a way that took a second to register: crushed clamshells.

The party was a fundraiser for a documentary on combating coastal erosion, newly severe at Montauk's downtown beach. An invitation from his friend Bruce had led Clancy to rent a car and drive the three hours from the city to get here. He was that desperate. Maybe he'd feel a stirring of interest—in a woman, in anything. The invitation was a sign: Fish or cut bait. Looking for signs was a habit left over from childhood, when he believed they were messages from his parents in heaven. In times of difficulty, he found himself searching for markers and omens, guidance about what he should do.

Now this. The façade of the restaurant glowed with a pink luminescence, the artsy lighting conveying a tone of understated elegance. The restaurant door, however, wouldn't give. He pushed harder. The door widened just enough for him to squeeze through the crush of partygoers, brushing up against tanned skin, silky garments, cascading hair. He gave his name to a slender woman, chic in a black dress, and made his way to the bar.

He gulped a beer as he watched the movement of women like birds of bright plumage in their cocktail dresses. People were clustered under fairy lights ensnared in glittery fishnets suspended from the room's cathedral ceiling. The lights swayed as the doors opened and closed, twinkling like undulating constellations above the guests' heads. He fidgeted with his tie, calmed by the knot snug against his throat, and kept an eye out for Bruce.

Bruce was a journalist for *You're Hot!* magazine. Clancy was an insurance claims adjuster. Despite their dissimilarities, he and Bruce had become close. Or Clancy knew, as close as he allowed himself to get. It was as if he had inherited a kid brother, the family that he, an orphan with no siblings, had never had. When Clancy's girlfriend Irene moved out the previous month, Bruce, who lived in the same apartment building in Astoria, had cooked him fiery chili and tried to fix him up with various women. It hadn't helped, but Clancy had to love him for it.

The alcohol had begun its slow calming magic when Clancy felt a hard slap, clinking his glass against his teeth. Bruce was his usual insouciant self, wearing a black shirt with garish swirls. Clancy, as always, was in chinos and carefully ironed denim shirt.

"Like it?" Bruce shoved a sleeve under Clancy's nose. The swirls consisted of words, upside down and sideways. "It says 'Fuck you' in twenty different languages."

Clancy laughed and shook his head.

A woman appeared from behind Bruce and slid an arm under his. "This," Bruce said, "is Dominique. She made all the arrangements."

"Hey." Dominique lightly touched Clancy's hand with her fingers. She was really Donna, Clancy knew, an aspiring actress working as an assistant to the filmmaker. She was quite tall, dressed in tight black capris and a white-sequined halter, which showed off glistening shoulders. Her hair was cut severely short, and she had large Bambi eyes. Clancy found her terrifying.

"So," Bruce said, sizing up their mutual lack of interest, "why don't I introduce you around?"

He led Clancy to a raised table in the back where the small documentary crew was settled. Everyone greeted Clancy and then went back to their conversation, buzzing about the Army Corps project. From what Clancy could gather, the project involved an artificial dune constructed of a heaping pile of sand-bags. Apparently, the Corps had excavated and damaged the natural dune, provoking outrage and a recent act of sabotage. The bags were slashed open, expelling coarse yellow sand.

Clancy downed his beer and felt the alcohol drift to the edges of his body, to all the nooks and crannies. He was only minimally conscious of the conversation, of Bruce's efforts to draw him in. An auburn-haired beauty offered him champagne from a tray of flutes, which he declined. With her shimmery green gown and wavy hair, she was like a mermaid flowing through dark and light shadows as she glided through the crowd. Around him people grouped and regrouped, like country dancers coming together, pulling apart, and puckering up. Kiss, kiss, kiss.

These partygoers were so young, so *on*. Clancy put his glass to his lips only to remember it was empty. He had to pace himself, to maintain the floating sensation, the pleasant distance. He snagged passing hors d'oeuvres, fending off self-pity. He'd resolved when he was young to never feel sorry for himself, and for the most part he'd succeeded. But Irene's departure had left him shaken, hollow in a way he hadn't felt since his parents' death. Lately he'd found himself drawn to his balcony, mesmerized by the movement of cars on Astoria Boulevard, craving the rush of air.

He excused himself and began a slow circuit around the restaurant, noting the polished wainscoting and the exquisite floral arrangements in large earthen vases set in recessed niches in the walls. Places like this used to make him feel out of his depth. But he had discovered he had the ability to escape notice, to radiate no heat.

He amused himself with guessing professions, all Hampton clichés: hedge-fund manager, art dealer, oyster shucker. Bruce had said there would be construction workers and surfers, politicians and town workers, schoolteachers and landscapers. The short-order cook was a volunteer fireman; the postal worker led a scout troop. Montauk, unlike the rest of the glitzy Hamptons, was that kind of town. *Realtor*, he decided, of an older woman in a silver sheath, as a tall young woman with a broad, smiling face and long, white-blond braid approached with a tray of scallops.

Silver Sheath pincered a napkin with two fingers of the hand holding her drink while lifting a scallop skewer with the other. "These storms are only going to get more frequent," she said to a woman in red, who arched away from the drippy sauce.

"A manufactured dune? Please." Woman in Red shook the ice cubes in her glass. "It's not about saving the beach; it's about protecting the motels."

A man in a blue blazer turned to the women. "The sandbag barrier will gain us time until we can retreat from the coast."

"Retreat?" A burly man pushed past Clancy. "Where are the businesses supposed to go? Sacrifice for the good of the community? I'll do that after I see you give up *your* house."

There was a crash, the sound of glass breaking, a second of shocked silence.

"What the—?" Man in Blue Blazer held up his hand, dripping with liquid.

People sprang forward to pull the burly man away as the film crew rushed over, camera bobbing. Shattered glass glistened on the wet floor. The blonde who had been serving the scallops reappeared with a broom and paper towels.

Clancy knelt and began scooping up shards. "What was all that about?" He took the dustpan from her hands.

"I'm not sure." She patted at the floor with a paper towel, her voice breathy with excitement. "That's the town supervisor whose drink got knocked out of his hand."

Clancy followed her to the kitchen with the loaded dustpan and handed over the wadded-up paper towels with glass to one of the workers. The red-headed beauty with her silver tray of flutes slid past without eye contact. He'd once known a little girl with the same unusual, deep auburn hair. She hadn't liked him.

"Thanks for your help." The blonde smiled as he held the door for her to maneuver back out with a freshly loaded tray. People were heading to the rear of the room. He joined the flow to a long table on which a curious array of objects was displayed: a lumpy ceramic bowl, an old edition of a wildlife book, and a large painting of the ocean depicted from behind a barbed-wire fence. The painting made him feel pitched forward into the ferocious sea.

"What do you think?" a voice asked. He turned to see the woman who had checked him in at the door. Her corkscrew-curly black hair was backlit, as if electrified.

"It's gorgeous, but . . . disturbing somehow. You?"

"Well, I was quite disturbed when I painted it!" she laughed. "That fence was the bane of my existence."

"You're the artist? The fence isn't metaphoric, then?"

"It's a long story." She made a dismissive gesture.

"Tell me more."

She cocked her head, regarding him a moment, then stuck out her hand. "Julienne Bishop, landscape painter and owner of Bishops by the Sea." Her grip was strong.

He imitated her mock formality, giving her hand an emphatic shake. "Clancy Frederics, insurance claims adjuster. So, what's Bishops by the Sea, a gallery?"

"A little motel out in Montauk."

"Montauk." The word spiked a jolt of pleasure. It conjured up a man called Otto, who had, for a brief time, been his Big Brother. The father of the auburn-haired girl. Bruce's invitation had brought back a memory of the time Otto had taken him deep sea fishing. "I think I was there once."

"Can't have been Montauk, or you'd know for sure."

He noticed the dimple in her right cheek, and as she raised her glass, a wire-thin wedding band.

"I was very young, but I remember being happy." Happy memories from his childhood were rare, but this he would not mention.

"Well, it's changed, but still wonderful. Visit. It's only a few miles farther east."

"And the fence?" he gestured to the painting.

She pulled on a curl as if it were taffy. "One day I headed to the beach across from our motel and discovered a fence blocking access. The ownership of the land had changed, and the corporation that bought it had the fence erected. They wanted to build a half-dozen houses. Lucky for us, the parcel is restricted by old deeds. Unlucky for us, we and our neighbors had to sue to uphold our access rights. It cost us a fortune, but we won. You can see how the fence invaded my life."

Clancy recalled clinging to a chain-linked fence, shaking it with urgency to get into a playground on the other side. Which foster home was that? He remembered rust marks and the smell of metal on his skin.

"So, what does a claims adjuster do, exactly?"

The auburn beauty approached again, and this time Clancy removed two flutes, handing one to Julienne. "I investigate claims and determine if people should get a payout and how much."

"Do you enjoy it?"

Usually when he told people what he did, they changed the subject. "Actually, yes."

He liked the predictability and control. He enjoyed visiting homes and offices and making assessments, okaying the checks that brought new rugs, new roofs, peace of mind. Even so, he knew more than to bore anyone with the details.

"Julienne!" A woman with an overturned bowl of bright white hair rushed over.

Julienne put her hand on the woman's arm, as if to lower the volume. "Clancy Frederics, Grace Morgan. Grace is president of our local environmental group."

"SOS—Save Our Space," Grace shouted.

"We need to preserve our rural character or we'll end up like the rest of Long Island," Julienne explained. From the flush on her face, he saw how much this mattered to her.

Grace Morgan leaned into Julienne and began to whisper. Clancy took the hint.

"I'll leave you to talk." He wandered back to the objects on display and lifted the card in front of Julienne's painting. *Trepidation*. Under a bid for $300, he wrote $400. The idea of owning a painting of Montauk appealed to him. He crossed off the $400 and wrote $500 just as someone announced the auction would start in five minutes.

Clancy tucked himself against the wall to watch. The auction went quickly, starting with the bids on the lesser items. As the winners were announced, he felt increasingly keyed up, as if his fate might hinge on whether he won Julienne Bishop's painting.

The name, when called, was not his. The winning bid was $3,000, way out of his league. The flutes came his way again, but the champagne had no taste. The inside of his mouth had gone numb. He had tipped over the magic line. A foul mood was stealing over him. He had not won Julienne's painting—a sign. He should leave now, to be alone when the mood got too awful to bear.

Just then the air conditioning cut off to a chorus of groans.

"Sorry folks," a man said. "The summer of brownouts. Should be back on in a jiffy."

Definitely a sign to leave. Clancy realized he didn't know where he and Bruce were staying. He circled the restaurant, palms beginning to sweat. There was no sign of Bruce. Clancy spotted people passing through a side door and followed them outside.

Beyond the little patio was a bay dotted with small boats. In the distance, lights from a few houses traced the shoreline; the sky was swept with stars, as if by a paintbrush dipped in glitter. A soft wind caressed his skin, and the moist humid air caught his breath in an unexpected way; he suddenly felt like crying.

Bruce was leaning up against the railing, talking with a woman.

"This is Faye." Bruce pulled her to him.

They chatted, and then Clancy asked Bruce for the address where they were staying.

"Shit, I don't know. You'll have to find Dominique."

Clancy didn't want to find Dominique. He didn't want to go back to an unfamiliar house, to share a room with Bruce, giddy with sexual conquest. His dark mood thickened; he imagined himself on the highway, heading into the night, accelerating so fast he was flying.

He spotted Dominique coming out of the ladies' room. She grabbed his arm. "It's too damn hot. Everyone's going down to the beach! Let's get Bruce."

"Thanks, but—" There was a light tap on his back. Julienne Bishop.

"Coming along?"

Suddenly, a trip to the beach sounded like fun.

In a whirl, the group swooped out of the restaurant.

"We're carpooling," Julienne said to Clancy. "Ride with me. I have a beach sticker."

Hers was a small SUV. "I haven't gone for a midnight swim in ages," she said as they pulled out.

"Swim?" A walk, Clancy had assumed, maybe a bonfire.

"It's a full moon; we'll be able to see."

They drove several miles down a long straight road hemmed by low pines. "This is the Napeague isthmus, the umbilical cord connecting Montauk to the rest of the Hamptons."

"How close is the ocean?"

Julienne gestured toward an expanse of dunes that became visible as they emerged from the tunnel of pines. "At one point in geological time, Montauk was an island. With the next hurricane who knows, the ocean and bay could meet again."

The road forked, and a moment later she turned into a state park. A handful of other cars were pulling into the lot, the dozen or so partygoers tumbling out.

They giggled past the park office and the lines of tents and trailers and down a passageway through the dunes, which opened onto a wide expanse of beach. The full moon made a swath of shimmering white light on the water.

"Let's do it!" someone shouted, and everyone was suddenly racing, kicking up sand.

Clancy sprinted after Julienne, his feet fighting the soft sand, arms flailing. At the water he bent over, laughing. Everyone was shedding clothes, flinging themselves into the surf, shrieking.

"I'm not a strong swimmer," Clancy said.

"It's really calm." Julienne was out of her shift in a second, a quick flash of skin illuminated, and then she was diving in. The moon shone on the water, the low rolling tumbles, the susurrating waves that rose up in the dark and with a low boom, became froth at his feet.

Clancy followed. The water stung his legs and sent shock waves to his groin. The water was so cold he covered his crotch with his hands. A swell came toward him. For a moment he froze, and then he ran into it clumsily, hurrying to dive under before it knocked him around. Its power thrummed over him, and then he was above the surface, his mouth full of saltwater, spitting and laughing.

The water churned with bodies. A few people were floating just beyond the breaking waves; others were bodysurfing toward shore. Exhilaration ripped through him. He leapt up with each wave, threw himself backward onto them, dove under them. He was buoyant in the saltwater, the moon and stars an infinity overhead as he lay on his back and floated.

"Big one!" someone yelled. He looked up to see a black mass bearing down. His exhilaration turned to terror, and he was flailing toward the wave, trying to swim under it but being pulled as the wave sucked everything into itself. He tried to dive under but was too late. The wave smashed down and hurled him over and over, spun like a weightless bit of seaweed. Then he was being swept along at horrendous speed, sand scouring his body. He couldn't get his breath, and he knew he was going to die. He fought to come to the surface, gasping for air. Another wave slammed him back underneath, and he was again dragged along the sand, shells scraping his skin, lungs bursting.

Someone called his name. Someone was slapping him and rolling him over. His stomach heaved and a burst of water spewed from his mouth. He sputtered and came to. The face of someone he liked but couldn't immediately remember came into focus. Julienne.

"Jesus, Clancy, you scared the shit out of me." It was Bruce's voice, but Clancy could see only a blur of legs.

"Are you okay?" Julienne's voice sounded shaky.

"I think so," he croaked. His throat hurt. Faces were leaning over him. He was suddenly conscious of his nakedness. "Could you get my clothes?"

"That was a wicked wave," Julienne said. "I'm really sorry."

Clancy tried to sit up, hands over his groin. Julienne, oblivious to his embarrassment, kept talking and apologizing.

Finally, Bruce brought his clothes and helped him stand. Clancy fumbled, trying to get his pants on. His chest was sore, his wrist throbbing. He felt arms hoisting him up from behind and carrying him back to the parking lot, like a holy man surrounded by pilgrims. At the top of the passageway, he was finally released.

"You're banged up," Julienne said. "My motel's close by. Let me put you up."

"Good idea." Bruce's arm was draped over Faye's shoulder. Without him, Bruce could have their room to himself.

Clancy turned to Julienne. "That would be great. Thanks."

Julienne said, "Stay put," and went to bring her car around. Everyone drifted off, calling out their goodnights.

As he waited, he stared at the ocean. The moon was partially obscured now by clouds, the ocean inscrutable. His terror was receding. As he stood listening to the lapping of the water—the calming breath of the sea—his earlier exhilaration gradually returned. He felt gratitude. Gratitude to be alive. Gratitude that he wanted to be alive.

He hadn't known he was capable of feeling such joy.

CHAPTER 2: Julienne

B ishops by the Sea was a bungalow colony of gray-shingled cabins trimmed in pastel colors, peach or yellow or blue, set back from the road on a rise of land, with clusters of asters and Montauk daisies just beginning to bud. Julienne and Rob lived in a matching cedar-shingled ranch at the top of the rise. The cabins, scattered helter-skelter below, were joined by crushed rock pathways bordered with native grasses. The same families returned each summer, claiming their favorite cabins—the one closest to the beach or the large one with a view of the woods.

Within hours the children of the guests got to know each other. Their parents let them roam free to play hide-and-seek among the bushes or throw a Frisbee on the lawn and breathed a sigh of relief to be left to enjoy their coffee or their cocktails. Later, everyone made their way across Old Montauk Highway and down the path through the dunes, a colorful awkward parade, children in shorts and flip-flops, beach pails in hand, parents encumbered with chairs. In the late afternoon they returned for showers and to meet over the barbecue grills.

From their living room window, Julienne and Rob kept watch over their son Max and their guests' comings and goings. During the summer, as she did the piles of laundry or the bookings, Julienne had time only to glance at her studio or steal a moment to stand at the door and inhale the scent of dust and dried paint. Over the summer, her unfinished canvases stood against a wall, backs to her, so she couldn't feel their reproachful stares.

Now it was fall. The beach plums were ripening along the coast, and soon she and Max would go cranberry picking in the Walking Dunes where right this very minute, hidden in the wet swales, the cranberries were beginning to form. Finally, with summer over, she could get back to work. She was ready for something new, but she didn't know what. She felt a gathering inside her, a kind of energy stirring.

The morning after the party, she woke eager to spend time in her studio. But it was Saturday: family breakfast. And there was her guest to think about. Her body gave an involuntary shudder at the memory—the man curled into himself on the sand, fetal and still.

When she told Rob what had happened, he shook his head and said, "I'd have thought you'd have more sense."

Rob grew up in the dullness of the suburbs, whereas she had spent every summer of her life here. Her aunt and uncle owned the bungalow colony, and she grew up with activities—bonfires in the dunes, wandering solo in the woods, night swims—that came with more than a bit of risk. Still, she didn't want to argue. She and Rob were out of sorts with each other lately, and she didn't have the energy to deal with it. She'd been annoyed with him for not coming to the party—she wanted to get a sitter, and he preferred to stay home with Max. She went for the swim, rather than come home, partly to spite him.

Rob put his arm over his face and dropped into sleep. She sat on the edge of the bed and removed her shoes with a thud and massaged her aching feet, remembering her neighbor's comment when Julienne sold her a $200 ticket to the party.

"I miss the old potlucks. We didn't have to wear heels to those!"

It wasn't just the parties getting upscaled. Even here in East Hampton's easternmost hamlet, big money was moving in. Fancy eateries replaced family restaurants, celebrities tore down modest homes to build showpieces, and international conglomerates scooped up mom-and-pop motels like theirs.

At the party the night before, Grace Morgan mentioned a parcel of privately owned open space called the Moorlands, one of Julienne's favorite places, was up for subdivision approval for eight houses. Julienne sometimes went there to paint when the winds were too cold coming off the ocean. The grassy meadow was sheltered on three sides overlooking Fort Pond Bay near where her cousin Billy lived. She liked to set up near a large rock, a glacial erratic, and look down on the distant woods where she had spent happy hours of her childhood summers playing with Billy.

Rob was still sleeping. She yanked on sweatpants and headed to her studio at the back of the property. The door creaked as she opened it; dust motes flew into her face. The air held a faint scent of linseed and turpentine.

Julienne turned her unfinished canvases face out and plopped into her large, upholstered chair. She picked at a bit of dried cadmium red on the tattered arm cushion and eyed the lineup, her annual post-summer assessment. Her energy seeped away, like the chair's stuffing. As always when she was away from her work too long, getting back to it required effort. She was a rusty screw resisting its groove.

The beach, then. Just the sight of the water would wash away the gunk, the pathogen-thoughts. She grabbed her painting things and headed across the road, down the path, and to the hollow surrounded by contorted pines on the flattened top of a dune, where she liked to set up. She dropped her tote and headed to the water. To spiral down to calmness, she needed to walk.

The waves were coming in at an oblique angle, folding one on top of the next. In the distance two draggers plied the water, their masts sticking up like pencils behind the ears of a distracted editor.

A few gulls were lined up, facing the wind. They occasionally pecked at the sand with tiny munching movements. A lone fisherman rocked back on his heels to cast. Blues and striped bass usually hit the shore this time of year, but this fall was uncharacteristic, the water unusually warm.

She headed west, placing her feet in the indentations made by others; her footprints would be covered in turn. *We're all ghosts*, she thought, tromping heavily to press each foot as deeply as possible.

She walked as far as an old, gray-shingled cottage, which had remained unchanged as long as she could remember. Next to it, a new house with sharp angles and glass, perched like an imperious eagle on the bluffs slowly eroding beneath it. She turned her back to it. She wanted to pretend the town wasn't changing, that it could retain its essential self. But she feared soon there would be one home too many, one more small home supplanted by a large one, and the foreground and background, the elegant balance of home to landscape, would reverse. The time would come when the built environment would irrevocably dominate the natural, and the essence of the place would be lost.

This was one of the reasons she joined the environmental group SOS. There wasn't one big environmental disaster looming, like toxic sludge or tainted drinking water . . . it was "death by a thousand cuts." The week before, she had volunteered to remove invasive weeds from Fort Pond. The plant growth had been incremental, and now the pond was choking, fighting for survival. As a trickle of water seeped in through an almost invisible crack in her left boot, she thought, *How easy it was to change from one kind of place to another.*

She took off her flip-flops and stepped into the foam, sending dozens of sanderlings racing off on toothpick legs. Behind her in the cliffs, come spring, swallows would poke small holes in the soft clay for their nests. Birds came and went, year after year. They migrated, bred, returned to the same trees, same cliffs, same stretches of brush, staking out their territories, singing their proprietary songs. Fighting over turf.

They were like humans, when too many occupied the same habitat. An image for a painting flashed in her mind's eye, a crowd of birds jumbled on top of each other, pecking in fury, superimposed over human beings crammed into a landscape.

She reversed back up the beach. She picked up a deflated red balloon, a tampon container, a sippy cup lid, and a coil of frayed yellow rope that the heavy weather of the previous week had trapped in the wrack line. So much still washed up, despite the laws against ocean dumping. As she walked back, she gathered a smashed straw hat, a tennis ball, and a turquoise sneaker, size 5½, decorated with fake jewels.

At her painting spot, she wiped off her feet, encrusted with sand like a sugar donut, and slipped on her flip-flops. She checked her watch. She had time for a few color washes. Maybe holding a brush and going through the motions—the sensation of bristles against the texture of the canvas, the pull of the paint—would release something, like gristle from a throat, and free her up.

She plunged her brush into her jar of water, squeezed out a few dollops of paint, and swirled tiny dots of cadmium blue and umber into the wet brush hairs. She laid long even strokes across a small canvas. It felt good to have her hand in motion, to feel the connection with the surface.

Just twenty minutes of work settled her. As she dropped off her tote at the studio and dumped the debris she'd collected into the garbage can, the turquoise of the sneaker against the pink of the straw hat arrested her. Rob and Max were waiting, but she couldn't resist . . . she fashioned the thick rope around the perimeter of the hat, secured the bejeweled sneaker in the center, and bouqueted the balloons on top.

She plopped the hat on the head of the manikin that stood sentry near the door. The fake emeralds and sapphires winked at her. There. At least she'd made *something*.

Julienne arranged oranges, apples, strawberries, and melon on the counter. She heard Rob's purposeful footsteps. Without turning her head, she said, "We'll feed him breakfast and then I'll take him to get his car."

When Rob didn't respond, she glanced over her shoulder. He was leaning against the door jamb, hands in pockets, black-and red-checked wool jacket open, hair ruffled. He merely shrugged. So, he was still irritated with her, too.

The front door slammed and a moment later, Max appeared. "You won't believe how big the hole is!" His pale skin was flushed.

After their neighbor's recent death, her heirs had put her home up for sale. The new owners hadn't wasted a second tearing down the old house. A few days earlier, loud noises drew Julienne and Rob outside, where an enormous yellow backhoe shoved its metal claw into the ground like a ghost crab, burrowing in and leaving behind a pile of extracted dirt.

"I don't want you hanging around the excavation by yourself," Rob said to Max. "I'll go with you after breakfast."

Julienne picked up an apple and peeler. "Max, can you go to Apricot and ask the man there to come to breakfast? His name is Clancy."

"I don't know him."

"If you want us to let you watch the work, it would be nice if you would do as I ask."

Max thumped out.

Julienne finished with the apple and put an elbow on the counter. Rob's face wore the closed expression that signaled something was up. He crossed to the table and pulled out a chair. "I'll prep the eggs in a minute."

"What is it?"

He ran a hand along the surface of the kitchen table, an old door he had refinished and placed on legs salvaged from the dump. "He's getting cocky. He's stopped asking permission before he does things."

Rob believed in keeping a tighter rein on Max than she did.

"He's getting older. We can cut him more slack, don't you think?"

"Just the opposite. He's a preteen. This is when kids really go astray."

"Astray?" She laughed and tossed the apple peels into the compost bin.

He flushed. "You're too cavalier, Julienne. There are dangers here, like anywhere. You're too dismissive."

"Kids these days are so sheltered and protected. They don't develop inner resources or real judgment. You've said yourself you want him to be independent."

"Fair enough. But we haven't been paying close enough attention this summer."

"We? You mean me, don't you?"

His mouth pursed in amusement. She bristled, but he was right. "I'll keep a closer eye."

"It's not just that." He looked down at the table.

"What?" She pulled up a chair. She couldn't read his expression.

"I heard something troubling." He paused. "There's a rumor going around that it was SOS that slit open the sand-bags on the beach."

"That's ridiculous."

His face didn't change expression.

"You can't really believe . . . Us—sabotage?"

"You're new to the group. Is it possible that one of the members went rogue?"

"No, not possible. Where did you hear this, anyhow?"

"Actually, it was from your cousin."

"Oh."

"I didn't ask Billy where he'd heard it," Rob went on. "It's a problem if people suspect SOS of something like this. It may not be such a good idea to be part of a group perceived as that radical."

"SOS is just trying to safeguard the environment. Unless you call that radical."

He didn't rise to the bait. "Just remember this impacts me, too."

He meant the chamber of commerce. As motel owners, they were part of the business community, and the business community was often on opposite sides of the issues from SOS. Even accepting help from SOS with their lawsuit over the fence had put them at odds with a few of their closest chamber friends. Julienne went back to the sink and yanked down the cutting board.

"I know you want to give back to SOS, but wouldn't you rather spend what time you have on your art?"

It was a low blow. He knew how much she wanted to be painting. As if he sensed he'd gone too far, his tone became conciliatory. "Couldn't you be supportive without being publicly associated with them?"

She leaned against the counter and folded her arms across her chest. "When did you become so afraid of the chamber?" She hadn't thought he cared what any of them thought.

"I'm not afraid. I'd just rather not deal with their innuendoes." He hesitated. "Your family goes way back; you can get away with taking any stance you like. I'd like to fit in more. Is that so hard to understand?"

He was her husband. How could she not have known that despite their time here, he didn't feel like a real local? She'd sensed what she thought was restlessness all summer but ignored it. To be honest, she'd ignored him as well. She was too busy; they'd both been so busy. "I'm sorry, I didn't realize—"

"I know how much you love this place, Jules." He got up and came over to her, but didn't put his arms around her.

She was afraid to ask what, exactly, he meant. She picked up the paring knife and held it over the jumble of fruit on the counter. Her hand shook, as if she had a tremor. She thought they were a team and felt the same way about their lives. She thought he loved it here as much as she did. He went uncomplainingly about the chores and the upkeep; he was handy with tools and woodworking, enjoyed surf fishing with his buddies. Yet these weren't passions that gave his life purpose.

When she didn't respond, he moved past her to take the plates out of the cabinet. She glanced out the kitchen window, at the sloping lawn, the cluster of cabins, and the sea beyond. The water had gotten rougher than even an hour before. The sea was infinitely changeable, calm and twinkling one hour, dancing and galloping the next. This place meant everything to her. People probably wondered how she could paint the same thing day after day, but it was never the same. She questioned many things about herself and her art, especially whether she was any good at all. But what she didn't question was her subject. The landscapes of Montauk, its bays and inlets, its dunes and pale whispering grasses, its open and constantly mutating skies, its ever-changing seas, obsessed her: The play of light on the ocean and the landscape. She didn't care that her brand of landscape painting was no longer fashionable. All she wanted was to study and paint the effects of light in all its exquisite unknowable variations on the land-scape she loved.

Sometimes, when she was working well, a little part of her worried she cared about this more than anything or anyone.

She'd been the one who wanted to make a life here. She thought he agreed it was the perfect place, wild and beautiful, to raise their son. Now, watching his expression as he placed the plates on the table, a Roman candle of fear flared from her gut to her throat. She picked up the knife and hacked clumsily into the melon, splattering seeds and pulp.

There'd been no actual decision to live here forever. If after all this time Rob felt he didn't belong, or if he was no longer happy, would he want to leave altogether?

CHAPTER 3: Clancy

Clancy became aware of sunlight on his face and a vaguely familiar sound he couldn't place. He lay with eyes closed, trying to stay empty and yielding and float back to sleep. The sound teased, reminiscent of distant traffic.

He sat abruptly; a sharp pain stabbed his rib cage. The small room, window, furniture—none of it was familiar. As he told himself to calm down and breathe deeply, he heard a thudding sound. His mind made the connection . . . the ocean. He was in Montauk, in one of Julienne Bishop's cottages.

He sank with relief against the pillows. The not knowing where he was hadn't happened in years. In his childhood, in the group homes and foster homes, he often awoke in confusion and panic. He'd learned to orient himself before bed, to tell himself, "You're with the McCormick family. They seem nice. They have a black Lab," so that he would wake up clear and intact. Eventually the disorienting episodes had stopped. Now he lay a moment longer, waiting for the aftereffects of his panic to subside, unnerved to have it happen again, after so long.

It was probably the midnight swim and near drowning, more traumatic than he wanted to admit. The pain in his chest spoke to this. He should probably have gone back to Amagansett with Bruce.

He glanced around the room, noticing thoughtful touches he had missed the night before: the skylight over the kitchen area, a sitting alcove with two chairs and a wicker table grouped near a bay window. Next to a stack of *Edible* magazines were a scented candle and a small box of wooden matches, cornflower blue with *Bishops by the Sea* in bright peach lettering. He would ask Julienne Bishop for a few more. He'd been collecting wooden matches since childhood, using them to make tiny structures. Even now he sometimes made them, just for fun.

He went to the window. The bungalow was at a slight elevation, overlooking brambly vegetation, the shock of the ocean in the near distance. It looked very different from the black force of the night before. Nearly flat, it was lit with shards of light, which jumped from place to place in little explosions.

He set up the coffeemaker and dressed. Maybe he'd put off meeting up with Bruce and have breakfast in town and see if it was anything like how he remembered it. He went back to the window. Far out he could see the beginnings of the swell and followed as the waves drew closer, dispersing into plumes of foam. Maybe he'd just sit all day and watch the waves.

The coffeemaker beeped. He poured himself a cup. A young, dark-haired boy was coming down the pathway. He took a step, then stopped and fingered a flower, took a step, and tied a shoelace. He stood a moment staring at the ocean. He leapt up as if to shoot a hoop. He took a few more steps.

Clancy sipped his coffee. The boy was now outside his door. Clancy waited, but there was no knock. The boy was motionless, as if the fates had plunked him there and he didn't know why. Amused, Clancy watched to see what he would do. After a minute he took pity and slowly, so as not to startle the boy, opened the door.

"Hello there."

The boy had dark hair and pale skin. He cleared his throat. "Excuse me, sir, are you Mr. Clancy?"

"Yup, that's me. What can I do for you?" His voice came

out ridiculously hearty, as if he was trying too hard to sound appropriately adult.

"My name is Max. I have a message."

"Thanks." When the boy just stood there, Clancy said "What is it?"

"My mom said to come over for breakfast."

The dark-blue eyes, thick lashes, and thin face. Of course. The hair, although black, was completely different—stiff and straight. That must be the husband.

"Just let me get my shoes."

As they walked up the curving path, Clancy realized Julienne had put him in one of the largest bungalows, situated for the best views. Each had a different color trim on the windows and doors, and everywhere bushes were beginning to bloom with white, daisy-like flowers.

"This is a very pretty place. Do you like living here?"

Max came to an abrupt halt and looked at Clancy as if appalled. "I love it!"

"I can understand that."

Max frowned, nodded, and marched off. *Intense kid*, Clancy thought. Intense, as he himself had been as a boy, with a kind of confidence Clancy knew he lacked, but which he had also noted in Julienne. "What do you love most?"

Max's eyes narrowed, as if he was gauging whether or not Clancy was making fun of him. Then, seeming satisfied, he said, "The woods. And the animals."

"Animals?" Clancy said. "Fish?"

"No," Max said, "like foxes."

"Foxes? At the beach?"

"Deer, rabbits," Max continued. "All kinds of birds. Other stuff. In the woods."

"There are woods here?"

"My mother could tell you," Max said, evasive all of a sudden. He gestured to the Old Montauk Highway. "This was an Indian trail. Later, when white people came, they used it to drive the cattle to pasture."

Cattle? What an imagination the kid had.

Their home was of the same cedar-shingle style as the cottages, only larger. Max opened the screen door and held it just long enough for Clancy to get in before letting it slam.

"Thanks, Max. Especially for telling me all this stuff."

Max gave that short, quick nod of his head again, with what seemed like slightly less wariness. "I could show you my arrowheads."

Clancy felt a leap of pleasure. "I'd like that."

Max raced down the hall, nearly colliding with Julienne coming out of a doorway.

"Whoa!" Julienne seemed less glamorous, more boyish, in daylight; he guessed she was a few years older than his own thirty-six. She was dressed in jeans and a tank top, which exposed the boniness of her shoulders, and her mess of curls clearly uncombed.

"Clancy, welcome. How are you feeling?"

"Only a little sore. Thanks for inviting me. This is quite homey," he said, as they passed through the entryway, which held pegs for coats, a bench covered with shoes, and assorted overflowing bins.

"It's a disaster," Julienne laughed. "The mess drives Rob crazy. I seem to reserve all my creativity for my painting, and the house suffers. Then again," she led him into the living room, "we have this." A picture window ran the length of the room.

"Wow." They stood for a moment gazing out. From this elevation and angle, the entire line of breakers stretching east was visible.

"Come into the kitchen." She began to lead the way just as Max, returning from his room, blocked their path.

"Here." He held up his cupped hand to Clancy.

"Not now, sweetie," Julienne put her hand on his shoulder. "Clancy came for breakfast."

"It's fine," Clancy said. "I'd like to see."

"Okay, but don't take too long. Kitchen's this way."

Max unfurled his fist. A reddish-brown, rock-like object lay in his palm.

"Is this real?"

"Of course! A real Indian here made it hundreds of years ago."

"I've never seen a real arrowhead before."

"Hold it." Max held it out.

The arrowhead was fluted and chipped on its sides, the chips amazingly regular. Clancy ran his finger along the edge. The point was quite sharp. It felt like the stone it came from, cold and hard. He remembered the cold smoothness of marbles he used to collect as a boy, the sound as he rolled them in his hand, and someone he couldn't remember saying, "a beauty," and how his chest had ached with pride.

"This is a beauty, Max." He handed it back, gratified to see Max's smile.

In the large bright kitchen, Julienne was at the stove, the sun highlighting errant wisps of hair around her head like a halo. Scents of coffee and browning meat made Clancy's stomach spasm. At the counter, a man leaned over a yellow ceramic bowl, whisking. He wiped his hands on the dish towel tucked into his belt and held out his hand. "Welcome. I'm Rob."

He had the same bristle-like hair as Max, and his eyes held the same quiet reserve. Like Clancy, he was medium tall, but more solid, muscular. His grip was strong but not competitively so. Still, this was the kind of man who knew how to chop wood and repair toasters. Something in Clancy deflated.

"Sit and relax," Rob said. "It'll just be a minute."

Clancy watched them go about their well-practiced family ballet. Max set the table, laying the silverware with great concentration, folding and refolding napkins, glancing up at Clancy every now and again. Julienne squeezed oranges by the sink one minute, then tossed the skins like hoop shots into the compost bin across the room. Rob chopped cheese and added it to the froth of beaten eggs, then poured it into a gigantic pan with a sizzle.

Watching them, Clancy felt he was being fostered by a new family. How did this one do things? What did they expect of him? What were the rules? The inside jokes he'd never get? Abruptly he stood to help.

"Sit, Clancy, sit." Julienne brandished a dish towel at him, but he ignored her and gathered up the plates, with colors like the trim of the cottages—robin's egg blue, apricot, and yellow—and brought them to Rob for loading up. They passed the juice and the Irish brown bread, which Julienne made a point of saying was homemade in town, and dug in.

Clancy took a forkful of egg and oozing cheese. "Fabulous," he said, trying to pause between bites.

"Julienne tells me she nearly drowned you last night. My wife has a reckless streak."

Rob's slightly patronizing air irked Clancy. "I was having so much fun I forgot to keep my eyes on the waves. My own stupid fault."

"You nearly drowned?" Max leaned forward.

"He got caught in a wave." Julienne frowned at her son's eagerness. To Clancy she said, "It's nice of you to defend me, but really, I feel responsible. You were uncertain, and I egged you on."

A flash of dark wave, the coldness of the sand. He shook off the memory. "If it hadn't been for that, I wouldn't be here now, enjoying this extraordinary breakfast and wonderful company."

The doorbell rang.

"I'll get it." Rob placed a hand on Julienne's shoulder.

She tilted her face to his. Clancy thought of Irene. *Did she ever smile at me that way?*

"There's no real passion," Irene had said, adding the words that stung. "You don't even know it's not there, do you?"

Before Irene, he had been the one who left, sometimes not even saying good-bye to the foster families as he followed the social worker out the door.

"Running a motel, it's rare we get through a meal without an interruption," Julienne was saying.

Rob returned with a giant in a flannel shirt and knit cap and the young woman with the white-blond braids who had been passing out the scallops at the party.

"You're the man who helped me sweep up the glass last night!" Her face lit up, reminding him of a sunflower—one of the few he knew the name of.

"And you're the queen of scallops." Clancy put out his hand. "I'm Clancy."

"Molly Lundgren, Billy Linehan," Julienne said. "Billy's my cousin."

Billy gave Clancy a brief nod. He placed his hands on Max's shoulders. "How goes it, urchin?"

"Coffee?" Rob asked.

"Nah, we just came to get my junk."

"I'll give you a hand." Rob followed them out.

"Since his parents died a year ago, Billy's been raising his little brother Jonah, who's Max's best friend," Julienne refilled Clancy's coffee cup. "He and Molly met recently. She's very sweet, as you can see, so I hope it lasts. He's had a hard time."

Rob returned alone. "Billy's going to be leading the scout troop from now on. Otto Lansky's stepped down. Says he's getting too old."

"It'll be good for Billy to take charge of something," Julienne said.

"Otto Lansky?" Clancy said, stunned. "I knew someone by that name once."

"Really? This one's a retired cop." Julienne went to the refrigerator and removed a large bowl.

"The man I knew was a cop." It was Otto who had taken him to Montauk as a boy. "I wonder if it could be the same man. Maybe he retired out here."

"I'll get his phone number if you want to look him up." Julienne began dishing fruit salad onto everyone's plates.

"That'd be great." What an astonishing thrill it would be to see Otto again.

"Clearly you were meant to come to Montauk." Julienne smiled and punctuated the remark by popping a strawberry into her mouth.

CHAPTER 4: Molly

A t the docks on the north side of the Montauk peninsula facing Block Island Sound, Molly Lundgren found a summer job at a fish market.

Molly fell in love with Montauk even before she fell in love with Billy. She was in love with the way the sand dunes drifted to the ocean's edge, the way the clam and mussel shells crunched underfoot at the shore near the Point, and the way her skin smelled after a day in the salty surf, baked in brittle sunlight. Most of all she was in love with the harbor, with the thick coils of rope, the lobster crates massed near the fishing boats, the stench of dead fish and dried-out seaweed, and the flavors of lemon, salt, and grease of the fried clams she had every day for lunch at the Promised Land bar. Theresa Nolan, the bartender, had become like an older sister and told her which of the boys were okay and which to steer clear of.

She packed out fish to be trucked into the city, stocked the display cases, and helped out at the counter. It was heavy, sloppy, exhausting work, but when she left each day, she felt strong and complete, and she slept at night as if she were falling down drunk. She never wanted it to end. And then there was Billy.

She couldn't believe the way her life had spun into this new and thrilling alignment. Billy and his little brother Jonah had grown up on Fort Pond Bay, among families of fishermen who had lived there for decades. Billy worked the charter boats during the season and crewed on draggers in between. His parents had died the previous year, and he'd taken his kid brother to spend the summer with relatives in Wisconsin, the only summer he had ever been away. If she hadn't met him the day after Labor Day, she wouldn't have met him at all. And now she was moving in with him. She'd never done anything so wild and improbable in her life.

"Unload these, will ya?" Ernesto, a coworker, broke into her reverie.

He cuffed her on the arm, but she could barely feel it through her thick sweatshirt. She nodded, wiped her hands on her soiled white apron, and leaned her weight against the dolly, shoving it with all her strength along the wooden floorboards, her rubber boots making wet, sucking noises.

"You look like a madwoman," Vince teased as she pushed the dolly against the swinging doors into the shop.

She laughed, slipping on thick rubber gloves. In the display case, the light caught and reflected the sparkles of freshly chipped ice. She began to lift the fish by the tail and lay them down with expert flips of her wrist. Those for filleting she set aside for Vince, who would soon instruct her in that art. Over the summer she had sold fish and lobster and hauled, mopped, and cut. She'd learned to gut, leaving on head and tail, and learned to scale so skillfully not a wispy flake remained. Now that she was staying on, Vince said he'd teach her how to make the clean slice under the head, insert the sharp, thin blade, and with only a few deft motions, remove fillets.

She took the dolly out back and left it near the dock, which was busy with men—for it was only men who worked here—unloading the tuna, thicker than her waist, and recoiling the ropes and emptying the buckets to the plaintive cawing of the gulls as they wheeled overhead and dove for scraps. Rounding the spit of land poking into Block Island Sound, the boat Billy was on, the *Cora Marie*, was coming in. As she watched it make its stately way, circled with gulls like tiny white flags, like a flock of angels, she felt as if the buoys floating on the water bobbed around inside her, little capsules of joy.

Lucky, lucky, lucky.

———————

She owed meeting Billy to her best friend Rachel, who came up with the idea of getting jobs on the East End for the summer. If they had to work, they might as well work where they could party, she had argued. Rachel found work at a fancy health spa and met all kinds of people. By people they meant guys, of course. Molly met guys, too. Ernesto and Vince dragged her after work to join the motley bunch that gravitated to the Promised Land.

The day after Labor Day, Molly and Rachel had gone to the beach.

"I don't know if I can bear to leave. I'm as trapped as a porgy in a gill net," Molly said.

She enjoyed fishing terminology, like "snapping bait on the main line," and "putting fish in the box," though she had only a fuzzy idea of what any of it meant.

"You're not seriously considering staying?" Rachel wiggled her bikini to line up below her belly piercing and glared at Molly over her sunglasses. "It won't be like this in winter. It'll be cold and nasty and deserted. There's nobody here."

"People live here year-round," Molly said meekly. "Fishermen."

"Only people who've given up on the world would stay here year-round."

Molly raised herself up onto her elbows and squinted at the water.

"Do you have the time?" A guy in striped board shorts smiled down on them.

Molly shielded her face from the sun. "Sorry," she started to say, but Rachel had already swung herself into a sitting position and was digging in her bag for her phone.

The guy dropped into a squat, spraying sand. Another, bigger and taller, stood nearby. He stared at her so intently she felt she grew larger with each second that passed under his gaze. *I'm an ox*, she thought. *A big, blond milkmaid*. Rachel, small and dainty, was chattering away.

"Sit already." Rachel pointed to the quiet boy, backlit from the sun. "You're making me nervous."

He lowered himself to the blanket. Molly shifted over to make room, reaching for her cover-up. He eyed her as she pulled it tightly around her.

"I'm Billy. You should always wear green."

Sweat was pooling in her armpits, an itchy trickle. "I've never really liked green. I don't know why I bought this."

"You look like a sea goddess." He drew out the word "goddess" as if he liked the sound.

"Salad dressing," she said.

At his puzzled look, she explained, "You know, Green Goddess salad dressing."

It was the most ridiculous conversation she'd ever had.

They spent the rest of the week together. Billy said he'd never known anyone he could be quiet with the way he could with her. He boasted to his friends how strong she was and how easily she hauled the heavy, ice-packed crates of fish. Billy, too, was big; even stretching herself to her tallest, the top of her head only reached his ear. For the first time in her life—on the docks and with Billy—she felt comfortable with her body. It was as if she'd spent her life among Lilliputians and only now was in a world properly proportioned.

Billy liked her scruffy from work, sleeves rolled up to

reveal bruises, and blood under her fingernails. He shook his head at the flowery print dress she wore for their first date and gave her some of his oversized shirts.

"See," he said rotating her to face the mirror. "You're so sexy when you look tough." She didn't see sexy, just the contrast of the dark shirt with her thick, paintbrush-straight white-blond hair. Billy liked it when she wore her hair down and he liked when she plaited it into a long braid, swinging it like a rope to tease her.

That week together made all the difference. If she hadn't met Billy, she might have left Montauk when her summer job was over. Billy tipped the balance.

When Molly told Rachel she wouldn't be driving back to Roslyn but was staying on at the fish market and would be moving in with Billy, Rachel shrieked, "Are you completely out of your mind?"

But Molly knew there was more than a little envy at the romance of it all.

———

Molly and Billy settled into a corner booth at the Promised Land. While they waited for Kathy, their waitress, to take their order, Molly studied Theresa, as if her ease and maturity could be learned. Behind her, bottles gleamed green, ruby red, amber, complimenting Theresa's colors, her auburn hair, tawny skin. Molly wondered what it must feel like to be so beautiful. Theresa seemed indifferent or even bored by it. She wore jeans and flannel shirts, no makeup, her hair piled up and held by a large clip. Her face wore an expression of absent concentration, a faraway look, as if she was listening to music no one else could hear.

As if she felt Molly's gaze, Theresa turned and smiled. Theresa didn't talk much about herself, and Molly sensed there was a lot under the surface she didn't share. No matter what the customers threw at her—bar quarrels, spilled beer—Theresa remained calm and unruffled. Bonnie Raitt was singing, "She's Nobody's Girl," and Molly thought, *that's Theresa exactly*.

The door flew open with a thud. Stu and Porgy and a few other fishermen blew in like a fresh squall.

"Get off your ass, Theresa," Porgy shouted. "You've got thirsty customers!"

He was round and fleshy like the fish he was nicknamed for. Theresa gave him the finger, and Porgy reached across the bar and grabbed it and put it in his mouth, making Molly cringe.

Theresa extricated her hand, took the bowls of chowder from Kathy, and brought them over to Molly and Billy. The bowls tilted slightly on the uneven shellacked planks of the tabletop.

"You should get another job," Molly said.

"Better beer than fish!"

"None of this twosome shit!" Stu dove for the booth, butting Molly with his hip to slide over. His scruffy beard and gold stud gave him a rakish pirate vibe.

"How's it going?" Billy asked.

"The fluke are taking their sweet-assed time migrating, even with this wind." Stu took a gulp of his beer.

"What makes them migrate?" Molly asked.

"Depends on what they eat, which depends on water temperature." Stu licked foam off his mustache. "If it's too warm, they wait before coming. If there's a storm, they might overstay. A domino effect. Everything affecting everything else."

"Do you think I could learn to be a fisherman?"

Billy and Stu choked on their laughter.

"What's so funny?"

All summer long, as Molly listened to the fishing talk, an ache grew inside her. She wanted to know what it felt like to gaze in every direction and see nothing but ocean. She wanted to know what it felt like to bait hooks and watch the long lines play out over the water. She wanted to feel the thrum of the motor under her soles as they rode the rough channel between the Point and Gardener's Island or fished Valiant Rock in the area they called The Race.

"It's tough physical labor," Stu said.

"I'm strong. Billy will tell you that."

"She's an Amazon." Billy raised her arm to show off her muscles. "Babe, there's barely enough work for the ones who are left."

Stu leaned forward. "Species are declining. Sizes, catches are smaller. You have to go farther out to find fish."

Molly felt a spike of anxiety. The ocean heating up was bad for fish, for everything, but could people destroy something as powerful as an ocean?

"And the regulations," Stu continued.

"Don't get us started on the regs." Billy stood and tucked in his shirt. He glanced at Molly's still full glass and gestured at Stu. "Draft?"

"Draft it is."

"For a fisherman, he doesn't talk about it much," Molly said to Stu.

Billy would tell her things if she pressed him, like how the ocean floor looked through the depth finder, but then it was as if he got snagged on thick netting and shut down.

"You know how his folks died, right?" Stu pulled at his beard.

"Pneumonia?"

"Exposure. They fished too late into the season and got caught in a bad storm. His mom got sick, and they didn't have health insurance. Didn't go to the doctor. After she died, his dad was a mess."

"Like how?"

"Billy didn't tell you?"

She shook her head and took a quick swallow of beer.

"He went on a bender. Slipped and fell off the rock jetty. Hit his head."

Her hand flew to her mouth. She heard the crack of head against rock and saw the limp body floating in the water.

"It wasn't Billy who found him." They both glanced over at Billy, leaning against the bar. "Still, it's gotta have a big effect on him. No fisherman likes to admit when he's spooked. I'm sure he wouldn't be keen on you anywhere near serious water."

Molly realized she was holding her breath and let it out into the silence between them.

Stu ran his hand over his beard. "Don't go telling him I told you. You know how he likes to keep things close to the vest."

She didn't know that, actually. Billy was so open with her. She toyed with a packet of oyster crackers. Of course, there would be much about him she had yet to learn.

There wasn't anything about her he didn't know, though. Nothing important. She glanced around. The bar was full of people who had known Billy all his life, people who undoubtedly knew things about him that she couldn't even guess, people who might, in some ways, be even closer to him than she was.

"Hey." Stu put his hand over hers and squeezed, as if he knew what she was thinking. "He's a great guy. It's good to see him happy again. He's lucky to have you."

Lucky, lucky, lucky.

After work Molly waited outside the motel where she and the other workers had been housed over the summer, her belongings in two duffels at her feet. Billy pulled up with a screech, jumped out, and enveloped her, his mouth all over her face like a puppy's. She laughed, pushing him away. He wore a blue wool cap, a cap that contained in its smell the secrets of the sea. His eyes had seen horizons she could only imagine, and his salt-roughened hands, which touched her so gently, had battled with shark and tuna and swordfish and cod.

She climbed in, dumping her duffels atop the nest of seaweed-encrusted coils of rope, metal buckets, and other gear. The seat springs bit her bottom as they drove from the dock area through the residential streets to Flamingo Road and then onto Industrial Road, flanked on one side by Fort Pond and on the other by Fort Pond Bay.

"Don't expect too much." Billy had rented out his house while he and his little brother Jonah were away and had only just reclaimed it. He figured the rental income would compensate for losing a season of fishing and give Jonah a chance to be among family after their parents' deaths. They drove over the railroad tracks to where the road dead-ended at the bay. A line of bungalows faced the water, boarded up for the season. They drove briefly along the water and then entered the woods.

"Jonah knows I'm coming, doesn't he?"

Billy hadn't wanted to introduce her to his brother too soon. She wondered what an eleven-year-old boy would be like.

"He's stoked. I told him how terrific and gorgeous you are."

"Oh Billy, now he'll be disappointed."

"You're an idiot, you know that?" Billy said.

They arrived at a grassy clearing, with a weathered bungalow fronting the bay. Beyond the house, she glimpsed a rocky beach and a small boat tied up to a short pier.

"Oh my god, it's paradise!"

"You're sure not going to feel that way when you see inside. Remember, this place dates back to the fifties."

Billy had told her his house was situated within a small community of fishing families, but because of the way the shoreline curved and the vegetation, she couldn't make out the houses nearby. "It's so private."

"That's why it's worth a fortune now." He pushed open the door, its screen ripped and sagging, and waited for her to precede him.

Molly took a step back. "You'd never think of selling, would you?"

Billy took a moment to answer. "I guess not. But the money's pretty tempting. There's been a developer nosing around."

"You'd have to be crazy to give this up."

Billy touched her cheek. "Come."

The door opened directly into a kitchen. The ceilings were low, the wallpaper a faded flower pattern. Flanking a porcelain sink were open, wooden shelves. Framed photos were grouped on the wall, black-and-white shots of men standing in or around water and boats. Molly followed Billy into a narrow corridor, which opened into a living room and a set of uneven stairs to a second floor. Molly didn't think she had ever been inside a house so old.

"Jonah! Get your ass down here," Billy shouted.

A tall, skinny boy thudded down the stairs. He skidded to the bottom, slipped, and fell. Billy let out a guffaw.

"Billy!" Molly reached out a hand to Jonah. "Are you okay?"

The boy made an indecipherable gargling noise in answer and struggled to his feet. He had the same square and stubborn jaw as Billy's, but his brown hair was light where Billy's was dark. He began to pick at a scab on his elbow.

"Stop," Billy said.

Blood oozed from the scab. Jonah examined it with satisfaction.

"Would you like to show me around?" Molly asked Jonah.

Jonah immediately brought her upstairs, where two small bedrooms were tucked under eaves, a bathroom in between. Billy's room faced the bay, while Jonah's fronted the forested area through which they had driven. Cutout photos of sharks, dolphins, and whales papered his walls.

"I like dophins and whales, too," Molly said. "Sharks, I'm not so sure."

"This is a hammerhead." Jonah ran a finger down the glossy paper. "That's a great white. They mostly hunt at night. Sometimes you can see one from the beach. Whales, too."

"Have you ever gone whale watching? We could go sometime."

Jonah raced back downstairs. "Billy! Molly's gonna take me whale watching!"

Jonah isn't going to pose a problem at all, Molly thought. *It's like we're already a family.* She wrapped her arms around herself and gave a little squeeze.

Lucky, lucky, lucky.

———◆———

Molly leaned against Billy as they settled on the edge of the dock, legs dangling into the water. The bay was lit with the retreating sun, the sky pale over rose-tinged clouds hanging just above the horizon. Molly slid her hand through the water, still warm from the day's heat, and tapped her heels against the wood. Billy rested his head on her shoulder. A feeling like honey spread through her body.

"What do you want more than anything else?"

Billy thrust out his lower jaw in the way he did when concentrating. "Me personally? Not something like world peace?"

"Right." Molly smoothed down the wiry black hairs on his forearm. He leaned back on his elbows. "What do I wish . . . I wish you'd come here and let me put my arms around you."

Molly obliged, her back against his chest. He covered her breasts with his hands.

"Holy mother of God." His breath on her neck was moist and warm.

"I'm serious."

"So am I."

"Answer my question."

"Okay." His hands on her breasts went slack. "I'd like to have enough money so I wouldn't have to worry."

"That's reasonable." Molly waited for him to ask her. She wanted to tell him how, with him, she had everything she'd ever wanted, especially what she hadn't even known she wanted.

"It might sound reasonable, but it isn't. You think if you work hard, you get ahead, but that's a hoax."

"How do you mean?" She twisted to meet his eyes over her shoulder.

"My parents were always struggling with the bills. If we got ahead one season, we fell behind the next. The ones born ahead stay ahead. People like us race their whole lives and barely stay in place." Billy made a sweeping gesture at the opalescent sky. "This is wasted on us. We're too busy worrying about how we're going to buy shoes and repair the roof. But with money . . . Can you see how everything would be different?"

Molly was raised in a middle-class family up island; she had never known true want.

"Why'd you ask such a strange question anyways?"

Molly traced his cheekbone with her finger. This wasn't the moment to talk about her happiness. She'd keep it to herself for now, husband it like the perfectly intact conch shell they'd discovered on the beach.

"I was reading a fairy tale. The one about the fisherman and the golden fish. He throws it back in exchange for having his wish come true."

CHAPTER 5: Clancy

The warm September air washed over Clancy as he drove back to town along the hilly coastal road after Julienne dropped him at his car. Being away from the city, with its familiar noise, dirt, and energy usually unsettled him, but today he felt as buoyant as the butterfly kite bobbing in the distance over the ocean.

The town was slightly familiar from when he'd been here with Otto as a boy—the feel of the place but not the particulars: bakery, pizza parlor, fudge shop, T-shirt store, deli, bank, and the tall tower of a building standing guard over a town green with its little gazebo. He parked at a town lot and walked on a path to the beach, where he sat on an upended log to watch the ocean.

He'd been about Max's age, maybe a bit younger. His childhood memories were spotty, and he had repressed most of them, even the good. The good only hurt more, highlighting what had been missing the rest of the time.

He didn't believe it when the social worker told him. It was always the younger children who were picked for outings. He wasn't talkative or charming. People didn't warm up to him. He'd had more than enough awkward encounters with strangers. But a pal, a Big Brother, sounded different.

The man was more a father's age than a brother's, but that was okay. Something about him put Clancy at ease.

Clancy was seated in one of the armchairs grouped around a wooden table in the common room of the reform school. The man towered over him, and as if this made him uncomfortable, he lowered himself into a chair as if to shrink closer to Clancy's size. He placed his hands and forearms flat on the armrests and moved them forward and back a few times, then stopped, self-conscious. His fingers began to flick at the fabric, sending up little specks of fiber. His expression was friendly, but the action of his fingers was dismissive.

"Take that!" the fingers seemed to say.

Clancy watched, trying to get a sense of this man who had come to take him out and be his pal. Maybe his fingers were saying he hated the brown-and-beige upholstery as much as Clancy did.

He was soft-spoken, this man, as he told Clancy about himself. He was a Nassau County police officer. He had a wife and a daughter, a girl a few years younger than Clancy. He had hoped for a son, too, but he and his wife couldn't have any more children.

"Do you like baseball?"

Clancy didn't know how to answer. The words lay between them like a discarded object neither knew what to do with. What little baseball Clancy had seen hadn't interested him, but he didn't want to ruin his chances with this man.

"Me, either," Otto said. "What do you say we go for a drive?"

Clancy jumped up. This was more like it.

Now he shifted on the log and squinted in the sun. The water wasn't as calm as it had been that morning. The wind ruffled its surface, catching the sun in the facets of the waves. He tried to recall where he and Otto had gone and what they had done that first day. He remembered the big car, the beige leather seat, the feeling of floating over the highway, and Otto's smooth way of turning the wheel.

In the following months, it didn't matter what they did as long as he got to go out with Otto. Otto came every month, and they'd go somewhere new: the North Shore, the South Shore, the park, the racetrack, the bowling alley. He remembered the long drive to Montauk, and Otto shaking him awake as they entered the town. The climb up the lighthouse had made him dizzy, and after that, on the boat, he had become queasy from the buckets of chum and smell of diesel fuel from the outboard motor. Capping off each outing was an ice cream soda at an old-fashioned drug store on the outskirts of Queens.

Clancy ran his hand along the velvet surface of the sand. When had the outings with Otto ended? When had they lost touch? There were a few cards and letters, and then nothing. It was twenty-plus years ago.

Clancy stood, brushed sand off his pants, and pulled the napkin with Julienne's hand-drawn map from his pocket.

He drove along Second House Road and made a left onto Dewey Place. The road gained slightly in elevation, and he slowed, looking at house numbers, until he spied a mailbox with Lansky written on it. The trim ranch-style house was as unpretentious as the man he remembered.

He slowed as he reached the door. A chime tinkled in the breeze and a bird of some kind—bigger than a sparrow, but with a hint of red—chirped around a feeder. He pressed the doorbell.

Through the glass he saw a man coming toward him. He was backlit, so his features were obscured, but something— the slope of the shoulders, the way he moved—sent a ripple of certainty through Clancy. When the man reached the door and Clancy could actually see him, he was no longer sure. This man was less imposing than the Otto Clancy remembered. He looked shrunken, clearly frail. His head seemed to wobble, as if his neck was too scrawny to hold it up. His face had a drawn, tight look.

"What can I do for you?" The man's tone was neither friendly nor unfriendly. The eyes, though smallish and penetrating, seemed familiar, despite the crepe-y lids.

"I'm sorry to bother you, but I think we knew each other once. I don't know if you'll remember me, but my name is Clancy—"

"You!" The man thrust back the door and put his hands on either side of Clancy's shoulders and squeezed. "My God," he said, "Clancy Frederics. My God. I never thought I'd see you again. Of course I remember you! Come in, come in." Otto led him down a long hall and into a living room, moving with a shuffle so slow Clancy found it hard not to trip on his heels. "What can I get you, son? Coffee? Tea? Soda?"

"Nothing, sir. I just had a big breakfast."

"Call me O, like you used to." Otto gestured to the couch. "Please sit." He lowered himself into a bulky recliner. "How did you come to find me?"

"Purely by accident," Clancy said, and explained. "Of course, until I saw you I couldn't be sure."

"I wrote but the letter came back, so I called. They said you'd been placed with a family. I didn't want to interfere."

The hurt of losing Otto washed over him, even after so many years. Clancy leaned forward. "I wrote you, too."

"Never got it." Otto shook his head. "When I retired and moved out here, my mail was supposed to be forwarded, but some stuff never reached me. Bad coincidence. I'm sorry."

"Me, too."

"Did it work out for you . . . that family?"

Clancy looked away. The light in the room was dim, throwing shadows over the dark furniture, and there was a slightly musty scent, as if the room hadn't been dusted in a while. He didn't want to admit he didn't even know which foster family it might have been. "Not really. But it's all so long ago."

"Tell me what you've been doing with yourself. I've always wondered what became of you, what you made of yourself. Married? Kids? You still making those little match-stick houses you were so good at?"

"You remember that? Yes I make them once in a while. No to the marriage and children. Hopefully someday." This was Clancy's stock answer, what he knew he was supposed to say, what people wanted to hear. What he really wanted, what he would be allowed to have, was not yet clear to him. "I work as a claims adjuster for a big insurance outfit. I like it. I live in Astoria, work in the city."

"Good for you, good for you." Otto leaned back in the recliner, palms flat on his thighs in the position Clancy remembered from long ago. But now he sat like an old man, legs spread apart, knees nearly to his chin, his body collapsed into itself.

"Tell me about you," Clancy said. He was feeling a little shy, reconciling this Otto with the man he remembered, and reconciling his childhood self with who he was now.

"Oh, not much to tell," Otto said. "You sure I can't get you something?"

"I remember you taking me here. That fishing trip. Had you been planning then to move?"

"No, but once I had my twenty-five years on the force, we moved out here. I got my real estate license and did that for a while. The fishing was the best. Do you fish? Remember all I taught you?"

Clancy laughed. The blood on his fingers. The round staring eye of a dead fish. "Oh I remember."

"It was a good life," Otto said, sighing.

"Was?" Clancy felt a spike of concern.

"I'm just getting old, is all."

This was so clearly apparent Clancy could think of nothing to say. "I remember you had a wife and a daughter."

"My daughter lives locally. Theresa Nolan. She took her mother's maiden name. My wife passed away twelve years ago."

"I'm sorry," Clancy said. Otto must be lonely, with his wife gone, living alone. It struck him that even as a child, he sensed Otto hadn't just been assuaging a young boy's need. He suspected they had shared an inherent loneliness.

"Car accident. She didn't suffer more than a second, the doctor said."

Had Clancy ever told Otto a car accident was what had taken his parents? Fast, people said, it had been fast. He understood at the time the words were meant to comfort him but not the meaning behind them. Had his parents flown more swiftly to heaven than most people? Or maybe they didn't have time to linger, to say goodbye, or to take him with them. If they had loved him—and people always told him how much his parents loved him—why didn't they take him to heaven, too?

"I remember about your parents," Otto added.

Clancy gave the dismissive wave that always sprang unbidden when people offered their sympathy for his loss.

They fell silent. Clancy looked around, casting for a new topic. The room was furnished with well-worn sofas and chairs, newspapers were piled on a coffee table, and framed maps hung on the walls. A large TV stood on a cabinet in a corner.

"Very homey," Clancy said, for the second time that day.

"I'm comfortable," Otto said, something grave in his tone. "Come outside with me?"

With difficulty, Otto stood and struggled to open the slider door. He gestured for Clancy to precede him onto a small stone patio. Beyond was rolling terrain, a bay visible in the far distance.

Clancy was astonished. "Is all this yours?"

"Gosh, no. The mowed bit around the patio is all. The rest is preserved, the eastern end of Hither Woods. It's real dry now—been having a drought—or it'd look a lot greener."

Clancy let his eyes drift over the expanse, the sun a warm mantle on his shoulders. A sudden gust set the chimes tinkling. He wondered if the West looked something like this. It felt strange to be alone with all this space. He also wondered if this was how ranchers felt in the midst of such emptiness.

"Come see my garden." Otto led him to the side of the house where a plot, filled with greenery, was defined by low stakes and mesh fencing. Otto dropped suddenly to his knees, alarming Clancy.

Then Otto pinched some dirt and said, "Feel."

The blackish dirt was soft and warm in Clancy's palm; it gave off an intense damp smell.

"It's taken me twenty years to get dirt like this," Otto said. "Horse manure, fish guts, chopped leaves . . . you name it." He grabbed Clancy by the elbow and hoisted himself back up. "See these? Best tomatoes you'll ever eat. I'll give you some to take."

"What's all the rest?"

"Lettuces, squashes. Those are pumpkins beginning. Peas. All organic. It's one thing the eco-crazies are right about. The marigolds keep away the bugs."

"How's that?"

"You smell them." Otto made a face.

Clancy put his nose into the petals of burnt orange and burgundy and inhaled the odd spicy odor. "I like it, actually."

Otto snorted. "I have a flower garden, too. Just zinnias and asters now."

"You really enjoy this."

"I love the land, working it. There's nothing like it."

Clancy nodded, but except for the time he had dropped Irene's houseplant and the pottery container broke, he wasn't sure he had even touched soil before today. He glanced around. The earth was covered with soil. It was the ground beneath his feet, yet he had no memory of ever bending down to feel it.

Otto swayed slightly.

"Are you okay?"

"Just need to rest a moment." Otto indicated with his chin. "In the shade there."

Clancy led him to a set of chairs under a small grouping of trees.

"Would you like me to get you some water?"

"I'm sick, Clancy. Dying, actually."

Clancy grabbed a chair back. "What?"

"Prostate."

"Oh Otto, no!"

"I'm comfortable," Otto said, the words taking on new meaning. "My doctor's giving me as much pain medication as I need."

"There's nothing—?"

"Nothing that will cure it. I've refused treatment. It'd only gain me a little time, and that time would be spent in a hospital. No, this is where I want to be." He gestured, and Clancy took in the golden fields, the distant woods, and closer, the stalks of red tomatoes.

"I have no regrets." Otto scanned the woods and water in the distance. "At least not about that." His mouth turned down in a spasm of bitterness.

Clancy didn't know whether to push him to say more or to let him be. "I guess we all have regrets," he said lightly, though if asked, he couldn't have said which among his choices were the faulty ones, the ones he would later come to regret.

"Mine's a doozy." Otto's eyes shifted to Clancy and away. "Cost me my daughter."

So he wanted to talk, then. "What do you mean?"

Otto put his gnarly hands on his knees. "After my wife and I moved out here, I fell in love with another woman, Bonnie, a neighbor. It grew slowly between us and by the time I realized what was happening, it was too late." Otto's eyes seeped at the edges.

"That must have been very difficult."

Otto lowered his head. "I don't believe in breaking up a marriage. I loved Mary Elizabeth; she didn't deserve to be thrown out like the trash. Bonnie never pressed me for a divorce; she felt as I did. That we had to honor our commitments. She and I saw each other all the time. In town at the post office, that kind of thing. And occasionally . . . we allowed ourselves to be together." He ran a hand over his face, as if erasing his emotions.

Clancy considered asking again if he would like a glass of water but didn't want to interrupt.

"I must have slipped up, or my wife sensed something. She confronted me. I didn't know how to lie; I bungled it. She was devastated. She jumped in the car and drove off. She crashed before she even got into town, the curve in the road just at Fort Pond. My daughter never forgave me for her death or for marrying Bonnie afterward, even though we waited. My daughter won't speak to me. Not even after Bonnie herself died. So . . ." he straightened and looked directly at Clancy, "now you know."

Clancy pulled closer, the chair scraping against the patio stones, and put his hand over Otto's. To be old, alone, and dying with such sorrow. What a bitter end.

"I'm so sorry."

"I do so wish we could be reconciled before I die."

"Does she know you're sick?"

Otto just shook his head. Clancy thought again of the little red-haired girl who had stared at him from the doorway of Otto's living room when he visited, who wouldn't play with him despite her father's coaxing. There had been something steely and tough about her that had impressed him.

"No one except my doctor—and now you—knows. There's a reason I can't get into, but that's how it must be."

Clancy nodded, puzzled.

"Chickadee," Otto said suddenly. He waved in the direction of the tree, where birds were swooping in and out. "They're very trusting. They'll even eat out of your hand."

They watched the birds in silence. The air was so fragrant, the sun so warm, the birdsong so pleasing, it didn't seem possible Otto could really be dying, and dying soon.

"Please, tell me about your life," Otto said. "What are your passions?"

Passions? Clancy couldn't name any passions. He launched into a description of his job, told a few stories about the woman who filed claims every year, each one more inventive than the last, and his boss's antics. The lines in Otto's face smoothed, and he laughed a few times, so Clancy talked more than he normally would. But seeing Otto's eyes begin to close, he stood to go. Otto insisted on walking him to his car.

"It was wonderful seeing you again," Clancy said. "I wish there were something I could do for you."

"Kind of you," Otto said.

"I want you to know it meant a lot to me when I was a kid. I don't know if I ever told you." Clancy reached out to shake his hand, but instead Otto opened his arms wide to hug him. They stood that way a moment, Otto patting him feebly on the back.

"Take care of yourself," he said.

Clancy got in his car, drove in a tight circle to reverse direction, and was about to call out goodbye when he saw Otto waving wildly. He rolled down the window.

"Did you mean it when you said you'd like to do something for me?"

"Anything," Clancy said.

"Would you go see my daughter?" Otto rested a gnarled hand on the car.

"Of course. What do you want me to do?"

Otto's face flushed. "You absolutely must not tell her I'm sick. Promise me that. Just feel her out. Gauge whether she might come around. See if she can be convinced to talk to me."

Clancy had a sinking feeling. He was not a persuasive person. "What reason should I give for going to see her?"

"Tell her you remember her from when she was little. Just be friendly, don't push it. Don't mention you saw me. Then let me know what you think."

"Of course, O, I'll be glad to. How do I contact her?"

"She works at a bar on the docks. The Promised Land."

On the way back to town, Clancy slowed as he passed Fort Pond where Otto's wife had spun off the road. It was hard to imagine tragedy on such a day. The afternoon light glowed with a richness of color he rarely noticed in the city. Along the coastal road to Bishops by the Sea, people jogged and walked, coming and going from the beach with chairs and children. Everything shimmered.

Before going to his bungalow, he dropped off the bag of tomatoes on Julienne's doorstep. The tomatoes were all sizes and shapes, with shades varying from orangey red to yellow, some with small cracks Otto said were from the heat.

Clancy bit into a cherry tomato; it burst sweetness into his mouth.

CHAPTER 6: Otto

Otto was drained, exhausted, but he didn't go inside until he had watched Clancy Frederics drive down the hill and away. It had been such a wonderful, unexpected pleasure to see this boy again, whom he'd cared about so long ago. Clancy was one good thing he had done, one thing he could feel proud of. He remembered how as a boy Clancy talked so softly he was nearly inaudible, and yet despite his reserve, there was a freshness to him, an openness Otto found quite striking. He remembered the way Clancy would stare at him, drinking in every word. Not like Theresa, with her darting eyes and body trembling with impatience. He tried to imagine their meeting; it was like sending a steady egret to beguile a swift sandpiper.

He went to the back of the house, wanting a last look before he gave in to his exhaustion. His gaze took in his garden and the fields and bay beyond. The sun was high and bright, harsh on the grass and bramble, sapping moisture, shriveling them almost before his eyes. He would not live to see snow blank the fields, ice crystals sparkling the grasses, or whether a mockingbird would nest in his shrubbery again come spring. He needed to make decisions quickly. Yet he was at a loss. He thought of himself as a simple man. Simple tastes, simple values. How had his life gotten so complicated?

Moving the slider to let himself into the living room took most of his strength. When he recovered, he continued and held on to the back of his sofa until he reached the kitchen. He rested a moment against the doorframe. This room reminded him the most of Bonnie—the pale-yellow Formica with the teal trim and the matching teal accents around the windows. This had been hers, this little house on the downward slope of what was called Montauk Mountain, one of the loveliest spots in Montauk. It had girly touches—frilly curtains, and crocheted covers on the spare toilet roll—yet he felt at home in a way he never had before. He and Mary Elizabeth, like others who had moved to Montauk after they retired, felt like outsiders. By marrying Bonnie, who was born and raised in the area, he was welcomed inside the club. Theresa had been eighteen at the time of her mother's death and twenty when he married Bonnie. He'd been sure she would come around. She hadn't. He had been thrown out of the Promised Land bar trying to talk with her an embarrassing number of times. When he moved into Bonnie's house and offered Theresa the house she'd grown up in, she turned him down. When he sold it, she'd refused the money it brought. When Bonnie's brother Harve asked him to come in on a business venture called The Moorlands Development Co., he invested the money Theresa had refused and put the Moorlands shares in her name.

Otto had been thrilled and flattered to become a partner in Moorlands LLC. They'd held the land as an investment and watched property values go up, biding their time. Otto had felt like a man on payday jiggling the coins in his pocket, feeling flush. Besides himself and Harve, the other principals were Tim, a close friend and retired community college teacher, Gaspar, a wealthy surfer, and Pete Walker, big in county politics. Pete had died the year before and his son, Pete Jr., had inherited his shares. An election was coming up, and the

Democrats, who were in power, were rumored to be considering a moratorium on development. Even the Republicans were making noises that growth had to slow. Pete Jr. was pressing them to develop or sell the land. He said that if they didn't get their approvals now, they might lose the chance for years.

To maintain their options, they had gone along with Pete's urging to get preliminary approval, though they were not in agreement about putting in a subdivision. Harve passionately advocated for affordable housing; Tim was pushing for open space preservation. Gaspar had crazy ideas that changed every week and didn't bear consideration.

Otto wanted to leave Theresa a hefty inheritance, but he thought Pete Jr. was an officious little prick and was disinclined to do what he wanted.

He poured water into a small plastic bottle fitted with a strap he put over his neck so he could use both hands to traverse the long corridor to the bedroom, one palm pressed against each wall. He wondered what Theresa would make of all the things he'd kept of Mary Elizabeth's. He hoped she would understand he was honoring her mother's memory because he had loved her very much. There was the soft wisp of a chiffon scarf, as delicate as the lightest tissue, as yellow as chiffon pie. There was an assortment of photographs, cards, and letters Mary Elizabeth had written him, some from before they were married. What he treasured most was a pin. It was just inexpensive costume jewelry, a ballet dancer whose gold skirt was studded with tiny blue stones. The dancer's leg was lifted, her arms extended in joy. This was how he liked to remember Mary Elizabeth—the sweet sensitive girl, lighthearted, full of life—not the broken woman, split open and anguished, whose body he'd had to identify.

He curled his fingers around the pin; it felt hard and cold, as hard and cold as Theresa treated him. If nothing else, surely she would accept this pin after his death.

Otto steadied himself against the bureau. The pain was approaching, like the sound of a far-off train. The pain would pick up speed and soon overwhelm him, but he didn't want to take his pills yet. He needed to think things through . . . what the sudden reappearance of Clancy in his life might make possible. There was still time to reconcile and ask forgiveness for all the ways he knew he had failed his daughter.

He sat on the edge of his bed and removed his pants, letting them fall to the floor. He took a few deep breaths and then launched himself fully onto the bed. He tried to relax and ease into the pain rather than fight it. He had to stave off as long as possible the time when he would have to go into hospice, which meant living with as much pain as he could, resisting the little pills that brought relief. But if he waited too long, he'd be sitting up in bed as he had this morning, pillow against his chest as if to ward off a blow, his face slick with sweat.

He'd asked that the group meet within the next two weeks to vote on what direction to take. If Pete Jr. knew Otto was dying, he'd find a pretext to delay the vote until after his death. Then, since neither Tim nor Harve would budge on their positions, Pete would prevail by persuading Gaspar to his side. Otto had to make up his mind quickly. He wanted to die in peace, knowing he had done the right thing.

Otto took out a pill and removed the cap of the water bottle.

He swallowed, closed his eyes, and pressed his head back against the cushion. If Theresa would take the shares, his dilemma would be solved. Maybe, just maybe, Clancy could work a miracle.

Otto thought of the great Montauk chieftain, Wyandanch, who had fought a fierce war against the Connecticut Pequots. The Pequots had kidnapped Wyandanch's daughter on her wedding day and spirited her away. Wyandanch had gone to a powerful white man, Lion Gardner, for help. Gardner had negotiated with the Pequots, and Wyandanch's daughter was returned. In thanks, Wyandanch had given Gardner an island, which still bore his name.

Maybe Clancy would be his Lion Gardner and return his daughter to him. Maybe this place he had tended could be passed on and tended by her in turn.

CHAPTER 7: Clancy

Clancy didn't remember the dock area as being quite as extensive from when Otto had taken him fishing. He was surprised by the number of marinas, the fishing boats with rigs, ropes, and thick rusted chains, and the small yachts and speedboats.

He briefly watched the men haul off boxes of fish and hose down decks. Then he made his way to the nondescript ramshackle building called The Promised Land, where Theresa Nolan worked. A sign over the door said, "Locals Only."

Although it was only 5:00 p.m., it was dark inside; none of the early evening light made its way in. The room had low ceilings and wood paneling, and the bar dominated almost the full length of the room. There were a handful of tables with placemats, salt and pepper shakers, and ketchup bottles. He chose a table underneath a scary-looking fake shark. He hoped it was fake. Opposite him three men sat side by side at the bar watching soccer on a TV mounted in the corner. This early there was no one else in the main room. He saw an open doorway to a kitchen and another door at the opposite end of the bar. It led to a back room from which he could hear voices and the sound of a game in progress, maybe pool.

After a moment, a woman emerged from the back and, seeing him, headed over. He realized she was the redhead in the glamorous gown who had been dispensing champagne at the fund-raiser.

"Want to see a menu, or are we just drinking today?" She was in black jeans and T-shirt, her long hair pulled up and secured with a clip perched on her head like a large insect. Despite the sloppy look she was ridiculously gorgeous, and for some reason this made him want to laugh. Her face was a perfect oval, the skin pale and creamy. It really was too much. Most remarkable were her eyes. They were a curious golden topaz, but instead of conveying an expected tawny warmth, they were as cold as the coldest blue.

"A Samuel Smith's, if you've got it. And I'll take a look at the menu, thanks."

When she came back with the beer, he said, "You're Theresa Nolan, right?"

She took a step back. "Who wants to know?"

"You won't remember me, but we met as children. I'm Clancy Frederics." He stuck out his hand. She folded her arms over her chest, refusing his hand. He ignored the slight and went on. "I saw you at the party last night. I thought I'd look you up. Your dad used to take me out when he was with the police. I had dinner at your house a few times."

He waited for a flicker of recognition. She'd been a scowly little girl, peering from behind sofas and doorways. It hadn't been clear if she had resented him or was simply curious.

"You expect me to believe you remember me from what, twenty-five years ago? Give me a break."

Startled by her antagonism, Clancy lowered his beer before taking a sip. She swung on her heel and returned to the men at the bar. Clancy picked up the menu, but the letters blurred. This was proving more awkward than he'd expected.

When she came back to take his order, he was ready.

"I looked up your dad. He mentioned you were living here. That's when it clicked why you seemed familiar."

"Bullshit. My father sent you."

"There are other reasons a man might want to drop by."

If he was hoping for some softening, some effect of the flattery, he was disappointed. She'd heard it all before.

"Drop it, friend," she said, mildly. She grabbed the menu and stalked off.

Clancy nursed his beer and watched her behind the bar, chatting with the men and ignoring him completely. He didn't even know if she would take his order. He felt stupid and gauche and debated whether to leave. Finally she headed back and slapped down a check.

"Look, I'll go," he said, "but can you just give me one second?" She narrowed her eyes and crossed her arms, but at least she didn't move away.

"Even if it were about your father, would that be so terrible?"

She looked into the distance for a second, then yanked the chair opposite him and plunked down. She crossed her arms on the table and leaned forward, and he could almost convince himself dragon smoke came from her nostrils.

"Let me see if I can get through to you. I want nothing to do with him. Got it?" She scraped back the chair and stood up.

Clancy sat shocked and dumbfounded. She had what he'd felt the loss of all his life, and she just threw it away. His throat burned with the urge to play Otto's trump card.

"He won't live forever," he said, his voice shaky. It was as close as he could come without betraying Otto's confidence.

"Believe me, the only place I look forward to seeing my father is in his grave."

Clancy recoiled with a quick intake of breath. "How can you be so cruel?"

She stalked off. He withdrew a bill from his wallet and threw it on the table.

As he reached the door she called out, "Don't come back."

Outside, it was beginning to get dark. His stomach was growling. He followed the movement of people into a large outdoor plaza bordered with tubs of flowers and a complex of restaurants and shops with names like Pirate Booty and Ocean Pearl jewelers. At a takeout window, he ordered a combination plate of fried clams and grilled tuna, which came with an ear of corn and paper cup of coleslaw.

He settled at a picnic table and watched boats, twinkling with lights, motor into the harbor. All around him were families with excited children. A gull cawed an agonized cry, chasing away another. With a swoop of power wings, it descended on a French fry and made off with it to a nearby roof.

Clancy deposited his paper plate in a garbage bin and started back, passing the ice cream stand. He thought of the ice cream sundae Otto always bought him at the end of his visits and got in line. In front of him, a little girl rested on her father's shoulders, heels tapping his chest in impatience.

She cried out, "Chocolate sprinkles, chocolate sprinkles!"

As the cone was handed up to the girl, still on her father's shoulders, Clancy decided he would have chocolate sprinkles, too.

It was fully dark now, and the sound of the fishing boats as they thudded against the wooden pier with the movement of the tide intensified. He licked his ice cream, enjoying the sweet crunch of the sugar cone, and followed the girl and her father back toward the parking lot, surrounded by other family groups heading to their cars. It had always been hard for him to understand families, coming as he did into the middle of them and leaving so soon. Their dynamics were so peculiar and puzzling. He thought of Otto, lying in bed, alone, sick, in pain, wanting what he would never get. Clancy's throat closed over the cold ice cream. He had failed Otto in the only thing he'd ever asked of him.

Tomorrow was Sunday, when he would return home.

He finished his last bite and walked back to his car. He drove the dark streets through town and then along Old Montauk Highway to Bishops by the Sea. As he walked to his bungalow, the moon slipped from behind a cloud, full and luminous, and he was reminded of the night before, of his terror and exhilaration. Otto was the closest to a father as anyone, and he was dying. Clancy stood a moment and watched a cloud slowly approach the moon and pass over it. Perhaps the moon was a sign. He couldn't deliver Theresa to Otto, but perhaps he could deliver himself.

He'd never truly been needed before. He'd never truly had anything to give.

CHAPTER 8: Theresa

Theresa Nolan watched Clancy Frederics cross to the door and slam it shut. Under her fingers, the surface of the bar felt slick. She gave it a wipe, threw down the rag, and headed to the ladies' room.

She had vowed never to speak to her father again; this jerk, with his saccharine memories, wasn't going to change that.

She remembered Clancy from those childhood visits; she resented him even then.

Her father had said, "He's an orphan. I want you to be nice to him."

What she remembered thinking was, *Let someone else be nice to him, you're my daddy.* Her father had always been distant, and when he began to bring Clancy home, it had become clear: Her father had wanted a boy.

She bent over the sink and splashed water on her face. Her cheeks were flaming the way they always did when she was angry, flushed almost the color of her hair. The day her world fell apart, the day her mother died, she told her father he was a betrayer, a liar, and a killer. As she saw the shame in his eyes, she realized the balance of power between them had shifted. She was steel, she was diamond, focused to a bright, hard point. She would not soften.

That had been twelve years ago, when she was eighteen. She got a job as a waitress and trained as a bartender at the

Promised Land. She liked how it nestled up against the dock, close enough to smell the fish remains and to trip over the odd coil of rope or the three-legged dog that hung about. It was a rough, homey bar like a thousand other dockside bars, with wood-scarred tables and dirty fishnet hanging from the ceiling. She liked its unpretentiousness, and its anonymity. She liked living at the funky trailer park on the outskirts of town, liked the feeling of being on the tip of the island, the edge of the world, close enough to fall off. But there were times—times when she was reminded of her father's presence or when men got to her—when she feared somehow she'd be driven away from this place she loved.

As she returned from the ladies' room, Marty, the owner, emerged from the back lot via the kitchen, an unlit cigarette dangling from the corner of his mouth. He was built like a keg of beer, in his mid-fifties, and showed every second of it. He glanced down at Theresa's breasts and said, "Nice shirt."

Theresa turned her back and refilled the bowls of nuts and goldfish. Despite her disrespect, Marty wouldn't fire her because she was popular and could work any bar she wanted on the East End.

Kathy rushed in with her usual apologies for being late. The place was beginning to fill, mostly with fishermen. First the old-timers, who were too old to go out much but who never tired of telling stories or complaining about how much better things used to be. Then the young Turks, fresh off the water, boisterous and boastful, stinking of sweat, oil, and fish guts.

The hard-core regulars would line up at the bar, watching sports with one eye and her with the other. Sometimes she felt like a caged animal, performing for a circus audience, or a croupier, dealing napkins.

"Who was that guy you chased away?"

Sky slid onto a stool, Sky with his sky-blue eyes. He was protective of her, under the misapprehension that because she'd slept with him a few years back, theirs was a special connection. She was happy to let him think so. Ever since she'd given up her promiscuous ways and found refuge in the Church, she kept her true self tucked away, like a stone wrapped tightly in a square of moleskin. Her true intimacies were with God, and the sand, cliffs, and ocean in which He was reflected.

Still, she liked Sky. She liked looking at him, too. He claimed to have descended from an Algonquin who had married one of the early British settlers, and he had the broad high cheekbones and strong brows of native peoples. But his hair, which hung straight to his shoulders, was a coppery blond, striking against his blue eyes. His nickname had as much to do with his airhead personality as his eye color. He was never without the blue bandanna he wore headband-style, in solidarity, he said, with his ancestors.

"Just some jerk."

"I worried he was hassling you."

"Not like that." She lifted a glass off the overhead rack and slid it under the tap. What had Clancy Frederics really wanted, she wondered. Why play emissary for her father, if that was what he was doing? Foam poured up and over the edge of the glass—an amateur's mistake. She wiped the glass and slid it across the bar.

"I hear the fishing's been slow." She couldn't have cared less but keeping up with the waters was part of the job.

"Yeah, everybody's freaked."

Only once had she gone fishing with her father. After he had taken that boy, she begged him to take her, too. He showed her how to cast, his hand cupping her elbow, guiding her arm up and back. These days, if she spied her father at the post office or the grocery store, she out-waited him or turned away. He had given up trying to speak with her, so why would he contact her now?

There was a shout from the dart game in the back.

"Sky, you're up," someone called out.

Sky saluted Theresa with his glass and moved off. Will and Choppy took his place before her at the altar, ready for her to dispense Communion.

An hour or so later, the door opened and Cody stood in the doorway. Cody had been circling her all summer but hadn't cast his line just yet. Despite her efforts to be celibate, she must give something off like pheromones.

Kathy, catching her expression, asked, "What do you have against him?" When Theresa shrugged, Kathy said, "Seems pretty nice to me."

Theresa knew it unnerved everyone that although she seemed to like men, and they liked her, there was never a boyfriend. Nobody could stand a woman alone, not if that was the way the woman preferred it.

Kathy placed a hand on Cody's arm. "Good to see you!"

"Glad somebody thinks so." Cody grinned at Theresa.

He was big, with shaggy hair and beard, like an oversized teddy bear. He slid onto a stool. She was irked by the pull of attraction.

"The usual?"

Cody nodded. She rubbed lime around the rim of a glass and placed a bottle of Corona in front of him.

"So," he sipped. "Wanna hear my news?"

"Of course." She wiped the surface of the bar.

"When I came out here, I was at what is commonly called the end of my rope—bad divorce, no money, no job."

"Welcome to Montauk, haven for battered souls."

Her tone had more of an edge than she'd intended, but Cody threw back his head and laughed, choking on his beer.

"Careful." She passed him a napkin.

"Anyhow," he wiped his mouth, "I just lucked out. I got a job at the fish hatchery."

"Hey, that's great. Really."

"I'm psyched." He took a sip. "It's a pretty cool place. Ever been?"

"They took us in grade school."

"Why don't I give you a tour sometime?"

"That's okay, but thanks for asking."

"No sweat." He hopped off the stool, wiping a dribble of beer from his beard, face pinking from her brush-off. She felt a twinge of remorse.

The night went as nights did at the Promised Land Bar, except she couldn't lose herself in the work. Usually she felt like a dancer, melting from one movement to the next, lifting glasses with one hand as she poured with the other, pivoting to the cash register. Tonight she couldn't find the groove.

At 2:00 a.m., having finished the last closing tasks, she paused at the door before locking up to make sure no drunken idiots were hanging about. She slipped on her jean jacket against the cool night air. The jacket was a survivor, just like she was. It was what she had on when she left home, and she'd kept it alive by sewing and patching. She wore it over T-shirts on summer evenings and sweaters in fall and spring. In winter, she layered it over a thick, hooded sweat-shirt and under a plump down vest.

All was blackness beyond the illumination shed by the bar. The sky was matte, with no stars or moon. She leaned against the wooden doorframe, breathing in the tangy air, the metallic taste of late-night fog off the water. She heard nothing but the low tumbling of wood against resin, boats against their moorings. She let out a heavy sigh. There was no one. Had she expected her father to be lying in wait? Cody? Clancy Frederics? She slipped into her jeep and pulled away.

The road from the docks was empty of cars. At the inter-section with the main road, she turned left toward the Point, passing a jeep stabbed with fishing poles like acupuncture needles. Within a mile came her turn-off. Her headlights swept the potholes and bumps of the long dirt road and bored into the blackness. The road ended with the surprise of the trailer park, a small community of mobile homes they called the TP. She cut her lights and proceeded at a crawl to the easternmost trailer in the back row. Between the trailer she rented and the Point lay miles of preserved land, an area of forest, cliff, and wetland, crowded with mountain laurel, holly, tupelo, and other trees she couldn't identify, home to deer, red fox, and the elusive endangered blue-spotted salamander.

Theresa savored the darkness and the quiet. At night, the ocean was dominant; she let its lullaby calm her before heading inside. Just as she needed to be in the thick of the noise and chaos of human beings at the bar, so also was this utter solitude essential. She didn't reflect on this seemingly contradictory aspect of herself or much else that made her who she was.

Inside it was as orderly and trim as the hold of a meticulous sea captain, the bed tightly made, the kitchen Formica gleaming, the salt and pepper shakers and sugar bowl lined up in a row, as if snapping to attention.

She made herself a PB and J, poured a glass of milk, and ate staring out at the darkness, letting the peace of the ocean, dune, and wild sea grasses wash over her, driving away thoughts of men and her father. She longed to concentrate her soul to its essence, like a grain of sand, pure and tasting of salt. She lifted a quahog shell from the windowsill and ran her finger along its satiny purple-and-white interior. This was what she longed for—to hone and polish her soul to such simplicity, such purity.

———•◦••◦•———

In the morning, as on most days, Theresa walked along the beach below the cliffs to Mass at Our Lady of the Sea. The wind had scalloped wavy ridges in the sand. A few men faced the ocean, fishing poles angled provocatively from between their legs.

She reached the line of motels perched just behind the controversial artificial dune on the downtown beach. At the party, when a reporter had asked for her opinion, she'd turned so abruptly she sloshed Prosecco on his sleeve. The sabotage to the dune had been hers.

When the recent storm scoured the sand off the artificial dune and exposed the unsightly heap of bags, like padded bras on the unnaturally endowed beach, she had been outraged. The beach was sacred, and it had been despoiled. The town, the environmentalists, and the chamber talked a good game about working together to find a better solution to erosion, but she doubted they'd come to any consensus. She'd gone late at night and plunged a large boning knife into bag after bag, slicing them open with savage glee.

What she hadn't known was all sand was different. Like Goldilocks's porridge, it had to be just right. At the party, she overheard people talking and was horrified to learn the coarse yellow type she unleashed was incompatible and so heavy, it would clump and settle when it made its way into the ocean. She needed forgiveness.

She entered the church, blessed herself, and stared at the light coming in through the stained-glass windows. The daily Mass kept her grounded. After she had left home and was on her own for a few years, her life began to unravel. One day, to get out of the rain, she had slipped into the church. The peace and calm quieted her, and she began to visit frequently. It wasn't long before the pastor, Father Molina, approached her and asked if she'd like to talk. Something about him, his gentleness, won her over. Over time, he helped her see that she wanted to turn her life around, to stop her careless behavior with men. She began to understand an incident with her father when she was very young had triggered her promiscuity. Still, she couldn't share what had happened with Father Molina. She couldn't yet face it head on and forced the memory to the edges of her consciousness.

After Mass on the way back along the shore, she spied a neighbor, Beach Bum Barry. BB stalked the beach with a metal detector, looking for lost treasures. She often saw him when she was out walking or working on a project of her own, planting beach grasses to shore up what was left of the low dunes in front of the TP. The work had become for her a form of spiritual practice. Sometimes she could almost hear a hum, as if the universe was communicating to her, essence to essence.

She suspected she and BB were both chasing something ephemeral, with little chance of success. Yet they kept on.

"Red Rose—" his face glowed "—you're looking gorgeous."

"That's what you always say."

"Have you heard the news?" He made a woeful face.

"Beer cans left on the beach again?"

"Worse." He hitched up his pants over his ample belly. She'd have thought all the walking would have slimmed him down, but no. "The town won't let us keep the rock wall."

"Then we'll have no protection." The recent storm that scoured sand off the large artificial dune in town had also damaged the dunes that fronted their community. The TP had massed boulders along that stretch of beach to shore them up.

"Just saying what I heard." The red veins on BB's nose were more noticeable than usual. *He must be near sixty*, Theresa realized. Somehow, she'd never associated an age with him; he seemed eternal, like the beach itself.

"I'm sure you're worrying for nothing." BB often got more worked up than he needed to.

"No, Theresa, you're wrong." The use of her name startled her; BB only called her Red Rose. "Everyone's upset." The breeze whipped the wisps of hair on the top of his head into a mini-cyclone, which had her momentarily mesmerized.

"Who's everyone?"

"The board."

"Who's president now?" She never went to meetings. "That guy in the pink trailer? Treetops?"

"Joe Tretorn?"

"Yeah, him."

"Let's go see him."

Theresa threw her arm across BB's shoulders, and they headed up from the beach side by side, passing rows of trailers, some fronted with pebbles or native grasses, others with patches of grass. Most trailers were decorated with beachy kitsch—buoys, a mermaid sculpture made of driftwood—but a few were upgraded, bought by people as weekend getaways. This irked her. Although she had put a little money aside each month to someday purchase a trailer of her own, prices remained out of reach.

Joe Tretorn was a short stocky man, fiftyish, completely bald. He greeted them wearing a red bathrobe that clashed painfully with the Pepto-Bismol pink of his trailer. He held a cup of coffee, his face mushy, as if he'd just awakened.

He invited them in and gestured to the little kitchen nook. He pulled on a shelf that folded down to become a countertop cutting board, from which utensils dangled, and extracted two coffee mugs.

"Clever," Theresa said.

"Made it myself." People in the trailer park delighted in showing off their improvements, as if competing for a prize in the most creative use of small spaces.

"So . . ." He poured them coffee. "You want to know what's happening. Gosh, how popular I've become since serving on this board. You should come to meetings, Theresa." He spread his fingers on the table, which was tiled in mosaic pieces to depict a harbor scene.

Theresa placed her mug on a large white sail. "I work nights." Issues like plans for the community room or the landscaping didn't interest her. "Why is the town making us remove the boulders?"

"We never put in for a permit. Hard structures aren't allowed. Supposedly they increase erosion further down the beach."

"How come they allow the fake dune downtown, then?"

"Sandbags are considered 'soft.'"

Theresa just looked at him.

"I know. In any case, the downtown beach project was the feds, not the town's doing."

She stroked the glaze of the cobalt-blue boat with a forefinger. "What, then?"

Tretorn took her hand between both of his and pressed it like a panini. "We're setting up a meeting and asking for a permit. If that doesn't fly, we'll appeal. We have any number of ways of fighting this."

Fight? Theresa thought. *What power do we have?* A slant of sun angled through the window, glinting off the metallic in the tile.

"We got no money for lawyers." BB jostled his cup in agitation.

"Don't freak out just yet, okay?"

Tretorn rested his forefingers against the puffy pouches beneath his eyes as if to flatten them. "Let's see what happens when we meet with the town."

Theresa thanked Tretorn for his time and then parted company with BB outside. She retrieved her wagon with her tools and flats of American beach grass and wheeled it down to what was left of their beach. It was just a paltry strip, mostly pebbles and a smattering of broken shells and scraggly vegetation. When she'd first come, there had been a wide stretch of sand, but the oceanfront wasn't even passable now except at low tide.

What they needed was a proper shoring up of the area, something like her small efforts to plant beach grass but on a grand scale. She'd suggest this to Tretorn.

She had chosen a section of dune to work on farther down the beach from where the boulders had been placed. Although she'd planted bare root plugs in neat rows at the proper angle to the water and wind, most of the plants hadn't gotten established early enough to withstand the ferocity of the storm. The few strands that remained looked sparse and forlorn.

She heard a cry. A gull was bent over a crab, grasping it in its beak and shaking it, then dashing it against a rock to extract the meat.

She gathered up the tattered plants and knelt in front of the dune. She would be just as tenacious, she thought.

Like Sisyphus, she'd begin once again.

CHAPTER 9: Clancy

Stepping outside his bungalow, Clancy startled a deer browsing in the bramble bordering the road. He and the deer stared into each other's eyes before it bounded away. The deer reminded him of Theresa—still, alert, skittish. Clancy was on his way to see Otto now and dreaded telling him of his failed encounter with his daughter. The day matched his mood, clouds thick and unmoving, air heavy.

Otto came to the door and leaned against the wall; his skin seemed even grayer than the day before. Clancy followed him into the living room.

"I've been up for hours, thinking," Otto said. "You talk first. I assume it was no good, or you'd have already said."

"I'm sorry, Otto. Theresa was really resistant. I was shocked at her level of anger."

Otto sagged deeper into his lounger. "It was just a faint hope, really."

Clancy wished there was something comforting to say. "Maybe if you reconsider and let her know about your health?"

Otto moved his hand in the air as if to swat away a bit of dust, but the gesture lacked force. "No time."

Clancy winced at his implication. "I've decided to stay out here for a bit. I could use the break, and it would give us some time together." He had arranged with Julienne to rent his bungalow indefinitely and told his boss he needed to be with a dying friend. He had more than enough vacation time accumulated.

Otto's eyes filled with tears. Clancy put his arms clumsily around him and the chair. He smelled the musty fabric of the upholstery and the faint, strange odor of Otto's skin. Otto's body felt limp. Then, as if injected with starch, he stiffened and gently pushed Clancy away and wiped his eyes.

"I'm sorry. It must be the drugs."

"I think you're incredibly brave."

Otto shook his head. "Not brave. It's just that I need to see something through. But right now, I have to be in bed. I feel done in."

"Let me help you."

Clancy half-lifted Otto from his chair and walked him to use the bathroom and then into the bedroom. Otto lay shivering until Clancy covered him with a blanket. "I need those," Otto pointed. "Two." The bottle was on the night-stand. Clancy fetched a glass of water and handed Otto the small white pills. Morphine, 5 mg.

Otto fell asleep, his breathing a low snore that was so soothing, Clancy drifted off for a few minutes. He awoke to the sound of the wind rattling a branch against the side of the house. Outside the sky had darkened, and the tomato plants in the garden swayed on their stakes, leaves trembling.

"We need to talk." Otto had awakened.

Clancy turned from the window. He pulled his chair closer to Otto's bedside.

"I appreciate your gesture, but I've arranged for hospice. It's all set up, for when my doctor and I agree. I don't think it'll be too long."

"I'm sticking around anyhow."

Otto reached out and squeezed Clancy's hand. "Okay, then. Hospice will take care of the body. You can help me with the soul, if you will."

"Otto, I'm in no way religious."

"That's not what I mean. There are decisions I need to make. Big ones. I think talking will help. Everyone else has a stake in it one way or another and can't be objective. I feel as if you were sent to me at just the right moment."

"I'm glad." Listening was something he could do, something that had, in a way, defined his life.

"I've always believed ownership is sacred," Otto said. "I've always believed if it's my land, I can do with it what I want, and no one should have a say in that."

"Is there some problem with your place here?"

Otto shook his head. "There's a parcel of land owned by Moorlands Development Corp. Years ago I was asked to join a partnership to buy it. It's eleven acres. It's just beyond what you can see from the back of my house, adjacent to Hither Woods. The identity of the principals is secret, and that's kept pressure off us. The idea was to sit on it, let it build in value." Otto shifted his position and winced, his breathing becoming audible. "One of the partners died last year, and his son inherited. He pushed us to file an application to develop, to protect our options. There've been rumors the town may put a building moratorium in place. The five of us are to meet soon. Without me, the one who wants to develop will prevail. I need to die knowing that I've left behind something good. I'm just not sure what that is."

"You're not sure what you think would be the best use of the land?"

"Right. My buddy Tim is for preserving the land— saving it for the birds and the bees. My brother-in-law, Harve, wants it for affordable housing. Another, Gaspar, has a new idea every two minutes. He's talking about a holistic healing center—some sort of cockamamie." Otto rolled his eyes. "Pete, the aggressive one, wants to develop or cash out. None of them will budge, so whoever I side with, wins."

"How much time do you have to make the decision?"

"Plenty, if it weren't for being sick. To develop there'll have to be an environmental impact statement and a public hearing. On the other hand, if I decide in favor of affordable housing or open space preservation, we'd withdraw the application to develop and sell to the town."

Otto's head fell back on his pillow. His skin looked pasty, with a light sheen of sweat. Clancy suggested tea. The pilot light on the gas range had gone out, and there was some spilled water around one of the jets, so he wiped it up with a paper towel and then fished for the box of Bishops by the Sea matches he'd pocketed to get the flame going. When he returned to the room, Otto was asleep again. Clancy left the tea by his bedside with a note that he'd call later and tiptoed from the house.

He stood a minute gazing out into the far distance where Otto had gestured the Moorlands parcel to be. He tried to imagine showpiece homes or an affordable housing complex, but both were hard to envision. He wondered what happened to deer and birds and mice and whatever else lived in woods and pastureland when a parcel was developed. Did they all crowd into other places, or did some die off? He knew so little about the natural world. It had never seemed particularly important.

He glanced at his watch; time to meet up with Max. When he had arranged renting his bungalow with Julienne, he had offered to take Max on an outing.

As he passed through town and along the coastal road, he wondered if this—this sense of obligation and duty mixed with affection—was what it felt like to be part of a family. Whenever he told people he'd been orphaned, their eyes would fill with sympathy; they'd been relieved when he said he had lived in foster homes. The word "home" had such resonance. Yet he'd never felt at home. The group facility was terrible, but he preferred it, preferred being with other boys who had suffered losses like his own. It was the foster homes that were unfathomable, odd fiefdoms, places he wasn't sure he wanted to be enfolded into. Each time he'd been fostered, all he'd wanted was to get away.

Julienne answered her doorbell, rag in hand, smudges of gray paint on her chin.

"Am I too early? Sorry to interrupt your work."

She followed his gaze to the rag and laughed. "I didn't realize I was still holding this. Come on in." She opened the door wide. "Max is really excited."

"He's a great kid."

"He likes you, too." Julienne smiled. "He usually wanders about on his own. I don't know if I mentioned it, but he was severely asthmatic as a little boy, and we home-schooled him for the first couple of years. Except for Jonah, he doesn't have close friends."

"I'm sure he'll catch up," Clancy said, then paused and added, "but what do I know?" He hadn't ever caught up; he was friendless until college. He shivered, recalling the hostility, the fistfights, the bugs placed under his pillow to torment him.

Max came running from his room.

"Ready to ride?" Clancy asked. He'd seen an ad for horseback riding at the county park.

"Yes!" Max rubbed his hands in glee. Clancy and Julienne glanced at each other and laughed. Then Julienne grabbed Max to her and hugged him hard, kissing the top of his head.

Clancy found he had to look away.

CHAPTER 10: Otto

From the way the back of his house was situated, Otto couldn't see his neighbors on either side, as if he were alone in the universe. The expanse of meadow in the distance seemed to shimmer in the light, a movement so subtle he imagined a native hunter, bow aimed at a rabbit hiding in the grass. The Montauketts had lived on the peninsula until driven out by the end of the 1890s. When woody vegetation encroached on the open downs, they set the fields on fire, making it easier to spot small game to hunt.

His legs trembled; he gripped the edge of the doorframe to steady himself. He didn't have the energy to cross the room to the light switch, and the room had the soft glow of the inside of a church. He remembered the rasping sound as he yanked down the kneeler to sink into prayer, the smooth feel of the wood under his hands as he gripped the back of the pew in front of him, the texture of the worn, red-velvet seat cushion. For a moment, he longed for that solace. Religion had gone by the board after Mary Elizabeth died.

He moved hand over hand to the living room and sagged into his chair. He hoped he hadn't been wrong to postpone hospice. Maybe he wasn't going to be able to hold out as long as he needed to. He put a lined pad on his lap.

Dear Clancy,

I wish there were time to explain why this decision about Moorlands is so important. Things seemed so much simpler when I first came to Montauk. Or maybe there simply wasn't as much opportunity for greed to show its hand.

He felt an intense pinch like a stapler in his chest. The pain lasted only a minute, but he was panting, his face wet with sweat.

He picked up the pen and went on.

CHAPTER 11: The Fire

The orange glow in Hither Woods lit up the sky, a strange trembly shimmer, visible even as far as the docks. Fishermen were the first to call in the alarm; the volunteer firemen among them abandoned their gear and gunned their trucks toward the firehouse. Downtown, the storekeepers, post office clerks, and gas station attendants looked to the west, momentarily puzzled at the direction of the light, until seconds later the eerie sound of the fire alarm made it clear.

At Bishops by the Sea, a mile south of the woods that were burning, Clancy slept soundly in his bungalow. Up at the house, Rob was in the shower, and Julienne went to wake Max up for school. At the window to check the weather, she detected the faint odor of smoke and saw a diaphanous glow over Hither Woods, plumes like fog drifting their way. As the alarm pierced the morning silence, she raced through the house closing windows, afraid the smoke would trigger an asthma attack in Max.

Several miles east, far from Hither Woods, Theresa sat with her back to the cliffs. Too wired to sleep after work, she had headed down to the beach, walking in the dark, the half-moon light gilding the water. She pulled a down comforter around her and settled in to watch the sunrise, trying to catch the precise second when the night became day, when the first tinge of light appeared, that imperceptible shift. The light became so bright she had to shield her eyes, unaware that behind her the sky was fierce with a different kind of glow. This far away the sound of the fire alarm was too faint to hear over the thudding of the ocean.

———•◦••◦•———

The fire's glow shot through Molly and Billy's bedroom window, rousing them from sleep. Billy, a volunteer fireman, leapt up. From where their house was situated, he could see bright orange flames shooting up above Hither Woods close by. Seconds later came the shrill sound of the fire alarm.

"Get dressed, quick." He shoved his T-shirt into his pants and yanked his reflective coat and helmet from the closet. "I can't tell which direction it's moving."

Molly leaned over for a kiss, but he flew past her down the stairs.

Billy jumped into his truck and accelerated so hard, his wheels spewed chunks of dirt. He raced up Navy Road, over the railroad tracks and onto Industrial Road, the fire bright in his rearview mirror. There had been a legendary fire, decades before, when a spark from a Long Island railroad train burned acres of Hither Woods. At the intersection with Edgemere, police vehicles lined the road. The traffic light at the firehouse was flashing as a heavy rescue pumper peeled out, sirens shrieking.

Billy was assigned to one of the crews of six to dig a ditch about twenty feet out and along the perimeter of Hither Woods. They piled into a fire truck and headed back the way Billy had just come, passing his driveway and going the half-mile farther to the parking area at the eastern end of Hither

Woods near the pier into Fort Pond Bay. Flames were visible, coming from the interior of the woods. Conditions had been dry, and the fire seemed to be moving quickly, gobbling up understory, dark smoke billowing their way.

Billy bent over his shovel and dug in. Within minutes his skin felt hot, and he was soaked with sweat. He kept an eye on the flames as he dug, muscles burning.

"Harder, harder," the crew leader called, and he bent again.

A short while later, another crew joined theirs, and they continued to work, inching along, digging into the dry brambles and grasses on the outskirts of the woods, piling the dirt, resting a moment, shoveling again.

After several hours, the fire was extinguished and the chief drove up to say they could pack it in. Billy leaned on his shovel and wiped his face on his soaked shirt. A wide swath of meadow between the ditch and the woods was charred and flattened; trees at the edge of the woods were shriveled and black. He felt nauseated by the destruction.

Billy climbed stiffly into his truck, lower back aching. As he passed the intersection of the road that led up to the height of land near where Otto Lansky lived, he wondered if the fire had reached the meadow bordering his house. He'd been to see Otto just a few days earlier to pick up his scout troop files.

Otto's car was in the driveway; Billy decided to check up on the old man. From Otto's house only a bit of the fire damage was visible—a fringe of singed grass and a few blackened pines in the distance, though a smoky haze clouded the air. Billy pressed the doorbell and ran his tongue over his teeth, tasting the ashes that filled his mouth. He rang the bell again. He rubbed his nose on his sleeve; his insides were probably full of smoke and dirt and even the residue of burned trees and grasses.

No answer. He stood a moment, uncertain. No one in

Montauk locked their doors. He hesitated, then pushed. The door swung in soundlessly.

"Otto? It's Billy Linehan. You okay?"

He could hear only the faint ticking of a clock. He closed the door behind him and started toward the kitchen. The acrid scent of the fire permeated the house. The place was dark; he ran his hand along the kitchen wall until he found the switch. The light sprang on, and he jumped back in fright. Otto lay on the floor on his back, his right arm on his chest, as if pledging allegiance, his eyes and mouth open.

News spread quickly of Otto's death, reaching the post office, the grocery store, and the pizza place. The town's pace shifted; everyone found time to spend a moment on the checkout line or in the bank lobby.

"Did you hear? Otto Lansky is dead," the post office clerk said to the fourth-grade teacher, who came in to mail a package.

"Otto Lansky." The teacher passed on the information to the liquor store owner as she paid for a bottle of chardonnay.

Townspeople were advised to wear masks when outside, although the autumn's stiff winds would remove the smoke quickly. There was no word about how the fire might have started, but its severity was blamed on the unusual dry weather of the past month.

"We're lucky not more of the woods were affected," Tonya at the coffee shop said, carafe paused at a dangerous angle.

Along the Old Montauk Highway a workman, repairing a roof leak, remembered how he'd gone once with friends to hunt deer in Hither Woods not far from the area that was now scorched. He remembered the evening chill, the talk around the campfire, the sharp unfamiliar taste of beer. He remembered the thrill of hanging out with the tough crowd, the fear of getting caught because hunting season hadn't yet opened. The roofer paused to reload his nail gun, smiling to himself. They hadn't gotten caught or gotten any deer, either, but it was one of the best memories of his youth.

The clerk behind the counter in the drug store found herself thinking about the boy who had taken her for a walk once after school. They had crossed the meadow now destroyed by the fire and then, just where Hither Woods began, he cupped her chin and kissed her. The boy had grown into a man who worked at the Ford dealership in Wainscott, only a casual acquaintance now. She had never forgotten that moment, the golden light on the meadow, the softness of his lips.

———— ·•··• ————

The call from the police awoke Theresa after just a few hours' sleep. From outside the trailer, a piercing sound entered her consciousness. The trailer park lay underneath the flyway, streams of birds heading south for the winter.

She listened without a word, then placed the phone face down on the windowsill. What bird did that piercing sound belong to? Her father would have known. Her father used to put a finger over her lips so she wouldn't make a noise. She would scan the foliage, the branches, searching out a shape, a movement, and eventually she would see what he saw.

"Notice the bird's size," he would say. "Notice the shape of the tail and especially the beak, notice where the bird is perched. High on a branch? Deep in a thicket? Pecking along the ground? Clinging to the tree bark with its feet?"

A sense of loss swept through her like a gust of wind, stopping her breath. Her father was dead. The bird trilled again. Sweet. Achingly sweet. He was gone. What she had wished for had happened, and she would not be able to ask him anything ever again.

She had hated him. She was sure she had hated him. She should not be feeling ripped apart by the call of a bird.

The wind slammed the door against the body of the trailer as she stepped out. The sky far out over the ocean was blue, most of the haze from the fire already dissipated. She pulled up the hood of her sweatshirt and lowered her head into the wind like a prizefighter. Swallows were doing wheelies in the air currents. She climbed over the boulder barrier and headed east, walking alternately on sand and on small rocks that rolled underfoot, clacking and hissing as the surf came and went in its ceaseless, tireless way.

She settled on a log nestled into a hollow of the cliff face. Erosion had scoured the cliffs as if a giant had run fingernails deep down its slope. Every day, every minute, pieces of the peninsula crumbled into the ocean. The loss was infinitesimal to the naked eye, but it was measurable . . . as much as 100 feet per century, some said. She wondered if over time the entire peninsula would disappear.

Theresa waited to be soothed by the ocean's motion, but she felt hollow, as scoured inside as the cliffs. Waves hissed among the pebbles like angry gossips, then turned their backs on her, offering nothing. Why, when it was her father who had died, did she feel as if it was God who had forsaken her?

———◦•✦•◦———

Julienne and Max were at the kitchen coloring. Max's book had horses and ranch life. Hers had intricate, vaguely Moroccan designs. They shared the crayons between them. Max had been irritable all day, annoyed she'd kept him home from school. Although the forest fire had subsided by late morning, the smoke still hung in the air, and she didn't want to chance an asthma attack.

The phone rang, and she passed Max the purple crayon as she got up. It was Billy. "You okay?" she asked. "It must have been pretty intense today."

"Yeah, but that's not why I'm calling." He told her about finding Otto's body.

"Oh no," Julienne said, choking up.

"Why are you crying?" Max asked, when she turned back to the table, wiping her eyes.

"Mr. Lansky has died. I'm so sorry, sweetie." She put her arms around Max and pressed his head to her. They were quiet a moment, and then she remembered. Clancy.

He had seemed happy since reconnecting with Otto. She hated that she was going to have to shake him up with this news.

Outside the air smelled singed, and a layer of smoke drifted high overhead.

———

Clancy was tying the shoelaces of a new pair of sneakers with bright yellow laces. *Why not break out of my usual rut*, he'd decided. He was sore from the horseback riding but energized. He collected expertise and experiences the way Max collected artifacts. At one foster home, he'd learned to cook spaghetti and meatballs. In a housing project in Queens, he'd played marbles, and he still had a jar filled with the most special ones he'd won. Now he could add horseback riding to his tally. These small things pleased him, as if, added up, they consti-tuted a real life, a life of worth and meaning, of consequence.

There was a knock: light, clipped, discreet. Not Max's thump and not Julienne's usual *rat-a-tat-tat*. But there she was, agitating a curl, twirling it, and letting it rebound, a habit with which, even in just these few days, he had become familiar.

"Clancy, I have awful news."

"Come on in." He stepped aside.

She entered but stayed just inside the door. "I'm so sorry to tell you this, but Otto is dead."

"Otto?" Clancy said, stupidly. "I just saw him yesterday. He was fine." Otto had not been fine, but surely not so close to death. Clancy felt as if his clothes had become concrete.

"You'd better sit down. You've gone white."

"I'm all right." His hand went to his throat. Her eyes followed the gesture. He dropped his hand.

"I know you hadn't seen him in all these years, but it's still a loss."

Clancy nodded, throat constricting. He wanted in the worst way to cry, to be gathered up and comforted. He turned away.

"My cousin Billy is a volunteer firefighter and dropped by to check on Otto. Billy said it might have been smoke inhalation because Otto's place was downwind of the fire. The police are calling the death suspicious until they know for sure."

"Suspicious?" Clancy took a step back.

"They took the body to be autopsied. So any service has to wait. I'll check in with you when I learn more." She rested a hand on his shoulder. Though it was the briefest of touches, the back of his neck tingled in response.

CHAPTER 12: Clancy

The next day, long after the fire was out, the rains came. Clancy hadn't noticed the weather turn. The air itself seemed to ooze water; it didn't seem directional, sky to ground, but was simply everywhere, as if the bungalow were underwater. It perfectly matched his mood, mourning Otto.

Julienne hadn't gotten back to him about the arrangements. Clancy considered calling the Promised Land bar, but he doubted Theresa would claim the body. That task would likely fall to the brother-in-law or to the partner Otto said was his closest friend.

On the window ledge was Clancy's growing pile of matchboxes. He emptied some matches on the table and moved them around with a finger. He'd make Max a little pavilion, like the one on the village green.

The first matchbook structure he'd ever built was a house. He had carefully applied glue to the matches to make squares, then attached the sides of the squares to each other, pressing and holding them together just so. Figuring out openings and extra stories was a brain tease. It was the perfect hobby; he could play undisturbed in small spaces, a closet or an upper bunk, and his creations were small enough that he took his best ones with him each time he moved.

It had been a long time since he'd built something. He fanned out the matchsticks to create triangles, attached them to a paper backing for stability, and then formed them into a tented hat to create the top of the pavilion. He enjoyed figuring out how to put things together. He remembered when he first understood he had a talent for it—with LEGOs, which he encountered at one of the foster homes. The LEGOs belonged to the boy in the house.

The boy's parents said, "Ian, please share," and Clancy saw the red-hot light that pulsed in Ian's eyes and said quickly, "I don't like that kind of toy."

One afternoon, Ian was at a party and his parents were watching TV. Clancy stood looking at the yellow and red and blue pieces heaped on the floor of Ian's room. He made sure Ian's parents were engrossed, and then picked up two pieces and clicked them together. He picked up another, then another, working rapidly, tongue hanging from his mouth. Minutes passed. He forgot to listen, to be alert.

"Wow."

Clancy dropped the piece he'd been holding. "I'm sorry!"

"It's fine, Clancy," Ian's father said. "We want you to share Ian's toys. He has more than enough."

"No, they're his. I just wanted to see what it was like."

Ian's father came closer. "You're amazing at this. How did you make those turrets? Marge! Come here. You have got to see this!"

Clancy felt the tears gathering in his throat. He knew what would happen. How could these grownups not understand?

Now Clancy brought the pavilion roof to the windowsill to dry. The rain had become softer, lending a dreamy quality to the world outside.

He had waited until Ian's parents went to bed and then disassembled his creation. But Ian's parents told Ian what Clancy had done and pressured Clancy to make a new one. Afterward, Ian did everything he could to torment Clancy.

Ian's parents didn't want to give Clancy up, he knew that. But in the end of course they did. They couldn't send Ian back, after all.

Turning from the window, Clancy realized, *I can purchase my own damn LEGOs*. He'd go into town, rain or no rain. He grabbed an umbrella and headed out to his car. He'd just turned on the engine when his phone rang.

"Clancy Frederics? This is Detective Tobias."

The detective explained they were investigating Otto's death. Apparently Clancy was one of the last people to see Otto alive.

Clancy drove slowly into town, present and past sadness overlapping like a wave—Otto, those of his childhood—accompanied by the dirge-like rhythm of the windshield wipers.

The police station was tucked away behind stores in the center of town, easy to spot with the patrol cars parked outside. Clancy entered a small waiting room. A clerk glanced up from her phone conversation and put a hand over the mouthpiece.

"I'm here to see Detective Tobias."

She led him into an investigation room, and a moment later two officers joined him and introduced themselves. Detective Tobias was short, middle-aged, and compact. Thin and with a head of unruly hair, Detective Barola, the junior officer, towered over him like a stalk of celery. They indicated a seat for Clancy and settled on the opposite side of the table. Tobias leaned forward.

"According to Billy Linehan, who discovered Mr. Lansky's body, you left Otto a note. How did you know Mr. Lansky?"

"He took me on outings when I was a boy. I recently reconnected with him." Clancy folded his hands before him on the table. "I visited him at his home Saturday and then again on Sunday."

"I'm very sorry for your loss. What was the purpose of your visits?"

"Just social." He interlaced his fingers.

"Is that what brought you to Montauk, Mr. Frederics?"

"No, I came out for a party on Friday night. Julienne Bishop invited me to stay at her bungalow colony for the weekend."

"What time was your visit with Mr. Lansky on Sunday?"

Clancy loosened his fingers. "I came around eleven and left a little before one. I'd promised to take the Bishops' son Max horseback riding."

"How did Mr. Lansky seem when you saw him?" Tobias asked.

Clancy cast his mind back to the day before. The teacup by the bedside, Otto's face, so weary even in sleep. "He wasn't feeling great. I made him tea and helped him to bed."

"He was in bed when you left?"

"Yes. He had fallen asleep."

"His body was found on the kitchen floor."

Clancy recoiled. He had assumed Otto had died in his sleep. "I guess he must have gotten up."

"Did you see a pill bottle with morphine tablets?" Barola asked.

"Yes. He asked me to give him two pills."

"Do you know why he would have been taking such a drug?"

"He said he was in pain. He told me he wasn't in good health. Have you checked with his doctor?"

The two detectives exchanged glances. "Was he depressed, do you think?"

A cold feeling came over Clancy. It took him a moment to answer. "He had some things on his mind, but I don't think he was suicidal, if that's what you're asking."

"So he wasn't depressed?"

"Did the pills have something to do with his death?"

"We can't comment on that. Is there anything else you can tell us?"

"I don't think so."

"If anything occurs to you, please give us a call." Tobias handed Clancy his card and walked him out. As he opened the door for Clancy, Tobias said, "Have you visited Hither Woods while you've been here?"

"No. I've never been there."

Tobias held his gaze, then nodded and stepped out of the way to let Clancy pass.

Outside the rain had cleared, leaving the air heavy and wet, but Clancy no longer felt like buying LEGOs.

He was just hanging up his wet jacket in the bungalow's bathroom when there was a knock. Julienne must have heard he'd been at the police station. He opened the door with a smile, then flinched. It was the detectives.

"Sorry to bother you, but we have a few more questions. Can we come in?"

"Of course." He stepped aside.

Tobias scanned the room. "Look at this." He gestured with his chin at the windowsill where the little pavilion sat drying.

"A hobby." Clancy removed the newspapers off the chairs for the officers to sit, but they continued to stand.

"I see you have quite a few of these distinctive Bishops by the Sea matches." Clancy followed Tobias's gaze to the tower of the peach-and-blue boxes he'd amassed. He said nothing. Tobias let the silence build. Clancy knew the trick, yet he felt his anxiety rise.

"One of these boxes was found next to the stove in Mr. Lansky's home."

"I had to light the pilot under the kettle to make him his tea. I must have left one there."

"Mr. Lansky may have died of smoke inhalation."

The words hung in the air; it took Clancy a moment to understand Tobias's meaning. He felt a swell of panic. He had once set a fire, an attempt to get away from a foster home. Surely they couldn't know about that.

Tobias was studying his face. Clancy pressed his palms against his thighs, willing himself to appear unruffled.

"Did you know Mr. Lansky made you both a beneficiary *and* the executor of his will?"

Stunned, Clancy's hand went to his throat. "That doesn't make sense. We hadn't seen each other in years. Not until this past weekend."

"Yes," Tobias said. "It seemed . . . surprising . . . to us, too."

Even though Tobias's tone was mild, Clancy flushed from the insinuation. He began to rise from his chair.

Tobias lifted his palms as if to stay a rearing horse. "Please, no need to take offense. We're investigating a suspicious death here. We have to ask uncomfortable questions. So, Mr. Lansky didn't tell you he was making you his executor or a beneficiary?"

Clancy stood anyhow. He and Tobias were toe to toe, eyes locked. "That's correct."

Tobias took a step back. "The lawyer who's handling Otto's estate is a Ms. Jewel. You'll want to give her a call." He went to the door, Barola at his heels. Then, as an afterthought, he said, "The will's a doozy."

"Wait. Explain what you mean."

Barola gave a rueful shrug. "Sorry. Gotta leave that for the lawyer."

Clancy's hands shook as he punched in the number for Ms. Jewel; he got voice mail. He decided to walk over to the house to see if Julienne had learned anything about Otto's funeral service.

"Did something happen?" she said when she answered the door, scanning his face.

"The police. I don't know why they keep questioning me."

He followed her into the kitchen. She poured him a cup of coffee, and they settled at the table. The coffee, mixed with his fear, tasted bitter. He was plunged back into childhood, when authorities came to exert power and shake up his world.

"I can't tell if they're investigating Otto's death or the forest fire. Or if they think they're connected." His words came out in a rush.

"Breathe." She got up and stood behind him. "Breathe." She pressed her hands efficiently up and down his back. "Come on, breathe with me."

He wanted to ease against her and forget everything. He took a few long and steady breaths. When he opened his eyes, she was back in her seat, staring at him. Her face did not contain the expression of warmth he expected.

"Sorry," he said. He seemed always to be saying sorry.

"You looked like you were going to have a panic attack. That's a technique I do with Max. His asthma."

"They made a big deal of the fact that I have a stack of your matchboxes."

She looked puzzled. "All I know from Billy is they aren't sure whether Otto died of natural causes."

"Otto told me he was sick, but he wanted it kept secret. He was taking morphine. Maybe the police think he took too much." Clancy took a quick sip; the coffee went down the wrong way, and he coughed. "I gave him his pills, but I don't think . . . at least I hope—"

His throat clamped up and he coughed to clear it. "I just gave him what he asked for—two pills."

A wary look came into her eyes. She made a dismissive gesture, as if to disperse his troubles into the air. "I'm sure you're worrying for nothing."

"He made me a beneficiary."

An expression of alarm darted across her face. "Look, we had a good lawyer for our suit over the fence. He's local and knows how things work out here. He's not a criminal lawyer, but I'm sure he can help."

"I'd be very grateful," Clancy said. His cup clattered as he put it back into the saucer.

Julienne left to get the lawyer's number. When she returned and handed him the slip of paper, she seemed distant, as if his falling under suspicion was some sort of breach. Feeling unwelcome, he thanked her and left. He needed air. It was the suffocating sensation from childhood, when he was in a home he didn't want to be, the sensation that built until he had to run away, running no matter how impossible he knew it would be to succeed, knowing in the end they would find him and drag him back.

———

The lawyer lived nearby. Clancy walked over along the coastal road, passing a hodgepodge of houses, the older ones small and plain, the newer ones glass and premium wood siding. The rain had cleared out all the humidity, leaving the air fresh and the sky swept of clouds. He turned up Lincoln Street. He spotted the house, which had a set of stairs on the outside leading up to a deck. The lawyer was waiting, beer in hand; he gestured for Clancy to come up. His dark hair was damp, and he was dressed in a T-shirt and floral board shorts.

"Eddie Frey. Just got back from surfing." His hand was cold from the bottle. *A surfing lawyer*, Clancy thought. *Just what I need.*

He was about Clancy's age, mid-to-late thirties, tanned and fit. Clancy declined his offer of a beer, and Frey flung himself into a low-slung chair. "So, what's this all about?"

Clancy took his time in the telling. The lawyer stared at him over his bottle, tapping the rim against his teeth without saying a word, until Clancy finished. Then he took one long swallow and placed the bottle down with a click on the patio table.

"Tobias did the interview? He's okay. Since we have no idea what's led them to rule this a suspicious death, there's no way to get out in front of it. You didn't know Otto was going to make you executor or put you in his will?"

"No, we had completely lost touch. We reconnected only last weekend."

"Since you say he was sick, the autopsy will likely show he died of natural causes. I'm more concerned about the forest fire and their focus on the matches. Let me see if I can find out whether they're calling in the Suffolk County Arson Squad. In the meantime, don't panic, don't go anywhere, and don't do anything about any of this. I'll nose around."

Clancy thanked him and headed back. He walked on the ocean side of the road alongside the brambles and was soon distracted by birds, busy among the bushes. Some, with white stripes on the sides of their tails, would wait until the last moment to fly off as he came abreast of them, as if it were a game. The pressure in his chest began to ease.

As he rounded the bend to the motel, he saw a squad car pulling up into the parking area and froze. The policemen got out, slamming their doors. Clancy's leg muscles tightened. Fear churned in his gut. He ached to sprint away, but they had spotted him.

"I'm afraid we need yet another moment of your time," Tobias said as he approached.

Clancy wondered if he should call the lawyer. Sweat pooled in his armpits.

"We looked into your background. Turns out your fingerprints are in the system. Had a difficult childhood, did you?"

"What does my childhood have to do with anything?"

"Perhaps you've forgotten the incident that led to your being taken from a foster family and put in reform school? Arson is a Class 1 felony."

"How—?" Clancy's skin was suddenly hot.

"Your juvenile records were never sealed."

Clancy swallowed. He felt like a child again, with an overwhelming urge to run. His hand went to his throat, but there was no tie to tighten and make him feel secure. "I was just a kid, and it wasn't much of a fire. There were no charges." He struggled to calm himself. "I'm getting my lawyer on the phone."

"You've gotten yourself a lawyer? That was fast."

"Yes, I got a lawyer." He backed away, fumbled in his pocket for his phone.

"No need to call. Just answer truthfully and we'll be out of your hair. Why did you set that fire when you were a boy? Did it make you feel powerful?"

"It was a ploy. I was miserable and desperate. I just wanted out of there."

"You set a fire because you wanted to leave a perfectly good home and go to a reform school?" Tobias's voice had thickened with mockery.

Clancy looked from his closed-set dark eyes to Barola's light-blue ones. He saw the eyes of hunters, of clever men sizing up their prey, assessing the weight, the fat composition of a choice piece of meat. Men like these, men who undoubtedly grew up in happy, warm comfortable homes, would never understand how it felt to be brought in like a stray cat. To have his things stolen and jokes played on him and the soles of his feel scorched with cigarettes after they tied his hands behind his back, just for sport. He would have burned their whole fucking house down if he could—anything to get out of there.

And he had gotten out. He had gotten out and survived and made a life for himself, and these two know-it-all policemen were not going to take that away from him.

"I'm sorry," he said, calmer now. "I'm going to insist on having my lawyer present."

The two men glanced at each other. "That won't be necessary. Good day."

He didn't move until he saw them drive away. He was shaking so badly he couldn't get the key in his door. Still, he had won. For the moment, at least, he had won.

———◦•◦•◦———

Frey said he had an appointment, but he could give Clancy fifteen minutes. This time Clancy drove over, and Frey ushered him into his living room. It was decorated with minimalist furniture in tones of gray and white, the walls covered with enormous photos of waves. Clancy found it soothing.

"Why in hell didn't you tell me about setting fires?" Frey was now dressed in a rumpled beige linen jacket and jeans, hair slicked back from his forehead. He plopped on the couch and gestured for Clancy to sit.

"Well, it's embarrassing, obviously."

"Tell me what happened."

"I was twelve, with a family I hated. So I got into trouble."

"You set the fire deliberately to get caught and sent to reform school?"

"I didn't think about where they would send me. I just wanted out. They had two older boys who tormented me. Check my records. I ran away from every foster home. That one was the last." He waited, and then added, "I set a fire in their kitchen garbage can. To be honest, I was shocked it actually worked."

Frey frowned. "Did they bring charges?"

"They called the police, but the social worker convinced them not to press charges." Clancy took a deep breath. "Apparently, my fingerprints are in the system. It never occurred to me to have my records sealed."

"Any other fires? Anything else I should know about?"

Clancy ran a finger over the nubby texture of the couch. "No. But there's something else that might be relevant. Something Otto told me in confidence."

"Anything you tell me is privileged." Frey uncrossed his legs and leaned forward.

"Otto was part of a group that owned some land. He said if it got out that he was dying, his partners would hold off on a decision for what to do with the parcel until after his death. Otto wanted to be part of the decision, so he was keeping his cancer a secret. He asked me to talk with his daughter. They were estranged, and he wanted to come to terms with her before he died. I got nowhere with her. Theresa Nolan, a bartender. She really hated him."

"Oh, I know Theresa, and that they were estranged, but I didn't realize it went that deep. Good, that may be something we can use." The lawyer straightened. "Give me the partners' names." He whipped out a small notebook. "No idea what it may mean, but we should get all the background we can."

"I don't know the surnames, but one is his brother-in-law, Harve. Another's a retired teacher, Tim, and the third is the son of one of the original partners, someone prominent out here, Pete something. I don't know what the fourth one, Gaspar, does."

"I'll see what I can dig up." Frey got to feet.

Clancy followed him down the stairs. Opening the door to a silver Mini with bright purple detailing, Frey said, "The autopsy and toxicology will be another week or so. Don't worry, I'm all over this."

"I really appreciate it." Frey's confident air relaxed the tightness in Clancy's chest.

Frey leaned out of the car window. "If it's bad news, it'll be time to find you a criminal lawyer."

The coils retightened inside Clancy's chest.

CHAPTER 13: Julienne

Overhead, the clouds bunched and thickened, darkened in tone, threatening rain yet again, but Julienne went down to the beach anyway. She worked rapidly, with short brushstrokes, to capture the changes in light and color. An ominous yellowish tinge began to saturate the sky. She dipped her brush into acid green.

In the distance, she saw a man walking up the beach and for a moment thought it was Clancy. She felt comfortable with him so quickly, which wasn't typical for her with men. But the police interest in him this past week made her uneasy.

"It was odd him showing up out of the blue . . . and then this happening," Rob said the night before.

"He didn't 'show up' out of the blue. I invited him."

Rob just shrugged.

Maybe her wariness was because Clancy was so guarded, literally buttoned up. To visit Otto, he had worn a tie, pushing it against his Adam's Apple as if he wanted to throttle himself, and she'd joked, "You'll kill yourself if you keep that up."

He'd blushed and laughed.

The day before, when she went to bring him fresh linens, he wasn't there, and she used her key to go inside. His clothes were still folded in his suitcase, and his toiletries were grouped on one side of the sink, as if he wasn't sure he had permission to take up space. On the table in the kitchenette, there was a collection of beach artifacts: a jingle shell, a skate egg case, a black-speckled rock.

There was something very sweet about him but also a little sad. He carried himself stiffly, something self-protective in his posture. *He's like rhubarb*, she mused, sweeping her brush to form a stalk-like shape, tough to break down, needing to be combined with sugar. Maybe he just needed some heat—the warmth of love—to break him open into full flavor.

On a whim, she had clipped a pink zinnia and placed it on the pile of towels. She couldn't remember the last time she'd had an impulse to do something like that for Rob.

Pink, she thought now, mixing white into magenta. She used cobalt blue to trace a thin line here and there with a mere bristle hair, the subtlest underlining of a wave. The man on the beach came into her field of vision again, walking with a child. He was nothing like Clancy, she realized. He had the partially shaved look so popular these days. Why did those hipsters who left on a few days' growth irritate her so much? She dipped her brush into the water jar and then into the hardening paint to release a watery pinkish mix. Clancy was clean-shaven, no hint of hipster. She'd noticed his preppy clothes, dull brown shoes. Did all these style choices indicate he was politically conservative? Then again, his sneakers sported bright yellow laces.

She wiped her brush and stood back to eye her painting. She had felt a different kind of unease when Clancy seemed to be hyperventilating and she had stroked his back. Her impulse was motherly, but then their eyes locked, and she was briefly mesmerized by the flecks of green and gold in the hazel. His expression had been searching, grave, and she perceived a kind of stature and presence she hadn't sensed in him before.

The man and the child moved past, two dark shadows she painted into her canvas with a few strokes. Otto Lansky came to mind. The last time she'd seen him, he looked crumpled and worn. His eyes, enfolded in wrinkly skin, had the watery look of old men's eyes. There had been a light still burning in those eyes, she thought, like a residual spark in a charred bit of wood left over from a bonfire—harmless under the sand until it burned your foot.

There was a sudden stillness as the wind died down, as if holding its breath before letting loose, and she felt a drop of rain. Above, thick clouds bunched closer, and the drops came more quickly. Sighing, she slid the canvas, barely dry, into her carryall. At the top of the bluff, she turned back to the ocean, committing the colors and configuration of the clouds to memory until she made it back to her studio.

Several hours later, Julienne stepped out of her studio. The sun had come back out and hung low in the sky, glittering the drops on the foliage and intensifying the colors. She breathed in the fresh scent of moist earth the rain had released.

The short walk back to the house was a useful transition, a way to ease out of her concentration and into the everyday world. She was greeted with the smell of sautéed onions, something simmering on the stove. Rob was in the living room. He smiled up at her from the couch and put down his book.

She bent down for a kiss and dropped onto the sofa next to him. "Work went well. Thanks for picking up Max. How was your afternoon?"

"Good. The rain had stopped by then, so we hung out watching soccer practice. I threw together some chili." Rob picked up his book, then put it down again. "The police paid Clancy another visit."

"This is getting weird."

"I'll say."

"You're irritated I invited him to stay here. But you can't think—?"

"It's hard to know what to think. He comes. There's a fire. Otto dies. Are any of those connected? Right now the police are probably just getting what information they can, and we shouldn't be concerned that we're harboring an arsonist or a murderer." Rob met her eyes. "I'm just uncomfortable. He seems to be something of a pet project."

She held back a flare of irritation.

"And I don't like him giving Max presents."

"Anything besides LEGOs?"

Rob shrugged. "A little thing he made for him."

Max was at his desk, staring into the distance. She followed his gaze to the wall, where open shelves displayed his treasures: beach ephemera, dried seaweed, adventure books. On the floor was a partially finished construction out of the LEGOs Clancy had purchased for him. She had said Max couldn't accept the gift, then conceded when Clancy argued it was his way of thanking them for helping with his legal troubles.

"Hey darling boy." Julienne put her arms around Max. He smelled of the coconut soap that hung from a rope in their shower and was shaped like a whale. She didn't know how much longer he would allow this kind of physical proximity and hugged him every chance she could.

"How was school?" She ran her hand over his bristly hair, then released him.

"Good. We got to see a movie in Mrs. Morgan's class about the native peoples."

Ah, that explained his dreaminess. Max was enthralled with Grace Morgan. Julienne found it hard to reconcile the engaging teacher who taught in the local school with the acerbic leader of her environmental group. Julienne thought Grace herself was a force of nature when battling for the environment.

Julienne sat on the edge of his bed as Max told her the story of the Montauketts, who had taught the white settlers how to capture whales and spear fish in exchange for help in defeating their enemies. Eventually the Montauketts had been driven from their land.

"We have to write an essay saying if we think the Indians were right or wrong to sell their land."

"Did you talk about how the Montauketts thought about land and ownership?"

Max nodded. "They didn't believe in private property. Land was for everybody. Do you think the settlers knew they were tricking them when they made the deal?"

"That's a good question. What do you think?"

He frowned. "I kind of think they'd have to know? They cared just about themselves. Maybe they didn't mean to expose them to the germs that killed them, though."

"I guess it's complicated."

"I'd rather I was a Montaukett, not a white person."

"I understand." Julienne stood. "Hey, maybe you could help out at the new Indian museum; you could learn some of the skills they practiced. But first, dinner." As she passed to the door, the sense of unease snagged her again, like a thread caught on a nail. She glanced around, confused at what triggered it. Her breath seized.

On the floor, behind Max's LEGOs construction, was a miniature pavilion, the gift Clancy must have made him. She stared, skin tingling.

Matchsticks.

CHAPTER 14: Clancy

Water pressed down like a hand, bubbled like seltzer in his nostrils. Clancy flailed his arms and legs to no avail. The pressure on his chest became intense, and he made scissor-like motions with his arms, kicked his feet, struggling for air. He saw spots in the darkness; his brain seemed to explode. Thick strands of seaweed filled his mouth, slick and salty. With a final effort he heaved his body upward.

He awoke to the sound of the phone, heart pounding like the surf, covered in sweat.

"It's all over the news. I couldn't believe when I saw it. You're trending, man." Bruce's voice was so loud Clancy moved the phone from his ear. "What the fuck is this all about? Tell me everything."

Clancy turned on his laptop and pulled up the newspapers Bruce was referring to. "Fire . . . or Overdose . . . May Have Led to Death of Montauk Resident" said one headline. Clancy wasn't pictured, but he was mentioned by name as a subject of police "inquiries." He was described as "a former acquaintance who recently reappeared in town," and in another article, as "the recipient of Lansky's charity when he was an orphan." The neighbors who witnessed Otto's will the night before he died were quoted as saying Clancy had been named executor because Mr. Lansky "trusted him with his life."

The implication was infuriating. Clancy slammed the laptop closed. "I had no idea he would make me a beneficiary."

"If the guy altered his will for you, it doesn't play well."

"I don't care how it plays, as long as I'm exonerated."

"We need positive spin, that's key."

"What are you talking about?"

"Don't worry, my editor's given me the go-ahead. Of course it has to be an exclusive."

Clancy stiffened. "I haven't been talking to you for publication." How had he not seen this coming?

"You need this, good buddy. They're making hash of you out there. I'm going to turn it around. You'll be golden by the time I finish."

"Oh Jesus."

"That's right. Saved, too!"

"Seriously, Bruce, we need to go over what you can and can't say."

"Deal. I'll transcribe this and send it along and you'll let me know."

"You recorded this?"

"Well, yeah." He sounded sheepish. "Sorry. Should have mentioned that."

Clancy grabbed his jacket and headed to the beach, but the weather had changed again. He was cold, and the wind whipped particles of sand into his eyes. It occurred to him he could leave. The police hadn't said he had to stick around until they finished investigating. Surely whatever was necessary for him to do as Otto's executor could be done from Astoria. He would feel badly to miss Otto's funeral, but maybe it was for the best. He could imagine the hostility the community would send his way.

He'd settle his bill and go home. He was troubled by the awkwardness he felt the last time in Julienne's presence, anyhow.

She was just opening her door to go out, hair and shirt caught by the wind. Her appearance was distracted, disheveled. What was it, exactly, that he found so attractive about her? She was like the wind itself.

"Clancy! Frey's been trying to reach you. The autopsy and lab reports came in and show Otto died of prostate cancer."

Only in that moment did Clancy realize quite how afraid he'd been that, in giving Otto the morphine pills, he'd inadvertently caused his death.

She grabbed him by the shoulders and shook him. "Hey, it's great news."

A streak of yellow traversed her left cheekbone. He didn't answer. They stood facing each other, her hands on his shoulders. He suddenly wasn't so sure he wanted to go.

She gave a little laugh and moved back. "Oh, and this." She handed him a blue Post-it Note. "She said she tried your cell with no luck. Otto's lawyer."

"I've been named executor for Otto's estate."

"So I'd heard. He must have really trusted you."

That phrase again. He bristled. "He knew I was a claims adjuster; maybe he figured I'd be good handling these kinds of details."

"I didn't mean to imply . . ." She colored. "I'm just glad the cause of death is settled. Anyhow, the funeral is tomorrow, now that the body's been released. It's at the Catholic church."

Back at the bungalow, Clancy returned Otto's lawyer's call and set a time to come to her office the day after the funeral. Ms. Jewel said Otto had arranged for a funeral home in Amagansett to handle his remains and paid for everything in advance. There would be no viewing, just the funeral.

Clancy called Frey. "You heard they established cause of death?"

From the silence in response, Clancy knew there was something else. "What is it?"

"They've called in the arson squad."

Blood thudded in his ears. He fidgeted with a box of matches, spilling the sticks all over the table.

Frey's tone was clipped. "If what you've told me is true—and I believe you—you have nothing to worry about. Even if they determine it was arson, there's no reason for it to be tied to you just because you had some Bishops by the Sea matches."

Clancy gathered the matchsticks and slid them back into the box.

"How long before—"

"Not long to determine if it was an accident. If arson, that's another story."

He could remain under suspicion for quite some time. Clancy began straightening the room. He bundled the newspapers, wiped the little dinette table, refolded his shirts. He went to the window. The sky was full of glowering clouds, and the ocean had become even more agitated, the tops of the waves sheared off into spray. He stood motionless. It was soothing to watch the seesawing motion, the waves' advance and retreat, a kind of self-hypnosis.

He had tried to hypnotize himself as a boy. He had found an old watch on a chain that he pretended had belonged to his father, handed down through generations. He longed for information about his parents, but there was no one to ask. Early on he ceased questioning the social workers; whatever his family history may have been, he finally accepted it was lost to him. Untethered, he was free to imagine what he liked. So, he imagined a father with this large, ornate watch.

The watch was a gold-like metal, round with an etched design. It had a button that when pressed made the lid fly open. What a satisfying sound! The loud click, the popping open. He did it over and over, a dozen times a day, and the thrill never wore off. The watch face was depicted in Roman numerals, gold on white, the slender hands also gold. They never moved, but that hardly mattered. Ten minutes to three.

Clancy would dangle the watch in front of his face. Back and forth, back and forth. "Your eyes are feeling heavy, you are going to sleep now. You are going to remember." He would close his eyes and fall back upon the pillow. Sometimes he would dream, and he liked to think these were special dreams, ones that hinted at his life from when his parents were alive. The watch had given him hope, so it had given him strength. Just holding it brought serenity, a feeling of connection.

His hands tightened on the windowsill. There was nothing that could calm him today. He was angry; angrier than he could ever remember being. He swept his arm out, sending the stacks of matchboxes on the windowsill flying. Some landed on the floor, some on the coffee table. He breathed heavily, shocked at himself, but the physical action felt good. He was innocent, innocent of harming Otto, innocent of any attempt to profit from his death, innocent of the fire.

Since coming here, since the terrible beauty of the beach in the moonlight, he had known a new kind of peace; he would not let them take that away. He wasn't going to run. Not this time.

<hr />

They brought him in for questioning a few hours later. They took him to East Hampton, so he figured things must be serious, and left him in an interrogation room while he waited for Frey to arrive. The shakes started at his head, traveled down his body in a huge, convulsive wave, and began all over again.

He paced the small room clockwise, then counterclockwise. The room reminded him of grade school cafeterias, with stained light-green walls, metal folding chairs, crappy light fixtures, and a wooden table in the center. If he were convicted of arson, he'd spend God knew how many years in yet another institutional setting. His stomach seized. The crappy food, the dinginess, the bilious colors. Panic rose in his chest, the fear that his whole life would be like this, and he'd never escape.

The urge to sleep was like a wave pulling him under. He sat down and put his head on his arms, but he kept seeing the eyes of the policemen, the eyes of the reform school director.

That had been a hard place, and yet he had survived. He remembered the cold of the wood floors when he got out of bed at night to grope his way to the bathroom. He remembered the sound of other boys' crying, and the wish that he, too, could cry. Instead, there was a terrifying hollowness, as if there was nothing inside his chest, and he balled up a towel and hugged it to him, pressing it against himself to fill that cavity.

"Why do you sleep with this towel?" the director snapped, but he couldn't possibly explain. He said it was in case he wet the bed.

"Nonsense, you've never wet your bed."

"That's why I don't!"

They took away the towel, and he tried to pee in the bed just to convince them, but he couldn't get himself to let go. He pressed his fists against his ribs and curled into the tightest ball he could.

Eventually, he knew, his whole self was curled up in that tight ball.

A rasping sound brought him upright. The door opened and an officer let Frey into the room. Clancy struggled to stand but the bottom of the chair leg caught on the sticky surface of the flooring; he stumbled against the table.

"Just sit," Frey said, pulling out a chair.

"Are they arresting me? How bad is it?"

"I don't know. They'll be in soon to start questioning." Frey drummed his fingers on the table. "I have to ask. Did you have anything to do with that fire? Even by accident?"

"No. I had nothing to do with that fire."

"Okay, good. Had to ask."

The door opened and Tobias and Barola took seats on the other side of the table, placing a folder in front of them. Barola switched on a recording device and stated their names and the time.

"Mr. Frederics, you've a known history of setting fires, is that correct?"

"It's not a 'history.'" He had knelt over the wastebasket, stuffed full of crumpled-up paper, striking match after match. He leapt back as the flames curled around the edges, smoke wafting up and slowly filling the room. "I—"

"Are you charging my client or not?" Frey said, cutting Clancy off. "Show us your evidence or we're out of here."

"Patience, Mr. Frey, please. We'd just like to clear up a few matters and then we can rule him out as a suspect. I'll ask again. Mr. Frederics, you have a known history of setting fires, do you not?"

Clancy glanced at Frey for direction. Frey had made a point of saying he wasn't a criminal lawyer.

"Go ahead," Frey encouraged Clancy.

"I set one small fire when I was a child. I had nothing whatsoever to do with this fire."

"You have a fascination with matches?"

"I enjoy using wooden matches to make small structures. I don't have a fascination with matches. I don't have an attraction to fire."

Frey placed a hand on Clancy's arm. "I think it's time to stop this fishing expedition."

"We found several items near where the fire originated. One has Mr. Frederic's fingerprints on them."

Clancy's heart jolted like a train lurching forward. "What object?"

"A metal container holding several boxes of Bishops by the Sea matches. Would you care to explain?"

Clancy couldn't remember any such container. How had his fingerprints gotten on it?

"May I see the fingerprint report please?" Frey asked.

Tobias considered a moment, then slid a folder across the table.

Frey paged through the report, frowning. He took his time, turning one page after another, slowly. His expression smoothed suddenly, and Clancy felt a flicker of hope.

"This says there were several things found near the source. A metal teapot and cups, for instance. Clearly this was some sort of camping spot. Has this even been ruled arson?"

"We're waiting on that ruling," Tobias said. "Again, how did Mr. Frederic's fingerprints get on the container if he was nowhere near?"

"Were his the only fingerprints?"

After a moment's pause, Tobias grudgingly acknowledged, "They were the only ones we could identify."

Frey slapped his notepad down on the table. "Whether Mr. Frederics or any other guests of Bishops by the Sea handled it, that container didn't start that or any other fire. You don't have fingerprints on the matches themselves. You can't even determine if that matchbox held the specific match that started the fire. This evidence is tenuous at best. We're leaving." Frey shoved his portfolio into his briefcase.

Tobias leaned back, arms crossed over his chest, but said nothing.

There was a discreet knock and the door opened. A uniformed police office waved a folder at the detectives. Tobias motioned for it and then drew out a report. He studied it, sighed, and passed it to Barola.

"Well?" Frey asked.

"Accidental."

"We're outta here." Frey motioned to Clancy.

Tobias leaned forward and stabbed the report with his finger. "Someone set this. We're going to continue investigating."

Clancy followed Frey down the hall and out into the parking area. Once outside, Frey did a fist bump in the air. His dark hair, spiky with some sort of gel, caught the light.

"I'm still shaking," Clancy said. "I can't thank you enough."

"This was probably caused by some homeless guy camping out in the woods. Forget the whole thing, it's over. Just a case of police overreach."

Clancy toed the ground with his sneakers, his yellow laces mocking him. He wasn't so sure Frey was right. There were too many unanswered questions.

"I'm an outsider with a past. If I were the police, I guess I'd suspect me, too."

CHAPTER 15: Theresa

Arches of wood rose to a graceful peak in the church. Theresa's chest expanded as it did when she crested the dunes and the ocean spread before her. As she followed the lines of the arches upward, she had the heady sensation of watching the movements of a gull, as if she, too, were gliding on a wind current.

The feeling lasted a moment, and then her chest bunched and contracted. She would have stayed home but for Father Molina, who had gotten special permission to hold a funeral Mass for her father even though he had not been a congregant. The church was crowded, and she longed to hide behind the wooden screen that protected the privacy of the sacristy.

With a loud chord from the organ, everyone pivoted toward the rear of the church as pallbearers entered with the casket. Theresa spotted Molly and Billy in the back and wished she'd thought to ask them to sit with her. The resonant tones of the organ found a matching vibration inside her; afraid she would cry, she bowed her head, her face in her hands. Father Molina began the Mass. She listened to the familiar prayers, the soothing cadences of his voice, its Latino lilt just barely detectible, and thought of the words of Jesus's teachings, the beauty of the language, and not of her father in the casket placed at the altar rail.

A bell rang out, and Father Molina invited everyone up to the communion rail. With so much resentment and anger in her heart, she could not receive the sacrament.

"Forgiveness will come," Father Molina often told her. "Keep trying, and one day it will come."

The day had not come, as Father Molina, her confessor, knew, not even with her father's casket several feet away. Yet Father looked straight at her as he held up the host and motioned to her with his head. She glanced at the crucifix. Those of her childhood, with Jesus's emaciated body and contorted face, were terrifying. This Jesus, suspended on thin wire, seemed to float in the air, arms wide and welcoming. Father Molina gestured to her again. Perhaps her father's death granted her an exemption. She approached the communion rail. The wafer melted on her tongue as tears slid down her cheeks.

After the Mass, on the front steps, she stood at the receiving line. Some, who knew the nature of her relationship with her father, strained for what to say. Molly came up beside her and slid an arm around her waist in support.

"He was such a giving man," a woman clasped her hand.

Theresa's face felt like a mask, her throat so tight she could barely breathe. She glanced over the woman's head and saw Clancy Frederics among those waiting to offer condolences. She glared at him until he walked away. Her face flushed at her rudeness, but she didn't regret it. She had been shocked to learn he'd been appointed executor of her father's will. Interloper. She remembered how it felt watching her father go off to be with Clancy when she was a child.

"We'll have fun on our own," her mother would say, and Theresa would pretend to like baking cookies or playing with dolls. She didn't want to add to her mother's pain at being, as she was, left behind, an afterthought. She'd felt a warm glow of satisfaction when Clancy was arrested, only to be disappointed when he was released.

Pete Walker, who had been a grade behind her in school and was now a local businessman, tapped her arm. "I'm very sorry for your loss. Can I speak with you very briefly?"

"I'm about to go to the cemetery."

"When you can. I'd like to discuss your father's business dealings. Here's my card."

"I'm not interested." She started down the steps.

He pressed his card into her hand. "Please. Call me."

She crumpled the card and shoved it in her pocket as Father Molina took her arm to lead her away.

The cemetery was on a hill overlooking Fort Pond, the site of the old Montaukett burial ground, its grave markers nearly indistinguishable from the rocks and small boulders scattered upon the open meadow. It was a sacred place, and as she approached the Council Rock, she sensed a vibration in the breeze, which swirled at this height of land. Clouds massed overhead, and at the far edge of the field three deer emerged, their silhouettes majestic against the backdrop of the bay.

Father Molina gathered the group around the casket . . . how insignificant and forlorn it seemed in this vast space. Father asked that everyone hold hands.

Eyes raised to the sky, he prayed, "Forgive Otto Lansky for his sins, Oh Father, and guide those of us still on earth to seek our own forgiveness. Open our hearts to your precious love. May he rest in peace."

"Amen," Theresa mumbled.

Everyone repeated their condolences and drifted off. Father Molina placed a hand on her arm. "You're doing the best you can. You'll get there in the end."

Theresa shrugged. Even saying "I hope so," was something of a lie.

"What will you do now?" he asked as they walked back on the gravel walkway.

Theresa didn't know whether he meant that day or in some broader sense. "Pete Walker approached me. He wants to discuss my father's business dealings." She kicked at a pebble and watched it roll a few times before stopping.

"Do you need help with some of that? If there's anything I can do, or with any of the arrangements, I'm here for you, Theresa."

"Thank you, Father. I'm supposed to meet with the lawyer about the will tomorrow. I don't want anything to do with his money." She felt a few drops of rain on her head; the air carried the musty smell of dampened soil.

"Do you really want to turn your back on your own legacy?"

"It's blood money!" She felt a drop trickle down her neck. She shivered and moved more quickly toward the car. "I hate everything to do with him."

The priest hesitated, then opened the door for her. He got in behind the wheel and settled his garments around him. They sat watching the rain splat the windshield. "You don't need to rush into any decisions just yet." He put the key in the ignition. "Give yourself time."

"I wish it would all just go away." Rain was hitting harder now, and the priest put on the wipers and lights but didn't set the car in motion. Theresa turned from the window and watched him think. She loved this about the priest, how thoughtful and measured he was. His face, clean shaven, was a beautiful shade of brown and with the sheen of soft, unmarked leather, although he had to be at least fifty.

"I know how much your situation with your father has troubled you. Still, try to be open to what this experience provides. Try not to shut the door just yet."

She couldn't answer. Since her father's death, memories had flooded in. The time he had taken her fishing, out on Navy Pier. The time he caught her making out with a boy and grounded her. The time she had told him she thought she'd like to be a biologist, and he'd said, "Don't be ridiculous, you're no good in science."

She wondered if these uncanny flashes of scenes happened to others after a death. She was afraid the memory haunting her, which she managed to suppress all these years, would overtake her like a wave.

"I'll try." She glanced away. "I'll try to be more open."

"Death has impacts on us we can't foresee. That's just the nature of it."

Father finally put the car in gear and headed out of the cemetery. They were both quiet on the way back to the church, where she had left her jeep.

"You know," he said, pulling into the lot, "some people are drawn to this area because of their love of the ocean. But for some it's a form of running away. Away from expectations and failures. Away from stress, or strife, or even other people."

"What are you saying?" Her hand rested on the door handle but she didn't open the door.

"You've said you want to be close to God. That may require pushing against your own boundaries."

"I don't understand."

"Sometimes I think you're determined to block the love that could fill your life. It's as if there is a rocky shore surrounding your heart, keeping you from the ocean's life-giving water. From love."

Theresa felt her face flush. That rocky shore was her protection, her safety.

"Try, Theresa. That's all God asks."

CHAPTER 16: Clancy

Ms. Jewel's office was downtown above a sweatshirt store. Overlooking Main Street, her windows had views across one- and two-story buildings to the ocean only blocks away. The office had a gleaming wooden floor with small hook rugs, a couch covered in dark-green corduroy, which currently provided comfort to a Golden Retriever, and a mission-style desk, from behind which Ms. Jewel stood and extended her very slender, very chilly hand. She was slight and intense-looking, with a dark suit and black-framed glasses.

"Thank you for coming, Mr. Frederics. I hope you're not allergic to dogs? That's Ralph. You might prefer the chair." She indicated a straight-backed antique.

"No, I'm fine." He chose the couch and put a hand on the dog's head.

"We're waiting for Mr. Lansky's daughter. Coffee?"

While she poured, he stroked the dog's silky ears. Max had told him this was his favorite breed. Poor asthmatic Max.

"I'm sure this has been a difficult time for you," Ms. Jewel said hesitantly.

He glanced up in surprise, the dog's ear still in his hand. Her eyes had gone to her desk, where he saw *You're Hot!* open to Bruce's article. It had come out just after he'd been released by the police. Bruce had written an up-by-the-bootstraps, poor-boy-makes-good kind of story, painting him as a loving friend to Otto and a victim of police prosecution. In Bruce's telling, Clancy was a regular Dicken's character. David Copperfield, probably.

"I'll be happy to put it all behind me." The arrest and article had thrust him into public view, forced from his usual cocoon of anonymity.

"I'm sure." Her eyes were sympathetic.

The door was flung open. Theresa Nolan stopped short, like a startled deer. Her long hair was a tangled mess over a beat-up jean jacket.

"Ms. Nolan, please come in," Ms. Jewel said. "The wind is something fierce today, isn't it? This is Mr. Frederics. Tea? Coffee?"

Theresa declined the offer and after a moment's hesitation, took the chair Ms. Jewel indicated, swiveling it so her back was to Clancy. He lowered his face into the dog's fur.

Ms. Jewel plaited her fingers and put her hands on top of the desk. "I have to say this will has some very peculiar aspects. Bear with me."

Clancy stole a glance at Theresa's profile. Did she feel a shred of remorse at her treatment of her father? Her face held a dark, closed guardedness that might have been anything—guilt or anger or merely discomfort.

"I should explain Mr. Lansky stated he chose Mr. Frederics as executor because he would have no financial stake in the outcome of business decisions he's leaving to him." Ms. Jewel glanced again at Theresa for her reaction. Theresa's back stayed rigid.

"Now, as to the house, I'm afraid it's a little unorthodox. Mr. Lansky has left it to you, Ms. Nolan, but there's a condition. It's yours only if you choose to live in it. He doesn't want the house sold or torn down, though improvements are allowed."

"I don't want it." Theresa's voice was firm, harsh.

Clancy was taken aback, but the lawyer seemed to expect this reaction. "Your father anticipated your feelings. The will specifies that you have a month to reconsider, but if at the end of that time you don't want to live in the house, it goes to Mr. Frederics."

"What?" Clancy jerked forward.

Ms. Jewel's gaze remained fixed on Theresa. Her shoulders stiffened. "I won't change my mind."

"Fine," the lawyer said, "but we'll honor the time requirement." She swiveled her chair toward Clancy. "Mr. Frederics, if it comes to that, there are conditions for your assuming ownership as well." She gave him a brief smile. "In order to take possession, Mr. Lansky stipulates you must live in the house at least part-time. I understand you currently live in Queens. Assuming you don't move to Montauk, he mandates one-third of your time be spent here."

Clancy was stunned. "This doesn't make sense."

The lawyer merely nodded. "If neither of you takes the house, he has provisions for the creation of some sort of trust, but he makes it clear this is not his preference. He wants the house to be inhabited by someone he loves. Separately, there are other assets. Ms. Nolan, you are beneficiary of your father's share of a parcel of land owned by a partnership called The Moorlands Corporation. However, Mr. Frederics, as executor, will be making the decisions regarding the disposition of that property. Although the parcel received subdivision approval, the partners are considering other options. It will be some time before that issue is resolved and there's any kind of payout for you."

"I won't take anything from my father."

Ms. Jewel gave a loud sigh and leaned forward, her hands splayed on top of her desk. "As you'll see in the sidebar accompanying the will, your father makes a point of explaining that his share of the Moorlands parcel was purchased with the proceeds of the sale of the house you grew up in, which had originally been bought with your mother's family's money. In essence, that money was solely your mother's and not his." She sat back.

Theresa didn't as much as shift in her chair.

The lawyer shuffled her papers and smoothed them with her hands. "There are bequests to various individuals and organizations, as well. I think that's pretty much it. I have copies for you both."

"Can I go?" Theresa stood.

"Yes, of course." This time the lawyer seemed taken aback. "I'll be in touch in a month if I don't hear from you sooner. At that point, we'll deal with the paperwork. In the meantime, feel free to call with any questions."

Theresa mumbled her thanks and left, addressing neither word nor glance at Clancy.

"Phew," Ms. Jewel said. "That was awkward."

"They were estranged. I guess it's complicated."

"The will itself is complicated. Mr. Lansky wrote the codicil in handwriting and called his neighbors in to witness it the night before he died. He also had a letter for you about the Moorlands parcel that he began but, sadly, didn't finish. I'm hoping he shared his thoughts with you in person about that?"

"We began to talk about it, but then he died."

"Hopefully you can get some guidance from the other partners. I'll help in any way I can." She handed him an envelope. "What he wrote about you is very moving."

"I don't know that I'm qualified to act as executor, to make these decisions."

"He trusted you to be his emissary. He was sure you'd make good decisions." She walked him to the door. "I'll be in touch once I hear from Ms. Nolan. If she chooses to keep the house, there's a bequest to you. If not, the house is yours, assuming you meet the conditions. Meantime, look all this over and call me when you're ready."

As soon as he was downstairs Clancy leaned against the plate glass front of the liquor store, gathering himself. He couldn't take in what Otto had done: his extraordinary generosity on the one hand, and on the other, inserting Clancy into the complexity of the Moorlands situation and, in essence, pitting him against Theresa.

If she didn't take the house . . . He briefly thought of Otto's garden, the feeling of the dirt in his fingers, of the breeze stirring the leaves of the cherry tree over the patio. He shook his mind free. A young couple in cutoffs and T-shirts passed, arms entwined. A man in waders and a stained sweatshirt emerged from the pizza parlor with a box. Clancy could smell the fragrance of garlic from several feet away. An older woman strolled up the street, cajoling a tiny, white dog as a young boy whizzed past on a skateboard. This was an isolated funky town far from everything he knew. Would he want to make it a major part of his life?

What was he thinking? Theresa would take the house. She'd be crazy not to, crazier than he already thought she was. He walked to his car. He needed to put these thoughts from his mind, take care of business for Otto, and get back to his own life.

The clouds had broken up while he was in the lawyer's office, the sun muscling its way through. Even with the car windows shut, the wheezing sound of the wind was audible, buffeting the car as he drove. Clouds created different patterns of shade on the roadway, and occasional puddles indicated it had rained here, although it hadn't in town.

Wind whipped his hair into his eyes as he made his way to his bungalow, bending the last of the colorful flowers around the bungalows nearly to the ground.

Max came from behind his house, a long stick in one hand. He pulled back his arm as if the stick were a bow. Clancy watched the imaginary arrow shoot across the sky.

If he were to inherit Otto's house, Max could visit. Clancy imagined standing in the doorway, Max rushing toward him, and for a second he felt the presence beside him of a dog that strained to leap forward in greeting. A Golden Retriever.

Max gave a shriek, like an Indian war whoop, and leapt into the air. *A strange boy*, Clancy thought. Then again, he, too, had been a strange boy.

His heart thumped oddly. He went inside and sat in the rocker without putting on the lights. He was shaken by this vision of himself—a man with a home, a dog . . . a child?

It was as if the wave that had knocked him down had changed him in a cosmic way, and he was caught up in a strange vortex over which he had no control.

 *Late Autumn*

GOLDENROD GROWS IN great profusion this fall, brightening the dunes along the ocean. Beach plum ripens, while in the swales of the nearby dunes, cranberries begin to form. Cloudless yellow sulphur butterflies flutter at the edge of the surf in a long, pale-gold ribbon.

Yet the monarchs fail to arrive. Other autumns they seem to materialize out of the air: first a single butterfly, then a second, and within hours, an undulating shimmy of orange and white and black drifts west along the dunes.

The town's natural resources employees know what is awry in the natural world: the drop off in songbirds, the disappearance of right whales, the rising of the oceans. But they are overwhelmed with local concerns—the increased nitrogen in the bays, and the wreckage in the forest understory from grazing deer. Migrating butterflies are beyond their purview.

At the docks, it is the catch that has everyone worried. The fall species have been slow to arrive, and boats are fishing longer hours to meet their quotas.

By mid-October, the air grows heavy and foggy. There are two new hurricane warnings, Derek and Evelin, though in the end, neither arrives.

All seems suspended . . . waiting.

CHAPTER 17: Molly

At the fish market, Vince told Molly that by the end of the month they would be cutting back to just three days a week through the holidays, and then would shut altogether until spring. It was what they did every year, but she hadn't known. Seeing her face, Vince kept saying how sorry he was.

"It's okay, Vince, really."

Not much would stay open in Montauk over the winter. Maybe she would apply to Kmart for holiday work, though it would mean a thirty-minute commute to Bridgehampton. She had majored in psychology but never figured out what to do with her degree—even if she weren't living in a quasi-rural area without a wide range of options.

On the way home, she passed the edge of the woods and fields where the fire had raged the previous month. It was desolate, with blackened tree limbs and grasses. Even the soil appeared scorched. She would never forget Billy's face, covered in soot and sweat. He had been exhausted and shaken, having found the body of Otto Lansky. She was relieved Otto had died of natural causes and that Clancy, the nice man who was staying in one of Julienne and Rob's bungalows, was no longer under suspicion. She couldn't get over how he had knelt to help her sweep up the broken glass at the fundraiser.

She turned down the rutted road to their house. As she reached their clearing, she was uneasy to see a fancy white car, out of place beside Billy's beat-up truck. The developer angling to buy the house had been leaving messages, asking to stop by. Billy hadn't returned the calls.

She ran her eyes over the curled-up shingles, the mold darkening the top of the door under the eaves where sun didn't reach, and the sagging wooden steps. The house canted slightly, but its small proportions were reminiscent of fairy-tale cottages, dormers like jaunty eyebrows over the windows.

In the living room, Billy and another man were talking. Billy stopped midsentence as she walked in, and she couldn't read his expression. The man, dressed in a soft charcoal V-neck sweater, rose, hand outstretched.

"Theodore Miloxi." His face was thin and very tan, a few age spots gracing his cheeks.

Molly sat next to Billy on the couch. From outside came the cough of an outboard motor.

"We were talking about your lovely property here," Miloxi said. "Billy tells me you're opposed to selling."

Molly shot a glance at Billy; he picked up the white rock on the coffee table they used as a paperweight and began shifting it from one hand to the other. She turned back to Miloxi.

"It's not my call."

"He cares what you want." Miloxi smiled. "How can I change your mind?"

"It's been in Billy's family for generations. It's his legacy, his brother's legacy." Her words tripped over each other.

"Ah, sentiment." Miloxi nodded, as if saying, *Ah, foolish youth.* "You could get something far nicer with what I would pay you. A beautiful new home. Start fresh."

Molly's jaw set. Had Billy told him they had been talking about marrying, eventually trying for a baby? The motor coughed again, and through the window behind Miloxi's head, she saw a small boat passing by. When she said nothing, he continued.

"My dear, my company has big dreams for this entire stretch of waterfront."

"Build around us," Molly said.

"I don't think so." Miloxi chuckled, as if amused by an adorable child. "Property taxes are going up. Why not cash out and get a much nicer place, set yourselves up in life?"

Billy stood abruptly. "We'll give it thought."

"The faster you sign, the better. Hold out, and it'll cost you." Miloxi moved swiftly across the room and shut the door decisively behind him.

"Oh my god," Molly breathed.

Billy's face was flushed. "He's such a prick; I wouldn't sell to him if I had a choice."

"You don't have to sell, do you?"

Billy ran his hands over his face. "I'm just trying to be responsible. He's right that it would be the smart thing. I know you don't want me to."

"Billy, it's not my decision."

"We're together now, Molly. We decide together."

Outside, the boat motor abruptly died.

———————

Billy was quiet during dinner, and Molly didn't press him, deciding they should wait until Jonah was in bed to talk things through.

She sat with Jonah while he did his homework and then went upstairs to ready him for bed while he kept up his usual chatter, a torrent of words about school, Max, and his favorite teacher, Mrs. Morgan.

"Did you know that it's the seahorse daddies that have the babies? Tiny seahorses emerge from their stomachs. Did you know that whale's breath is called blow, and it sometimes makes a rainbow?" She smoothed his hair and smiled.

"I didn't know that." How she loved his snub-nosed, freckled face. She called him a little munchkin, which he thought was because he was always snacking. Even by the way his left brow was neatly bisected by a scar—noticeable only because the soft fuzzy hairs stopped and then started again—had he stolen a place in her heart.

Tonight, she only half-listened as he told her about the Nature Club and the school greenhouse and the baby quail they were caring for in the classroom.

Billy was sitting in the living room facing the TV when she went back downstairs, but he hadn't turned it on.

"Billy, I was thinking. We should tell Julienne about this developer. Maybe her environmental group could help."

"I don't want them all up in our business."

"What's wrong with SOS? Getting advice can't hurt."

He shrugged. "Listen. Mike asked me to sign on for the season." Mike was the captain of a trawler that fished for cod.

"That's good—right?"

"It would be a lot of money . . . if there's fish. Now that you and I are together, I need to think about doing something else."

"You love fishing!"

He didn't answer. Once she'd asked him if he would ever want to captain his own boat and he'd said no, but nothing more. Maybe he didn't love fishing as much as she'd assumed. Or maybe it had to do with his parents' deaths. She hadn't brought that up. She thought she should let him tell her when the time felt right.

"What other work would you do?"

"Not sure. I just want to be around more."

She picked up the rock paperweight and traced its veins with her index finger, surprised by the keenness of her disappointment. Sometimes when she was alone, she pulled out the photo albums stacked in the bookshelf beneath the window seat in the living room and paged through old black-and-white shots of his family going back to the 1950s and '60s. She would daydream herself onto the water, feeling the heaving waves, the infinity of horizon. When Billy came home stinking of fish, bits of seaweed in his waders, she would coax details from him as she rubbed lotion into his chapped hands and he leaned against her, eyes closed. She, too, closed her eyes, imagining the lines spooled out from the boats like long, skinny eels on top of the water, sun brilliant on the waves.

"What fascinates you so?" he asked, but she couldn't explain. There were no words.

". . . a job with regular hours," he was saying. "If we're not selling the house, I gotta fish until I figure out some other way to make a decent living."

She felt the sting, even though she knew he wasn't blaming her. "I don't want you to do what doesn't feel right." She ran a thumb over his eyebrows, pressing hard on the bone underneath, stroking away his worries. "Sometimes it's as if you don't care about all this."

"I almost think it means more to you."

"How can that be? It's your family history."

"I got memories here, Molly. It's hard for me, sometimes."

Molly felt heat rise to her face. How had this not occurred to her? That what were for her treasures—the times out in their rowboat, sitting on their little pier, watching the life on the bay—were for him tinged with pain. "I'm sorry," she whispered, chastened.

He pulled her to him and buried his face in her neck. "You're my family now, Molly. Home is you and Jonah. The rest doesn't really matter."

Molly tightened her arms around him. She wanted to hold onto this place, not just for herself, but for him and Jonah. Yet that might not be what they needed. Maybe she was just being selfish.

There was a note slipped under their door from their closest neighbors, Joel and Martha, inviting them to a meeting to discuss the offer from the developers. Afterward, Molly and Billy walked back to their house along the water. Theirs was the last home before Eddie Ecker Park began.

"It looks like there were only two houses in favor of selling," Molly said.

The tide had gone out, leaving behind thick knots of seaweed and bits of shell strewn about. As they walked, she kept her eyes on the ground for shells. She pocketed some of the large clam shells that were fun for her to paint with Jonah and a striking scallop shell, dark-red in the ridges.

Billy rolled his shoulders a few times, which he often did when he was uncomfortable. "I don't really trust Joel and Martha."

"Why?" Molly turned too abruptly, twisting her ankle. The shoreline was rocky, making walking difficult.

"Something happened years ago that pissed off my parents." He picked up a few stones and jiggled them. "I can't remember the details, but my parents said they weren't trustworthy. What are they really after?"

"You mean beyond just thinking it was a good idea to get everyone together?"

There had been about ten neighbors, and they'd taken turns talking, everyone indicating whether they were or weren't open to the idea of selling. Molly had been relieved when most seemed reluctant to sell.

"They're kind of slick, don't you think? What if they want to sell and are gauging where we're all coming from so they can feed that information to Miloxi?"

"That would be diabolical!" Molly hated to think so badly of anyone. "You really think they would do that? Work with him behind the scenes to figure out how to pressure the ones of us that don't want to sell?"

"I wouldn't put it past them." He loped a stone in a high arc toward the water.

Molly was silent, absorbing what he said. One of the women, middle-aged with a disheveled and bitter husband, an Iraq war vet, had seemed wishy washy. "Do you think Allison and her husband can be swayed?"

"Everyone can be swayed, Molly."

"Some people stand up for things. Principle matters to some people."

Billy hurled a second stone at the water. "No," he said, forcefully. "Everyone can be bought. It's only a question of price."

"That's not true," Molly started to protest, but the words caught her throat. Did he mean himself, too, then? She didn't dare ask.

CHAPTER 18: Theresa

It was the time of year when the sun glazed the stones along the shore and transformed the beach grasses into shimmering sheaves of wheat with plumes of platinum. As she walked to church, Theresa couldn't resist picking up a few stones and putting them in her pocket.

After Mass, she stopped in to get Father Molina's advice. She had not yet checked back in with the lawyer for her father's estate.

Father Molina's office was small, with an old wooden desk and several comfortable chairs. He listened attentively, long tapered fingers forming a steeple, tapping the tips lightly together, as she filled him in about the terms of her father's will.

He rocked forward in his chair. "Is there no way you could make yourself comfortable in the house? Renovate, so it would feel more like your own? I hate to see you turn your back on this, Theresa."

She was taken aback by his vehemence. "It sickens me," she whispered.

He closed his eyes briefly as he took in a long breath.

"Explain again what happens if you don't take it?"

Theresa shifted uncomfortably. "There's other money that would come to me. The lawyer said my father was a co-owner of some property. They're developing it or something, and once that happens, I would receive a portion of it."

"You'd be willing to take that?"

Theresa looked down at the threadbare carpet. Its once brilliant reds and yellows, Mexican in flavor, had faded to a blur, as fuzzy as her thoughts. "The lawyer made a point of saying my father purchased his share with money that was my mother's, not his."

"So, in your view it's not tainted?"

"Do you think that would be wrong? It still passed through his hands."

"Theresa," Father Molina said somewhat sharply, "surely—" He cut himself off. "It's not my place to tell you what to do, but as your counselor, I urge you not to be hasty, to give this more thought. I would go as far as to say . . ." He hesitated, lips drawn in.

"What, Father?"

"Not taking the house could be considered a sin of pride."

Her eyes smarted.

"I know how you felt about your father, and I respect that, even though you have never shared with me the deeper cause. Perhaps it's time?"

"He betrayed my mother, I've told you."

"We both know that's not the extent of it." He leaned forward, and she caught a whiff of breath mint. "The depth of your feeling alone tells me it goes further."

She began to deny it, then shook her head. "I'm sorry."

"It's okay. Though I hope you'll be able to share it with me someday, to relieve your mind and soul. But consider perhaps this is your father's way of trying to make reparations. And to refuse—"

She stood abruptly. "I'll think about it, Father, I promise."

Outside it had gotten chillier, and she tightened the strings of her sweatshirt hood around her face as she headed back along the beach. Talking with Father Molina hadn't helped. Her brain felt as snarled as the dried, black seaweed along the shore. She couldn't untangle the clot of feelings related to her father, or what held her back from accepting his gift. Until now her anger had felt pure and simple, honest and legitimate. Since his death, something had mixed in, something that made it murky, like sand churned up in the ocean that wouldn't return to the sea floor and settle.

She was so lost in thought she didn't see her neighbor BB until he was almost upon her, detector in hand.

"Red Rose!"

BB appeared tired, with circles under his eyes. His hair was sticking up and snarled. "We have to remove the boulders. We'll wash away, and the town will let it happen."

"We're not going to wash away, BB." She suppressed a laugh.

"Yes, we will, and no one will care. Everyone thinks we're riff-raff."

"I'll go see the board president again, okay?" She patted his shoulder to reassure him.

◆◆◆◆

Joe Tretorn answered her knock, yawning, a fist-sized patch of red on one cheek.

"Sorry, I don't mean to disturb you." *What did this guy do for a living anyway?* He wasn't that old. How could he already be retired?

"Come on in. I'll make some coffee."

"No need."

"Au contraire, I need."

"Sorry."

"Stop already."

"So," he settled opposite her with two mugs, coffee press, and a small pitcher of milk, "what's on your mind?"

"Is it true we have to remove the boulders?"

Tretorn's eyes were puffy but genial as he peered at her over his mug. He took a sip and ran his hand over his bald head, as if he'd forgotten he had no hair to smooth. "You really should come to the meetings."

"I'm not a group person."

"Fuck that. You're just not willing to put in the time."

"It's not like I have anything to contribute. I have no experience with these things."

"Think any of us does? We're all learning." He shook his head. "Okay, speech over. The town wouldn't budge on the permit. They've slapped us with violations. But we're not removing the boulders. They'll have to take us to court to force us."

"But eventually they'll win?" She became aware of the *plunk plunk* of a faucet drip.

He lifted his cup and sipped. Theresa gulped her own coffee too quickly and burned the roof of her mouth. "This is just buying time?"

Tretorn set down his cup. "We're gonna do everything there is to do."

"Right."

"Come to the next meeting."

"And that will help how?"

"It'll make you feel better."

"Yeah, right," Theresa said dryly. "Thanks for the coffee." She took her mug to the sink and washed it.

She walked back to her trailer along the crushed gravel walkway. Hers was one of the oldest in the community, white with aqua trim and awnings. She had draped fairy lights around the door and lined the walkway with glow lanterns, mason jars filled with white pebbles fitted with solar lids that lit her way after dark. This was her home, where she wanted to be. Even if they lost their beach, this was where she wanted to be.

She yanked open her door so hard it squeaked in protest. She knew it was foolhardy to reject her father's offer of his house, yet she couldn't bring herself to inhabit the same space as the woman who was instrumental in her mother's death. She was stuck, as trapped in her feelings as one of the moths that found their way into the trailer, only to waste its energy beating it wings against the window. She gently pinched their tiny wings, took them to the door, and released them.

If only someone could do that for her.

———————

At 4:30 p.m., it was already so dark inside the bar that Theresa had to feel for the peg on the back of the kitchen door to hang up her jean jacket. She called out, "Marty?" but there was no answer, so she started the setups for Kathy, who was late as usual.

Molly appeared just as Theresa was opening the door for business and handed her a plastic bag. "Scallops."

"Thanks! I'll put these in the fridge."

Molly often brought Theresa treats from the market at the end of the day. When she returned, Theresa poured Molly a tall glass of Pellegrino and slid over a bowl of goldfish.

"Any news about the TP?" Molly asked.

"The town won't let us keep the bulkheading."

"I'm so sorry. What will you do?"

Theresa shrugged. The door opened and a few of the usuals walked in. Cody slipped onto the stool beside Molly and kissed her on the cheek. As he grabbed the goldfish bowl, she stood up.

"Hey, I'll give it back. Don't leave on account of me."

Molly laughed. "Duty calls. Gotta pick up Jonah."

"Thanks for the scallops," Theresa called after her. She poured Cody's Corona and adjusted the lime slice. "So, what's hatching?"

"You know they don't actually hatch like chickens, right?" A bead of moisture from the beer glistened in his beard. He wore a green Irish sweater, which matched his eyes.

"So why isn't it called the Spawnery, then?"

"Ha, such a clever girl." He took a sip. "Lots of guys hit on you, I know."

Theresa grabbed a micro cloth and began polishing a glass.

"Look, I'm not like those other guys. I'd really like to get to know you." He leaned forward. "It doesn't have to be a big deal; we could take it slow."

Theresa kept her eyes on the cloth, twirling it inside the glass. "Not a good idea, Cody."

"I know it'll sound arrogant, but I get a vibe that you like me, too. Can you tell me what it is I'm doing wrong?"

She felt her face warm and turned slightly away. "It's not about you. I don't date."

"What do you mean, you don't date?"

"I'm not interested in a relationship," she said shortly. "Just how I am." She busied herself with the maraschino cherries. One dropped on the bar, and as she reached for it, Cody covered her hand with his. For a split second, she relaxed into his hand before she caught herself.

"Please," she said.

He didn't release his grip.

"Damn it, Cody." She yanked her hand away, ducked under the bar, and stalked off to the bathroom.

She cupped water over her face, but the cold didn't help. She could still feel the imprint of Cody's touch. She'd been celibate for over a year, but she could sense the lure of the bait, taste the metal of the hook in her mouth.

When she emerged, Kathy gave her a searching look. "Whatcha say to Cody?"

When Theresa didn't answer, Kathy shrugged. "Okay, your business. A pitcher of sangria."

Theresa took out the containers of cut-up apples and oranges. The bar door burst open again. Stu, Sky, Choppy, and the rest of the gang crowded up.

"Overfishing, bullshit. It's pollution." Will was grousing.

He was one of the old-timers, wizened and scruffy. He loved to get everyone worked up. When he talked, his Adam's apple moved up and down his throat like a bead on a string. He was one she needed to keep an eye on. He downed Jack Daniels like it was lemonade.

She busied herself with pulling drafts, sliding coasters and snacks everyone's way, and tuning out the grumblings that were as thick as cigarette smoke: how unfair the allocations were; how poorly the government collected data; and how this politician or that bureaucrat was in the pocket of the sports fishermen, who were all in the thrall of the environmental organizations. The conflicts in this town weren't just rich outsiders versus working-class locals; they were more nuanced—between commercial and sport fishermen, fishermen and surfers, environmentalists and small business owners. Tonight, she barely paid attention, frazzled by Cody, her father's will, everything.

Around 11:00 p.m., a man she didn't recognize came in. He ordered a Stoli, straight up, no ice, and left a ten-dollar tip. She noted the sharply pressed khakis and dress shirt, the clean, trim fingernails, so he wasn't a fisherman or dock worker. There was self-assurance, almost insolence, to the looking-over he gave her as he turned away and headed to a back table. A few of the charter boat captains nodded to him deferentially. Maybe DEC? The Department of Environmental Conservation was seen by many as an irritant, closing areas to shellfish, placing restrictions on species, boarding boats to search for illegal catches.

The man sauntered back up to the bar a short while later. "Stoli, straight up, no ice."

"I remember." No bartender worth her margarita salt would fail to memorize a client's drink. Again, he wouldn't take the change. She shrugged and shoved the bills into the tips jar.

She restacked the coasters, tidied the napkins. She had developed her own personal ballet, an economy of motion to spare her body, but by the end of the night, she'd be in pain: back, legs, shoulders. She mixed herself a G&T and knocked it back below the bar. When she stood up, Sky was hopping onto a stool, pretending not to have seen.

"How goes it?"

"Okay." She toyed with asking him for a neck rub. Bad idea. "You?"

Sky leaned his elbows on the bar. "Nada." He tugged at his bandanna. "Money and fish, fish and money."

"You guys wouldn't be happy if you didn't have fishing to complain about." She mimicked, "Where are the blues? If the water doesn't warm up soon, we won't get any tuna."

Sky laughed and was quiet a moment. "It's serious, though. Striper action is zip. No lobsters, not even in Maine. Looks like the scallops are hit badly again, and no one knows why. People are talking about getting out altogether. It's scary."

"It's just cyclical, isn't that what everyone always says?"

"I hate to admit it, but the environmentalists may be right that the stocks are getting depleted. The ocean is heating up. And the fucking government! They can't regulate their bowels, much less the fisheries!"

Theresa laughed. "Is that guy DEC? Are they closing one of the fisheries?"

"He's not DEC. Some business type from up-island. Miloxi something." Theresa frowned. Miloxi was the name of the guy who had been bothering Molly and Billy.

As if he sensed her interest, the man pivoted her way. Eyes on her, he took his time putting on his coat, a beautiful camel's hair as out of place in the bar as a camel would have been. *I am powerful*, his look read. *You don't impress me.* It was not an attitude she was used to.

"Guy's dangerous," Sky said. "I can feel it. Don't be an asshole."

"Huh?" She and Miloxi were still locking eyes.

"Keep your distance."

Theresa tore her gaze away, registering what Sky had said. She could only laugh. "Don't I always?"

There was a shout from the back and a crashing thud.

"Shit." She started out from behind the bar.

Sky raced ahead to the back room. "It's Will," he called over his shoulder.

She'd forgotten to keep track and dilute Will's drinks as she usually did. It saved her trouble and didn't hurt him any. She'd been distracted.

"He's out of control." One of the boat captains stormed past her to the door. Stu and Cody grabbed Will and pinned his arms. Sky righted a tipped-over chair.

"We'll get him home," Cody said, shuffling Will to the door.

Theresa nodded her thanks. She didn't breathe again until the door slammed behind the men.

She'd messed up. If she had been paying attention, this wouldn't have happened.

She waited a half-hour, then brightened the lights for last call. It was a bit early, but she'd had enough. She tidied and mopped the back room and stacked the chairs. When she stepped outside, the quiet and the cool night air were a tonic. The sky was mottled, with a glow behind the clouds where the moon hid. It sailed into an opening, seemed to hover, and slid behind another cloud. The air was fresh, with hints of diesel and salt and fish guts, and she breathed in, over and over. She could never get her fill.

There was a car waiting in the lot; Cody stepped out.

She groaned inwardly but walked over. "Thanks for helping out in there."

"No problem."

"Well, good night." She turned to go.

"I just wanted to say . . . I understand what happens when someone breaks your heart. You don't want to try again."

"Nobody's broken my heart, Cody."

He held his ground a moment before stepping aside to let her pass to her truck. Her cheeks felt hot as she slid behind the wheel. He was still standing there as she gunned the motor and pulled away in a jarring burst of gravel.

Nobody can break my heart, she thought. Her heart was a tightly closed clamshell; only minute grains of sand or water could make their way in.

No one would ever get close enough again to touch it.

CHAPTER 19: Clancy

As the town came into view, Clancy felt a curious exhilaration, an unexpected sense of belonging. He stopped the car and watched as a flock of starlings zoomed skyward in an aerial display over Ford Pond Bay, a feat of exquisite choreography. On the surface of the water, two mallards toppled over every few seconds, tails tipped upward, as they fed on aquatic plants below.

He was returning to Montauk after a few days in the city. Nearing the end of his stash of vacation days, still awaiting Theresa Nolan's decision on Otto's house, he had gone into his office to work out a leave of absence, then taken Bruce out to dinner to thank him for forwarding his mail while he was away. Given how much Otto had done for him as a boy, fulfilling his wishes for the Moorlands felt more like a sacred duty than a mere administrative task. He wanted to allow himself sufficient time.

This would be his first time inside Otto's house since his death. Clancy had arranged to have the house cleaned professionally. He couldn't bear to see so intimately the details of Otto's last moments reflected in the tissues in his wastebasket, the stains on his sheets.

The house keys were heavy in his hand; the ivory-colored ring, in the shape of a whale, was smooth to the touch. Clancy wondered if it was made from a part of an actual whale, the word for which he couldn't remember. The door opened smoothly. He stood just inside, an eerie chill shivering his skin.

How peculiar to inhabit someone else's house again, like times in foster care when he was left alone and could venture into the parents' bedroom. He only wanted to absorb the aura, the little details that were clues to the people he didn't really know but who had for whatever reason chosen to be his foster parents. He'd note the hairbrush left carelessly on a bureau, the glasses dangling off a bedside lamp, little signifiers of intimacy. Now it was his obligation to snoop, to learn what he needed to take charge of Otto's affairs.

Clancy pulled out Otto's letter, the paper worn from the many times he had read it.

Dear Clancy,

Things seemed so much simpler when I first came to Montauk. Or maybe there simply wasn't as much opportunity for greed to show its hand.

I want to say how special it's been to have you come back into my life. It reawakens my belief in God, as if He has sent you. You've been like a son to me, even though it's been so long since the wonderful times we had when you were a boy. I think they probably meant more to me than to you. No matter. You were so brave in the face of what you had gone through. I could tell right away you were special, a wise and compassionate soul. Having met you again, I can see how right I was.

Clancy put down the letter; a mix of loss and love settled in his throat, swollen and prickly.

I'm sorry to burden you with this decision on the Moorlands parcel, but I can die easy knowing you'll accept it and find the right solution.

In love and gratitude,

Otto

Below, in different ink, the handwriting harder to decipher, was a broken-off sentence.

Clancy, I have an idea. I have to think about this, but a thought just came to me—

There was a smudge, an odd pencil drawing with squares and circles and hashtags, and only one word that Clancy could make out: "retreat."

What could Otto possibly have meant? A place of calm and peace? Maybe the word was "repeat." Clancy tucked the letter in his wallet and moved down the hallway. First things first.

The air in the house felt stale, so he opened a few windows. The lounger in the corner seemed shrunken, an awkward beast, without Otto to fill it. The small table and lamp beside it held an open, hardcover book, with glasses nearby, as if Otto had been reading just moments before. On the side wall stood an old-fashioned china cabinet Clancy had scarcely noticed the times he'd visited, filled with flow-er-patterned pitchers and creamers on the top shelves and bowls and platters on the bottom. He moved to the bookcase. There were a few novels and biographies of famous political figures, but most were about the region—history, photography, gardening, and coastal flora and fauna.

He picked up *A History of the Montaukettes*, which sat on top of newspapers and magazines the cleaning people had neatly piled up on the coffee table. He remembered the papers spread all over the table, which now revealed itself to be a specimen type with a hinged glass lid, filled with shells and rocks. He wished he could have asked Otto about all the topics he found so fascinating. It stung that Otto had died just when they'd reconnected, depriving him of the time to know him more fully.

He settled on the couch and paged through the book, handling what Otto had handled, hoping it would help him feel more comfortable being here. While he understood Otto wanted someone he loved to live in his home, Clancy didn't feel entitled to such a gift.

He got up and walked to the slider that framed the landscape of meadow and distant woods, where several deer with long graceful necks bent over the ground. He'd heard there were too many of them, destroying gardens and endangering motorists. *God, they're lovely though.*

Turning, he caught a rancid smell and traced it to a container of birdseed in a cup by the door leading from the kitchen to the garden. He took it out past the patio, where he and Otto had sat, to the garden. The air felt warm and humid for mid-October. What had been orderly when Otto showed it to him was now a mess of dead and dying vegetation. He flung the seed in a wide arc, then removed a few dried leaves from a tomato plant. Everything was brown or dull green; the only bright colors were the marigolds. Clancy did what Otto had the day he'd first visited—pulled off a petal and rubbed it between his fingers, then brought his fingers to his nose. He closed his eyes and inhaled the scent, spicy and delicious.

If he took the house, he'd need to do something with this garden.

He caught himself again. His task was to take care of Otto's affairs, nothing more. He headed back inside.

A small desk, made of some dark wood, stood in a small alcove off the living room, its surface bare except for a misshapen green mug with pens and pencils, a stapler, and a plastic paperclip dispenser. It had two drawers on each side of an opening for the legs, everything neatly organized. The top drawers held notepaper and envelopes, check books and bills. The bottom drawer on the left held hanging file folders labeled health reports, insurance, car and home, and other documents. Clancy had no idea what he should be looking for until he found a folder labeled Gang of Five and papers relating to the partnership that owned the controversial Moorlands parcel. A quick perusal indicated it contained no instructions for him.

Nothing he looked through helped him guess at Otto's eureka moment, but in the final drawer was something unexpected: a stack of notebooks, all the same but for color. He set them on the desk and opened one with a forest-green cover. On the first page was written ECOLOGY. Inside were dated entries.

"Silverods are the white-flowered goldenrod that can be found in Montauk woodlands."

"Dwarf pines are rare in the rest of Long Island."

The bright blue notebook was labeled WATERS/FISHING, the red, WEATHER & GEOLOGY, and a brown one was HISTORY: MONTAUKETTS, MILITARY, & GENERAL. All were partially filled with notes in Otto's precise, almost print-like, script along with newspaper clippings stapled to the pages.

Clancy turned on a table lamp and opened the history notebook.

Unlike the rest of the Hamptons, inhabited by the English since the 1600s, only Native Americans lived on the Montauk peninsula before the early 1900s, as early as 6,000 BC. Once the Europeans came, the peninsula was used to graze their cattle, and the first houses in Montauk were way stations for the cattle drivers.

So Max was not being fanciful when he told Clancy there had once been cattle in Montauk.

The Hamptons attracted artists seeking the special qualities of the light, wealthy families seeking vacation homes, and more recently, hedge-fund managers looking to park their money where it was sure to appreciate. Montauk's remoteness, along with the harsh winters, kept the year-round population sparse for most of the twentieth century. Early on, two wealthy men saw its potential and began to develop the peninsula, but circumstances foiled their plans. First, Arthur Benson purchased the entire peninsula in 1878. In 1925, Carl Fisher purchased all 10,000 acres. Envisioning a Miami Beach of the North, he built a boardwalk along the ocean and Tudor-style homes and offices in town, and bulldozed a channel from Lake Montauk into Block Island Sound to create a world-class marina and deep-sea harbor. The crash of 1929 and other woes put an end to his plans, and instead of a playground for the rich, Montauk became a fishing mecca and held fast to its rough-and-tumble aspect—

The doorbell rang with a sharp blast. Clancy's pulse raced. He knew the police would never figure out who started the Hither Woods fire; he'd remain under suspicion indefinitely.

But it wasn't the police. At the door was a stocky older man with a tanned and weathered face. He was wearing a baseball jacket and a Montauk Brewery cap.

"Harve Bender, Otto's brother-in-law." He grabbed Clancy's hand and pumped it. "For his second wife. I apologize for barging in, but I live nearby so when I saw the car, I figured I'd give it a shot." His diction was precise, in contrast with his relaxed look.

"Come on in. Would you like something to drink?"

"No thanks." He followed Clancy into the living room and stood a moment, taking it in. "A lifetime of history in here."

Clancy nodded. It crossed his mind that if someone were to look around his apartment in Astoria, they'd see little sign of his personal history, of what had bearing on his life.

Harve sat on the sofa and leaned forward, forearms on knees. "I'll come right to the point. I know you were named executor of Otto's will, so I assume you know about the Moorlands Group." He waited for Clancy's nod, then went on. "Otto and I were close, and he mentioned you before he died. I don't mean to be blunt, but you kinda came out of nowhere. I'd like to know who's taking over his shares—you or his daughter? We need a majority of the partners to decide what we're going to do with the land, and Otto's was the deciding vote. I want to express my views, if it's going to be you."

His tone was courteous but firm. Clancy liked his forthrightness. "Otto's daughter inherits, but I have the authority to vote his shares. I'm just beginning to go through his papers."

"Good timing then." Harve brought his hands together, his arthritic fingers like knobs of ginger root. "I want to convince you to vote the way I think best."

"I'm eager to hear you out. But I'll be voting according to what I establish were Otto's wishes."

"Fair enough." Harve nodded. "I wouldn't want it any other way. But him and me were close, and I'm pretty damn sure he'd have decided to vote my way. Look, you're new. You won't realize how much we love this place. We're a tribe of people who would do anything to live here. It's beautiful, of course. You can see that." His gaze went to the window. "But as much as we want it not to change, it must." He turned back to Clancy. "Humans are part of the ecosystem, too. This town needs affordable housing. We've got workers coming here from Melville and beyond, clogging the roads mornings and nights. It drives up wages. It drives up the price of food. Our young people can't live here. They have to leave because they can't afford it. It's at a point of crisis. People rent out rooms and basements they're not supposed to. Houses that are only big enough for one family are housing three. The environmentalists keep pushing to save open space, and this is what happens—an out-of-whack community for rich people."

Before Clancy could comment, Harve barreled on, his voice rising. "You got your firemen and teachers, the bedrock of a town, living miles away, while big fancy houses are sitting empty nine months of the year. That's what you got. So, I'm telling you—and I know in my heart Otto would agree—a development of reasonably priced houses is what this town needs, and the Moorlands is the best place for it. Hell, it's the only place. The environmentalists have sewn everything up. There isn't another large parcel left." His skin suddenly flared, mottled and red.

One thing Clancy had learned through his work was how to let silences settle, to resist the pressure to agree too readily. He waited and then said, "Harve, I appreciate what you're saying. I'm here to protect Otto's interests, and I need to inform myself first. I'm just going to have to take some time on this."

Harve sighed, the color receding from his face. He leaned back against the sofa cushions. "I do get a little emotional. My son and wife and only grandkids just moved away."

"I understand," Clancy said, though family was the last thing he understood.

Harve took a breath and pulled himself to his feet. "I appreciate you hearing me out. Let me know how to reach you. The Planning Department just notified us our application warrants an environmental review. That has to happen before things go forward. Even so, we'll be holding a meeting of the partners soon, and of course, we'll need you there."

"I plan to stay another month or so." Clancy handed Harve his card. "I appreciate you giving me the time I need to make a decision."

"Fair enough. Oh, and will you give us your word that you won't divulge the identity of the partners? We don't need any heat brought on us from the community."

Clancy saw him to the door. He had imagined the process would be as complicated as making a claims decision—weighing the evidence, using well-worked out parameters and precedents. He hadn't expected it to get quite so emotional.

He went back to the living room. Outside the deer had come closer, and there were more of them. They didn't seem to feel his eyes from behind the slider glass. He watched for long minutes, filling up with their beauty, letting his heartbeat slow.

———◆◆◆———

A few hours of going through Otto's papers and skimming his notebooks clarified nothing. Clancy was beginning to have an uneasy, out-of-his depth feeling. If only Otto had lived even a day or two longer.

He arrived back at Bishops as Julienne and Max were stepping out of their house. Max came running over.

"We're going for a hike. Wanna come?"

Clancy glanced at Julienne. He'd been keeping his distance.

"Come, please." She sounded sincere.

"I've never been on a real hike."

"About time, then!" Julienne smiled.

They set off down a trail through gnarly trees Julienne said were shadbush, Max in the lead, the light flickering through the lattice of branches. The brilliance of the autumn colors had faded by now; the brambles' berries were going from red to yellow, and the air was filled with a heady scent of decaying leaves.

Max ran on ahead, waving a crooked branch he was using as a hiking stick. The trail was rutted and lumpy with roots and stones that wanted to trip Clancy up.

Julienne said something over her shoulder that Clancy couldn't catch.

"What?" he said and stumbled.

She caught one of his pinwheeling arms and laughed. "I'm sorry. I shouldn't laugh."

"I forgive you."

"I'm glad." She said it seriously, as if she meant something more. Maybe she regretted her wariness toward him after he'd come under suspicion.

The trail went downhill through a stretch of overarching holly trees. He liked walking through the tunnel of branches, liked how the sun threw dark and light patches on the ground. Julienne was quick and athletic in her movements, arms pumping as if to a metronome. He imagined she was a tomboy when she was young.

As they walked, he was aware of sounds: the slight rustling of their feet and an occasional bird call and a distant rumble of ocean when the path dead-ended at a T. Julienne briefly disappeared from view. A moment later he emerged from the trees to find himself at the edge of a low cliff above a sheltered cove.

Julienne threw out her arms. "Ta-da!"

"Wow." He'd no idea the woods led to the coast. The ocean spread out before them, with the town to the west and an expanse of low vegetation to the east.

"Come this way!" Max lifted his branch. They reentered the woods and headed east at the T. After a few minutes, the trail opened up again, revealing a sweep of headland and a low compound of modest, white structures like something out of rural Ireland.

"That used to be Andy Warhol's estate."

He was astonished. "Warhol? I'd expect something far grander."

They headed down to the water's edge. Looking back up from the beach, Clancy saw how the cliffs were scoured and fluted, as if raked by the fingernails of an angry giant.

"I've never seen anything like this."

"They're called hoodoos." Max danced back up from the water's edge.

"Why don't you tell Clancy what causes it."

"Wind and erosion, right, Mom?"

"That's right. The lighter stuff washes out, leaving these formations."

"Max is really precocious," Clancy said to Julienne as they continued on along the beach. "It amazes me how much he knows."

"When we homeschooled him, every walk was a lesson. We're so fortunate. Living here is like a science lab." Julienne picked up a slender length of driftwood. "It was a lot of work, but it was special for me, too, like reliving my summers here growing up."

"I get it."

"It's important to me that he—that future generations— have this. That we don't screw it up." She stirred the sand with the stick.

"Screw it up how?"

"This was just a fishing village less than seventy years ago. Even with the growth of the fishing industry and tourists, it kept its essence. Growing up, you'd go clamming off someone's beach, or pick cranberries in the dunes, or ice skate on the pond." She paused. "Now it's gotten so popular, it's like a different kind of erosion. It's wearing away the fabric of the place, forcing people out. I don't know half the people I see on the street."

Clancy didn't know anyone he saw on the street where he lived, either, and he liked that just fine. "Can anything be done?"

She poked with her driftwood stick, moving small rocks around. "Good planning and zoning, if there's the will to do that. It's hard for politicians to write strong-enough legislation. Too many people benefit from the growth. Too many wealthy donors." Her tone was bitter.

They'd reached a cove where the tide had brought the water nearly to the base of the cliff. Their only way forward was over a slurry of small rocks interspersed with boulders.

Max leaped from one rock to another. Teetering slightly, he said to Clancy, "Know why there's so many rocks?" He pointed with his stick. The cliff, topped with a scruff of vegetation, concaved in below. Small clumps of soil held onto bits of foliage, like a bald pate with a few strands of hair. "The water hits the cliffs, takes away the soil, and the rocks come tumbling down."

"Is it just a natural process, then?" He asked Julienne.

"Yes, but the erosion is accelerating because of sea level rise. You've heard of those islands in the Pacific that are disappearing? This whole peninsula could end up under water someday, too."

"It seems very futile when you put it that way."

"Well, our species could stop the behavior that's driving climate change." She flung her driftwood stick into the distance like a spear. She glanced at him and away. "Sorry. It just makes me crazy."

On the other side of the cove, the shore was sandy again.

"Chocolate!" Max shouted, heading toward a large drift-wood log.

"Our turnaround spot." Julienne linked her arm through Clancy's, as if determined to be cheery, releasing it when they reached the log. "My parents got me to go on hikes by promising me chocolate—a tradition I deeply believe in." She pulled a huge bar out of her pack. Clancy popped a square in his mouth, letting it melt against his tongue. The sun appeared and disappeared behind clouds, glazing the undersides of the waves.

Max ran off to poke along the wrack line, his sweatpants pockets bulging with his finds. Clancy felt a sense of peace settle over him, a kind of drowsiness. He leaned back and closed his eyes, listening to the rumble of the ocean as it differentiated into separate booms and hisses, Max's laughter sailing over it.

"I see why you love this so much." He shifted onto his side to face her. "And why you're called to paint it."

"I don't know what I'd do if I had to leave."

"Why would you have to?"

She rolled a small pink stone between her fingers. "Sometimes I worry that Rob's not so happy here."

"Is there somewhere else he wants to be?"

"Not that he's said." She gave a laugh. "It's probably my guilt talking because staying here matters more to me than anything." She shuddered. "Even saying that aloud . . ." She placed the stone back on the sand.

"There's nothing wrong with loving this," Clancy said.

The wind had picked up a little. She untied her sweatshirt from around her waist and pulled it on. "I seem to be doing all the talking. You haven't told me much about yourself."

"I've had a very ordinary life, I'm afraid."

She narrowed her eyes, as if trying to gauge the truth of things. "An ordinary life, maybe, but I think you're far from an ordinary man. I mean to plumb those hidden depths!"

She said this with mock seriousness, and he laughed, but a discomfiting shiver rippled over him. It was almost as if she was flirting with him.

Max barreled into them, jetting a spray of wet sand.

"Yetch!" Julienne cried. Sand freckled her face.

Clancy pulled a bandanna from his back pocket. He leaned over to wipe her cheek, then checked himself and handed it to her instead.

CHAPTER 20: Molly

L ight rain fell, fog drifting in wisps off the bay. Molly moved away from the window. Jonah was at the kitchen table with his notebooks, his heels kicking the legs of his chair in metronomic concentration.

"How about we cook something special for dinner?"

"Cool!" It amazed her how much Jonah enjoyed cooking. He'd begun helping with the cutting and chopping, and they progressed to experimenting together, going through cookbook recipes step by step.

"Lasagna?"

She took out fresh onions, peppers, mushrooms, baby spinach, and all the leftover cheeses in the house. There were a few anchovies in a jar, so she took them out, too.

"What did Mrs. Morgan talk about today?" She sautéed the onions while Jonah mixed the ricotta and mozzarella. His teacher, whom he adored, was the same woman Julienne described as a "real firebrand," the head of her environmental group. Grace Morgan had already found out that the international outfit Miloxi represented made deals all around the world.

"We're learning about the whale business. When the colonists came, they wanted the whales because they were very luca . . . luca-something."

"Lucrative?"

"Because of the oil from the blubber. After they killed the whales, they boiled them. They got the Indians to do all the work because they knew how. The Indians only killed whales for food, but the colonists killed them for commerce. So that's why there are almost none left."

"I never heard any of this before."

"Mrs. Morgan says people don't know the history that's right under their noses." Jonah wrinkled his own. "I like history. Do you?"

"I like the history you tell me."

"Did I tell you that a long time ago the town was close to here and not where it is now? There was a giant hurricane, and the whole town was destroyed."

"When was that?"

"A long time ago. We could be due for another one, Mrs. Morgan says."

Molly smiled at the way Jonah channeled Mrs. Morgan, using her language, changing his voice. He said this with relish, but it made her wonder if he was preoccupied with loss.

The day before, they had paged through old family photo albums. There were men with traps and drift nets and wooden dories . . . his grandfather and uncles. In one picture, a group of men and one woman stood on a dock, an enormous striped bass laid out on a wooden table lined up against a yardstick. Jonah had leaned into her, his breath warm on her neck.

"That one's my dad and that one's my mom."

Molly froze. She should have realized looking at the album could trigger painful memories. "I'm so sorry you lost them."

Jonah had buried his face in her neck. She ran her hand over his head, the hair soft against her skin.

The onions were done. Jonah slid them into the cheese mixture and spread it over the first layer of noodles in the baking pan. They topped it with tomato sauce and spinach and began the layering process again.

The sound of Billy's truck came from outside. A minute later, he was in the kitchen, holding his wet boots off to the side as he kissed her.

"We made lasagna!" Jonah said.

"Smells wonderful." Billy ran a sweat-shirted sleeve under his nose. His face was red from the wind, his skin moist from rain.

He's better-looking than anyone has a right to be, she thought, admiring his thick black brows and short, straight nose. As she turned back to the stove, he put his arms around her waist from behind, rubbing his chin on the top of her head.

"Gimme body warmth."

Jonah came bounding over. As Molly drew him in, Billy disengaged.

"Jonah, my man," he said, "there's a game on. What do you say we watch a little TV before dinner like true-blooded American males?"

"Sure, Billy, my man." Jonah drew himself up, grinning.

Billy was sometimes abrupt with Jonah, pushing him away, asserting his claim to Molly. Other times, like now, as if hurt by Jonah's attachment to her, Billy would leave Molly behind to have his brother to himself.

She sighed. She understood. As they walked out of the kitchen, something about the way Billy's arm rested on Jonah's shoulder, while Jonah's went around Billy's waist, pierced her heart. They were lone survivors of a storm, bound by trauma, the Lost Boys of *Peter Pan*. Sometimes the three of them together felt whole and good, a solid entity, but other times she felt too central, their Wendy, a little afraid of losing herself in the process.

After dinner, Jonah went upstairs to finish his homework, and Billy and Molly settled in the living room. The rain was now making tiny *pings* against the window.

Billy reached for her hand. "Mike wants to head out again. Okay with you?"

"How long would you be gone?"

"Ten, maybe twelve days."

She let the thought settle.

"Molly?"

Her last day of work at the fish market was coming up. "I was thinking I would apply at Kmart. I guess that could wait until you're back."

"We could get by till spring without you working if we make good money on this trip."

If, she thought, but didn't say.

———

As soon as Billy left a few days later, the weather turned. The ferocity of the wind came as a surprise, but everyone just shrugged and said, "That's Montauk."

If she forgot a hat, her hair was whipped into a cyclone of strands stinging her face. She worried about Billy, miles from shore, pitching on heavy seas, lashed by wind and rain. She tried not to think it was her fault because if it weren't for her, he'd sell the house and have enough money to get off the water for good. The developer had called again, and she told him they were not interested. When he kept arguing, she hung up on him.

She and Jonah went to the beach or the woods after school, but with the sun setting early, the walks were short. Once indoors, Jonah talked as he did his homework, scrunching his face close over the paper. He talked through dinner, and he talked as they cleaned up, and he talked as he got ready for bed. But then she shushed him and took a book from his bookcase to read aloud. He put his head on her shoulder, and she breathed his scent of eraser and bubblegum toothpaste. She missed Billy and she knew Jonah did, too, but there was something precious nurtured in the space Billy left behind. Sometimes she stayed in bed even after Jonah fell asleep, listening to his breathing and imagining she was on the boat with Billy, together on the slicked-down surface, staring up at the stars, sharply etched in the inky blackness.

———•·••·•———

By the middle of October, after Billy had been gone a week, decorated scarecrows began to appear around town—an octopus reading a prayer book in front of the church, a surfer holding a board in front of the sports shop, a mermaid scarecrow made of trash. Jonah decided to be the Tin Man for Halloween. They punched holes in cans and ran fishing line through, and then she stitched the cans to an old thermal shirt.

Billy got in touch to say they were heading home; the captain didn't want to take any chances with an impending storm. On TV, the weather map appeared with blue-black Van Gogh swirls. Molly watched the bay being whipped by the wind and measured the distance from the shore to the house in her mind.

She drove Jonah to school, drizzle hitting the windshield. Children raced for the doors, schoolbags smacking their backs, heads lowered. Above, the clouds didn't seem to be moving, but from the direction of the ocean came a low keening sound.

All day she paced, uneasy, as the wind picked up and finally, as if in a pique, the sky opened up. Torrents of rain were unleashed, rain that fell so heavily she couldn't see the bay. She soaked beans for chili, set up a pot for rice, tidied the house for Billy's return, and rushed to the window every few minutes. The bay seemed to be rising before her eyes. Panicked, she dialed Julienne.

"There's not much you can do. You have quite a bit of

frontage; it's not likely the water will get anywhere near the house."

Molly ran the dishcloth along the counter. "I've never seen rain like this."

"At least the wind's died down a bit. When's Billy back?"

"Soon. Before nightfall."

"Keep an eye on it, and if the water gets too close, call. You guys are welcome to stay here."

Molly made hot chocolate and stood by the window with her mug. At first, she thought she was imagining it, but the water seemed to have stalled about twenty feet from the edge of what they called their patio, a flat area on which they had laid pavers. She rested her head against the window with relief.

Seconds later came a series of doorbell rings, and Billy was calling out, "Molly Molly Molly!"

She flung herself at him before he could remove his wet clothes, and they clung like two shipwrecked victims, water pooling on the floor around them.

The rain continued for two days. People kept saying it simply couldn't go on like this. They flew in through the back door of the drug store, rain gear flapping, to get their morning papers. In the post office, water from dripping umbrellas made soggy messes of the tossed-away circulars that tumbled from the recycle bin.

Molly drove to work down their rutted road, skirting deep potholes filled with water. At the dock, business was unbearably slow.

"Florida." Vince paced behind the counter. "Palm trees and piña coladas. Coconuts. Pools and piña coladas. Pink walls, pink sands. Piña coladas."

"I thought you loved it here," Molly said.

"Of course I do." Vince leaned against the wall and crossed his arms over his chest. "I work my ass off all summer. Vacation, here I come!"

"Does everyone leave?"

"Everyone who can. All the seasonal—shop and motel and restaurant owners. Over the school break, a lot of the teachers and parents with kids go away, too. Costa Rica, Mexico. When the winter comes, oh baby. You'll see. No one in their right mind can stand it through the winter."

The bell tinkled. A last customer. Molly weighed out fish and closed out the register. Dusk came early now. She thought of the long winter ahead, days alone in the house while Billy was out fishing and Jonah was in school. She wondered what she would find to do with herself.

Outside the clouds had lifted a bit, a subtle brightening. She decided to drop in at the Promised Land before heading home. It was so early, only a few bar stools were occupied. She plopped next to Cody; Theresa slid over the bowl of goldfish.

"How's the hatchery?" she asked Cody. She loved hearing about his work there.

"The spat's coming along." The spat was what they called the shellfish babies. They grew them in tanks and then, come spring, transplanted them in local waters to develop.

"Maybe I could try something like that?" She popped a goldfish in her mouth. "You know, catching clams or scallops."

"You don't exactly 'catch' them." Cody bit his lip with a smirk. "They're not running away from you. They just nestle along the bottom."

"Well okay, but what do you think?"

"Sure. You could even do it commercially; you just have to get a license. You might want to get a sense of what's involved first."

"How?"

"Well, the hatchery asks for volunteers when we put the spat out in the water in the spring, and then to monitor over the summer."

"Oh my god, that would be so awesome!"

Cody laughed, and she saw him glance over her head. "Maybe you could convince your friend here to volunteer, too."

Molly twisted around on her stool, but Theresa had moved down the bar.

"What's her story?" Cody asked. "She told me she doesn't date. Do you buy that, or is she just blowing me off?"

Molly hesitated. "I think I'd know if she was seeing someone."

He put his hand on hers. "Put in a good word for me, will you?"

Cody was such a sweetheart, it was an easy favor. "Of course."

"Come visit the hatchery. I'll show you everything."

⊸••⊷

Molly went online to learn what she could about the hatchery program. In past decades, shellfish, once so plentiful on the East End, had died off almost completely, maybe because of run off from surrounding land where too much fertilizer was used, maybe from warming waters due to the changing climate, maybe a combination of factors. The hatchery program was instituted to try and bring them back.

Over dinner, Billy didn't say a word as she told him about it, just scooped out casserole onto his and Jonah's plates, eyes fixed on her face as he chewed. When she finished, he was silent. She was puzzled and deflated by his reaction.

"Don't you think it would be really cool? Maybe Jonah could help, too."

"Could I?" Jonah jumped up.

Billy put his palm on Jonah's head and pressed him down into his seat.

"Billy? What is it?"

"Couldn't you find something to do on land? You're not a particularly good swimmer."

"What does swimming have to do with it?"

"Working on the water is dangerous." He crossed his arms over his chest and tilted back in his chair. "You know that fishing is one of the most dangerous professions there is?"

"This isn't fishing. This is just helping put some platters of spat into the water."

"Platters?"

"Well frames, boxes, whatever."

He just raised his eyebrows at her.

"It's really shallow water, Billy. I go out in the rowboat all the time."

"You don't go out alone."

He had no qualms about being on the water himself; it was whoever he loved being on the water that freaked him. He still hadn't opened up to her about his parents. Maybe this was the time to push him to do so.

"I didn't know you worried so much about this."

He began to clear the table. "Fine," he said, his back to her. "Do what you like."

"Billy!" She was frustrated. "Of course I won't if it upsets you."

"I want to!" Jonah wailed.

"Hey, I have an idea," Molly put a hand on Jonah's arm. "How about we visit the hatchery? We'll take a tour and see the tanks. We don't need a boat." She looked over Jonah's head at Billy to see if this would pass muster.

Billy tossed the dish towel over his shoulder and reached for her. "That's my girl," he whispered in her hair.

She hugged him back, though a leaden feeling settled in the pit of her stomach. She wondered if she should be so accommodating. Yet something in her couldn't bear to cause him pain.

CHAPTER 21: Julienne

Julienne walked uphill from the eastern slope of Hither Woods to the Moorlands parcel. The subdivision proposal was on the agenda for discussion at that morning's SOS meeting, and she wanted to take photos and a short video, a 360-degree view of the area, to bring to the group. The ground was barren and brown with the season, a range of color from ochre to near-black. Julienne was pleased to see that the fire, which had started in the interior of the adjacent woods, hadn't caused much damage, just a few blackened skeletons of trees and patches of scorched earth where the parcel bordered the woods. She sat a moment on the large boulder, soaking up the quiet. It would be such a shame to see this peaceful and secluded place carved up by housing.

On the way to the meeting, she picked up a walnut Danish ring, Grace's favorite, as a thank you for looking into Molly and Billy's situation with the developer. Grace was affectionately called TOB behind her back, tough old bird. She was known for intimidating everyone . . . everyone except her sixth-grade students, Max and Jonah included, who adored her. She confronted officials to do their environmental duty; she pressured harried townspeople to become involved in civic affairs. She harangued teenagers, who just wanted to be left alone to party on the beach with their six-packs, to get off the dunes because of the ecosystem's fragility.

Rob found Grace impossible, but Julienne admired, even revered her. She had such guts. If not for her help when they were confronted with the fence, their motel business might have been seriously impacted. Julienne had joined SOS in gratitude and did anything Grace asked—sitting at tables with brochures, selling cupcakes—whatever it took. The surprise was that she liked it. She liked feeling involved and having a group to discuss issues facing the hamlet.

Meetings were held around Grace's beat-up dining table. Stacks of files and newspapers were piled in the adjacent living room, the group's de facto office.

"Okay, folks," Grace began, her hair bright-white in the light coming in over her shoulder. "Let's discuss whether there's further action on the Moorlands that we should take now that the Planning Department is requiring an environmental impact statement."

"We should pressure the town to purchase the property for open space," Travis, a long-time member, said. "Do we know if they are willing to sell?"

Julienne looked to Grace expectantly, but Grace shook her head. "We don't have that information."

"Who exactly constitutes the Moorlands Group?" Stefan broke in. "The town only certifies ownership of these LLCs. They need to be made public who they are. We've all heard about the real estate transactions in Florida where dirty money was being laundered. With all these deals in the luxury market, all the money sloshing around, it could be happening here."

Julienne glanced again at Grace. Was this plausible?

"Let's not get sidetracked," Barbara, a lawyer, interjected. "We entered our comments on Moorlands when the application was submitted. There's nothing for us to do at this point. We don't know of any special geological features, rare trees, archeological significance, right? The EIS will uncover anything compelling."

"The real issue is density," Travis said. "We should focus on pressuring the town to move forward with a moratorium."

"We already have a reputation for being too radical," Barbara countered. "Remember the rumor that we were responsible for slashing the sandbags on the downtown beach? Pushing for a moratorium might be a step too far."

"Isn't it just plain wrong to sit back and watch one of the last parcels of open space become more luxury housing we don't need?" Lucy, one of the group's youngest members, said, her voice squeaky with emotion.

"And it's such a beautiful spot," Julienne said.

There were murmurs of support, more discussion, and then Grace suggested they move on. "I'll see if I can find out if there's a chance of the town purchasing the property. I'll do some digging."

———————

The bump and grind of heavy equipment next door, what Rob dubbed the Black Box for its austere lines and black siding, had been halted for days by the heavy rain. With work resuming, the noise seemed to Julienne even louder, like the death throes of an enormous beast, unnerving her. Accidentally she knocked a juice glass against the side of the sink and it shattered. She stared at the soap bubbles tinting red, a sunset blooming in the water. Then the sting registered, and cursing, she wadded her hand in paper towels and went in search of gauze and tape.

She called the town to complain—the third time in as many weeks—even though she knew the town would do nothing about the noise since the construction was approved. Then she went out on the deck, holding up her hand to stop the bleeding. The noise was slightly diminished on this side of the house. She stared at the roll of the waves, so tame from this distance, the fishing boats like toys on the horizon. *Be one with the beauty*, she told herself. Instead, she fixated on the Montauk daisies massed along the front of the deck, stalks limp and sprawling, and well past their peak of whiteness. Her spirits refused to lift.

The phone rang. She grabbed it just before her friend Laura hung up.

"Sorry, I was out on the deck."

"You, relaxing? Not possible."

"The blasted noise distracted me, and I cut my hand. I'm busy coagulating."

Laura gave a pig-like snort. "I know it's last minute, but I'm calling to invite you over to dinner tonight. Stan caught a mess of blues this morning. We'd love to share the bounty."

"Wonderful! I'll run it by Rob in case he has plans I don't know about."

Just as she hung up, the phone rang again, this time Billy. After her meeting she'd left him a message to call her so she could fill him in about what Grace had learned.

"Could you stop by before it's time to pick up the boys from school?" Billy asked. "The developer keeps calling."

"Of course." With her cut hand, there'd be no more painting today anyhow.

Julienne headed down Second House Road until she came to the lumberyard and made a left onto Industrial Road. She liked the area's rough-and-tumble vibe, liked that there were still solidly working-class parts of town. As she crossed over the railroad tracks and along the shore of Fort Pond Bay and into the dark canopy of woods, she remembered how forbidding and exciting they seemed when she and Billy were kids.

Julienne and her parents stayed at the bungalow colony owned by one aunt and uncle, she the sister of Billy's father. The families had been together all the time. Julienne hated returning to the city every fall and envied Billy for living in Montauk year-round. She hadn't realized how much less affluent the Linehans were than the Bishops and how tough the fishing life could be. She'd longed to live as Billy did . . . barefoot in and out of boats and water, allowed to roam at will, confident and accomplished outdoors. This was the life she wanted for Max.

Now Billy was struggling to raise his little brother on his own, while she, having inherited the bungalow colony, had it so much easier.

She turned into the dirt driveway and parked next to Billy's truck. Crisp brown leaves were piled in neat pyramids, and a rake leaned against a large oak. As she walked to the front of the house, facing the bay, she was taken aback by the beaten-down grass and mud that showed how close to the house the water had come in the recent storm. Though the house was set back, it wasn't much above sea level.

"The rain really did some damage, didn't it?" she said, scraping her sneakers on the mat before entering the kitchen.

"Seems like there are more storms, and worse ones, than we used to have." Billy took her jacket.

Molly greeted her with a hug. "I was thinking we could make some kind of berm with plantings. You know my friend Theresa, from the bar? She does stuff like that and said she'd show me."

Julienne was momentarily distracted by Molly's astonishing coloring, all pinks and golds, like a ripe peach. There seemed to be no shadows to Molly, no hidden edges. She radiated goodness.

They settled in the kitchen, where a plate of jelly croissants waited.

"From the bake shop? You shouldn't have!" Julienne bit into one and moaned.

"Epic, right?" Billy said.

Julienne wiped her mouth of the dusted sugar and put a teabag into a mug while Molly poured over the hot water.

"Grace said there's nothing illegal in this developer offering to buy any or all the homes along here. The good news is that zoning will curtail what he's allowed to do." Julienne wiggled her tea bag in the water. "She said I should ask you what kind of development he's talking about—houses or condos?"

Billy and Molly glanced at each other. "He didn't say, did he Molly?"

"This is zoned residential?" Julienne asked. "Not resort?"

"I'm pretty sure," Billy said. "I guess I'd better check."

"Could you explain zoning?" Molly asked.

"It governs what's allowed to be built where. If this is residential, then only houses can replace houses. There is a chance, though, that if they purchase all the homes along the shoreline, they could get it treated like an open-space subdivision. Then some kind of condo or co-op development could go in."

"With the pressure he's putting on everyone, I'll bet that's what they're planning." Billy glanced over at Molly.

Julienne's tea was cool enough to sip. "It's lucky you're right up against Eddie Ecker Park—a bit of a buffer."

"A development would change everything." Molly looked stricken, and she clasped her hands together tightly. "He made it sound like he'd make our lives miserable if we don't sell."

"Are any of your neighbors considering selling?"

Billy nodded and cut the last croissant in thirds and passed a piece each to Molly and Julienne.

Julienne immediately popped hers in her mouth, but Molly left hers untouched.

"One, a guy who lives with his mother, told Billy he wants to live on his own. If his mom takes the deal, it would mean only us and one other couple holding out."

"It wouldn't be a bad idea to consult a lawyer."

"I don't have money for a lawyer, Jules."

"I have a lawyer friend, the one who helped Clancy. I'm sure he'll do me a favor."

Molly clasped Julienne's hands. "Thank you!"

They raised their tea cups in unison and sipped. Then Billy turned to the clock. "Time to pick up the boys."

Julienne followed Billy out. As they reached their vehicles she asked, "Are you as solid as Molly is about not wanting to sell?"

He glanced back at the house, where Molly stood in the doorway. "Let's talk at the school." They drove the curving back roads to the school, then stood leaning against her car. They faced the athletic fields, watching the upper grades stream out.

"I keep thinking maybe this is too good an opportunity to pass up," Billy said, hands in pockets, not meeting her gaze, "but Molly loves where we live. I do, too, of course." He ran a hand over his mouth and chin. "Right now, our property taxes aren't outrageous. We haven't been assessed in ages, but that's coming for sure. If we sold, it would set us up for life."

"But where would you go?"

"Nowhere. I'd stay in Montauk."

"You think you'd get enough to buy here? It's gotten so expensive."

"We're on the water. That's top dollar, right?"

Julienne toed the ground with her sneaker. How unfair this was. While she and her cousin were each in possession of valuable property, their circumstances were vastly different. She and Rob had a thriving business, but Billy had only his own labor. She could understand the appeal of cashing in and getting a better perch in life.

"You still want me to see what else I can find out?"

Billy nodded, then straightened. "Here they come." Jonah and Max were running toward them, jackets flapping.

"I love Molly. I want to do what she wants. But I have to think of Jonah, too."

Julienne started to say, maybe that isn't what Jonah needs. Yet it wasn't her place to argue how the value of the life they had, the wild natural area and living in the woods and on the water, was greater than the kind of security big money could supply.

———◆·◆·◆———

Laura and Stan's house was in Culloden Shores, an area with one of the most distinctive histories in Montauk. A development of 200 holiday houses was created in the 1960s on a sandy stretch of land near the docks. The homes, called Leisuramas, came fully furnished, including toothbrushes in the bathroom, and were sold through Macy's department store. People would ride the elevator to the ninth floor to see the scale models and put down a deposit. Within months, a new house was theirs.

Laura's parents had purchased one as a second home and later opened a gift shop and lived in Montauk full time. After they retired, Laura and Stan moved into the house and took over the store, which carried candles, scented oils, and mermaid-shaped soaps. They'd recently redone the house; the first floor was now an open plan, with a huge, fabulous kitchen. Laura greeted them at the door, wielding a wine opener.

"No Max?"

"We dropped him at Billy's."

Laura was trim and birdlike, with sharp features and quick movements. Her husband was not much taller, and meatier. He worked as a bookkeeper and was an avid surfcaster. The two couples had gotten friendly through the chamber of commerce, though only Rob attended meetings these days. Since having joined SOS, Julienne was persona non grata. She was grateful Laura remained a steadfast friend.

"I'm surprised the blues are still running this late in the season." Rob helped Julienne out of her jacket and handed a bag with wine, cheese, and bread to Stan.

"I was hoping for stripers, but the waters are still too warm."

They settled in the living room facing the fireplace. The house was done in pastels, with turquoise and white throws and pillows on beige leather couches. A large glass jar of sea glass was on a side table, and a basket of shells sat atop a bookcase. On the walls were several large paintings, including a small one of Julienne's, the reflection of a piping plover in the water, a ruffle of wave just beyond. It was all a little too studied for Julienne's taste.

"You've done a lovely job," she said.

"Thank you!" Laura blushed. "That means a lot coming from you."

"Me?" Julienne glanced at Rob. "Our home, sad to say—"

"You're an artist. I just try and make things pretty."

"You have a terrific eye," Julienne insisted.

Over dinner, talk turned to the recent flooding and how the synthetic dune was holding up in the vulnerable downtown area.

"So far so good," Stu said, "though all it will take is a big storm to rip it to shreds."

"Will the motels ever consider moving away from the shore, do you think?" Julienne asked. After Hurricane Sandy, there had been buyouts along the coast of Staten Island and other areas, and those shorelines had been restored to their natural state. The idea of something like that was discussed at SOS, but only in the most wistful, wishful of terms.

"You're kidding, right?" Stan laughed. "The business community would go to war over that."

"What's happening with the construction next door to you?" Laura changed the subject, passing a platter of roasted broccolini for emphasis.

"The house is massive." Julienne lined up three spears on her plate.

"They're putting in a movie theater and a gym," Rob said. He waved a broccolini stalk. "This is all delish, by the way."

"Such an energy suck," Julienne said.

"Modern homes are more energy efficient, no?" Stan asked.

"That's offset by their size. Not to mention the water usage with extra bathrooms and swimming pools that reduce the water table." Julienne put down her fork.

"Fair enough." Stan raised his palms in surrender.

They moved back to the living room for dessert. Once she'd served everyone coffee, Laura cleared her throat, and her eyes flit from Julienne to Rob. "We have an announcement." Her pale skin got blotchy, and she took a sip of water.

Julienne leaned forward. "Is everything okay?"

"We're moving away."

"What?" Julienne felt a sharp kick in her stomach, like when she was pregnant with Max. "You just fixed up this place!"

"We figured either way, stay or go, it made sense to improve it."

"I'm floored! Why?"

Stan drew himself up. "Face it, Montauk is not the place we once knew. Just what you were saying . . . all this new building. And the people. I mean, I fall over laughing when I see a woman walking downtown in heels. Here? And those guys with the silly little hats? I used to know the names of every business owner in town. Everything used to be in locals' hands. It's getting so corporate."

"There's so much else," Julienne said. "The beaches, your beautiful shop."

Laura covered Julienne's hand with her own. "I'm tired, Jules. I work my ass off all summer, work through the holidays. When Jennifer was home, we were tied in to the school and her activities. We'd like to travel while we're still young enough. We can sell the business and this house and not have to work another day in our lives."

The silence boomed in Julienne's ears.

"Where will you go?" Rob asked.

"We got a year's rental on a condo in South Carolina. We'll see how we like it. You have to promise to visit."

Julienne threw her arms around her friend. "We'll miss you so much."

As soon as they were in the car and driving away, Julienne burst out, "I hate this!"

"I know."

"They're moaning about the new rich sweeping in and then they up and sell? He complains nothing's like it used to be. Then why not stay and fight what's happening?"

"Can you blame them for grabbing the golden parachute? It's hard to expect people not to do what's in their personal self-interest."

"Think what they're giving up!" Julienne's eyes pricked with tears. She was surprised at her level of fury. "And they're contributing to the very problem they're complaining about!"

"I understand that's how you see it."

"You don't?"

"I don't mean that."

She couldn't see his face in the dark. "Well, what then?"

"You're just a bit hard on people, that's all."

She knew she should pull back, not hammer at him with all this ferocity, but she couldn't help herself. "Don't you agree there's something wrong with all of it? These market forces . . . they're running rampant."

"What, you're challenging the capitalist system now?" Rob laughed.

She faced the window. "Maybe. Maybe I am."

"It's been good to us."

She became silent as they drove down deserted winter streets and through town.

"I know you'll miss them. We'll miss them. I think that's maybe why you're so upset." He reached for her hand. "Everyone out here will be confronted with the same thing, ultimately." He slowed as they approached their driveway.

He was right, she realized. Their situation would be exactly like Laura and Stan's in less than ten years, when Max would be graduating from college. It frightened her to think of it. They owned what had become valuable property, just the luck of being in the right place at the right time. Although they made only a modest living, their motel and the land it was on, once just a basic mom-and-pop, was now worth millions.

They were quiet getting into bed.

"Come here." Rob pulled her toward him, then rolled her onto her stomach, and began to massage her shoulders and neck.

She was tense with anger and despair and felt coiled tight. As if he knew, his touch was especially gentle. She willed herself to relax, to feel. Neither had initiated sex in a while; she didn't want to turn away.

CHAPTER 22: Clancy

Outside the bungalow window, Clancy's view was almost completely obscured. Dense fog transformed the world into an impressionistic painting; it was all pale grays, a smear of brown beach bramble, white where the ocean should have been. He grabbed his jacket and headed outside, needing to move. Ms. Jewel had just called to tell him Theresa Nolan was not taking the house. It was his if he wanted it.

Scraps of white chiffon drifted from the direction of the water, thin streams of smoky white dancing in the air currents. As he reached the crest of the dune, visibility vanished, and he was enveloped in whiteness.

He headed blind toward the sound of the ocean. It was oddly thrilling to be walking when he could hardly see, focusing on the ocean's beat. At the water's edge, he could make out only the lacy frill where the waves melted into the sand. The air smelled both metallic and salty; he inhaled deeply. He loved the fog's invisibility cloak. He was buoyant, free, and insubstantial.

Nearby came a sound, and he started. A figure was coming up the beach. He didn't recognize Julienne until she was almost abreast of him.

"I thought that was you," she said.

"This fog is unbelievable."

"We get it every now and again. When the ground is warmer than the air, or the other way around, I can never remember. Walk?"

He fell into step beside her. He was closer to the water's edge than she was, and the sand sloped at this point in the tide cycle, so she was upward of him. The fog lent a curious intimacy.

"How's the painting these days?"

They had had no interaction since their hike at Amsterdam Beach the week before. Occasionally, he had a glimpse of her going or coming from her studio. She walked so fast it was almost comical, head of corkscrew curls bent down, mouth working, as if in intense conversation with herself.

"I'm into the swing of it now. You seem busy, too. Dealing with Otto's affairs?"

"Yes, going through his papers." There was a lunch meeting with the partners the next day, and after that, he decided, he would talk with her about Moorlands. He didn't like keeping his role secret, and he wanted the benefit of her knowledge. "I just heard from the lawyer . . . time's up with no word from Theresa Nolan."

"She's not going to take the house?"

"Looks like it."

"You'll be in Montauk!" She grabbed him in an impromptu hug.

"Not so fast," he laughed. "I'm not sure what I'm going to do." He didn't know if he would want to live a significant portion of time in Montauk and how he would balance that with his job if he did.

"I really hope you'll take it," she said, in a more measured tone.

"Won't that make me a pariah in this town? An outsider who lucks into a house he doesn't deserve?"

"You can't worry about what people think. Though I should warn you about Theresa Nolan. She's got a reputation."

"Not a problem," Clancy laughed. "She's not my type."

"That's not what I meant, though rumor has it she swallows men up and spits them out like so many watermelon seeds. I meant she could change her mind and say she wants the house the minute you say you'll take it. I'd hate anyone I care about to be hurt by her."

Off balance by her expression of affection, Clancy didn't notice how close he'd gotten to the water. There was a hiss as a wave swamped his sneakers and the bottom of his jeans.

Abruptly Julienne reached down, and for a moment he thought she meant to do something to his pants. She'd spotted a small starfish. She handed it to him.

He ran a finger over the surface. It felt coarse, stiff, its tentacles curled upward. "Should I throw it back?"

"Too late for that one. Sometimes there are masses of them all along the wrack line. I've no idea why. Keep it."

"Thanks." He slipped it into his pocket.

"Ready to head back? I should get to work."

"Sure," he said, though he'd have preferred to continue walking together.

At their approach to the motel, lights sprang on. It was just the motion sensors, but it made him feel welcome.

"If you take the house, I guess you won't be staying with us much longer."

Clancy hadn't thought that far ahead. "If I decide to keep Otto's place, I'll need to clear it out, maybe have it painted. If it's okay, I'll stay on here a bit longer."

"Of course!" She gave his arm a brief squeeze.

Fingering the starfish in his pocket, he watched her make her way up to her house. She had a kind of simplicity, like a tree that had lost its leaves, so her structure, her elemental self, was visible. He could sense her ambition, the limbs reaching up for light and air and water. She was a thirsty creature, yet thoroughly self-sufficient.

The light went on in her kitchen, and first Max and then Rob appeared in the window. He waited until Julienne entered the frame. She grabbed Max for a kiss and played matador with a dish towel. Clancy laughed. *She makes me happy just looking at her*. And then, *Oh no*.

———•-•••-•———

The next morning, Clancy waited until he assumed Julienne would be in her studio before going up to the house to drop off a book he'd gotten for Max. The awareness that his feelings for her went deeper than he had acknowledged to himself threatened to ruin everything . . . being around her, even staying at Bishops by the Sea.

He replayed their conversation on the hike, when she mock-flirted with him. In his mind, he saw Rob as a cutout figure, an outline, and himself stepping into that space, filling the role of husband and father. The image brought on a heady mix of longing and dismay. He recoiled against any schism in her relationship. He wanted affirmation of marriage, of the family unit, its preciousness.

He was leaning the bag with the book against the door when it abruptly opened.

"Saw you from the window," Julienne said, Max at her side. He was in PJs, pale-blue flannel with prancing horses.

"I didn't expect you to be home."

Max held up his inhaler.

"I think it must be the fog." Julienne made a face.

Clancy handed Max the book, an illustrated guide to horses. "It was on the free pile at the library," he said, to forestall an argument about buying Max too many gifts. Max held the book in both hands with the reverence of a book-seller for a rare edition.

"How sweet! Rob had to go to Town Hall, so I'm hanging with Max. Coffee?"

Clancy debated making his excuses, then followed Julienne to the kitchen, Max pattering alongside, a slight wheeze audible. A sketch pad, coloring book, and box of colored pencils lay on the table.

"I'm happy to stay with Max this morning if you want to go to your studio." His lunch meeting with the Moorlands partners was not until 1:00 p.m.

A look of naked hope crossed Julienne's face. "Oh, I can't let you—"

"I'd enjoy it."

"Maybe just for an hour." She gave in easily. "Have some coffee first."

The phone rang. "Go ahead and take it," Clancy said.

Julienne smiled and gestured at the coffee pot with the phone as she picked up.

He filled a mug and stood over Max as he paged through the book. "Look, this is like the one I rode at Deep Hollow!"

"Exactly!" Clancy was happy the book was a success. He heard Julienne say, "Moorlands? Good to know."

"Moorlands?" he asked, as she returned to the table.

"A large parcel that's up for development. We discussed it at our last SOS meeting. We're hoping the town might buy and preserve it."

"Why do you think it should be preserved?"

"Surely you know the answer? Open space has intrinsic value. It protects our groundwater, means less infrastructure . . . so many reasons."

"You wouldn't want it for, say, affordable housing?"

She raised her eyebrows. "I'm surprised you'd think of that, not being from here. True, a lot of young people and workers can't afford homes here. Convincing developers to build affordable is tough, though. Not enough profit." She sighed and picked up her mug. "We don't even know if the owners would be willing to consider selling to the town to preserve. We don't know who we're dealing with. It could be local guys or it could be an international consortium." She hesitated. "Or a money-laundering operation."

"You're joking?"

"Moorlands is owned by a limited liability corporation. Those don't have to disclose who they are. This is such a hot market, it's totally possible dirty money is involved."

Clancy pulled up the knot of his tie so close to his throat, he coughed.

Julienne passed him a glass of water. "You really have to stop trying to kill yourself."

She went off to her studio and Clancy and Max went into his room to play with his LEGOS. Clancy had bought Max several sets; he'd wanted to capture the feeling of total abundance and awe he'd felt when he had first encountered them.

They sat on the floor and worked together, deciding on colors and patterns, what they should build, who should do what. There was such joy in playing. For Max, it was more about the imagination. He made up stories and characters. For Clancy, it was the physicality, the pleasure of snapping pieces together, seeing something take shape.

"Mrs. Morgan showed us where the fire was," Max said abruptly, not looking at Clancy. "It looked like Halloween."

Clancy realized Max had been constructing a red vehicle, which maybe had brought to mind a fire truck. "What do you mean, Halloween?"

"She took us into Hither Woods for Nature Club. She showed us the burned trees. Like black skeletons." Max was sounding breathy again. Clancy hadn't heard him wheeze all the time they had been playing.

"It's upsetting, I know."

"She said the police know someone made a fire in the woods. When they find out, will they put him in jail?" Max chewed on his lip.

"It was just an accident. Nobody's going to jail."

"If I tell you something, will you keep it secret?" Max's eyes were intent.

"You have my word."

"I think it was me." He said it in a whisper so low Clancy barely heard him.

Clancy put a hand on Max's arm. "Why would you think that?"

"I made a fire in the woods one time."

Clancy took a moment to take this in. "You were careful to put it out, right?"

"I thought I was careful. I poured water over it. I can't really remember!"

Poor Max, anxious and blaming himself. Clancy squeezed Max's shoulder. "Something much bigger started the fire. It wasn't you. I'm one hundred percent sure."

Max grabbed Clancy's hand and kissed it.

The sign in the window read, HELP WANTED: MUST BE ABLE TO SHUCK CLAMS. A bar ran along one side of the room, and everyone glanced up as he walked in—guys in dirty sweatshirts with unruly hair who looked as if they had honed their alcoholism from an early age, and one woman holding court. He was ushered into a dining area with historic photos on the walls, parents and kids settled in at booths, and plastic baskets with paper liners, limp fries, and half-finished glasses of soda scattered across the tables.

In the corner farthest from the window, Harve waved him over. He was dressed more formally this time, in slacks and a beige pullover.

"Clancy, let me introduce you. Pete Walker," he indicated a man of about thirty, short and wiry, whose hand snapped out for a brisk shake.

"Gaspar Diggs."

A man with a skimpy gray ponytail, soul patch, and tightly fitted bike shirt, said, "Glad to meet you, man," and gave him a fist bump.

"And Tim Turchi."

Otto had told Clancy Tim was his closest friend, so Clancy had been curious to meet him. Tim half stood and gave Clancy's hand a warm clasp. He was tall and big, dressed conservatively in a crisp plaid shirt. He slid over in the booth to make room.

"I visited Clancy a few weeks back," Harve began, nodding toward Clancy, after they'd given the waiter their orders. "I explained our situation. As you know, Clancy is executor of Otto's will and Otto expressly left him full voting authority of his shares."

Clancy read suspicion in the men's faces. He tugged at the knot in his tie.

"I don't want to hold things up for you gentlemen. Still, I can't vote on anything until I'm sure I'm carrying out Otto's wishes."

"Well what's the problem?" Pete Walker asked bluntly. He face was narrow, somehow feral. "Didn't Otto leave instructions?"

"I'll know more when I finish going through his papers." Clancy said it firmly to keep a defensive edge from his voice.

Harve stepped into the impasse. "How about we all lay our cards on the table? We'll be given the go ahead with our subdivision plan as soon as the Environmental Impact Statement is complete. I propose we revise our application and instead sell to the town for workforce affordable housing."

"That's just plain stupid." Pete lifted the ketchup bottle and smacked the bottom with his palm. "That's like giving away all the profits gained from holding onto it all these years."

"It was your dad, not you, holding on to it," Harve snapped.

"Gentlemen," Tim said. "We're all friends at this table."

Clancy, having noted a look of distaste cross Tim's face at Pete's comment, found it interesting that he chose to play the peacemaker.

"Where do you stand?" Harve turned to Gaspar.

Gaspar twirled an asparagus spear into some kind of aioli and popped it into his mouth. "I want to throw something out. I've been reading about attractions in other places that could work here."

"Gaspar, it's a little late for this," Pete said.

"It's not. You convinced us to file this application just to have it in place, in case of a moratorium. We never agreed we were going to subdivide or sell to a developer. And Clancy needs time to get up to speed." Gaspar gave Clancy a toothy smile. Otto had called Gaspar a flake, but perhaps he was shrewder than he appeared.

"What do you have in mind?" Tim asked.

"You know how we all mocked Gurney's when they went upscale for charging the crazy amounts they're charging? No one's laughing now, right? They've got the whole spa thing going. Their clientele is the yoga and seaweed wrap set."

"You want to build a spa?" Pete asked.

Gaspar ignored him. "You know that labyrinth up by Hither Woods? People walk around it and meditate. That salt cave thing is doing great too, and think about the Koreans on New Year's, greeting the dawn at the lighthouse."

"Where are you going with this?" Peter interrupted.

Gaspar wiped his mouth with a napkin and dipped another spear. "It's a whole new kind of people coming out here—the searchers, I call them. Okay, so here's the pitch." He hunched forward, fingering his soul patch. "A holistic center! A place of spirituality and reflection. Maybe workshops on understanding and cultural exchange. Meditation and yoga, natch, but much more. We remarket Montauk. No longer the fishing capital of the world, that's kind of over, and certainly not the Jersey Shore party scene that's been pissing everyone off of late. No, we become Montauk, Malibu of the East!"

The silence at the table was absolute. From the looks on the others' faces, Clancy couldn't tell if this idea was completely brilliant or completely absurd.

"You're proposing instead of selling to a developer and becoming rich-rich, or doing the subdivision ourselves with glorious, architecturally significant, glossy, magazine-worthy homes that sell for millions of dollars and becoming rich-rich-rich, you want to build some kind of ashram?" Pete's voice went up into such a crescendo, the entire restaurant went silent.

Gaspar just smiled and crunched down on a stalk of celery.

"Let's wind this back," Tim said. "We'll give Clancy the time he needs, and then it's a simple vote up or down. And while we're at it, here's a suggestion. As you know, I'm in favor of preservation. Why don't we all circulate our proposals among ourselves to review, with pros and cons, dollars and cents."

After a pause, everyone nodded. Clancy spoke up. "I wanted to let you know I heard some speculation. Because you're an LLC, it's being suggested that money laundering could be involved. I thought you might want to consider going public with who you are."

"Money laundering? Give me a break!" Pete scoffed. He stood, shoving his wallet in his pants. "No, we're not going public. We don't want everyone jumping up our ass. This must be kept confidential, agreed?"

Clancy decided not to argue. It was better for him if everything, especially his role in Moorlands, was kept secret anyhow. He felt suspicious glances everywhere he went because of the fire and Otto's will. At the same time, he wanted to talk things over with Julienne. Perhaps he could trust her to keep it secret.

Outside the restaurant, Clancy dug out a business card and handed it to Tim, who would be in charge of distributing the proposals among the group. "I know you and Otto were especially close. I'd like to talk with you about him."

"Any time. He was a wonderful man."

"I want to do the right thing by him."

"I'm sure you will. This town meant everything to him. You are in a tough spot."

"You think it'll be difficult to determine how he would have voted?"

"No, I mean because there's no consensus among us, as you saw. You're the monkey in the middle."

 *Winter*

WINTER COMES ABRUPTLY this year, a sudden dip that takes everyone by surprise after the mild autumn and days of intense rain. In the woods, the red berries of shad and Russian olive are like crystallized candy on the stiffened branches, while shallow-pooled kettle holes freeze thin crème brûlée crusts of ice. The beaches are hard with frozen sand, and hoary grasses transform the dunes into shaggy buffalo.

At the harbor, boats are shrink-wrapped and ghostly; on the beaches, where the grasses are stiff with frozen salt, gulls stand huddled, beaks to the wind. Trees are silent of summer's melodic song, their bare branches whispering to themselves, while on the ground, skulking in the bramble or briar weed, feral cats, coats thickened, hunt mice. Cars move sluggishly through town, a solitary retiree sits over his newspaper in the library, and the check-out clerks in the grocery store grow bored. You can walk for hours along the beach or the woods and never see another human being. Outside after dark, you might think you are someplace far more remote, the Adirondacks, perhaps.

In December, when dusk turns El Greco blue, the lighthouse is outlined in thousands of holiday lights, magnificent against the darkening sky. People gather in reverent clusters, taking photos with icy fingers, leaving only as stars emerge in the sharp cloudless night.

CHAPTER 23: Clancy

Clancy was used to New York winters, but not this kind of winter. The wind was brutal, a keening, moaning, malevolent beast, stinging his face, numbing his feet.

Still, some mornings were glorious at the bungalow colony. He had never before watched the sun come up. At this time of year, it began its rise at a point on the beach just visible from his cottage. A flush of color would soak into the darkness, and he would sit with his coffee and watch as the tiny speck of red slowly . . . so slowly . . . eased up, until the globe sat on the horizon with the majesty of a queen upon her throne. Gulls wheeled in excitement as the pinks and oranges spread, and he watched, eyes stunned and burning, his chest filling with emotion. It seemed to him there should be a musical accompaniment. Something as magnificent as this deserved its own symphony.

With the holidays approaching, Clancy went into several gift shops in town, trying to find a present for Julienne. He wanted something special but not inappropriately personal, and it was proving impossible. He finally decided he'd get her an art book from the Met when he went back to Astoria for the holidays. He planned to extend his leave of absence for several months, given how slowly things were progressing on the Moorlands.

As he was leaving the gift shop, he overheard a conversation about the holiday lighting of the lighthouse and decided to visit. It was just getting dark, and as he approached, the lighthouse seemed to spring up out of the darkness, spectacular on the cold and otherwise desolate night. He parked and stood absorbing the scene, the wind blowing his hair back from his face. He listened to the thud of distant waves, overcome by the grandeur of the iconic structure ablaze and brilliant, as if taking a stand against the forces of darkness.

⁕

The image of the lighthouse stayed with him while he was in the city. He had an enjoyable time at his company's office party and on Christmas with Bruce and his friends, but the image of the lighthouse, or the beach, or the meadow behind Otto's house would suddenly flood his mind and throw him off balance. Montauk was like a dream, something to cosset like one of the rocks he picked up on his beach walks and kept in a pocket to wrap his fingers around.

Once back in Montauk, he learned there were no results yet from the mandated environmental impact study on the Moorlands, and the partners had not yet shared their proposals. He settled into a routine of heading to Otto's house midmorning each day to burrow into his papers and files and read his notebooks. Given Otto's careful recording of Montauk's flora and fauna, his gardening notes and bird-watching, Clancy would expect Otto to be in favor of full preservation of the parcel. Yet Otto had said he was conflicted and confused. It was both tantalizing and frustrating that he had not had the chance to explain. Day after day, as Clancy pored through the material, he found no notes specific to Otto's reasoning and had nothing direct to go on.

It was time to talk individually with the partners.

Tim gave Clancy directions to his house on a tiny peninsula on Fort Pond called Shepherd's Neck. Clancy quickly got lost among circuitous narrow roads, many with small stucco cottages clustered as if in a twee English village. He was curious to see the inside of one of the tiny Tudors, but Tim's house was an ordinary ranch.

Tim ushered Clancy in with a little bow and sweep of his arm. There were shoes and boots in the entryway, so Clancy removed his own and padded behind Tim, who wore backless slippers, into a large living room. Couches, chairs, and tables were arranged in front of windows that gave a view over the pond and the wooded hills, dotted with homes, in the far distance. In the center of the pond, improbably, a few branches seemed to be sticking straight up out of the water.

"That's Brushy Island," Tim explained. "Those branches are all that remain of a tupelo tree that was once twelve feet high. Cormorants often settle there. As sediment fills the pond, the water rises. The island will be totally gone soon." He looked down at his slippers. "Like so much else. Anyhow, what can I get you to drink?"

When he returned with two glasses of water, they settled in front of the window. "Let me know how I can help." Tim's eyes, narrowed by folds of aging skin, were kindly.

"I'd appreciate some insight into Otto. You're in favor of preservation and were his closest friend, yet he had reservations about going that route. Do you know why?"

Tim rested his fingers on the edge of the white, lacquered coffee table. "It's actually pretty simple. Otto—as I'm sure you know—was compassionate and community minded. Harve's point of view, in favor of housing for the young people and workers in the hamlet, weighed on him pretty heavily. And another factor was that he wanted to do right by his daughter. The most bang for the buck is if we sell to a developer or do the subdivision ourselves, Pete's agenda. Selling to the town would get us less."

"Why? Isn't the value of the land the same no matter what?"

"Everything is based on the assessed value, yes, but the town usually can't afford that much. If we vote to preserve, we'd have to negotiate downward. One thing for certain is Otto wouldn't go for a holistic center or any of the other ideas Gaspar has floated. In my heart of hearts, I believe he would have chosen preservation."

"Did you know he asked me to talk with his daughter before he died? He was hoping for some rapprochement. She was quite hostile. Maybe he wanted to know her wishes before making his decision. It was only after she refused to see him that he had the lawyer write the codicil to have me vote the shares."

"I didn't know that." Tim took a sip of water. "Theresa and I attend the same church, but she's something of an enigma. Even so, since Otto didn't leave the deciding to her, neither should you." He glanced at Clancy. "Have you considered that you may not be able to divine what he would have wanted? That you might have to make an independent call? He obviously thought you'd be a good and impartial thinker. And for whatever reason, he wanted an outsider—forgive me for calling you that—to tip the balance."

Clancy was taken aback. He hadn't considered he might not be able to discern Otto's wishes and it might fall to him to decide the best course of action.

Tim put down his glass with a clack and leaned forward. "Have you heard of the term 'continuity of habitat'? It's about not breaking up land into too many parcels. Fragmentation can kill species—separate them from their water source or their breeding grounds. You lose diversity and over time only a narrow set of species survive. You end up with, say, nothing but deer and raccoons. Whole systems lose complexity. We're reaching our carrying capacity out here—the number of organisms an area can support in a sustainable way. If you add more homes and roads and sewage, it increases the burden. I appreciate Harve's point of view, but I don't want to add to that burden."

"I hear what you're saying." This was all new to Clancy, much he would need to think about.

Tim ran his hands over his head, smoothing back his thick gray hair. "It's hard to express why I think all this is so important. You probably think it's nuts to expend so much energy on such a small area, however precious, when most places don't even have the luxury of space *to* preserve."

"I think what you're saying is that even if this is only one small area, the small areas in the aggregate add up to something bigger and more essential?"

"Exactly! Can you see your way to voting for preservation?"

"You've been very clear, very persuasive. I just need to give this more thought. I hope you understand."

"Let me know if there's more information I can give you to make the case."

"I will. I really appreciate you taking the time to talk with me," Clancy stood. "Getting your proposals should help clarify things. I'll be meeting with Harve and Gaspar—and Pete, I guess—in the next few days."

Tim walked Clancy to the door, staying silent as Clancy put his shoes back on. He shook his hand brusquely. "I appreciate the tough spot you're in, as I said. Pete Walker is a blunt instrument. He has none of his dad's finesse. He'll pile on the pressure. Be prepared."

———

Harve had struck Clancy as the kind of man who didn't know how not to be honest, who wouldn't distort Otto's views to match his own. He seemed sincere in the way Otto had been sincere. The two men seemed very old school, honorable and caring, in a way that struck Clancy as rare.

He and Harve made plans to meet at a coffee shop in town that stayed open through the winter. Clancy parked next to the single office tower near the town green, one of several buildings he'd learned from Otto's history notebook had been built by developer Carl Fisher. Clancy wondered what the town would have been like had the Depression and poor business decisions not derailed Fisher's ambitious plans.

The town had a '50s feel, and the coffee shop reminded him of diners he'd grown up with in Queens: small Formica tables, a counter with stools, and cheap travel posters on the walls. The sole waitress gestured at him with her coffee pot. He turned his cup—the thick, white serviceable fare of innumerable diners—to receive the coffee, as Harve walked in.

"Tonya, how are you, my dear?"

"Busy as all get out, as you can see."

They both laughed, but it probably wasn't funny. A place like this wouldn't be popular with the trendy types who were moving into town. Its days were likely numbered.

"The usual?" Tonya asked Harve.

"I think I'll go a little wild. Rye instead of white."

Tonya laughed again and slapped Harve on the shoulder.

Harve turned to Clancy. "Here are my numbers." He pulled a folded sheet of graph paper from his breast pocket. "I'm having someone else verify them." He slid his proposal across the table.

Clancy folded the paper and slipped it in his chest pocket. "I'll give this a careful look. What I'd really like right now is to hear your take on Otto, on a personal level. What kind of man you feel he was."

"But you knew him."

"Only as a boy."

"Well, he had community spirit. He volunteered at the Senior Center, and the food pantry, and also with the Scouts."

"So, people-oriented?" This made sense. After all, Otto had volunteered to be a Big Brother.

"In truth he was a bit shy. Not really outgoing."

Harve paused as Tonya delivered their breakfasts. Clancy cut into his omelet with the side of his fork. Cheese oozed out.

Clancy thought of the notebooks filled with flora and fauna and Otto's garden. "Would you call him an environmentalist?"

"Gosh, no, those weren't his people."

"How do you mean?" Clancy asked.

"He was a lifelong Republican. Out here, that means small business. Though I have to say," Harve dipped a corner of toast into a yoke, "the Party strayed from our values. Otto and me, people like us, felt stranded."

"Did he become a Democrat then?"

"Never. Out here the parties are all mixed up. You'll get Republicans in favor of tight regs on water quality, Dems fighting to keep the government from meddling in the fishing industry. I hopscotch all over the ballot these days. Otto, too."

"So you're saying he felt out of sync with things?"

"It's hard to explain." Harve pressed his napkin to his mouth. "Montauk used to be called the Wild West. It was an afterthought, a stepchild of the Hamptons. Out here, you did what you wanted with your own property. There was more than enough of it. People saw ways to make a living from what's special about this place—like the charter boat captains, guys who figured out they could make more money taking other people fishing than fishing themselves. Anyone could find work. Hire on for a season or a year, good pay in summer, get by in winter. Island culture. Everyone believed in live and let live."

Clancy nodded, though he had no idea what this had to do with Otto and his values. "Otto told me he believed people should be able to do what they want with their own property. Is that what you mean? How would that have impacted how he would have voted?"

Harve shook his head. "Montauk's a fishing community. Now many fishermen can no longer afford to live here. Heck,

Otto's own daughter lives at the trailer park, did you know that? Where does someone like her—the people who give this town its soul—get to live? Don't you think, above all, that's what Otto would have cared about?"

Clancy, just about to take a sip of coffee, set his cup back down. "What do you mean, a trailer?"

"There's a mobile home community east of town. Been there forever. A place like that would never be allowed now."

Theresa, in a mobile home. This made it even more inexplicable that she refused her father's house. It made it even harder for him to consider accepting that gift. Clancy drained his coffee.

"Sorry, I do go on," Harve said. "But really, Clancy, how can you vote otherwise than for affordable housing?" He pulled out his wallet, but Clancy put his hand over it.

"On me."

Clancy walked back across the green to his car, deep in thought. It was after he told Otto that Theresa wouldn't be reconciled that he added the codicil. With Theresa unlikely to accept the house, Otto might very well have cast his vote for affordable housing, as that might have benefitted her. Or perhaps he'd have opted for the larger payout a development would bring. Clancy beeped his car open. Either way, why not say so? Why the mystery? And the enigmatic drawing and the word "retreat." How did they fit in? Perhaps the drawing was meant to represent the trailer park where Theresa lived, the arrows an indication that she should move—retreat—elsewhere. Clancy slid behind the wheel.

This was only getting more perplexing.

———•◦•◦•———

The next day, Clancy met with Gaspar, who suggested a health food café in the center of town, which seemed to be a hot spot for the young hip set with their nose rings and painted hair. Gaspar ordered a kale and walnut salad and Clancy a chicken quesadilla. They settled in the cheerful space in the rear, backs against throw pillows.

Gaspar shook dressing all over his salad, drenching it. Clancy doubted Gaspar would be able to taste the greens themselves.

"He was a great old dude, but like, not exactly forward thinking. I get how the old-timers want to hang on, really I do. I love this place, I love its funky vibe, the whole dive bar and retro beach feel. But change is inevitable. We have to harness that. You hold on too tight and you ruin the thing you're trying to save. That's an actual quote but I can't remember from who. You catch my drift."

Gaspar stabbed his bamboo fork into the dripping kale a few times before securing some, then stashed the fork in his mouth. He chewed vigorously, soul patch wiggling. Clancy cut his quesadilla into neat squares and popped a piece in his mouth. He chewed and considered.

"Did you get the sense Otto leaned toward preservation?"

"I wouldn't say that." Gaspar whipped his fork around the bowl. "I don't recall that at all."

"I understand you had some other thoughts for the parcel before this latest one you're proposing. What did Otto think about your ideas?"

Gaspar went back to poking at his salad and waited until he secured a leaf before speaking. "Otto was respectful. He listened. He was considering my thoughts. He may not have got it, but . . ." a large piece of kale dangled, "you're young, from the city. You get it. Beautiful landscaped grounds, chimes ringing out." The kale made it to his mouth, and he swallowed, closing his eyes briefly. "Yoga, story circles, a juice bar . . ." He opened his eyes. "I know you're trying to do the right thing by Otto, but it seems like he didn't leave you any instructions. You can vote whatever way you think best? As I see it—" he dabbed his mouth with a napkin "—my solution brings in the big bucks, which should make Pete happy, and would save a goodly percentage of green space, too. That's pretty much a win-win as I see it."

Clancy considered, his own fork in midair. It made a weird kind of sense. "Why wasn't Pete on board, then?"

Gaspar narrowed his eyes briefly. "Pete's stuck on his own proposal. My ideas are visionary, harder to support on paper. I'm working on that. I'm getting some numbers from other resort areas that have gone in this direction. So, what about you? What do you need to see from me to be convinced?"

"I'm not sure, Gaspar. I promise to seriously consider your ideas. I look forward to seeing whatever you come up with."

———•◆•———

Clancy headed back to his car, unsettled. Each of the men's arguments were compelling, even Gaspar's. And, to be thorough, he should meet with Pete. He sighed.

He was dispirited, out of his depth. He pulled on his seatbelt. He would read every piece of paper and notebook in Otto's house. And maybe the men's presentations would help. He started his car. The last thing he wanted was for Tim to be right, that he wouldn't be able to divine Otto's wishes and would have to use his own judgement. He had no stake in the outcome and no expertise. Who was he to say what the best use of land should be? Land, the concept, was beginning to seem very complicated, full of nuance, its meaning and purpose far more variable than he'd have thought—had he ever given it thought.

He headed back to the bungalow along the coastal road, driving hard through its dips and turns. The driving calmed him. He just had to give this time, surrender to the process. The road was lovely even now, in early winter, when everything was drab and brown, just the merest hint of color, orange berries on beach bramble. There was so much more sky here than in the building-cluttered city. And the ocean. When Julienne said it was different every day, he hadn't understood, but he'd come to see how true that was. Some days it boiled with whitecaps, some days it was dimpled, and some days, if the sun hit a certain way, it twinkled all over with pinpricks of light. Even the sand and the shape of the beach differed from day to day, to a degree that astonished him.

In his cottage, he settled into the rocker at the window. The ocean was agitated; the tops of the waves sheared off into great plumes of spray. As he rocked in time with the waves, it reminded him of how he had pretended to hypnotize himself as a boy.

He foraged in his suitcase for the small box that held the watch. Should he try it again? Maybe all the information he'd gathered would dance within him in some kind of alchemy, and he'd wake up knowing what Otto would have wanted.

He sat back, held the watch in front of his face, making it sway, repeating the incantation. "Your eyes are feeling heavy, your lids are closing, you're going to sleep." Obediently he closed his eyes. The watch slipped to his lap. He dreamed.

CHAPTER 24: Theresa

Theresa awoke to the sound of a loud motor outside her trailer. She pulled aside the curtains to see at least a half-dozen residents walking determinedly toward the shore. She'd forgotten today the barrier of rocks would be removed. The TP had lost their court battle, and the fines had gotten steep. She hurriedly pulled on sweatpants and jacket.

Residents were standing in a loose circle, silently watching. Theresa drew alongside Joe Tretorn, who was wearing a pink-and purple-striped beanie that contrasted to his grim expression. The excavator dug into the wall of boulders; the ease and speed with which the metal jaws grasped and dumped the rocks into the waiting truck was shocking.

"This sucks."

Tretorn kept his eyes fixed on the bulldozer. "It gets worse." The lines on either side of his mouth deepened.

"How can it get worse?" There was a loud mechanical groan as the jaws nudged again among the boulders.

"We heard a rumor the town may be considering condemning the property."

"What does that even mean? Condemn it for what?" Theresa snapped, as if this were his fault.

"It means seize the property." His tone was clipped, as if he were biting off the words.

"How can that be legal?" She shouted to be heard above the noise. Residents owned or rented their homes; the land beneath was held communally.

"It's called eminent domain." He faced her. "They've done it other places."

"But why?"

"No idea. It's just a rumor at this point."

"What do we do?" The pile of rocks was nearly depleted.

"Rally the community. This place is a unique piece of Montauk history. People won't want to see it go."

"People think we're a honky-tonk blight on the town. No one's going to 'rally,' Joe."

"Try not to be such a cynic."

If they were forced out, there was no way she could afford to live anywhere else in this town. She felt momentarily dizzy as the enormity of what she had done, in relinquishing ownership of her father's house, hit her, and she grabbed Tretorn's arm for purchase. It hadn't occurred to her that it wasn't just their beach that could be lost but everything.

The clanking intensified; there was a loud rumble as the rocks rolled against each other in the vehicle's maw. The odor of diesel was nauseating. Theresa felt her eyes tear. Their little cove looked so vulnerable without the protection of the rocks, the front line of trailers dangerously close to the water.

———•◦•◦•———

Theresa had been avoiding Pete Walker since her father's funeral, ignoring his calls and the messages left for her at the bar. It suddenly seemed wise to find out what he wanted.

"Your timing is perfect." His voice on the phone was hearty.

Pete Jr. had been a year behind her in school, and she remembered him the way you remembered boys who were younger—not at all. He invited her to meet him at the Clever

Clam, a low-key standby near the train tracks along the Napeague stretch that had been there for decades.

As she drove to meet him, she wondered if his choice signified he wanted to make the point that they were both locals. Maybe he just didn't want to be seen together.

The sandy area abutting the train tracks that served as an outside patio during the summer was empty, metal tables and chairs stacked up and covered with beige tarps; there were only a few cars in the lot. Pete was waiting at a booth in the back. He was shorter and thinner than his father, who had been an imposing man. Pete Walker Sr. had been the head of the chamber, town supervisor for two terms, and had a successful real estate business. She wondered what it was like to be the only son of someone so influential.

"Theresa." Pete Jr. clasped both of her hands in his. "Thank you for coming."

She slid in opposite him. The waitress, South or Central American like many workers throughout the area, brought over their menus.

"I wanted to say again how sorry I am about your father," Pete said. "As you know, I lost my own only last year."

His eyes locked on hers. She nodded. She very much doubted his feelings toward his father were anything like hers for her own.

"It's a tough thing." His eyes shifted away and back. "Moorlands . . ." he took a sip of water, ". . . was my father's dream. It's important to me, too." She waited, unsure what he was trying to say. "Well, let's order first."

They made small talk until the food came. Pete placed his side of fries generously between them with a wave at her to help herself, and leaned forward, all business now. "I inherited my father's shares. You should have your father's. It's that simple. It's wrong that they've been taken away from you."

"They haven't been taken away, exactly." Theresa hesitated, then reached for a fry. "The value's mine. I don't really care that the executor will vote them." She pooled ketchup on her plate and dipped her fry. "Why does it matter?"

Pete pursed his lips. "It has to do with how much money the project yields. How the shares get voted will impact the payout."

"I don't understand." She hadn't given this any thought.

"High end, beautifully designed houses will fetch a premium. My father envisioned an estate of six or seven homes, each on an acre."

"So what's the issue?"

"There isn't a majority of the partners in agreement about the parcel's future." She waited, and he finally went on. "A couple of them have other ideas."

"Like?"

"One wants open space. Another affordable housing. With either of those options, there'd be significantly less money."

Theresa took a moment to digest this. "What does the executor want?"

"He says he's in favor of whatever your father wanted. That's not necessarily in your best interest. You should have a say in the disposition of the property."

"I don't mean to be blunt, but why do you care?"

"I think you and I have common goals." He slid the fries closer to her with a small smile.

She wanted to resist his effort to win her over, but the fries were too tempting. She selected another, crunchier fry and popped it in her mouth. Clearly, he didn't have the votes for what he wanted and expected she would fall into line with his wishes. "Open space, affordable housing. Those are worthwhile."

"But time-consuming. You wouldn't see a payout for quite some time."

"And luxury housing? Wouldn't that take a while, too?"

His narrow face was avid. "We wouldn't have to design and sell the houses ourselves. We could sell to a developer. Like that." He snapped his fingers. "There's big money nosing around. Think of the group that created the Smuggler's Cove resort."

Theresa spooned up a bit of chili. She didn't know anything about real estate or whether what he said did or didn't make sense. She didn't want him to sense her ignorance. When she stayed silent, he put his elbows on the table and leaned forward.

"If you want a decent payout, you're going to have to get the right to vote the shares."

"And how would I do that?" She gestured with the spoon.

"You'd have to sue. I'd pay for the lawyers. All you'd have to do is sign."

"On what basis would I sue? My father's will was clear."

"Doesn't it seem odd that your father would give some stranger power over your future? Don't you think your father might have been coerced? Doesn't it worry you that Clancy Frederics was the last person to see him alive?"

The spoon slipped from her hand and clattered against the chili bowl. "You can't think—"

"Not necessarily. Though why were the police so interested in him? Perhaps Frederics took advantage of a sick old man and did you out of some of your inheritance. A judge or a jury is going to see the unfairness of that."

Theresa was stunned.

"Do it for the money, if nothing else." He leaned even closer. "Please?" He gave a crooked smile.

She pulled back. "I'll think about it."

The waitress brought the check. "I'll get this," Pete said.

"No." She didn't like to feel beholden.

"I insist."

She said a grudging, "Thanks."

Outside a car was pulling up, wheels scraping against the crushed stone. A woman stepped out and reached into the back seat to remove a baby from its carrier. Her red coat flapped open as she walked to the restaurant, cuddling the baby to her chest.

"Our fathers left us this legacy," Pete said. "I want to do mine proud." His eyes teared, and he grabbed his water glass to cover his embarrassment.

Theresa pulled on her jean jacket. There was a bitter taste in her mouth. No chance for her of making her father proud.

Walking to church, Theresa left clear depressions in the sand, as if asserting herself on the landscape. The sand had the winter crunch she loved. She wondered if there was moisture in the grains that froze to give it the hardness that made it easier to walk on. The wind created mist-like eddies over the surface of the sand, reminding her of a horse's mane swept back.

When she reached The Hangout, previously Sloppy Tuna, previously Mimosa, previous to that she couldn't remember, she headed up to the church for her meeting with Father Molina.

She scraped sand off her sneakers, entered the church, and blessed herself with holy water. The church held a reverent hush. She let the hush permeate her skin, calm her mind.

She slipped into a pew at the back. This was the Spanish-speaking Mass, and there were about thirty parishioners—landscape workers, restaurant cooks, store cashiers—all part of the backbone of the community.

She knew Father Molina helped the immigrants, most from Ecuador and Guatemala but from Jamaica and Eastern Europe, too. Out here jobs were plentiful, but housing was difficult. It occurred to her that if she were to have a say over the Moorlands parcel, perhaps that was what she could choose—housing for parishioners like these and herself.

She enjoyed the sounds of Spanish, letting them wash over her, her mind drifting through the sermon, only a few words of which she could understand. At the end of the Mass, after everyone left, she went up front to wait for Father Molina to change out of his garments.

"Ah, Theresa." He came out from the sacristy and took her hands. "How are you?"

She hadn't been in to see him for a few weeks, since Christmas, when he'd asked her to come to a feast he hosted for those without family who would otherwise be alone. She was not much of a cook, but she had helped whip up sweet potato soufflé and steamed string beans.

"Fine, Father. You?"

"Wonderful. And happy to see you." She followed him from the church and into his office. Rather than sit behind the desk, he joined her on the other side, their chairs swiveling toward each other.

"I hope you haven't regretted your decision to turn down the house?"

She shook her head. Too late now anyhow. "Do you remember the day of the funeral, I told you Pete Walker approached me?"

"I do."

Her seat squeaked as she swiveled toward the priest. "You know the executor of the will was given the right to vote my father's shares in the Moorlands parcel. Walker is one of the partners. He wants me to try and get the right to vote them."

Father Molina tapped his lips with his fingertips. "Have you decided you're willing to take the money that will come to you from that parcel, then?"

She shrugged. "There's a rumor the town might condemn the trailer park. If that happens, I'll be forced to move. So, if I don't take the money, I don't have a chance in hell— pardon me, Father—of finding someplace to live."

"I'm so sorry, Theresa." He wrinkled his forehead. "About Walker's request. I'm not clear how being able to vote the shares would help you."

Theresa gathered up her hair and fished for a butterfly clip in her pocket before meeting his eyes. "He said the only way I can get money quickly is if they sell to developers. The partners are not in agreement about that. The executor has the deciding vote. Walker's afraid he won't vote to develop."

"What do the other partners want?"

"Preservation. Affordable housing. Walker says those would bring much less money and take more time."

"I see." There was an odd expression on Father Molina's face. Did she seem grasping and greedy? She couldn't bear for him to think of her that way.

"You know it's not the money. It's—"

"Your home is threatened, Theresa. You don't need to apologize."

"Would it be moral to sue or threaten to sue? That's what he wants. And he asked me not to divulge that he's the one asking me to do it. That makes me uneasy, too."

Father Molina touched the tips of his fingers to his lips again. "It's not immoral, certainly. But what you say does give me pause . . . about Walker's motives. And given what you've told me about your father's will, I don't know whether you'd have a winning case."

Theresa hesitated. "Walker claims it looks suspicious that my father gave the executor the power over the shares. That maybe he took advantage of his weakened state."

"Do you believe that?"

Theresa picked at a thread coming loose from the sleeve of her jean jacket. The night before, she had covered yet another small tear with a patch of red plaid flannel. "No."

Father Molina sighed. "I wonder if there isn't a better way to accomplish what you need. I would imagine the partners could finance buying you out so you'd have your money sooner. Perhaps you could talk this over with the executor directly? Explain what you're up against. Maybe he'll take your wishes to heart. If your gut sense is right, he's got no axe to grind with all this. He's an outsider? It may be worth a try. If he's unsympathetic, then consider other options."

When Clancy had tried to talk with her at the Promised Land, she'd been anything but pleasant. He wouldn't likely be helpful to her now.

She sighed and stood up.

"Thanks, Father, you've given me a lot to think about."

"Anytime, you know that."

Outside it was colder, and an icy rain had begun to fall. She pulled up her hood and wound her scarf around her face and neck.

There were no good answers. She didn't like or trust Pete Walker. She trudged, head down, into the wind, the rain assaulting her. If she had taken her father's house, she wouldn't be in this predicament. She stomped along the beach. She had worked so hard to find a place of internal peace, a calm and balanced center. That center was coming loose, fraying. *How much longer can I keep stitching and mending?*

Theresa stood behind the bar, ready for the onslaught. Molly had organized a birthday gathering, and nothing got everybody out into a cold winter night like a party. Every two seconds, the door let in a blast of frigid air; the local guys showed how tough they were by leaving their coats in their trucks.

"Surprise! Surprise! Surprise!"

Billy's face was a cartoon caricature of shock, and Molly's was bright with pleasure. Kathy circled the room, setting food down on all the tables.

It was like summer again, with bodies clamoring and

crowding up in a mad dance, keeping her on her toes. Bills were flying so fast there was no point in closing the register. Finally, people settled down at tables and orders slowed, so she could chat a bit with some of the boys. She even gave Cody a smile. Encouraged, he hopped onto a barstool. He'd kept his distance ever since their exchange in the parking lot, for which she was grateful. The glow of the recessed lights above the bar highlighted the red and gold hairs of his beard.

Molly slipped in next to him, and they got to talking about the hatchery. Theresa thought Molly was doing it for her sake—trying to draw her in, to make her see Cody was a great guy and that she shouldn't be such a hard-ass—but then she realized Molly was totally into this stuff, the details of growing spat and how it would be seeded in the spring.

Theresa suddenly recalled a warm perfect day when her father had taken her to the bay for her first time snorkeling. She went under water, face down, forcing away her initial panic. She swam along, looking into the long grasses and along the ridges of sand. Her father pointed to where the shells rested. Later he taught her how to wield a clam rake, too, nudging the shells gently out of their tangle.

She brushed away the memory, and when she looked up, there he was at the door: Mr. F-ing Executor. Clancy Frederics.

As the party burned through the evening, she watched him. He stayed clear of her, not even ordering a drink. Perhaps Father Molina was right, and there was something she could say that would make a difference. She watched Clancy as if somehow, in the way he moved and talked, she could glean whether it was worth trying.

Billy's cousin, the one with the wild head of curly black hair whose name she couldn't remember, came over. "There's a shot called Chocolate Cake. Do you know that one?"

Theresa pulled out the vodka and Frangelico and whipped up two blenders' worth. She lined up the glasses and went down the line pouring. She shouted, "Free shots, Birthday Cake!" She did another round and knocked one back herself.

"You're quite the popular gal." She put down her glass. It was that developer, voice low, insinuating. How dare he crash the party? Molly had told her he represented a group of rich and powerful investors who made deals all over the world.

She took her time rinsing out the blender at the sink.

"Oh, so we're playing that game, are we?" he finally said.

"Not playing any kind of game." She finally poured his Stoli and set it in front of him.

He took a quick swallow, staring at her over his glass. "All of life is a game. Games of chance, games of power, games of risk."

"So what's yours, then?"

"Oh, what you'd expect. Money."

"Nice to have enough of it to play with."

"How about you, Theresa? Would you like some to play with?"

It jolted her that he knew her name.

"Depends on what we're talking about." Jittery energy quivered inside her.

"You know about me, don't you? Who I am, what I do?"

"If you mean do I know you're some kind of developer, then yes."

"I'm the kind who's backed by a group of rich investors. That's the kind of developer I am."

"Am I supposed to be impressed?"

"You should."

They stared at each other, a kind of checkmate.

"Little towns like these, they think they can make laws to keep out change. They can't. It's stupid and shortsighted. Greed is the human condition, it's in our DNA. It will always win out. The smart way forward is to cut the best deal. Use the leverage you have. Otherwise, it's just heartache all around. Like for your little friend. She's very sweet, and her boy is head over heels for her, but they'll cave in the end."

Theresa gripped the edge of the bar. "How dare you."

"Give your friend some sisterly advice," he went on, ignoring her outrage. "Tell her and her boyfriend to sell. I'll make it worth your while." He tossed back the remainder of his drink.

She put both hands on the bar. "Get the fuck out."

He laughed and walked away. Her heart was pounding. What could someone with unlimited sources of money do to make Molly's life miserable?

The evening slowed, as if time were an elastic medium that could stretch or contract at will. There was an intermittent crescendo of cheers from the back room . . . a dart game in progress. Her head was buzzing from the shots, and the base of her neck and shoulders ached. She was unnerved by the conversation with the developer and wondered what to say or not say to Molly and Billy. She looked at their happy faces, surrounded by friends. Tonight was not the time.

She scanned the crowd for Clancy Frederics but didn't see him. Pete Walker was heading her way. *Just what I don't need*. She curbed the impulse to duck under the bar.

"So Theresa, what's your decision?"

Around her people were leaning into each other in conversation; there was a loud happy hum in the air. Something rose up in her throat like bile. All these people belonged. Soon she might no longer belong. Soon she might have no place to go.

She gathered up a few dirty glasses. She thought of Clancy Frederics, the interloper, the orphan. She was an orphan now, too.

"I need an answer." Pete leaned over the bar.

She bent down and put the glasses in the rubber bin. She held onto its sides, head lowered, eyes closed, sickened. Perhaps Miloxi was right, and it all came down to greed in the end.

CHAPTER 25: Clancy

Clancy put down the book on the native Montauketts, one of several he'd taken back to the bungalow to read on this rainy day. Otto had marked a passage, about how the Montauketts had lost their land, with a little, pink paper flag. Could this be what Otto had had in mind by "retreat"— a place for descendants of native peoples, who had been cheated of their land, to return? It was an inspired idea; Clancy felt a leap of excitement.

It took only seconds to realize the idea was beyond far-fetched. Any Montauketts who hadn't died from disease had been dispersed across the country. There was no way of repatriating them to the Moorlands parcel, and farfetched that the partners would consider giving away the land anyhow.

Clancy rummaged for a piece of paper. Otto had written, *"An idea just came to me,"* as if a sudden unconventional solution had presented itself. Clancy decided he'd follow that lead and try brainstorming.

Just like an equation, there were three values that had to be solved for: first, a good return on their investment to satisfy the partners. Second, for Otto's goal, some benefit for the community. And whatever the idea, it had to relate to that one word: "Retreat."

Clancy leaned back in the rocker. What else could land be used for besides housing or open space that could provide benefits to a community? He supposed some municipal use—a waste treatment plant or solar array or wind farm. Perhaps an actual farm. Could any of these garner enough profit? He was doubtful. And none had anything to do with "retreat."

Frustrated, he picked up *The Military in Montauk: Army, Navy, Air Force*. Much of the preserved land in Montauk had at one time been military. Paging idly through the book, Clancy stopped at a photo of Camp Hero.

> *To protect it from enemy bombers and German spies in fishing boats, the Camp Hero base was built to look like a typical New England fishing village. Concrete bunkers had windows painted on them and ornamental roofs with fake dormers. The gymnasium was made to look like a church with a faux steeple.*

An entire fake village to fool the enemy. Fascinating. He continued reading, and a minute later a phrase seemed to shimmy on the page: ". . . with the military's retreat . . ."

Military retreat. Otto had been a policeman. He may have been military, too, schooled in tactical retreat. This could be it. Clancy's heart leaped, then stalled. He couldn't see any connection to the Moorlands. The military had sold off all its land on the peninsula decades before. Their retreat had already happened.

He threw down the book. His mind was balking. He wasn't going to get any further today. Outside the rain had stopped, and clouds were breaking up to reveal patches of light blue. Time to go to town.

He kept a running list of items to buy, mostly an excuse to eavesdrop on conversations. In the weeks after Otto's death he was aware of whispers and glances, but suspicion of him seemed to have died down finally, and the shopkeepers were friendly. It was fun to learn aspects of the town this way.

He visited the hardware and print shop and then headed to the post office, the trifecta of engagement. Today, though, it was almost empty. As he was leaving, he came face to face with Theresa Nolan.

"Sorry," they said in unison. Neither moved. With her hair in a high ponytail, she called to mind a skittish colt ready to bolt.

"Actually, I wanted to ask you about some things in your father's house."

She snorted. "I thought it was clear I'm not interested." She was bundled up in the worn jean jacket over a thick gray sweatshirt. She pulled the hood up and ducked her head as she tried to make her way around him.

He gave no ground. "I'm uneasy disposing of his belongings before you've seen them."

She gave a deep exasperated sigh. "I don't want anything."

"Maybe you'd like them donated to a charity? Or a church?"

She seemed taken aback. He remembered Tim Turchi mentioning she was a congregant of the Catholic Church where Otto's funeral Mass had been said. Clancy added a clincher. "There are some things of your mother's." Otto had set aside a yellow chiffon scarf, a red velvet shawl with gold embroidery, and several items of jewelry.

"How do you know they were my mother's?" She narrowed her eyes at him, those curiously distant, cat-like, topaz eyes. It struck him that the cold hardness he saw there might be something closer to fear . . . but of what? Something in him warmed to her a little. Defensiveness and self-protection were traits he knew well.

"Your father left a note. Look, why don't we set a time for you to come over. Or I can bring them to you."

"Let me think about it."

"I'll give you my number."

She bit her lip, but she took his card and shoved it into her pocket as she hurried off.

Set back from the road and atop cliffs fronting the ocean, the resort was well known, but until now Clancy had merely passed by while driving along the coastal road. The view was spectacular. Of course, this was the kind of place Pete Walker would choose for the partners to meet.

When Clancy had invited Pete to talk, Pete countered by calling this meeting for the whole group. The proposals were now circulated among them. Pete was sitting at a table overlooking the ocean, fingers drumming on the table.

"I remember when this place was a seedy, overpriced, tourist trap," Harve said, surveying the room.

"Still overpriced and still a trap." Tim Turchi squeezed Clancy's shoulder in greeting.

"Let's get to it," Pete said. "I called this meeting because our lawyer has informed me that Theresa Nolan is suing her father's estate for the voting rights on the Moorlands parcel."

"What?" Clancy's face went hot. His hand sought the comfort of his throat. He felt blindsided, furious that Theresa had had the gall to say nothing when they ran into each other earlier at the post office.

"What does it mean?" Harve asked.

"It means she doesn't trust Clancy."

"That's uncalled for." Clancy started to rise from his chair.

Pete stared him down. "She wants to get her money out. She's facing an emergency situation and needs cash."

Why hadn't Theresa come to him first? Clancy dropped back in his chair. He knew the answer. He'd been hated by the children of every parent who'd ever been kind to him.

"So," Walker leaned forward, "someone needs to agree to go forward with development or we'll be tied up legally for quite some time. She'll prevail in the end."

"Otto's will was witnessed and found sound." Clancy tried to keep his tone even.

"He was old and ill; that will cast doubt on his state of mind," Pete said. "It will be seen as just that his daughter vote the shares."

"Not necessarily," Harve said.

Clancy threw him a grateful glance. The food arrived; they took up their knives and forks.

"Is there any point in trying to discuss the situation with Ms. Nolan?" Tim asked.

Pete's knife clicked against his plate. "No. Her lawsuit adds to the pressure on us to move this forward. The application is going to be deemed complete any day and once the public hearing date is set, it'll sail through." He turned to Clancy. "You're just wasting our time."

Clancy recalled seeing Walker talking with Theresa at the bar the night of Billy Linehan's birthday party. There had been something in her body language suggesting an argument. He considered if Pete might be behind this move to force his hand.

Clancy stared into Pete's eyes. He understood Pete saw him as soft, indecisive, and easy to push around. What Pete couldn't know was how Clancy's upbringing had forged him. He was like a rock, a sedimentary rock, whose core had been built up, layer after layer, into hardness. He could not be bullied.

He put down his sandwich, half-eaten. "Thanks for lunch, Pete. I'll be in touch."

He walked swiftly through the restaurant and out the door to his car. As he was setting his phone down on the passenger seat, it vibrated.

"I'm urging you to think carefully about what you're doing," Pete said.

"I assure you, I am." Clancy revved the motor to drown out Pete's voice.

"The people in this community have long memories."

Clancy swiped down to end the call. He drove too fast along the coastal road, passing driveways to houses visible only from the ocean, enjoying the dips and turns.

Concentrating on the road calmed him. He rounded the bend and crested the rise where Bishops by the Sea sat atop the slight hill, its peach and blue sign newly painted and welcoming. He signaled, then jolted to a stop at the entranceway. A patrol car sat idling.

Detective Tobias was just getting out of the car. Spotting Clancy, he headed over, Detective Barola trailing. Tobias made a circling "roll down your window" motion. It took Clancy a second before he could loosen his grip on the wheel.

"How are you doing, Mr. Frederics? Enjoying our peaceful winters here in Montauk?"

"Have you come to tell me I'm no longer under suspicion?"

"Sounds like you're a little nervous about that."

"I'd like my name cleared."

"The fire was deliberately set. Just because there's insufficient proof to charge you now doesn't mean we won't later." Tobias leaned on the car.

"I did not set that fire."

"So you say. Still, unless we find another culprit, I'm afraid you won't be in the clear," Barola said.

They wouldn't look for a culprit, Clancy knew. He was too convenient a scapegoat.

"You should be careful how you act in this community," Tobias went on. "I'm telling you this for your own good. You're being watched."

Clancy waited until they had driven off to get out of his car, annoyed he'd let them get to him, had made him anxious.

Be careful how you act. The community is watching. Everyone had a history out here, connections like the roots of plants, all tangled up together.

Clancy was an outsider, resented by people who didn't even know him. Pete Walker was an important man; his father had been even more important.

Pete had sent Tobias as a warning.

I can fuck with you.

CHAPTER 26: Molly

"Montauk is dead in the winter," everyone said, and now, after the holidays and with the fish market closed, Molly understood. The sky at night seemed more intensely dark, the constellations sharper, the quiet quieter than during the summer and fall. She missed the calls of birds, the swish of boats going by. Now there were only the sounds the wind made when it rattled through the house or the soft lapping of tiny waves against the shore.

During the holidays, the shops and restaurants that stayed open decorated their windows: the florist with masses of poinsettias; the grocery with a large gingerbread house; and the gift shop with a pink feather tree hung with gold and silver starfish ornaments. The pavilion in the green was garlanded, balsams with colored lights lining the main street. Flyers advertised a craft fair at the church, a bake sale at the library, a musical performance at the grammar school. Now, with the holidays over and only locals around, the sight of a lone house here or there lit up in the dark only made everything feel more desolate.

On her last day at the market Molly mopped the floor while Vince wiped down the counters, and together they scrubbed the wooden worktables in the back of all traces of blood.

Vince helped her load the food to be donated into Billy's truck, then gave her an awkward hug and walked off with a wave. She pulled her jacket closer around her neck, tucked her hair under her cap, and stood a moment listening to the quiet. There was no one around, just the gulls wheeling overhead. The dock was all hers.

She drove to the church with the packed boxes. She didn't know who would get this food . . . maybe elderly people whose social security didn't go far enough or retired fisher-men who had nothing resembling a pension. Or maybe some of the immigrants who had put down roots and were living off their summer wages and doing odd jobs to make ends meet in the off season. She was beginning to understand that when the town evolved into more resort than fishing village, not everyone reaped the rewards.

For the first few weeks after her layoff, she found things to occupy her. She did house repairs, wielding a hammer to fix the saddle in the backdoor entry, using a scraper to edge under and flick off the lichen that had taken hold on a shady part of the roof. She bought a bookcase for Jonah and put it together, only having to redo one screw she put in the wrong place. She and Jonah cut branches from a holly tree in the woods and created a centerpiece on the kitchen table, its leaves and berries glossy in the light. They glued seashells on a small, fluted glass and filled it with stones. One rainy day she drove up-island to a mall and came home with a few finds.

The small kitchen caught the morning sun. Whoever had built the house had situated it well. Her new placemats, yellow with blue flowers, and matching yellow napkin holder brightened up the worn appliances and old-fashioned wooden cupboards. Three cooking pots in graduated sizes hung on hooks, newly shiny. The linoleum floor was scrubbed; the stovetop was pristine. She couldn't think of a single thing to do.

The wind gusted, rattling the window frames. The little dory, overturned, was pulled up on the bank, and out at the bay, the wind made baby whitecaps on the surface of the water. She'd given up the idea of work at Kmart in Bridge-hampton. It was too long a commute. With Billy fishing and Jonah to take care of, it made no financial sense. Spring couldn't come soon enough.

The hatchery wouldn't need volunteers for months. She'd taken Jonah there the day before, and Cody had given them a tour, explaining about the spat, how it was moved from one tank to another as it grew, the temperatures and the nutrients adjusted until the time was right to place them in designated waters to grow into adults.

"You are so lucky to work here!"

Cody finished writing a measurement on a chart attached to a tank by a chain. "What happened to your idea about harvesting scallops?"

"Billy's not crazy about me being out on the water." She lowered her voice. "He has some issues because of his parents' deaths. Keep that to yourself, okay?"

Cody's eyes followed hers to confirm Jonah was out of earshot. "What about growing oysters? That's done right from shore."

"Really? From shore?"

"There's a town aquaculture program. Doesn't cost much, and they even give you the oysters and the gear."

"That sounds awesome." Maybe Billy would be okay with that.

Cody went on to say that oysters tasted of the place where they grew—something called meroir. Their flavor was derived from the water and the microorganisms they filtered, and the ones from Long Island were saltier than those say, from the Chesapeake. Molly had a hard time swallowing the slimy creatures, but she loved the idea that when someone ate an oyster, they were, in a way, eating the sea.

Molly's thoughts were interrupted by the sound of a car approaching. She froze. Only after it passed did she let out her breath. She hadn't seen Theodore Miloxi at the party, but Theresa had told her about her conversation. The developer had left another message earlier in the week, and Molly worried he would show up unannounced.

She went again to the window. A woman was walking along the shore headed her way, swaddled head to knee in puffy down. She trudged forward, as if deep in thought, not even glancing at the water as the cormorants flew off as she passed. Then, as if feeling Molly's eyes, the hooded face turned toward her, and she came up over their lawn. It was Allison, who lived several houses to their east.

"Allison, hi, is everything okay?"

Allison pushed back her hood; her face was raw from the wind, and she swiped a mitten under her nose. "I just wanted to talk to you a minute. Is now good?" She scraped her sneakers on the mat; little specks of sand went everywhere.

"Sure, come on in." Molly was uneasy. Allison hadn't ventured into the cold for just a casual chat. "I have to pick up Jonah soon. Something to warm you up? Tea? Coffee? Or cranberry juice?"

"Tea would be great." Allison shrugged off her jacket while Molly filled the kettle. "Looks nice in here," she said.

"I want to fix it up a bit more, but it's kind of special the way it is, I think." As she reached for the tea cups, she caught Allison's wince. "What is it?"

"So, you're really planning to stay?"

"Oh." Molly was taken aback by Allison's accusatory tone. Not meeting her eyes, Molly filled the pot with tea leaves. "We love it here." She wanted to add, "Don't you?" but somehow that felt rude.

Allison said nothing. Molly placed the creamer with the dancing goats she had gotten at the church's holiday fair on the table.

"You're not just holding out for a better price?"

"That didn't even cross our minds!"

Allison shrugged. "There's more money in it for everyone if we all agree to sell."

Molly's hand trembled as she poured the tea into a strainer she held over Allison's cup. "I don't know how you can be so sure there'd be more money, unless he's put it in writing." Allison's expression was blank. "I thought you and Doug were staying. Have you changed your minds?" Her heart was racing, and her face felt warm.

Allison picked at a fleck of skin on her chapped lips, not meeting Molly's eyes. "We don't feel we can pass this up. It's kind of the deal of a lifetime."

Molly cradled the creamer. "You could sell anytime down the road if you need to. It's not like the house is going to go down in value. Like when you're really old." Her voice rose despite her intention to sound calm. "How can you give all this up?"

Allison glanced outside, but her expression didn't change. "I know it's beautiful and all, but there's more to life. I've never gotten to travel . . ." Her voice changed, the wistfulness gone. "I think it would be good for Doug to get away from here, if you want to know the truth."

There were rumors Doug was troubled, an addict. Molly thought it was unfair to make those assumptions just because he was an Iraq war vet. Maybe there was truth to it.

They were silent. Molly searched for something to say. "I'm sorry I don't have any cookies or anything." It seemed the conversation was over.

Allison stood. "Will you think about it?" She pulled up her hood. "You're kind of spoiling it for everybody."

———◦◦◦———

Jonah and Molly made spaghetti squash with a sauce of toma-toes, broccoli, and zucchini. He loved to fork up the golden strands of squash. He scooped masses of it onto a casserole dish, ladled sauce over it, and then they placed it in the oven to warm. Billy was fishing this week near Cox's Ledge where there had been a good run of cod, close enough to be home every night.

Molly was troubled by the conversation with Allison, and as if sensing she was distracted, Jonah leaned against her every now and again, pressing his body into her side, as if she were a tree and he wanted to feel her stability. She would pause, put her arm around him, and gently squeeze. They would stand like that for a moment, and then he would move off, resuming his chatter.

Molly greeted Billy in the back entryway as he hung up his waders and slicker, droplets of water still in his hair.

"Smells great," he said, coming into the kitchen, lifting his head to sniff like a shaggy dog. He ruffled Jonah's head in greeting.

After dinner, while Jonah settled in with his homework, Molly broached the subject of the visit.

"Allison came over today."

Billy, finishing up the dishes, placed the last plate in the rack and wiped his hands on a dishtowel. "Huh?"

"Allison." She gestured with her head in the direction of Allison's house.

"What did she want?"

"She and Doug have decided to sell."

"Shit." He leaned back against the counter. "Why?"

"She said because it's so much money, and she's always wanted to travel. Then she said it would do Doug good to be away from here. I think that's the real reason."

Billy ran his fingers down his face to rest at his jaw, as if his wisdom teeth hurt.

"Billy?"

"I'm thinking."

There was the sound of wind picking up outside and icy pellets hitting the windows. "She made it sound like everyone thinks we're holding out to get a better offer. She said if we don't sell, we're spoiling it for everyone."

"That pisses me off." Billy pulled out a chair and plunked down at the table. "It's classic, trying to turn us against each other. They can all make whatever deals they want. We're not stopping them." He began fussing with the salt shaker.

She put her hand on his to still his fidgeting. "What if he won't do a deal without all of us? What if we really are ruining it for everyone?"

"I don't believe it for a second. That would be a stupid way to do business. He'd make a bundle of money from even one of the houses along the shore here. This is just a way to pressure us."

"You think?" Molly was flooded with relief. Billy seemed committed to staying firm.

"I do." He rubbed his thumb up and down between her finger bones. "I guess it makes sense to check in with the others just in case." He sighed.

"Want me to talk with them?" She knew he wasn't crazy about the neighbors.

"Nah, it should be me."

"We can go together."

There was a sudden gust of wind. The icy pellets continued to hit the windows and there was a loud rattling sound.

A bang came from upstairs. "Molly! Billy! I'm scared."

"We're coming," Billy called out. He and Molly smiled at each other.

Later, after she and Billy each read Jonah a story and they'd all taken turns in the bathroom, after she had kissed Billy on his shoulder because he was already asleep, only then did she realize she'd forgotten to tell him her idea about getting an oyster permit.

CHAPTER 27: Julienne

News of a challenge to a will has cast an intriguing light on the subdivision proposal for the Moorlands Parcel, eleven acres in Montauk. The principals of the Moorlands LLC have been kept secret, but it's now been revealed that the recently deceased Otto Lansky was one of the partners. For many years, it's been supposed that Moorlands was one of the international investor groups that have been gobbling up restaurants and hotels in the area, but Mr. Lansky was a long-time resident; it's likely the other principals are as well. Apparently, the executor of his will, a Mr. Clancy Frederics, has inherited Lansky's role within the group, hence the suit, brought by Lansky's daughter, Theresa Nolan, a bartender at the Promised Land bar.

The parcel is zoned for as many as eight houses and the owners have every right to realize profits from their ownership—that's the American way. But these piecemeal applications, even when done correctly, have landed us where we are today—helpless to hold back the tide of rampant growth and overdevelopment. Some in the community, environmental group SOS among them, are urging the town to double its efforts to buy the property. We've been arguing for a while now that what's needed is an overarching plan for the future of our town.

The time for a moratorium, which both parties sadly
backed away from, is now.

—EDITORIALS, *The Coastal Clarion*

Julienne put down the paper, her emotions whipsawed. She
was thrilled the local paper had come out in favor of preserving the Moorlands parcel and a building moratorium. But
she was stunned by the revelation that Otto Lansky had been
a partner in the Moorlands Group and even more stunned by
Clancy's role. How could he have said nothing to her about
this? She took her coffee mug to the window and glanced
across the lawn at his bungalow. The unease she had felt
about him being named Otto's executor and the suspicion of
arson had warred with her gut sense of him. Yet even as she
had grown fond of him and was flattered by his interest in
her, she'd sensed something amiss, something he was hiding.
Now she knew what.

As if she conjured him, he emerged from his bungalow
and walked toward his car, carrying a cardboard carton. She
dashed out to waylay him, furious he hadn't confided in her.
Then her hurt feelings caught up with her and she simply
stood on her doorstep and watched him drive away.

She needed to work anyhow. She had a group show
coming up and hadn't decided which pieces to use. Her new
paintings felt like a jumble . . . not finished . . . maybe finished.
The sense of vulnerability was building, as it did before every
show. And now, when she had the whole day free to work, she
was too agitated to focus.

Only the beach would do. She loved the colors of
winter, the pearlescent sky, the hoary dun-colored cliffs. Her
walks let her spiral down into the place from which her art
derived, calming her, filling her with impressions to carry
back to her studio.

She had to admit that even before this upset with Clancy, she'd been feeling out of kilter, as if her bones and limbs, or perhaps her head and heart, were at odds. Her work was going in a direction that confused her; her strokes were bigger, she was using more paint, and sometimes she conjured glimmers of shapes, like malicious forces, weird algal forms, beneath her surfaces.

One day along the shore, there had been masses of sea-foam, the soapy-looking blobs of a yellowish-white that were caused by wave action and organic matter. She found it disturbing yet fascinating and painted it in her next work. She was pushing against something or pushing toward something; she needed to *act*.

She grabbed her old down coat from the closet and was mid-zip when the phone rang.

"Julienne!" Grace shouted. "Did you read the *Clarion*?"

Julienne unzipped and sat back down. "Yes. What do you think?"

"It's a gift, a golden opportunity. With the daughter suing, the subdivision is on hold. We can use this time to organize."

"You mean a petition?"

"That's what we need to think through. I'm calling an emergency meeting. Saturday morning, ten o'clock, my house. You'll be there." It wasn't a question.

Rob had offered to take Max to Bridgehampton Saturday morning, so she could get her work finished in time for the show. Still, this was important. And she knew what would happen after the meeting; she would be going door to door or standing outside the post office in the freezing cold, getting people onboard with whatever was decided. Instead of feeling irritated that this would take her from her work, she felt energized. Maybe this was the action she'd been craving.

Although the walk helped her mood, her work in the studio afterward didn't go well. She was scattered and unproductive. She tried to calm herself by cleaning brushes and organizing her paints. It was no use. She gave up and headed back to the house, still undecided about which of the pieces to put in the show, disgusted with herself.

She was preparing dinner when Rob and Max clomped in.

"Can you *please* remember to take your boots off outside?"

"Nice to see you, too."

To give her time to work, Rob had picked Max up from school. He had even volunteered to talk with Max's teacher about his science fair project. His face was raw and red from the cold. She was a hateful person.

"Sorry," she apologized. "Not a good day."

"No excuse."

"No."

To make up for her grouchiness she opened a bottle of wine and put wood in the fireplace. She handed Rob a glass, and they settled on the worn corduroy couches in the living room, facing the windows that in the rapidly fading dusk merely gave them their reflections. Rob let her rant about her work, which segued to discussing Clancy and the surprise about his connection to the Moorlands parcel. She became aware of Rob frowning and realized she had been talking nonstop, thoroughly self-absorbed.

"I'm monopolizing. Fill me in on your afternoon."

He waited to see if she was really ready to listen. "I had an idea for the entryway to Teal."

Winter was when they did small improvements to the bungalows.

"Tell me." She poured another glass of wine.

"You know how that flat roof always leaks? What about putting on a gabled roof and adding a skylight?"

As he talked, she watched his face come alive. She studied its familiar planes, the angularity she loved, the small scar on his upper right cheek where he had once cut himself when woodworking. She should paint him. Or charcoal might be the better medium, light and dark shadings.

"Would you like to see?"

It took her a second to refocus. When she nodded, he jumped up to get his sketch, as eager as Max when he showed her what he had picked up on his wanderings, as part of his homeschooling, to make him aware and observant.

"Choose just one thing," she'd say at the end of their beach walks. "Whatever you think is most special."

If she had known his room would end up overflowing with innumerable objects, kept in carefully labeled see-through boxes they purchased by the dozen, she might not have begun the practice.

Come to think of it, Max hadn't shown her any treasures lately. Come to think of it, she didn't recall him doing much wandering, either. Maybe he was outgrowing some of those preoccupations.

Rob bounded back in with a yellow pad. She'd have to ask him about Max; she'd been so immersed in her painting, she hadn't been paying attention to either of them very much at all.

———◦•◦•◦———

In the morning, seeing a light in Clancy's bungalow, Julienne walked over. There was a weak, winter sun, a milky yellow; the snow was holding off.

"So," she said, the second he opened the door, his normally tidy brown hair mussed, as if she'd woken him, "were you ever going to tell me?"

He grimaced. "Would you come in? It's kind of cold." He was wearing sweatpants and a long-sleeved T-shirt and odd gray slipper socks.

Neat stacks of files and books were piled on the dinette table; folded laundry and *The Coastal Clarion* were on the couch. He moved the files and gestured for her to sit at the table. "Coffee?"

"Sure." She glanced at the little Mr. Coffee machine they provided their guests, then saw a small French press he must have purchased himself. He scooped in a very dark roast and heated water.

They stood without speaking, staring at the press while the coffee steeped, as if that would make it go faster. Finally, he depressed the plunger.

"So you've seen the paper," Clancy finally said. "I didn't know it was going to be made public."

"Be that as it may—"

"I know, I know, I'm so sorry. Otto took me into his confidence. He asked me to keep his role secret, and I felt bound by my promise to him."

"Even after he died?"

"It's a bit complicated." He handed her a pitcher of milk. "Please believe me that I really wanted to tell you." The rich aroma of the coffee filled the room.

"The newspaper suggested that the shares in the corporation are yours?"

Clancy poured the coffee into two mugs and brought them to the table.

"Oh no. The value is Theresa Nolan's."

Her hands, wrapped around her coffee cup for warmth, went slack, her hopes dashed that he could help get the parcel saved.

"There's a decision about the parcel to be made, and I have a role in that because I'm executor. I've been educating myself." He gestured to the files and books.

This sounded more promising. "Educating yourself about what?" He was even more of a cipher than she'd thought.

"The principals are not in agreement about what they want."

"What part do you play, then?" She saw him hesitate and was irritated that even now he held back.

"Please understand this is still confidential. I get to vote Otto's shares. That's why Theresa is suing."

She felt a jolt of excitement. "Does this mean there's a chance of preservation?"

"A chance." He met her eyes. She stared back, trying to read whatever it was he was saying but not saying.

"What percentage are your shares? How many partners are there?"

He bit his lip; she felt anger flare again.

"Clancy, surely—"

"Julienne, I know that you or at least SOS have a particular point of view, and I'm trying to be impartial and do what Otto would have wanted. I'm getting pressured from all sides within the group. For right now, I have to keep all this to myself."

She had thought he was receptive, even sympathetic, to her passion, her arguments for preservation. Apparently, he found her heavy-handed. Offended, she plunked her mug down hard. "Wow. Really?"

"Please don't take it that way."

"I'm not taking it any way." She shoved her chair back and stood. She picked up the mug and with a flourish poured the remainder of her coffee down the sink.

"It's not that I don't trust you," his voice was pleading. "I just need to get my thoughts together."

"Take whatever time you like." She opened the door. "Fucking outsiders," she said under her breath, just loud enough for him to hear.

⬥

The anger fueled her work for over an hour before she brought it to heel. After how open and generous she'd been with him, the idea he didn't feel he could confide in her was infuriating. She was sloppy with her brush, paint flying, getting it in her hair, her face, the floor. She built up the surface of the canvas into a great chaotic blur of swirling color and mass. She began another with swirls of gray; there was a vague form coming from the shadows, from out of the fog: Clancy. As she continued to paint, her gestures slowed, and she made soft, feathery strokes. She was surprised to find a growing sense of tenderness and pity mixing in with her anger, as if she were accessing a deep well of something she sensed in him, perhaps loneliness, which kept him so apart.

She began to feel she should apologize. She went back to his bungalow, but he was gone. She thought a moment, then scribbled "Please come" on a postcard for her gallery show the next day and slipped it under his door.

———◦•✦•◦———

"A good day today, I see." Rob was tucking his shirt into his pants as she entered the bedroom.

She stopped. "How do you know?"

"On a bad day, your head is down. If you mutter at the ground, I know it's a *really* bad day. On a good day, you have your alert puppy look. Sometimes you shuffle your feet, as if you're hearing music."

Julienne winced. "How embarrassing." She sat on the edge of the bed. "There is a kind of hum I hear when the work's going well. Not a tone, exactly."

"The creative flow they talk about?"

"If only I could turn it on with a dial, like a radio." She got up and rummaged in her closet.

"Don't tell me you haven't figured out what to wear."

She had wanted not to wear black . . . such a cliché. Staring into her closet, there was the reality: nothing but black. Sometimes she thought she couldn't be a real artist because she didn't dress like one. No leggings and boots, no intricately tied scarves, no well-designed yet unconstructed flowing garments.

"You do know that unless you shop, something new won't magically appear?"

It was back to the black wool shift.

———

She and the other three artists arrived at Ashawagh Hall in the chilly afternoon, clouds bunching up thick and ominous. They rushed in, bundled in coats they stashed in the back. The gallery owner handed each of them a glass and made a celebratory toast, and they chatted while they waited for people to show up. With the nasty weather, Julienne worried that few would come, even though people were desperate during isolated winters for something to do. Then friends trickled in—Billy and Molly, members of SOS, even a few local motel owners and others from the chamber who were still speaking to her after her defection to the dark side. She was so touched, she downed two red wines in quick succession, chattered away, and thanked everyone for their kind comments, which weren't actually registering.

At some point, she saw Clancy enter the gallery. She rushed over, grabbing him as he was trying to take off his coat. "Thank you for coming! Do you forgive me? I'm so sorry for the way I acted."

He pulled quickly out of the hug.

"Jules—" Rob was at her side, "—sorry to interrupt, but the arts reporter wants to get a quote and a photo."

"Sorry, so sorry!" She giggled as Rob pulled her away; over her shoulder she saw Clancy raise an imaginary glass in tribute. At the last minute, right before the show, she thought, *What the hell*, and added the canvas she'd done of Clancy emerging out of the fog. They had placed it off on the side, leaning against the wall like an afterthought. She felt a moment's unease in case Clancy recognized himself, but why would he? Rob hadn't known and seemed irritated when she told him.

"Why would you be painting *him*?"

"Something about him touches me."

"Oh, really?"

"Not like that. A kind of sorrow."

Rob had just stared at her. "*Harrumph.*"

Now he steered her to the reporter, and Julienne clasped her hands in front of her and then at her sides, then back in front again, as they posed her next to one of her paintings. She was interested that they chose one of the ones she privately thought of as her "angry series" to stand next to. The black dress was perhaps a good choice after all, against the strong colors. The reporter asked her a few questions, and she found it hard to express herself. *Why, oh why, did I have that second glass of wine?*

Then again, perhaps because of the wine, she was happy with how her paintings were displayed on the gallery walls. One of the other artists was very conceptual, with austere works of fabric and yarn. Another painted life-size portraits in a hyper-realist mode, and the last created small canvases and boxes reminiscent of Joseph Cornell. Among all these, her landscapes seemed especially vibrant.

Time raced, and somehow the party was winding down. Molly rushed up to her. "Julienne, this was wonderful. Your work is wonderful!" Molly's cheeks had two bright spots the shade of earthy terra rosa. Julienne wrapped her arms around Molly. You just had to love her enthusiasm.

Julienne returned from the ladies room and noticed Clancy standing in front of the fog painting. He was motionless, his posture identical to that of the figure in the painting. A woman approached Julienne, but she couldn't pay attention, aware Clancy still hadn't moved. Her face warmed. A sick feeling flooded her. She felt ashamed, cruel, as if she had painted it to wound him.

She wanted to grab the painting and take it away.

CHAPTER 28: Clancy

Clancy stood before the small painting that leaned against the wall. Julienne's other canvases were large and fierce, with vibrant colors. In some, small creatures—an upended turtle, a crushed shorebird—struggled up through the thick paint. *Stranger to the Deed, work in progress,* was different, a swirling mass of grays, atmospheric, moody. He let his gaze move over the surface. He couldn't discern how she'd managed to capture fog. *Extraordinary.* It brought him back to the day they had walked on the beach together, the charged atmosphere of secrecy the fog created.

He bent closer. As if emerging from the canvas, barely visible, was a figure, a man, head slightly bowed, shoulders curled inward, as if to hold himself together, to hold in his loneliness, protect himself.

This was him. He took a sharp inward breath. This was how she saw him. Alone. Wounded.

He grabbed his coat and hurried from the gallery. Eyes prickling, he got into his car and shot out of the parking lot, nearly sideswiping a car coming in. The driver blasted him with his horn. Clancy pulled over, heart racing. His face was hot. He felt exposed and vulnerable under Julienne's intense painterly gaze.

Emotions swirled: hurt, embarrassment, and something else. He felt *known*. No one had ever looked at him so deeply. He stared across at the building that housed the gallery, a simple white structure situated on a triangle of land. It was called Ashawagh Hall, *ashawagh* the Native American word for "place where two roads come together." A coming together, a sense of community, was the feeling he'd had entering the gallery, feeling a part of things, happy to be among people he recognized, who welcomed him.

He'd been fooling himself. What community? He had gazed at the art, swirling the wine in his glass, making the occasional comment to people whom he vaguely recognized. As he thought about it, hands tightening on the wheel, he realized no one had been particularly friendly, not even Rob, who had quickly excused himself and moved away.

Clancy put the car into gear and eased slowly into the road. With the article exposing his role in the Moorlands parcel, there was yet a new reason for people to view him with hostility. He felt anew the prickles of the shame and grievance that had burned throughout his childhood. The weather matched his pained mood, with the dense cloud cover and grayish tinge to the sky.

He drove along the Napeague isthmus, emerging from its corridor of pitch pine forest to where the bay on the north and dunes on the ocean side were visible, acreage Julienne said was saved from development decades earlier. Where it hadn't been preserved, a cluster of enormous homes loomed so out of scale, they had the effect of shrinking the surrounding dunescape and dispelling the sense of vastness. The development was called Beach Plum.

"I can never understand why builders poetically name their developments after whatever they've just destroyed." Her tone was bitter. "Appeasement? Or evoking the spirit of the beach plums?"

His hand lifted off the steering wheel in an involuntary gesture as if to sweep the oversized houses away. This proprietary feeling surprised him. Apparently, he cared about this place whether or not it cared about him. It struck him that he wouldn't like to see the Moorlands parcel, albeit so much smaller, similarly diminished.

A moment later, the road forked and at the sign for the state park he pulled into the lot. He walked through the dunes, dull with winter-tired beach grasses, and to the water's edge. He hadn't been back since the night he had nearly drowned here. He began to walk, letting his eyes linger on the long sweep of the beach, focusing on the repetitive sound of the waves. He recalled something Otto had written in the green notebook, quoting someone called Octavio Paz, a poet. Paz believed people had lost their forefathers' deep connection to nature and consequently to the creative force of life itself. There was something more, about wild spaces and the human spirit and higher consciousness. As he walked, a sense of calmness came over him, and Clancy thought perhaps he understood something of what the poet had been saying.

In the distance, a heavily bundled-up man threw a stick for his dog. Gulls stepped fastidiously along the shore, turning their hard stares on him, holding out until he got very close before lifting off. Clancy felt his mood lift with their flight.

"Light and landscape have been Julienne Bishop's subjects since she began showing on the East End, but what seems new is an impetus to capture the ecological changes of Montauk. While she celebrates the natural beauty of the seascape, she presents a visceral sense of how this beauty is threatened by factors such as climate change, invasive species, and overdevelopment. Below the bold surface, shadowy figures—sick fish, dead birds—emerge. An enormous house teeters on the end of a cliff. Yet in a dab of bright light here, or a small child holding a mermaid's purse there, she allows a sliver of hope."
—Arts, Coastal Clarion

Clancy clipped the review and folded the rest of the newspaper neatly on a stack for recycling. He was grateful the reviewer had not mentioned *Stranger to the Deed, work in progress.*

He stood and gathered his things. It was time.

Otto's lawyer, Mary Jewel, had told him he was free to live in Otto's house while carrying out his duties as executor, but he had felt uncomfortable doing so. Now he would put aside his scruples and move in. It was past time to leave Bishop's by the Sea. He left a check and a note in Julienne's mailbox.

Theresa's challenge to the will had slowed the Moorlands process down, and there was no rush now for him to make a decision on the shares. His leave of absence was for several more months, and if Theresa prevailed, he wouldn't need to decide at all. A light wet snow began to fall while he was bringing his things to his car. On the way to Otto's house, he stocked up at the grocery and liquor store and grabbed a stack of empty boxes.

It took him just a few minutes to haul everything inside and put away the groceries. He stood in the living room, trying to decide where to start. Otto had left no instructions and Theresa hadn't called to arrange coming over to look at his belongings. Perhaps he'd have a yard sale and donate the proceeds to a local charity. For now, he'd pack up the small stuff and leave the furniture.

In the bathroom, he found a new set of towels in the linen cupboard and set out his own toiletries on the shelf under the mirror. He cleared out the hallway and bedroom closets, putting their contents in boxes, and emptied all the bureau drawers.

An antique oak cabinet served as Otto's nightstand, with a bottom enclosure and a skinny drawer above. Clancy opened the drawer, afraid to find painfully intimate signs of Otto's decline. But there were just reading glasses, honey cough drops, pens, and a nail clipper. He opened the bottom compartment and pulled out a few books and saw something wrapped in tissue paper. He sat on the bed to unwrap it. With shock, he saw that it was a tiny house with two windows, a front deck, and a steepled roof, painted in various shades of blue. His eyes filled. He remembered sitting beneath a window, newspaper spread out on the floor, as he carefully glued together the match sticks. He thought of Otto as he worked, wondering what color he would like the house painted. He remembered placing it in Otto's hands, saying, "You can open your eyes!" and the stunned look on Otto's face.

Clancy rewrapped the house and put it back where he had found it. Then he changed his mind and placed it on the bureau.

By late afternoon, half the living room was stacked with boxes labeled "Clothes," "Shoes," and "Miscellaneous." He glanced around, wondering what he could buy or do to make the place less fussy, lighter, should he decide to keep the house. Perhaps he could replace the living room sliders with an entire wall of glass. He'd only ever lived in apartments, with no call to give his imagination free rein.

He caught himself up. Too soon, too inappropriate. Suddenly he was overcome with exhaustion and hunger. He made a quick stir-fry and poured himself a glass of wine. He ate watching the snow fall, thicker now, no longer melting on impact.

After dinner, he turned on the table light near the recliner, considering which of Otto's notebooks to read. More history, he decided. By absorbing what Otto cared about, maybe he would come to know what he would have wanted.

Long Island, with its 180-mile coastline, was a rum-runners paradise throughout the 1920s. February 1925 was the first big raid on a dock on Fort Pond Bay, where

a party of 40 or 50 bootleggers and boatmen was taken
by surprise by county sheriffs.

The passage made him think of how Harve had described Montauk as the Wild West, too far from the rest of East Hampton to be bothered with. Otto might have been reluctant to go up against someone like Pete, who came from an old family. Equally, he might have found it difficult to side with the more monied types he'd perceive as tree-huggers. Clancy wondered if Otto's hesitancy in deciding what he wanted for the parcel might have been from such class-based and psychological hesitations.

Clancy fell asleep with the notebook open on his chest and awoke a few hours later, stiff and cramped. The world outside cascaded with soft, dancing snowflakes, drifting dreamily down. He went onto the patio in his bare feet. The snow shown brilliant in the moonlight, and the air had a tang of something fresh he couldn't put a name to, almost metallic.

He undressed and went to bed, imagining the snow blanketing the house like a down comforter.

In the morning, the world was completely transformed. The field behind the house was a blinding white; black boughs, traced in white, stood in sharp contrast in the far distance. The thermometer read twenty-eight, but in the brilliant sunshine, it felt warmer.

He made coffee, poured it into a thermos, and got dressed, putting on an extra pair of socks because he didn't have snow boots. He remembered seeing a pull-off for a trail right off the main road that led to the lighthouse.

A mile or so east of town, he saw the sign for the Shadmoor cliffs. There wasn't a single other car; his would be the first steps in the pristine snow.

The world glowed whiteness, thick mounds of snow on an infinity of branches. He locked the car, wrapped his scarf tighter around his neck, and pulled his socks up over the bottom of his jeans. As he stepped into the deep snow, it compressed under him; he had to lift his feet high as he walked to avoid too much getting into his sneakers.

He headed into the column of trees; the sun captured the snow crystals and shot light in every direction. It was hard going, and he felt silly with the prancing steps he had to take to keep the snow out of his sneakers, but it was fun, as if he were a child playing at being an explorer venturing into the unknown. The trail was wide and easy to follow, the air so clean he felt washed by it. The path dead-ended on the top of the low cliffs overlooking the ocean. Much of the sand was still covered with snow, and where it edged the sand, the contrast reminded him of vanilla icing on a donut.

The trail looped back along the top of the cliffs going west. The hamlet was charming in the distance, its low-scale stores and motels clustered together. Eyes dazzled by the blinding white and the shimmer of the ocean, he lifted his head and called out, "Yippee!"

Returning to the car, he realized he wasn't ready to go back; it would be exciting to see the view from the top the lighthouse.

His legs were encrusted from the knees down. He brushed off the snow and blasted the heater to dry his wet pants and socks as he drove. When he arrived at the Point, he was disappointed to discover the lighthouse was closed, so he walked down to the concession stand. That, too, was closed, but he was greeted with a sweeping view of Block Island Sound, the ocean hurling itself in great heaving waves on the boulders below.

A path led down to the beach, covered with rocks glazed with frozen sea. Gulls wheeled, crying their piercing cries, as he walked. Below the lighthouse, a revetment of enormous boulders encased in wire fencing served as a base flat enough to walk along. Not a single person was anywhere to be seen. He made his way carefully, afraid of slipping. He went as far as a protected cove sparkling with sun-struck snow, but the way down seemed too steep to navigate, so he reversed course, passing behind the lighthouse and then following a path down to the water's edge. He continued on, heading vaguely north, picking his way among mounds of stones and masses of different colored seaweed, telling himself he should go back but wanting to see what was around the next bend and then the next, wishing he'd brought a map and could pinpoint exactly where he was.

He reached an area with a set of very large rocks, a little kiosk up on a rise. As he continued toward it, he saw movement, as if the rocks were melting into the water. A black head poked out, and then another. Sea lions? Seals?

He stood motionless. The large black creatures, glistening in the light, clambered onto the rocks, draping themselves over each other, their noses pointed and twitchy with whiskers, their flippers long and graceful. His heart pounded.

He tiptoed up to the kiosk so he wouldn't frighten away the creatures. From the information panels in this viewing station, he learned that harbor seals came out to sun on the rocks in winter, usually at low tide. He watched them slide in and out of the water, imagining how the texture of rock and water must feel against their bodies. The waves and wind made a background hum, as if the air itself was singing.

One by one, the seals slipped back into the sea, and although he waited a while longer, they didn't reappear.

The sun was higher now, the snow already disappearing off the sandy parts of the beach. It struck him that the weight of pressure he had been feeling lately had lifted. He felt impossibly light, as if he were floating above the surface as he walked, and his mind felt clear and whole and empty. He wasn't at all tired. And he wondered if this was how a seal felt or a fox or a bird—just being alive to a given moment, one moment after the next, one component of a whole, like a grain of sand in the expanse of sand, or one leaf in a forest, one speck of the universe, part of some unfathomable mosaic.

He felt breathless with the thought, with a sense of touching something profound.

Whatever it was, whatever had happened, the seals had been a gift. A sign.

CHAPTER 29: Theresa

March in Montauk was always iffy, and this March was a tease, throwing out tantalizing hints of spring, the sun out and then disappearing, a few sprinkles, then clearing. Today, although it was warm, the wind was whipping up, as if the predictions of a storm might be correct. She had to decide: Take her new plantings out or try and bolster them with the seaweed mats she'd created, hoping that would be enough protection.

She got the idea after reading about wetlands reclamation work, where mats made of seaweed were used along the banks of streams and ponds to filter out contaminants. On a recent warm day, Molly and Jonah had helped her collect seaweed near the lighthouse. They wore high rubber boots and teetered among the rocks where masses of it grew underwater. It was too cold to wade out deeper but easier to gather what was washed up and mounded along the shore. Some strands were like thick, green, lasagna noodles, some red and feathery, and others had the round pods that were so much fun to pop. Jonah raced around stomping on them, though he went *"Phew"* at the briny, funky odor.

Creating the mats had been messy, and they were lumpy, smelly things, but they were the only idea she had left to try. She loaded them into her small red wagon and pulled it to the beach. If only she could filter out her anxiety the way the mats filtered out contaminants. Sloping up the face of their low dunes, the grasses she had planted swayed elegantly, fragile and delicate, in diagonal rows. At the base of the dune, she positioned a row of mats to create a base and then piled on masses of sand. Then she overlaid another row of mats, over-lapping slightly higher up the slope: mat, sand, mat, sand, working with just her trowel and her hands.

After she had finished three rows, she stepped back to survey her work. Even before the last storm, their dunes had noticeably flattened. If her plan didn't work, and the storm hit, the first high tide would take a chunk of the beach, and the second would eat away at the dune. All she could hope for was that this extra barrier would deflect just enough of the force of the sea.

It was Saturday and a few people were out walking, enjoying the unseasonable warmth. A few kids approached, curious. They wanted to help, and so she had them filling buckets of water and patting down sand over the seaweed mats as she continued adding rows.

A shadow darkened the area in front of her. Tretorn.

"So you *do* care."

She pulled her hair back from her sweaty face, refasten-ing her clip. "Of course I fucking care."

"Okay!" He held his hands up as if to ward off an assault. "I just meant . . . I guess we all do our part in different ways."

"Speaking of . . . any news?" She'd heard nothing further about the rumor of the town using eminent domain to seize the trailer park.

He hesitated. "Maybe something good."

She put down her trowel. "Really?"

"The town put in a request with the Army Corps for a beach nourishment project here."

"No shit?"

"Well, the wheels of bureaucracy and all that . . ." He shrugged, and she saw from his expression that while this was something, it wasn't really much of something; likely it would never come to pass.

"Right."

A sudden gust blew Tretorn's cap off his head, and they both raced for it. Clouds were massing on the horizon.

"Maybe the storm won't be too bad," he said. "They've been wrong before."

The wind made it hard to work, but she had nine more mats, so she kept on. One by one the kids lost interest and drifted away. Nothing was going well, not even the ploy with the Moorlands application. Clancy Frederics apparently wasn't caving in, and now they were in something called "discovery," which seemed to mean more waiting. She felt as roiled up as these twisted strands of kelp, and wished she'd never agreed to sue. She felt ashamed, knowing a lot of her motivation had been simply spite.

She wiped her sweaty face with her sleeve. The other day she had gone to the Moorlands property. Though just an ordinary meadow, the parcel was sheltered and quiet. The thought of trophy homes filling the space just seemed wrong.

She stood and stomped down on the mats to compact them. Pete Walker was paying for the lawyers, but she hadn't actually promised him to vote the way he wanted. There were many others like her who were struggling to make a living here. If she got the right to vote the shares, maybe she would push for workforce housing.

She brushed sand off her hands and put her trowel and bucket in the wagon. She didn't owe Pete any loyalty. Father Molina had probably been right. She was merely a pawn in whatever game he was playing.

———◆◆◆———

It was funny how whenever there was going to be a storm—hurricane, nor'easter, snow—everyone wanted to congregate at the bar instead of staying at home and off the roads the way they should. Some sort of human instinct, she guessed, to draw together in the face of an enemy that threatened the group from without.

Most of the fishermen were in. With the advance warning, the boats had turned back. The surfers would arrive late; they wanted the swells. They'd surf in the coldest of water, but they weren't crazy enough to stay out after dark in a storm. She placed extra bowls of goldfish along the bar, as if to summon Molly with her favorite snack. Sometimes she and Billy left Jonah with their cousin and came to the bar on Saturday nights.

"Red-haired slut!" someone shouted. She wheeled around, then, seeing Sky's laughing face, relaxed. It was the name of a drink, yet he got her every time. Sky was adjusting his bandanna, complaining about having to come in off the water just when they were into a mess of cod. She began pulling drafts. Will shuffled up to the bar; he talked about having had to put down his dog, an old mutt he boasted had the best sea legs on the docks. She spied Cody at the door and hoped he'd rescue her from Will, but he headed straight to the darts game in the back without even a wave in her direction. He probably had enough of being rebuffed by now.

A little while later, Stu and Cody emerged and headed her way. "Stu slaughtered me."

She passed them the peanuts. "Stu's the master. It's his English heritage. Generations of pubs in the Old Country."

"Skill, all skill." Stu lifted his bottle in salute and moved off to join the surfers' table.

Into the awkward silence, Theresa asked Cody, "Will the storm affect your work?"

"No, nothing's in the water yet."

"How big are the bugs now?"

"Almost three millimeters. Molly fell in love with the place. You should visit." Behind him, Theresa saw Theodore Miloxi heading straight for the bar.

Cody shifted his body to make room, but Miloxi didn't acknowledge the gesture.

"Maybe I will," she said to Cody, ignoring Miloxi.

Cody looked shocked. "Really? Anytime! Just let me know."

"Stoli, straight up, no ice," Miloxi interrupted, when Theresa continued to ignore him.

She poured the drink, taking her time, anger building. He left his usual excessive tip and walked away without a word.

"I guess he's loaded." Cody sounded jealous.

"He's a stupid fuck." She stuffed the bills into the tip jar.

"Jeeze, what did he do?"

"Guys like him, money guys. I hate them." Theresa grabbed Cody's Corona and swallowed most of it, then opened another for him. "He's messing with Molly and Billy's life."

"How so?"

"Pressuring them to sell, offering a boatload of money, getting all their neighbors in on it, too, so he and his 'investor cronies' can take over that whole shore."

"Molly never mentioned any of that. But it's up to them, right? I mean, it's not like he can force them?"

"All that money gives him so much power. What if he just buys up everything? That's not fair to the rest of us. Outsiders . . ."

"Hey, you're talking to an outsider."

"You're different. You respect the way of life here. You're not trying to bribe people just so you can make a fuckload of money."

Pete Walker, though, was no outsider, it occurred to her. His family went back generations. Yet in his way he—and she, too, if she voted the shares as he wanted—would be doing essentially the same thing.

She prised off a cap from another Corona and swallowed it in one go.

<hr />

Theresa waited until all the cars had left the lot before heading home. It was bitterly cold, the sky mottled. Few lights were on in any of the houses she passed, and the roads were empty. The wind was picking up, buffeting her truck. With the storm coming, she was glad her trailer was in the farthest row from the water, sheltered by the other rows. She gulped down her usual peanut butter and jelly and milk and climbed into bed, afraid she wouldn't be able to fall asleep given the eerie moans of the wind. But she was out in seconds.

She awoke to the sounds of knocking and the clatter of chimes. Outside she saw that her neighbor's awning was in tatters and banging rhythmically against the trailer, her chimes rotating in a swirling, tangled clot. A light rain had begun to fall. Theresa began to make coffee and noticed she had missed a message on her phone the night before. Pete Walker. She sighed, and called him back.

"It's a no-go," he said without preamble. His voice was raspy, the phone crackling with static. "Discovery's finished. The lawyer says this would move to trial now, except the judge let him know we don't have a shred of a case. Too many witnesses gave statements that your father was in his right mind. We could go to mediation, but that won't get us anywhere."

She was silent.

"You're got to talk to him," Pete said.

"The judge?"

"Clancy Frederics. He's a wimp. It's your only hope."

Your only hope, she thought, but didn't say. "He's not going to listen to me."

"Theresa, come on. You have certain advantages. Play them. From what I've heard, you know how."

Her face flamed. He knew her reputation of old. *Red-haired slut.*

Clancy agreed to meet her at the local health food café, but when she got there, it was closed. The pizza place was closed, too, as well as the printer and the hardware store, everyone expecting the nor'easter. She stood under the awning, just barely out of the rain. It was ridiculous to be out in this weather. Maybe he wouldn't even show.

Of course he would. He was a total fucking Boy Scout.

She saw a car pull up farther down the block, and then Clancy was headed her way with an umbrella over his head. How dumb could he be? The wind flipped it upside down in seconds, and he was sheepishly holding the spokey branches over his head.

"Nothing's open. Let's talk in your car." She followed him back to his navy-blue compact, the kind of car no local would think of driving.

He clicked the door open for her and as she slid in, the wind slammed it shut.

They spent a few seconds in a staring contest. Clancy's eyes were a dark hazel with flecks of gold. She was surprised he could hold out; she was a master at this. Finally, he conceded.

"Pete Walker pressured you into suing, didn't he?"

"He told me if you weren't going to sell to a developer, all this would take years."

Rain pelted the car, and she was reminded of the day of her father's funeral, sitting in Father Molina's car, when he was urging her to be more open to her father's gift, her inheritance, to let go of her anger. *If only . . .*

"Can I ask why you suddenly need the money, when before—"

"It looks like I'm going to lose my rental. If I have to move, I can't afford the prices out here."

"I'm sorry."

She remembered Pete's suggestion. Would it help to move closer, put her hand on Clancy's leg? He was attractive. She liked his slender face, with a mole on the left cheekbone, and it was sort of cute how his hair flopped into his eyes and he kept brushing it back. Rain slashed with such force, she could swear she felt the wet against her skin.

"I'll drop the challenge to the will if you'll let me have a say in the vote."

"We both know you're unlikely to prevail in this lawsuit, so that's not much of a bargain." There was laughter in his voice. Then his tone changed. "I've been reading your father's papers, talking to his friends. I need to honor your father's wishes and make the decision he would have wanted."

He sounded as if he was pleading with her to understand. She felt a flicker of hope. "You haven't made up your mind?"

"No, but what I'm clear about is two things: Your father didn't want the parcel developed and he wanted what was best for you." His voice became hesitant. "Look, I'll talk with the partners. There must be a way to get you your share. Give me a couple of days."

The flicker of hope died. Pete had said there was no way for the partners to buy her out. She stared at the pelting rain; the visibility was down to zero. "Whatever."

"I'm not any happier about all of this than you are." He bent his head toward his hands, resting on the steering wheel, then turned to her. "Do you want to rescind the agreement? Take the house after all?"

She was shocked. "You would do that?"

"Your father wanted you to have it."

"I can't. I just can't live there."

His voice rose. "What in the world could make you hate your father so much?"

"You think he was such a nice man, so loving."

"He *was* a good man. He *was* loving. And he loved you very much. He told me how much he loved you!" Clancy drew something from his pocket and handed it to her. "He set this aside for you." She hesitated, then accepted the square of forest-green velvet. She unfolded it carefully. Inside was the charm bracelet her mother always wore when she got dressed up to go out, and the ballerina pin Theresa had given her as a birthday gift, saved up from her babysitting money. The ballerina's gold skirt was studded with tiny fake sapphires, her arms stretched wide.

She felt wetness on her face. The ball of fury and sorrow and frustration inside her exploded. "He didn't see me! He didn't listen or believe me. He was stubborn and fixed in his ways and he wouldn't *budge*."

"About what, Theresa?" Clancy touched her, and a shiver raced down the length of her arm. She began to shake.

"I can't . . . I can't talk about it." Her sense of vulnerability, of coming undone, was terrifying. She grabbed the handle of the car. She couldn't breathe.

"Please, tell me. Maybe I can help. We can figure this out together."

"You? You were the golden boy."

"Theresa, I was an orphan. I lived in foster homes and institutions. Can you understand? I had nobody and nothing, except your father, and him for only a little while. I know it's different, but whatever your suffering is, I understand suffering. And I've survived, as you've survived." He paused, and said in a low tone, "I didn't realize until this moment how alike we are."

"Clancy." She was overcome with desperation. "Just let me vote the shares." She moved her hand toward his leg. He caught it and placed it firmly on the seat and pressed his own over it.

Something in her gave way. She covered her face, gasping and choking. Her collapse was terrifying; she was spiraling out of control. Clancy put his arms around her and drew her to him tightly. He spoke into her hair.

"Whatever it is," he whispered. "Just say it."

She let him hold her. She hadn't been held in a very long time, and it was an overwhelming relief to let go. She breathed into his jacket, her face moist, from tears or his wet jacket, she didn't know. He rocked her slightly and said nothing.

"My father had a friend," she mumbled into his chest. "He was like family. He came over all the time. He'd bring me presents and he would play with me, which my father never did. My father was the authority in the house, not a playmate, but Sam would let me climb on his back as if he was a horse or do puzzles." She choked up.

"One day . . . we were in the living room. I remember he switched off one of the lamps on the side table. It struck me as odd, I am just remembering that. He told me how cute I looked. I was pleased. I was wearing a new outfit, a plaid skirt and a white fuzzy sweater. Funny, I don't give a shit about clothes now. All of a sudden he pulled me onto his lap. It felt off, uncomfortable, but he was tickling me, making me giggle. Then he was sort of breathing into my ear, and then . . . and then."

She shuddered. Clancy's arms tightened around her. "Finish," he whispered. "You need to say it."

"His hand . . . he slid it up my skirt. It felt cold and rough. I was so young . . . ten . . . but I knew something was very wrong. And then I felt his fingers prying at the elastic of my underwear, at the top of my thigh." She coughed and took a few short breaths. "My father came in the room and yanked me from his lap so hard I stumbled to the floor. I tried to explain, but Sam told my father not to be mad, that I'd just been looking for attention. I was so shocked he'd lie like that."

"What did your father do?"

"Nothing. Absolutely nothing. When I tried to explain, he wouldn't believe me. That was the worst thing of all. He said I was a bad girl to make up such stories and that we must never speak of it again. He accused me of being coquettish. I sickened him. He never saw me the same way again."

Red-haired slut.

"Theresa, that's terrible."

She pulled away and wiped her face with her sleeve and shifted her back against the car door, finally able to look at Clancy directly. "It was my father who disowned *me*. He betrayed my mother. That's the kind of man he was."

Clancy started to say something, and she braced for his argument, but he surprised her. "I understand." His eyes held a pool of sadness. "I think that's why he wanted to talk with you. He knew he was dying; I think he wanted to make amends."

The rain was lashing the windshield, the storm intensifying. Stray bits of litter were flying down the street like confetti.

What if I'd let him make amends? Would I have been able to forgive him then?

Chapter 30: THE STORM

Noon

The wind swept sand along the beaches and into the air in ferocious eddies. Clouds were moving swiftly, beginning to clot on the horizon, dark masses gathering where only minutes before the sky was clear. Overhead was a thick, cottony gray mass; beyond, as if someone had drawn a line in charcoal, solid blackness.

The screen door crashed against its frame; Molly feared the wind would blow it off altogether. Whistling sounds put her in mind of an old aunt who had suffered from emphysema, terrifying her when she was a little girl.

After the balmy weather, the temperature plunge was shocking. They'd only just turned back the clocks. With the sun setting later, she and Jonah had been taking after-school walks in Hither Woods again. They'd even found a hollowed-out tree, a little cubby where a fox might be keeping its kits. Just yesterday they had gone with Theresa to the labyrinth, a spiral of rocks on the side of the hill near Hither Woods, and Molly found a moment to ask Theresa about Cody as she'd promised. Theresa had explained she was taking a break from men.

As they walked the spiral of stones and Molly took in the view—the fields, the woods, the bay—she was convinced she heard a hum, the Om of the universe Theresa had mentioned.

Molly was honored Theresa had taken her into her confidence and shared something as intimate as her spiritual practice.

Later, when she told Billy about the sacredness of the labyrinth he said, "Molly, you're so gullible."

The screen door slammed again. The storm was coming on quickly. The morning had been calm, and since the nor'easter wasn't expected to make landfall, she bundled Jonah up in a thick sweater under his yellow slicker and taken him to school.

"I'm surprised they didn't call it off," a woman said, pulling up her collar.

"It'll stay out to sea," a man said authoritatively. "The usual overhype."

Back at the house, the bay was now churning with wind-whipped whitecaps. The sky was great, gray lumps, and a light rain began to fall. Billy was still out on the water.

She brought inside the patio chairs and table that they'd put out only a few days earlier. In the tool shed, fifty-pound sandbags sagged in a dust-covered stack, but after the months hauling crates, she could lift them easily. She carried the bags one by one and lined them in front of the house, then stacked two more layers.

There were distant cracks like gunshots . . . branches breaking. She thought of Billy, the boat heaving beneath him, and felt herself sway. He hadn't called this morning, which meant they were too far out for a cell signal. She tried now anyway. When she had no luck, she called Bishops. Rob picked up.

"I can't reach Billy. They were fishing the Canyons. That's more than ten hours away." She tried to imagine the sharp cuts in the Continental Shelf where it dropped off into open ocean.

"His captain knows what he's doing," Rob said. "What about you? Would you like me to come over?"

"No, I'm set."

"You have sandbags? The boat's out of the water?"

"I pulled it out and tied it up to a tree."

"Keep us posted, Molly. Don't be shy if you need help."

A few minutes later, a text message came from the school saying that parents should pick up their kids as soon as possible. As she pulled up, Jonah came running out, raincoat flapping. Driving home through the woods, the rain sounded like hoof beats on the hood of the car. At the house, she was shocked to see the water covering the top of the dock. The rowboat was tossing about, as if trying to fling itself back into the water.

"Go inside!" she shouted to Jonah. The wind snapped back the hood of her rain jacket, and icy rain dripped down her neck as she raced to the boat. The water reached so far up the lawn that the boat was now in water. She should have tied it higher up the bank. She grasped the rope where she had attached it to a tree and tried to heave the boat farther up the slope. She was able to move it a foot or so, but the wind pulled against her, and the boat slid back down. Again she tried, edging backward up the bank, hauling with all her might, but she was unequal to the strength of the wind. It pulled her into the bay, water up to her knees. The water seemed to be rising before her eyes. With a sob, she let go.

She'd just gotten inside the house when the lights flickered and went off.

"Jonah!" she yelled. "We need to go to the shelter." She grabbed toiletries and underwear, stuffed a flashlight in her pocket, and hurried him to the car, heart pounding, then texted Billy to tell him where to find them.

4:00 p.m.

The sea bulged with swells of frothing water, the plumes speckled with bits of broken wood and flotsam. Crisscrossing currents crashed into each other in explosions of spray, ripping out dune grass

by the roots to the accompaniment of thunderous roars. Masses of
sea spume rolled along the beach, as if chased by Furies.

———◆◆◆◆◆———

Theresa sat in her truck for minutes to compose herself after
the conversation with Clancy, before heading to the docks to
help Marty board up the bar's windows. She drove so slowly,
the driver behind her honked and passed her with a raised
middle finger. She couldn't believe she had told Clancy.
Clancy, of all people.

She patted her swollen eyes dry and sprinted to the door.
As she and Marty lifted and nailed plywood over the windows, the physical labor began to settle her. They fought
against the intensifying wind and slashing rain.

"It's worse than I thought," Marty said. "Get on home."

Even with her wipers on their fastest speed, Theresa could
barely see, given the intensity of the rain. Although it was still
afternoon, it was as dark as dusk. Places where the road dipped
slightly were already flooding; she pumped the brakes after each
deep pool. There was an abrupt crack, and a tree branch came
down, startling her as it glanced off her roof. She was shaking.

Just outside her vision, something large and out of place
shot up in the road, and she swerved. Everything seemed to
happen at once. A thwack of impact and a sickening crunch
of metal. The air was sucked from her lungs.

The wind nearly tore off the door as she got out. It
whipped the hood of her slicker from her head, and rain
sluiced down her back. She had struck a deer. The doe lay on
its side, head askew, its tongue out, eyes like black marbles.
Even though the rain had washed the blood from a gash on
its side, there was still a pungent odor of blood and urine.

Theresa knelt and began to retch. The keening of the
wind mimicked her anguish. She touched the doe's neck and
felt the coarse, bristly hairs. It took a moment to penetrate.

The doe was cold; it must have been lying in the road before she struck it. She began to sob with relief that she wasn't responsible. She said a quick prayer and stood. There was nothing to be done.

She needed to get the truck off the road, but there was an enormous dent on the truck's fender. Tentatively, barely pressing the gas pedal, she angled sharply and backed up and then onto the shoulder of the road, shuddering as the front wheel reversed over part of the deer's body. The engine made a noise like metal inside a blender.

Theresa moved forward at a crawl with her flashers on. She curbed her impulse to pick up speed, continuing in slow motion until she reached the trailer park. Only then did she let out the breath she hadn't been aware she was holding.

There were a few lights on in the community. The electric poles hadn't gone down, at least not yet.

She pushed hard against the trailer door. Once inside, she pressed her forehead against the refrigerator, shaking with relief. The trailer rocked slightly in the wind. She thought of the dead deer, her poor damaged truck, her tender plantings, pummeled by the storm . . . and the futility of everything.

Julienne watched with trepidation and fascination as the storm built and the ocean became enraged, whitecaps farther out than she ever remembered seeing. She and Rob had taken the plywood window coverings out of the garage and attached them to all the ocean-facing bungalows. There was nothing to do but watch and wait and hope.

She made a pot of soup from the leftover vegetables in the refrigerator, and when darkness fell, the three of them settled in the living room to play Taboo, circled by candles and battery-powered lanterns. The wind whistled and shrieked, and every time there was a bang, they peered through the dark at the trees that bordered the property, which bent and swayed so low to the ground it seemed impossible they wouldn't break.

The captain decided to head back in rather than ride out the storm offshore. Billy tried again to call Molly but couldn't get a signal.

His share of the take would be almost four thousand, but he'd never do this again. Never. He'd had it. Some guys had saltwater in their blood. They saved until they could get their own boats, captain their own crews. They loved seeing the sun set over infinity, the thrill of the chase. But it wasn't in him. Or, rather, something else was in him, something that pushed against those things, something he might call caution, or fear, or premonition.

Whipped by the wind and soaked to the skin, the crew came in on pitching waves. Despite the storm, they unloaded the catch—that or lose everything—then raced to their trucks. Billy was cold and exhausted, his hands crisscrossed with cuts where his gloves had worn through. He turned on the ignition but just sat, shaking with chills. He blasted the heat and held his hands to the vent. The wind shook the truck, whistling through the windows. He'd experienced nor'easters before, but this storm seemed like another beast altogether.

He tried his cell again. No signal. He threw the phone on the seat. He should never have gone on this trip. Rain slashed the windshield, and the inside of the window fogged up. He put on the defroster, then pulled out, careening around turns, driving as fast as he dared. At the clearing, he saw Molly's car wasn't there. He fought the wind and rain to the front of the house. The bay waters were creeping up the slope toward the kitchen door, where piles of sandbags awaited.

Molly, his magnificent Molly.

Clancy sat reading, trying to ignore the sound of the wind, trying not to worry that the power would go out. He had food, a battery-powered lantern, plenty of water, and even filled the bathtub. This northeaster, much later in the season than was typical, had taken everyone by surprise.

The biggest storm ever to hit Montauk, he read, was the hurricane of 1938, dubbed the Long Island Express. At ninety-five miles per hour at its height, it flung cars and boats into the air like scraps of paper, and the entire village, then along the shores of Fort Pond, was wiped out. The downtown was rebuilt along the ocean, which in hindsight was a mistake as the shoreline development interfered with the natural ebb and flow of sand. Over time, erosion had become severe, hence the construction of the controversial artificial dune. Another catastrophic storm was overdue, they all said. This nor'easter might be the one. No one seemed confident the dune would hold up.

The light flickered but it held steady. Clancy was getting spooked. He put aside the history and picked up the binder with the Moorlands application. The environmental impact statement had been deemed complete, and he had gone through it several times already. The file included a list of the flora and fauna on the property, its ownership history, financials, maps, and photos. He had poured over this material, but it brought him no closer to a decision.

He walked to the slider. It was so dark now, he could see absolutely nothing, and his thoughts circled back to Theresa, the feel of intimacy as they sat in his car, enveloped in sheets of pounding rain. Their conversation had shocked him to his core. He had thought the world of Otto, idolized him, really. He couldn't fathom how Otto could have trusted the word of a friend, no matter how close, over that of his own daughter. It went against Clancy's sense of the man, and yet Clancy didn't doubt Theresa's account. A betrayal of her of this magnitude could explain the intensity and depth of the regret Otto had expressed, even if he hadn't directly acknowledged he had wronged his daughter.

Clancy closed the blinds against the darkness. He'd been equally shocked at the sympathy he felt for Theresa when she opened up to him, a radical reorienting of his perspective. It was like noticing a sliver of light, indicating an unsuspected hidden chamber, in what had appeared a solid and impenetrable wall. He cradled her in his arms to comfort her the way he'd always longed to be comforted.

He went back to the couch and began to tidy the papers. He would try and get the partners to go along with advancing her a payout. If they wouldn't or couldn't, there was no other option but to take ownership of the house, get a loan on it, and pay her himself.

He heard a loud thump and rushed to investigate. Lying on the patio was one of the birdfeeders. It must have blown against the house and made noise as it rebounded to the ground. His heartbeat relaxed, and he headed back inside.

There was a hissing sound, and then the lights went out.

10:00 p.m.

There was a hollow silence, as if the storm had swept even the people away. Even the ocean was quiescent. Trees lay toppled along the roads, powerlines limp, impotent.

They spent the night bedded down in the school gymnasium on a wad of blankets, Billy enveloping Molly and Jonah with his body. Every time Molly moved, Billy's arm tightened, as if afraid to lose contact.

In the morning they awoke to a morning clear and wind-less, with an intense blue sky.

Molly and Billy dropped Jonah off with Julienne and Rob and drove back to check on the house. They had to detour around where the ocean surge had breached the road near the grocery store, and then headed north toward the bay. Driving along Second House Road, they saw branches strewn everywhere. After Grandma's Beach and Navy Road, on the dirt road, tree limbs blocked their passage in several places, and they had to get out of the car to clear their way.

When they rounded the bend and could finally see their house, Billy let out a cry. A large piece of roof dangled over the upper windows. They raced to the other side, feet slipping in the mud and water. The rowboat was gone. The entire dock was gone. Windows that faced the bay were blown out, and fragments of yellow curtain and the vase Molly had put on the kitchen windowsill lay on the ground. Glass fragments were strewn everywhere, sparkling in the indifferent sunshine.

CHAPTER 31: Julienne

Julienne scrolled the online edition of *The Coastal Clarion*:

Reporters and photographers came from as far as New York City to cover what the meteorologists are calling the April Fool's storm, which began on March 31 and continued into the morning.

A photo of a swamped parking lot was captioned: *Water breached the town parking lot, now nicknamed "Little Fort Pond."*

A photo of a road with stalled cars had the caption: *The main road was impassable for hours after the storm subsided.*

And lastly, a photo of the remains of a house with a caption: *One of several homes that were lifted off their foundations, sections blown into Block Island Sound.*

———•◦•◦•———

The world outside their own window seemed unchanged except for a few Montauk daisy bushes damaged, a broken shutter, and a dangling section of gutter. In the distance, the chastened ocean rolled gently, as if the fury of the past two days had never happened. Still, from the calls that had gone back and forth all morning, Julienne knew the wreckage was everywhere. The bay side of town, the harbor area, and parts of downtown were a mess, trees upended, powerlines helter-skelter. It would take a while to assess the full extent of the damage. The reconstructed dune on the downtown beach was almost completely demolished, though it had given some protection to the buildings just behind it. Half the town had lost power.

She and Rob, up on their hill, had dodged a bullet. Not so for Billy and Molly. Her heart ached for them. Billy had broken down crying when he called to tell her what the storm had wrought . . . part of their roof off, windows blown out. They were meeting now with an insurance agent. Julienne had already made up the beds in the largest bungalow for them to live in until their house could be repaired.

She heard Rob's tread, heavy in work boots. They were going into town to lend a hand.

"Jonah and Max are busy fighting the battle of the Pequots and the Montauketts." Rob was smiling, pulling on thick leather gloves.

"You gave them your cell, right?" The boys were often allowed to be out and about on their own, but only for short spans of time. She and Rob would likely be gone all day.

"Yeah, and with a stern warning not to use it to download games. Ready?"

Julienne grabbed the loppers. The chainsaw was already stashed in the car.

At the community church, the volunteers were divided into groups. At times like these, everyone pulled together, rich and less rich alike. Julienne would help clear debris from the roads and load it into trucks. Rob went off with the chainsaw to help the town employees cut up the larger branches and trees that had come down. She saw Clancy across the room with a group that would be going house to house in the most affected areas to check on residents. She waved tentatively. Things still felt a bit awkward, despite their quasi-rapprochement at her gallery show.

By 4:00 p.m., Julienne was exhausted and ready to break for the day. Her back was sore, and she cursed herself for not bringing aspirin. As she waited outside the church for Rob, she put in an order at the pizza place and then called the boys. No answer. She was annoyed. They were likely playing outside and had left the phone indoors.

Rob's group pulled up. He jumped out of the truck as if he was still full of energy, his clothes and face covered with dark smudges.

He parked a kiss on her cheek. "How did it go?"

"Okay, but my feet and back are killing me. You look revitalized."

"Nothing like wielding a chainsaw to get the juices flowing."

"I ordered pizza. I called the boys, but they didn't answer."

"Time for another lecture."

On the way home, the warmth of the pies felt good against her legs. She closed her eyes and half-listened as Rob told her about all the downed trees and the piles of limbs stacked high along the sides of the roads for pickup.

They pulled up to the motel; no sign of the boys.

"I guess they're inside," Rob said.

"Boys!" She threw open the front door. "Food!"

There was no response. She turned to Rob. "Check in Max's room while I warm these up?" She had ordered pepperoni for the boys, usually not allowed, and another with veggies and extra cheese, because it was a pepperoni, extra-cheese kind of day.

Rob returned in a minute. "They're not here. Maybe Molly and Billy took them off somewhere? I'll give Billy a call."

"It's surprising they haven't been in touch, come to think of it." Worry was beginning to mix with her irritation. She began setting the table.

Rob punched in numbers on the phone. "Billy? By any chance do you have the boys? They seem to be AWOL." Rob made a thumb's down gesture at Julienne, then spoke into the phone. "Don't worry, I'm sure they'll be right back. How did it go with the insurance agent? Oh, shit. I'm so sorry. You'll stay with us as long as you need to." He continued to listen a few more minutes.

"How bad?" she asked, when he finished. She placed the pies on the table. As if on cue, each of them picked up a slice and began chewing.

"Bad. The insurance guy said that not only are the windows blown out, but the framing is wrecked. And more of the roof is torn off than they thought."

"Insurance will pay out, though?"

"Billy wasn't sure. He seems to have dropped some of his coverage."

She swallowed. "Well maybe there'll be some other kind of relief money available." She and Rob just looked at each other, knowing that was unlikely.

"Have they been in touch with the boys?"

"No. They're gathering up a bunch of their stuff and heading here."

"I'm starting to get worried." She grabbed her jacket. "I'll check my studio."

"I'll go down to the beach."

She ran up the walkway, her feet slipping on the gravel. Her studio was empty. She checked the tool shed and peered into the guest cottages, all unoccupied. No boys. She started to panic. She met Rob as he came back up the beach path, shaking his head.

Her pulse raced. "This is ridiculous. We better make some calls."

They called everyone they could think of, but no one had seen the boys.

"Would they have dared to go for a hike?" Julienne bolted to the foyer. Inside the front door, on the low bench where they left their footwear, there was no sign of Max's boots. "I can't believe this."

"Let's go." Rob headed out. "We should be able to find footprints with the ground this wet."

The north end of their property was bordered by low bushes and brambles; beyond it was the backyard of another property, and beyond that, the highway, on the other side of which was the southern edge of Hither Woods. At the perimeter of their property, Julienne pointed. On a narrow deer path through the brambles, two sets of boy-size boot prints were clearly visible.

"When I find him, I'm going to skin him alive," Rob said.

Julienne imagined him holding a miniature Max upside down like a dead rabbit.

Billy and Molly hadn't yet arrived, so Julienne texted an update to Billy, and they set off after the meandering footprints into the neighbor's yard and continued up to the highway.

Rob stood with his hands on his hips, watching as cars whizzed by, and repeated, "I'm going to skin him alive."

Julienne scanned the area. "They must have gone onto the trail you can access from Upland Road into Hither Woods and past the landfill." She pointed. "Max and I have walked in there."

They crossed the highway and followed the trail for a short way until the footsteps disappeared on the hard-packed ground. At the point where the trail forked, there was no way to guess which way the boys might have gone. They shouted, "Jonah, Max," and then pressed on, calling out at intervals and standing still to listen for a response, then continued down each of the other forks until these, too, broke off into yet other spurs.

Finally, they were stumped.

"I think it's time for the police," Julienne said.

Rob nodded. "It's going to start getting dark in a few hours."

⸻

Word reached every corner of Montauk. Two boys were missing. Though everyone was already overextended from helping out in the aftermath of the storm, dozens responded to the call to comb the woods. Voluntary firemen and the police stood around Bishops by the Sea, organizing teams of volunteers. Maps and flashlights were distributed.

Cars pulled in and parked haphazardly. Julienne felt calmer when she saw Grace Morgan marching toward her.

"I'll stay here in case the boys return on their own," she said, as a statement not a question.

Julienne felt a tap on her shoulder. Clancy.

"Max once told me about some bunkers in the woods that he and Jonah discovered. Maybe that's where they've gone."

Julienne grabbed Clancy's arm and rushed him over to where Rob and the police chief were conferring.

"Max mentioned he visits bunkers in the woods," Clancy said. "Does that make any sense?"

"There are old bunkers in Eddie Ecker Park," the police chief said. "That's nowhere near where they entered the woods, though. Still, worth checking out."

They regrouped and made a plan. The woods comprised more than 700 acres crisscrossed with extensive trails. The local hiking group would lead teams to branch out from where the boys had entered the woods, while Julienne and Rob would go directly by car to Eddie Ecker Park with the chief of police. She started to ask Clancy to ride with them, but he was already heading toward one of the search teams and she decided not to call him back.

Julienne couldn't stop fidgeting as they drove. Rob finally put his palm on her leg to stop the jiggling. They pulled up at Navy Pier on the outskirts of Hither Woods. There were dog walkers and a few fishermen. No boys. Visible in the far distance, where the fire had reached, were blackened stumps of trees.

The police chief consulted his GPS. "I have an idea where they might have accessed the bunkers."

A big man, he exuded a sense of assurance, which Julienne found calming.

"Coming from Upland Road and past the landfill, they likely would come out of the woods over the railroad tracks there." He pointed, then reversed the car and drove back along Navy Road to a pull-off she'd never noticed.

He stopped at a metal gate at the edge of the pull-off. An overgrown, cracked, concrete road was barely visible beyond the gate, leading into the woods.

"Hey, this is close to where Molly and Billy live!" Julienne said. "The boys might have figured out a way through Hither Woods to these woods, connecting them to each other." She was suddenly excited.

Just then, Billy's truck came careening down the road. Molly burst out before it had come to a complete stop. "You think they're in here?"

"Clancy said Max mentioned bunkers, and apparently there are some in here."

"Let's get going." The police chief grabbed a megaphone from the car and led them onto the old asphalt road.

The area was thickly forested and led sharply uphill. As they walked, they called out the boys' names every few minutes. They moved out of hardwood and into evergreens; it was suddenly quieter and darker, and Julienne became aware of the sounds of her own heavy breathing, the squelch of their shoes on the sodden ground, and the strong scent of muddy earth. She kept tripping over Rob's heels in her haste. Occasionally, Molly came abreast of them and grabbed and squeezed her hand.

The path led to a height of land that gave a view in the far distance of the entrance to Hither Woods, the bay still and lit below them with the soon-to-be setting sun. Molly pointed in the other direction.

"Look, you can almost see our house from here."

Only the remnants of their dock and a few pilings were visible. They pressed on, and moments later found themselves on the ridge of a carved-out bowl circled by woods.

"Wow," Billy said. "Who knew?"

"Former sandpit. The bunkers are near here." The police chief led them down the slope. He called out again through his megaphone.

They quickened their pace and around a bend appeared a concrete structure tucked deep into the side of the slope, its walls covered in graffiti. Julienne let out a cry. The police chief strode ahead, and she half-jogged to keep up, hair sticking to her perspiring forehead. The bunker was the kind of scary, beat-up place with no door and soil and plant life harvesting the roof. It was a place she would hesitate to enter but that would be a beacon to boys of Max and Jonah's age.

"Max, Jonah!" Billy yelled in his deep booming voice. As Julienne moved forward, the police chief blocked her progress.

"Please, Mrs. Bishop, let me go first."

Her heart smashed against her chest. Rob put his arm across her shoulders. She saw Molly grab Billy's hand.

The wait felt like forever.

"They're here and okay," the police chief called out from inside the bunker.

Julienne went limp against Rob. On the dirt floor, on a dirty rug remnant, the boys had clearly fallen asleep. They were now sitting up, hair mussed, befuddled.

"What possessed you to come here?" Julienne's voice quavered.

"We wanted to see everything after the storm." Jonah spoke rapidly. "We came to our clubhouse—where we play—and it was all gone. Burned. That's when Max realized . . . We were afraid, and so we ran away."

"Jonah, what are you talking about?" Billy yelled, as Rob was saying, "What clubhouse? What do you mean, burned?"

"The clubhouse is just . . . space." Jonah said. He and Max exchanged glances. Tears began to seep down Max's face. "Inside some trees."

"It was burned? You came here to hide? I'm not getting this." Julienne couldn't keep her voice under control.

Max's eyes were now swimming with tears. "Please don't be mad! We heat up water. On the cook stove. The old one from the camping set you threw away. I was careful. I promise! I didn't mean to do it."

"Wait. Are you talking about the fire in Hither Woods?" Molly was the first to approach the boys.

Shock kept Julienne rooted. Max was gulping for air, a wheeze audible.

"Max, are you saying it was you who set the fire?" Julienne said.

Jonah jumped up, his arms by his sides like a toy soldier. "Please don't put us in jail!"

"You're not under arrest, young men," the police chief said gravely. "But you gave your parents quite a scare by running off the way you did. Do you know the whole town is out looking for you?"

The boys bent their heads, two heavy flowers on thin-boy stalks, eyes downcast.

"I see you boys are sorry, and I'm sure your parents will find a proper punishment. But in the meantime, let's get you home."

——•—••—•——

The evening was an intense rush of hot baths, warmed-up pizza, and coaxing out the rest—the boys' hideaway in Hither Woods, the campfires they made. They hadn't been back to their hideaway during the winter, and when Max saw how the entire area around it was gone, burned to the ground, with the circle of stones remaining, they freaked out and ran away to the bunkers.

Having settled Molly, Billy, and Jonah in their bungalow, Julienne and Rob collapsed onto opposite ends of the sofa. She poured herself a second glass of wine.

"I guess we've given him too much freedom. *I've* given him too much," she amended. How was it possible they'd had no inkling of what Max was up to? She'd encouraged his roaming and exploring. Children needed to be outdoors to experience nature directly and to foster independence. Rob had only reluctantly agreed. He'd grown up in the suburbs at a time when parents kept kids close to home.

"I'm truly sorry." She waited, but he didn't chastise her.

"He wasn't hurt, that's the important thing." He got up to put another log on the fire. "I think he's learned his lesson. Thank God he's too young to face charges. Thankfully the fire wasn't worse."

"The fire." She shuddered. To think Clancy had been blamed when it was her own son. "We have to make it up to Clancy. And publicly." She was horrified and abashed.

"A letter in the *Clarion*?"

"And a thank you to everyone who came out to help." Julienne sagged deeper into the couch. "I'll apologize in person. Max will, too." She threw her head back and closed her eyes. "I'm completely wiped. I don't know what I would have done . . ."

"Don't go there, Jules."

"Still."

He lifted her legs to his lap and began to massage her right foot. "Just be grateful."

"Oh my god, that feels amazing." She leaned back, then sprang upright. "And Billy. What if their insurance won't cover the repairs?"

"Shush. Just close your eyes."

"What if insurers won't cover coastal homes anymore? I'm all for discouraging building on the coast, but the rich will manage to rebuild, and it'll be the regular people who will end up getting screwed."

"Julienne?"

"Yes?"

"Can you please, please, shut up?"

CHAPTER 32: Theresa

The morning after the April Fools' Storm, Theresa awoke with a jolt. The quiet was uncanny. Storm surge covered the entire pathway to the beach, trailers appearing to ride the skim of water like houseboats.

She pulled on boots and waded through the water to the beach. In both directions, the sand was completely gone, and what was left of the dune was ripped through, as if by a mighty cleaver.

She slogged along to where she had been doing her restoration work. Some of the seaweed mats were flung haphazardly on the slope while others were floating, coming and going with the tide. On the dune face, only a few strands of the grasses remained.

At the base of the dune, she picked up the tiny body of a sanderling. It had almost no weight, and its head was wobbly, partially detached. She touched the downy feathers with a finger. She could feel underneath where the bones were crushed and broken. It was hard to imagine the bird once raced on stick-like legs along the water's edge. She took a tissue from her jacket and swaddled the tiny body, crossing the sides over to form a neat packet, and placed it in her breast pocket, as if being near her heart would warm it back to life. She walked back to her trailer to bury the small bundle under a stunted pine tree. Then she went inside and called Pete Walker to tell him she was withdrawing her lawsuit.

In the following days, she reworked whatever seaweed mats were still viable, using her hands to mound wet sand around the remaining plugs of grass, tears of anger and frustration blooming now and again. She spread fiber mesh over the seaweed mats like a hairnet and shoveled sand on top. The storm season was over until fall. If they were lucky, the summer's littoral drift might help build the dunes back up.

Town board members came for a walkthrough of the devastation, and there were hopeful murmurings that federal money for a dune restoration might get allocated. Clancy contacted her to say he was working to get her the Moorlands payout and would let her know. Even so, Theresa felt an oppressive sense of hopelessness.

Occasionally, she allowed herself to imagine what she would do when she had the money to purchase a trailer of her own. An image of a room with pale wooden floors, high ceilings, and bright white curtains entered her mind, something she'd probably seen in an ad. She saw a sectional couch in heavy white cotton, and a hanging basket chair in the corner of the room, with a thick pillow patterned in a colorful tropical print. She closed her eyes and imagined a cat, smoky-gray from head to tail, with just a spot of white on its paws, leaping into the chair, setting it rocking.

She'd never made the trailer her own. She didn't want to waste money on something she didn't own. She'd put a red throw over the couch and tacked up two posters—one of surfers and one of the nearby bluffs—but those didn't mitigate the effect of the generic, used trailer, circa 1990. She'd never thought it would take so long to save up and never thought prices could escalate so rapidly. When her family moved to Montauk, a retired cop could afford one of the modest houses in town. Now only the hedge fund guys could pull that off.

A thump on her door broke her reverie. She glanced out the window. BB.

"Hey, what's up? Get another good find?"

He had been so excited the day before when he had unearthed a Swiss Army knife with his metal detector.

"There's a meeting. You gotta come." His foot on the bottom step jiggled. She hesitated. "Emergency—you *gotta* come," he repeated forcefully.

"For you, BB, I'll do it."

This would be a first. They fell in behind a stream of others hurrying to the community room. People grabbed folding chairs from where they were stacked against the wall and passed them out, setting them up in haphazard rows. The door kept banging open and shut as people entered.

Joe Tretorn did a cartoon-like double take when he spotted Theresa walking in. BB headed for the front row where the older residents were already seated, the ones who had been there since the early days, when the TP was all surfers and parties. It was hard to picture them going wild on the beach. Theresa leaned against the back wall.

"We have some unexpected bad news," Tretorn said. "A septic issue was spotted earlier today, and the whole system has to be inspected. It'll need to be completely cleaned and pumped. The tanks can fill up with silt and debris after storms when there's been flooding. Hopefully that's all that happened, and the pump-out will take care of it, but we could be looking at replacing the whole system. More immediately, there's a risk of sewage backup. The only way to prevent that is to relieve pressure on the system." He inhaled dramatically. "Reduce use."

There were groans throughout the room.

"I know, folks, I'm sorry. And because this poses a potential health issue, we think it would be wise to close completely for a bit. We know this is a hardship for our year-round residents, but we must ask you to work out plans to stay someplace else. We should know more by later today or tomorrow."

This was all just too much. Theresa left the meeting and went back down to the beach. She went east, rushing cove to cove to cove, stumbling over small rocks, as if to outrace what felt like a malevolent, almost biblical, curse: erosion, storm, and now sewage?

Where was she supposed to go? She couldn't even stay with Molly. Molly herself was homeless at the moment.

Finally, she stopped at one of the rockiest coves to catch her breath. She stared at the green sea lettuce swaying between the rocks in a tidal pool, following its gentle motion, taking long deep inhalations to slow her breathing. After a few minutes she threw her head back, stretched her arms wide, and slowly turned 360 degrees, searching the beauty around her as if for an answer as to where she could go.

And there it was.

CHAPTER 33: Clancy

On the wide sill in the kitchen, Clancy arranged and rear-ranged what was becoming a rock collection. It was surprising how many different types could be found on this part of Long Island. He had a sparkling flat gray one; a round, almost translucent, yellow one; a veined and marbled pink one; and his favorite, white with a thick band of green, as if seaweed had wrapped around it and become absorbed into the stone.

It was Max who had gotten him started on bringing back one specimen from every walk. Clancy had a horseshoe crab; orange, wafer-thin jingle shells; and the egg case of a skate, called a mermaid's purse, which he would have dismissed as debris. With the edge of a fingernail, Max slit open the black, crackling membrane to reveal an open chamber. All these things Clancy made note of in the empty pages left in Otto's notebooks.

Clancy heard Max and Jonah had been found, but no additional details. Julienne invited him over for lunch, saying she'd explain everything when he came. He was hoping to discuss the Moorlands parcel with her, but he worried it might still be too sensitive a topic.

The public hearing was now scheduled, and Julienne's environmental group was rallying people. A few days earlier, she had been in front of the post office with a petition in favor of preserving the parcel. He walked past without speaking because she was talking with someone, then saw her wince at what must have seemed like a slight.

His leave of absence was almost over, and with the Moorlands situation heating up, he had to come to a decision. Maybe he could learn something useful at the Town Planning Department. He should have just enough time to stop in before making it to lunch at Julienne's.

———•••••———

The clerk called over the planner on hand, a young man with a thin mustache and eager manner. The planner called up colorful maps on an enormous monitor and displayed the entire peninsula, the preserved parcels, and the residential sections. He described the zoning categories and talked about the overall vision of the town. From the excitement he showed as Clancy remained attentive, Clancy realized he must not often have such a willing audience. This work reminded him of his own, which he missed, with its guides, formulas, and finite factors to consider. Both fields were dry on the surface but represented so much life underneath.

There were multiple layers of complexity with so many systems, from waterways to flora and fauna and to roads and houses. They all interacted in complex, sophisticated ways. Overlapping worlds, of man and of nature. He'd never thought of towns in this way before. They were like living creatures or ecosystems.

"This was fascinating," Clancy said after an hour, standing up to go.

"I hope I've been helpful."

"You have," Clancy said with enthusiasm. Although there wasn't anything specific, he felt an odd sense of internal resolution, as if something had shifted, clicking into place.

Interconnections, he thought, walking back to his car. It was what resonated. Maybe he'd been approaching the decision the wrong way, a binary way. Affordable housing versus luxury homes. Holistic center versus preservation. Perhaps the answer lay in something more like the nebulous feeling he had right now, of everything weaving together in an organic way. *Organic*, he thought. *Garden.*

Something in him lit up, like one of those maps where you pressed a button to illuminate a town. He clicked open his car, laughing to himself. He wasn't making any sense.

———◦•◦•◦———

Clancy walked the gravel path to Julienne's studio. The bushes were beginning to bud, and there was a slight green tinge to the grass, although the air still had a sharp, chilly edge.

She was across the room in front of a canvas, her back to him, arm slightly raised, paintbrush cocked, conveying a paradoxical quality of stillness and energy. She radiated a sense of calm centeredness around an inner fire, like the paper lantern with a candle inside he'd once seen released over the ocean. He had been fearful it would burst into flames, but it just went higher and higher, like a beacon, until it vanished.

She started. "You're here!" She plunged her brush into a coffee can and wiped her hands vigorously on a rag. Her solemn expression took him aback.

"Work not going well?"

She reached for his hands. "That's not it." She grimaced. "Clancy, I'm so sorry. I have a huge apology to make."

"For what?"

"For one, my son. He'll be doing his own apologizing later. He started the fire in Hither Woods. Inadvertently. I can't believe what you've gone through, when it was Max who was responsible."

"*Max?*" Clancy's hands tightened on Julienne's. "What? How?"

She gently withdrew her hands. "He and Jonah apparently

had a sheltered place in the woods where they played. They sometimes lit a camp stove."

Realization dawned on Clancy. "That day Max and I were playing LEGOs? He seemed worried he might have set the fire. I didn't take him seriously. He has such an imagination. I'm sorry. I probably should have mentioned it to you."

"Probably." She frowned for a brief second. "But it wouldn't have changed anything." She pushed aside a stack of drawings and placed a tray with wrapped sandwiches at the other end of her long worktable. They scraped two wooden folding chairs across the floor and sat opposite each other. She passed him a bottle of water and untwisted the cap of another, took a long swig, then banged the bottle down on the table. "I'm furious with him for using matches, for not being careful. And most of all, for what this did to you."

He curbed an impulse to touch her and opened his bottle instead. "How did this come out? Wait—did Max run away *on purpose*?"

Julienne flicked away a fleck of dried blue paint. "They went to their play area, which they hadn't been to over the winter. Everything was burnt down to the ground. They realized what had happened, freaked, and ran away to the bunkers."

"Jeez, poor kid!"

"You're too sympathetic."

Clancy made a gesture of dismissal. "So that's how the Bishops by the Sea matches got there," he mused.

"Yes. They were in a tin box that had been in your bungalow."

"I don't remember it." Max must have taken it one of the times he visited Clancy.

"There were lots of fingerprints on it, not just yours. It was clear there was a kind of campsite. The police didn't have to treat you like a criminal."

Clancy rubbed his nose, which itched slightly from the dust and dried paint. He was tired of feeling like a victim. He took a long drink of water. "Thank goodness the fire wasn't worse or that Max wasn't injured."

Her eyes closed briefly. "I know. Apology number two. I'm sorry for being such a hard-ass about Moorlands."

There was a paintbrush under the table. Clancy retrieved it, then ran his finger along the brush's stiff bristles before handing it over. "I was more secretive than I needed to be."

"Can you tell me now, if it's okay to ask?" She offered him the tray.

There was no sting to the question. "Actually, I'd like your opinion." He took a sandwich from the tray. "I told you that each of the partners wants something different, and so whoever I side with, wins. It's Pete Walker who's pushing for the luxury development."

"Walker? A tough nut, from what I've heard." She took a bite of her sandwich; a dribble of tomato juice trickled down her chin.

"I've not been able to figure out what Otto wanted. And I feel an obligation to get the most money for Theresa, which may mean letting the subdivision go forward. That's why it's so complicated." He took a bite—avocado and tomato—as he waited for her response.

"Look, a subdivision means more infrastructure, more of a burden on the community. Not to mention the loss of habitat." She brushed her mouth with a napkin. "Land is irreplaceable. Maybe think of it that way."

"Even just a few acres of very ordinary land?"

"Even just a few acres of ordinary land." She gave him a slight smile. "You said you didn't want me pressuring you."

"I didn't want to give undue weight to anything you said before I studied the issue."

"What do you mean, undue weight?"

He just looked at her. Was he really going to have to spell this out? "What you say matters. Too much. I didn't want to let my feelings get in the way."

Her face suddenly bloomed with color. "Clancy, I'm sorry if I've—"

"No, not at all," he said hastily, "you haven't. Please don't worry." The way she had depicted him in her painting—sad, alone, wounded—had made everything clear. He harbored no illusions about the nature of her feelings for him, not anymore.

She leaned forward. "I feel warmly toward you, you do know that."

"And me, too. That's all I meant."

"Oh, okay, good." She dug her fingers into her curls. "Sorry for jumping to conclusions. God, how embarrassing."

Somehow, he was laughing then, too, her embarrassment dissipating his own. For a moment, he considered letting her believe she had simply been flattering herself.

"It'd be a different story if you weren't . . . you know. Then you'd have to fight me off."

He said it lightly, and she laughed, but her face colored again. They both glanced away and took refuge in their water bottles.

A shaft of light cut across the room, as if curtains had been pulled aside, a sign that he should leave. "Thank you so much for lunch. I'm really glad we had this talk." He stood.

"Me, too. Really glad. I'm glad we're friends again."

"You've been a tremendous help to me."

Julienne walked him to the door. He felt her attention wandering back to her work, so what she said next surprised him.

"You've made an impact on me, too."

"Really? How?"

"You've helped me see some things differently." Her expression was almost defiant, and her cheeks colored. "About, well . . . what really matters to me."

He nodded, studying her expression. Her marriage she meant. Possibly. He decided it wasn't wise to probe further. "I'm glad."

The door closed softly behind him. Outside the sky was shockingly alive with color. From here on the high point of land, he could see up and down the coast, and the sun at this time of year was setting far to his right. He stood a moment soaking it in, a mantle of peace, tinged with both relief and sadness, settling over him.

CHAPTER 34: Molly

The April Fool's storm made everything simple.

In the days after the storm, any lingering hopes Molly and Billy had of keeping their house were completely dashed. Their insurance claim was swiftly denied. To save money after his parents died, Billy had kept only flood insurance, and their damage was determined to be from wind and rain. Clancy helped them file an appeal but said their chances of succeeding weren't good.

Repairs needed to be done quickly or the house would be lost. Julienne and Rob offered to lend them money, but Billy felt uncomfortable accepting.

"We wouldn't be able to pay it back unless by a miracle we win the appeal," he said to Molly.

In the weeks after the storm, they tacked tarps over the areas of the roof where it was busted and put plywood over the windows. Molly had gotten good wielding a hammer and a drill, but even so, the damage and the increasing smell of mold made the house more depressing than she would have thought possible.

Finally, all they had left to do was pile up the loose planks that remained of the pier. Splintered bits of wood still washed back up even weeks after the storm. Their lawn was mud and smashed-down grass.

They stood at the water's edge. Billy ran a hand over his face. She'd never seen him so defeated. Lines seemed to have formed from his nose to his mouth overnight.

He started to say something, then just shrugged. She knew he couldn't bring himself to say the words, to disappoint her. It was up to her.

"We have to sell." She pressed her fist between her breasts, pressing the pain back into her body.

Billy raked his fingers through his overlong hair, creating two unruly clumps. He hadn't wanted to waste money on a haircut. "I know how much this place means to you."

She began to tear up and turned away so he couldn't see. If anything, the house had come to matter even more in the weeks they'd been living at Bishops by the Sea. Yet it wasn't her family who'd lived here for generations. Here Billy had stood as a little boy holding his father's hand, a father Molly would never know. Here Billy was lifted into his first boat. Here Jonah scraped a knee, his blood soaked up by the wood of the dock to dry in the sun.

Her own upbringing had been bland compared with his: a neighborhood where she could ride her bike up and down the block of lookalike ranch houses, all with the same rhododendrons and azaleas; and a school where the teachers paid attention to every child, their artwork displayed in the halls. She lived the epitome of the middle-class suburban dream, something she knew to be immensely grateful for. What she craved, though, was what she had found here. Billy's house was saturated with history, and living here, she'd been part of that. Living here she was connected all the way back, even if only secondhand. This past vibrated; this past carried her note. Yet this was not her legacy. What was needed was what would be best for Billy and Jonah.

"There's no other way." She put her hand on his arm. "You know it. I know it. It's what will give you—us—a new life."

"Are you sure?" His voice went up in pitch. "Are you one hundred percent sure?"

Her heart raced, and she pressed her fist against her chest again. "I guess it was inevitable. This just moves up the timing a bit, right?"

"Oh Molly." His face opened up, and he pulled her to him, pressing her into his sweat-soaked canvas jacket, its texture rough against her cheek.

"I hate this," he said into her hair. Then his voice changed. "I hate to let him win."

Molly's laugh was muffled against the cloth. "We're beyond concerning ourselves about him."

He sighed deeply and pulled back from her to stare into her eyes. "We'll find something great. My parents were friendly with Marge O'Shea, who works at Ocean Realty. Maybe she can deal with the whole thing, and we won't have to talk to him directly."

Ms. O'Shea's office was downtown, next to the florist. From the bunny rabbits and daffodils in the window, Molly realized with a shock it was almost Easter.

O'Shea came toward Billy, arms outstretched. She was tall, her hair in a glossy gray-blond French twist. She carried herself with the confidence of a woman who had been beautiful when young. "Billy, so good to see you. I've been meaning to reach out and see how you and Jonah are doing."

"We're good, we're fine," Billy said, his voice too loud. Even now, Molly knew, his emotions from his parents' deaths were too raw. "This is my girlfriend, Molly."

"Nice to meet you, Molly. Sit, both of you, please. Tell me how I can help."

"Like I told you on the phone, we had a lot of damage, much more than we can afford to repair. There's a developer,

Theodore Miloxi, who's been after us to buy the house. We don't know whether to sell to him or if there are other options."

O'Shea brought the two sides of her elegant cashmere cardigan together across her chest. "From what I've heard, his group has contracts in the works for several houses along your stretch of waterfront."

"Does that mean we have to sell to him?"

"In essence, yes. I doubt another buyer will want to get in the middle of that."

"Could you handle things for us, then? We don't want to deal with him directly."

"Of course, Billy, I'd be delighted to. I'm truly sorry you can't stay put, but with what they have planned, the area won't feel the same anyhow. At least this way, you're looking at a significant amount of money that should set you up in life."

———————

Their mood was somber driving back to Bishops by the Sea. They agreed to hold off telling Jonah about selling the house. It had been an especially unsettled time for him. He frequently woke Molly with nightmares, and she would sit up with him, listening to the sound of the ocean surf, a sound so different from the lapping waters of the bay, until he fell back asleep. Then she'd step outside to look at the stars to calm herself before slipping quietly back into the bungalow. Only Billy slept soundly, as if, now that they were giving up the house, all his cares had been relieved, a weight taken from him.

When Ms. O'Shea called to tell them the amount of the offer—1.3 million—Molly was staggered.

"It's crazy. The house is tiny and old!"

"It was always a teardown, Molly," Billy said.

Molly winced at the word, as if it were her own body to be torn apart.

They agreed to set aside $300,000 in a college fund for Jonah, another $200,000 for savings, and to use the rest to purchase a new house outright, all cash, no mortgage, because Billy's parents taught him that a mortgage was a noose around the neck. With no steady fulltime jobs, a mortgage was unlikely, anyway.

They headed back to Ms. O'Shea to look at properties.

"We'd like something on the water," Billy said, but O'Shea just shook her head. "Oh no, Billy, that's not possible."

"What do you mean?"

"Even if you were able to use the total from the sale, you couldn't buy anything on the water. With a mortgage you could swing a down payment on a more expensive house, but then you'd have steep monthly payments. You'll have to adjust your expectations just a bit. There are some nice places I'm sure you'll like."

She took them to see a small house in Hither Woods that had been newly renovated, but it was on a tiny lot without any land. They saw a modern home near the golf course that had no character. It became clear, as they looked at one listing after another, that they couldn't afford even a distant view of water. There was a house in Ditch Plain two blocks from the beach, but it needed a huge amount of work. The Realtor offered to show them a few houses farther west, but those would mean leaving Montauk, a deal-breaker.

<hr/>

Days and weeks went by, and still they didn't find a home.

"Stay as long as you like," Julienne and Rob said, but come summer, Molly and Billy knew they would need the income from the bungalow.

Ms. O'Shea urged them to rethink their numbers. "Just tinker a bit," she said.

Molly brought out the graph paper. "Should we alter the college fund or the savings, or both? After all, the house will go up in value." They talked late into the night, and the next day told Ms. O'Shea they could go as high as $800,000 and still afford the taxes.

In the afternoon she called, sounding excited.

"I think I've got one you'll be happy with. It's just listed for $795,000."

The house was a small two-story not far from the docks. It was on a slight rise of land and on a bigger lot than most. The deck out back overlooked the neighbors' trim lawns and wooden porch furniture. It was like any suburb anywhere. There was no hint of the sea or the scents and sounds of the bay and woods Molly loved.

"Landscaping would give you a bit more privacy," Ms. O'Shea said. "And there's plenty of sun if you wanted to put in a garden."

"What do you think?" Billy seemed excited. "Could we work with this?"

She nodded. It was the best they could do.

"You know, with sea level rise, it's smart to be away from the shore," he joked. "Eventually the water will come to us."

"We should get a boat, then," Molly joked back, but the words burned as they left her mouth. They'd never found their rowboat, just a washed-up piece of severed rope. She had rolled it up carefully and taken it with her when they left.

 *Spring*

THE HAMLET IS GOLDEN in the late afternoons when the parents pick up their kids from after-school activities. The landscapers and construction and retail workers are already heading west past the Hamptons, to the less fashionable towns where living is cheaper. For those lucky enough to make their home in this town, it's time to take the dogs to the beach for a run.

Shad festoons the hills and dunes with white blossoms, and the woods are filled with migrating warblers. Deep in the Point Woods, in the vernal pools, salamanders emerge from under the thick, matted leaf mast to lay their eggs. Skunk cabbages unfurl their leaves, while in the Napeague dune plain, the osprey carry new twigs to refresh last year's nests. By early May, the fluke are running, and deer have dropped their fawns.

CHAPTER 35: Clancy

The Moorlands Group had come together to walk their property, the men in boots, windbreakers, and light-colored pants tucked into their socks against ticks. Pete Walker carried a can of Permethrin and insisted on spraying everyone's legs. Lyme disease was on the rise; there were so many variants of tick-borne diseases, the doctors couldn't keep up.

Clancy understood ticks were the result of too many deer, the habitat seriously out of whack. Hunting was probably the only solution; even so, he bought a bumper sticker that read, SHOOT TICKS, NOT DEER.

"Wow, the border that got scorched by the fire is already revegetating itself." Tim gestured to the distance with a hiking stick.

"This parcel is not going to mushroom into a primeval forest. You think this acreage is worth preserving? For what? The fucking deer?" Pete said.

Clancy groaned. This would be so much easier without Walker.

Pete turned to Clancy. "We've waited long enough."

Without the familiar comfort of a tie, Clancy bunched up the fabric of his jacket against his neck. "I want to wait until the public hearing. I'd like to hear what the community has to say."

"Are you out of your fucking mind? The 'community' is never going to vote for a development!"

"Well, there you go."

"It's not such a bad idea to see how people feel." Tim poked with his hiking stick at the muddy ground.

"How people feel? How people *feel*? That's no way to make a business decision! I don't care that Theresa Nolan dropped her suit, *I'll* sue you—for being an asshole."

"Let's not overreact." Harve put up his hands. "It's not a terrible idea to gauge the temperature of the community. We don't want to make enemies of our neighbors."

Above came a honking sound. As one, they craned their necks to watch a flock of geese flying southeast in a tight formation.

"I know I've taken longer than you'd like," Clancy said, "but until the hearing, there's no reason to rush. I'll give you a decision within a week of that."

As he drove back to Otto's, Clancy had to admit Pete was justified in being annoyed at his refusal to make a decision. He wondered if it was indecisiveness that held him back or loyalty to Otto. Or sheer dislike of Pete Walker.

The other day, he'd gone for a walk along the coves near the lighthouse. He started at the trailer park, curious to see where Theresa lived. The mobile home community had its charms, a free and easy vibe he thought suited her. The legal complexities of getting her share of the Moorlands parcel had proved difficult, and so Clancy had done the paperwork to take ownership of Otto's house. The loan would come through soon.

His eyes followed the swishing movement of bright-green seaweed in one of the coves, where masses of mussels clung to the rocks just past the high-water mark. He'd never seen mussels outside a bowl before. He watched as the water surged against the rocks, awed at how tenaciously the little mollusks clung, the strength of their will against the ocean's pull.

Tenacity . . . a trait he admired. Julienne was tenacious in her fierce desire to keep Montauk the place she'd loved as a child, the muse to her art. Theresa was tenacious as well in opposition to her father. He, on the other hand, seemed to be refusing to budge for no ostensible reason.

Returning from his meeting, he walked to the patio on the side of what was now his house, drawn by the familiar *dee dee dee* of the chickadees, flicking their wings as they went back and forth from the feeder to a nearby branch. These days, the riot of bird song began around 4:00 a.m. and built to a complete cacophony. He would lie awake, concentrating, trying to commit specific songs to memory so he could look them up later. He'd fall back asleep and not be able to recall a single song come morning.

The meadow in the distance was turning a light shade of green, and the trees at the edge were fuzzy with new growth. Theresa's situation had forced his hand, and he felt both relief at having finally come to a decision as well as immense gratitude for Otto's gift. He realized he'd been growing attached. He'd bought seeds at the hardware store and was thrilled by how many birds flocked to the feeder. He enjoyed standing outside on the patio to experience the freshness of early morning, the warmth of midday, the bite of evening cold. He'd even been reading up on gardening, a way to honor Otto's memory, considering kale and lettuce, and, of course, tomatoes.

He walked over to the garden. The things coming up might be weeds; he had no way of knowing. Maybe they were destined to be zucchinis or cucumbers. He tugged at a grass-like stalk; it slid out from the earth easily. He sniffed but didn't get much odor. It was strange being so near to the ground, looking at it closely. He wasn't sure he wanted to encounter the worms and bugs that were underneath, but he was curious how it all worked. This blade of grass or nascent vegetable had the tiniest threads of root, so slender it seemed impossible it could serve a crucial function. And what about bacteria and all the rest, invisible and silent as they went about their work?

Otto talked in his notes about how he felt a deep connection and sense of spirituality from working in the garden, a sense of wonder at the natural world. The lyrics of a song came to Clancy with the refrain "back to the garden." Could this be what Otto meant by "retreat"? Retreat "to the garden?" Maybe he meant the word figuratively, as a symbol of a simpler, more innocent way of life. Maybe he meant it literally—Moorlands as a farm or a garden. The thought stunned him. He recalled his feeling after he spoke with the town planner, of interconnections, an organic approach to Otto's land.

He stood, still holding the blade of grass; it struck him he had overlooked talking to the one person who might know.

———————

Theresa didn't respond immediately, but her breathing was audible through the phone. Then she said, "Have you been to the Walking Dunes?"

She picked him up in town. Soon after they reached the Napeague stretch, she turned onto a narrow road and parked where the road ended abruptly at the water. The sand was a burnt-orange shade.

"Sediments of iron, from some old bog," she said.

In the distance the enclosed bay opened into the Sound. The quiet was almost absolute.

"It's so still," he said.

The surface of the water, the color of pewter, was as flat as cellophane stretched taut over a bowl. A few waterfowl rested out on the water near a boat. A fisherman in a plaid shirt raised a hand in salute.

"It's usually much windier," Theresa said. "It's popular with wind surfers. They skim along the water like ice skaters."

Clancy laughed at the image. He started down the beach, but she said there was a trail to follow first. She pulled two pamphlets from a small box attached to a post and handed him one, then led the way on a sandy path up through stunted pitch pines. She was wearing jeans and a long brown-and-orange-checked shirt that set off her auburn hair, which she had twisted on top of her head with a large clip.

The pamphlet was an illustrated guide with text and numbers matching small markers along a nature trail. They made a quick steep ascent and emerged on a ridge. A series of desert-like dunes stretched in all directions, great sweeping slopes of sand. A moonscape.

"This is impossible."

A quick smile crossed her face, and he saw she became even more beautiful when her face lit up. He was surprised she seemed so relaxed. He had expected she would be more awkward with him after their last encounter, when she'd told him about her abuse as a child. Instead, she seemed less distant, as if a layer of scales had been sloughed off.

He read aloud. "'Three coastal parabolic dunes, which reach heights of eighty feet, are in constant flux. They are walking in a southeasterly direction, devouring vegetation as they go.' I don't understand."

She pointed. "That's a pine in the process of getting buried."

Branches rested like vines upon the sand.

"We're literally walking on top of a bunch of sand-covered pine trees?"

She nodded. "Spooky."

She walked on, moving with the languid grace that was in such contrast with her brusque personality. They emerged from the dunes into an open expanse covered with tiny yellow blossoms. He felt as if they'd been transported into some other time and place.

"This is exquisite."

She startled, as if surprised he would be moved. Their glances caught and held, slender as filaments, a clear moment of connection.

"There are cranberries here in the fall. I gather some every year." The wisp of smile returned, and he felt, as if he were a tuning fork, a vibration, an uncanny sensation of knowing her.

They passed through bearberry and other low scrubs, and eventually the trail led back to the water. They continued along the shore, which curved toward the other side of the harbor, to the final narrow spit of land between the bay and the Sound. The sand here was chunky with stones, the breeze suddenly stiff.

A log was placed conveniently where they could sit with their backs to the wind.

"You wanted to talk."

She picked up a skimmer and with a deft motion sent it skipping. He followed suit, but his stone landed close by with a loud *clunk*.

"I wanted to let you know that we'll be able to get most of your payout. We won't know the exact amount until the decision on the property." He didn't want to let on that he was privately financing this with a mortgage against the house. "The money will be transferred to your account by the end of the week."

Her topaz gaze was like that of a cat's. "You could have told me that over the phone."

"You're right. I'm still at an impasse in figuring out what your father would have wanted for the Moorlands parcel. It occurred to me that I've asked everyone their opinion—friends, partners, brother-in-law, people at the town—and didn't think to ask you."

From her surprise he saw he'd fully broken the surface of her impassivity. "Me? You didn't want to let me vote the shares."

"Despite everything, I think you're the one who knew him best."

She turned away with an expelled breath. She picked up several more rocks and zinged them at the water. Off they went, skimming the surface, one, two, three skips each, in quick succession.

She finally sat down and turned to him. "What do you want to know?"

"I think your father wanted to find a bigger kind of concept for the property. Would that make sense?"

She removed her clip, shook out her hair, and secured it again. "Maybe. I've never thought about it, but he did talk about 'purpose' and 'community.' I mean, I think he tried his best with people, but we were an abstraction. Like I was 'daughter,' and he operated along some notion of what a daughter should be. So yeah, I could see him putting his focus on the whole of Montauk. A something 'bigger.'" She picked at a tear in her jeans. "But what, exactly?"

Clancy pulled Otto's letter from his wallet. "He left me a note saying he had a new idea. The rest of the sentence is gone. Some liquid spilled on it. Look at the final word."

She took the paper from him. "Retreat?"

"Any idea what it could mean?"

"Retreat from what?" She frowned, still picking at her jeans, enlarging the hole over her right knee. "No . . . sorry."

"Do you think he would have been in favor of a garden? A retreat back to nature?"

She threw her head back with a guffaw. "Way too hippie-ish. Impractical, too. Can't imagine the partners going for that. There'd be no money in it, right?"

She handed him back the letter, and her lack of enthusiasm deflated his own. He had been so hopeful she would say something to clarify everything.

He brushed sand off his pants and stood. "You've given me more insight, anyhow."

They headed back along the shore. The breeze had picked up and ruffled the water like a shiver on its surface, yet the air was warm for May. They removed their sneakers and sloshed along at the water's edge. He'd forgotten a cap; the sun on his head was intense.

She stopped abruptly. "Let's swim."

"Isn't it too cold?"

Theresa just laughed. He accepted her dare. Without another word, she stripped to a bikini and waded out. He pulled off his clothes, keeping on his underwear. The sand was like velvet on the soles of his feet. Her skin was golden in the light. She dove in, and her hair fanned around her like an anemone under water.

He swam out farther and farther until he warmed up. Then he rested, treading water and taking in the expanse of the bay, the distant spot they had walked to, the dunes lining the shore. He flipped onto his back and floated, listening to the lapping of water, the cry of a gull.

Theresa was out of the water, already hiking up her jeans as he swam back. She was matter-of-fact about her body under his gaze. He could tell she was aware of her beauty but somehow impatient with it.

He was slightly aroused and turned his back to pull on his pants.

"Clancy, what happened?"

Her finger, cold from the water, ran down his back. He was more shocked by her tone than her touch. It took him a second to realize what she was asking. His scars.

"A bit of a rough childhood."

"You weren't kidding, what you told me?"

"About suffering? No, I wasn't kidding." He gave a little laugh. "Reform-school boys. Sometimes they take it out on younger kids."

They were standing close; her face was almost white; she was clearly shaken. "But your whole back. Lashes? And cigarette burns?"

"The pain is long gone," he said, but at the words, he felt his eyes fill. Embarrassed, he bent down to pick up his shirt.

"Let me."

She held his shirt out and he put his left and then his right arms into the sleeves. He trembled suddenly with the cold. Then her arms were around him, and she held him tightly. Just holding. They swayed a moment in each other's arms.

The feeling of comfort was almost too much to bear.

CHAPTER 36: Julienne

Julienne searched through her closet, enjoying the clacking of the hangers smacking against each other as she slid them along the bar. She and Rob hadn't been out in ages. After the stresses of the storm and the crisis with Max, they needed a respite. Her hand stopped at a denim shirt-dress, and her mind shifted to Clancy; he often wore a chambray shirt this exact shade of blue. Her hand stilled on the fabric, thinking about the awkward exchange at the end of their lunch together in her studio. How heedless she'd been with him. From the start, he had been so attentive and admiring, and she had reveled in it. She hadn't considered the signals she might have been sending. Or maybe she didn't want to admit to her own attraction. Her face flushed. She shifted through a few more garments and pulled out a black, flowered skirt. Rob had always liked her in this.

She searched her bureau drawers for something to wear with the skirt. She had known things were a bit askew with Rob, but she hadn't wanted to deal with it, hoping things would right themselves on their own. This was a wake-up call. She had to ask herself, *What am I not getting from my marriage that left me so needy of Clancy's attention?* She sighed. Clearly there was work she had to do . . . work she and Rob had to do.

She was scrunching up her wet hair after her shower when he walked in. She smiled at him in the mirror. She needed to smile at him more. He was wearing a black shirt and pressed jeans.

"I love that shirt on you," she said.

His face registered such pleased surprise that she felt chastened.

"You look pretty hot yourself," he said, and she laughed, glancing down at her tatty robe.

"I just need a few minutes. Come give me a kiss first." He crossed the room. His lips tasted of salt and vinegar. "Potato chips!"

"Don't talk dirty."

She laughed, and something loosened inside her chest. Things could be put right. "Just wait till later," she whispered.

———◆·•·◆———

The party was sponsored by the chamber, a fundraiser for several of the family-owned businesses hurt most by the April Fool's storm. Dressed in her skirt and a silky top, with a shawl over her arm that made her feel elegant, Julienne took Rob's hand as they entered the recently refurbished Low Tide.

They were seated at a roomy banquette with a couple they didn't know well, Louise, a bank manager, and Jeff, a Realtor.

Louise glanced around and said, "They did such a beautiful job."

The restaurant, previously one of the funkiest places in town, with low ceilings and dark wood paneling, now had a pan-Asian menu and décor to match. Wallpaper depicted a trellis and vines, botanical tiles, and bamboo in large tubs.

"I sort of miss the old place," Julienne said.

"You must admit it was a dump."

"True, but I liked that you could go out back with your drink and kick off your shoes on the sand."

The waitress arrived with their menus. "How long have you been a Realtor, Jeff?" Rob asked.

"Got my license about fifteen years or so ago. I had no idea back then how hot the market was going to get."

Julienne couldn't tell from his tone if he minded. "How do you feel about that?"

"When I started, it was great. You were helping local families that wanted to sell, or people who had been coming here for vacation and wanted to buy. Now it's hedge fund guys and LLCs. Companies like mine are getting bought out by the big firms. Forces enormous competition."

"Are you in favor of a moratorium on building, then?" Julienne asked.

The waitress returned with a bottle of wine and offered it to Jeff. He took a taste, nodded.

"Not particularly," he said. "A bit overkill."

"The wine?" Rob joked.

"What do you think a moratorium would solve?" Louise asked Julienne.

"I think we've reached our carrying capacity, and a moratorium would give the town time to do serious planning."

"Look, change is the only constant. Development is inevitable," Jeff said.

Julienne glanced at Rob, wishing he would say something.

"You environmentalists idealize land," Louise said with a laugh. "Now look what's happened. Exorbitant land values that only the rich can afford. You have only yourselves to blame."

Julienne felt her face flame. Louise put her hand on her arm. "Just kidding."

"I just don't get why, if we all love what we have here, it's so impossible to imagine preserving it as it is." Julienne couldn't keep her voice from rising. There was silence.

Rob placed his hand on the back of her head; it was a gesture she usually found intimate. She twisted away.

"We don't mean to say that we want our town to become a fossil," Rob said. "We want a living, breathing place."

"Exactly," Jeff said. "Change can keep a community vital."

Julienne took a deep breath. "How can the town stand up to the big money without more controls in place?"

"It's a balance," Louise said. "Remember, a moratorium would hold up the projects of regular people, too. What's needed is scalpels, not blunt instruments."

"Take the Moorlands group," Jeff put in. "They're all locals who've held onto that parcel for over a decade. They have a right to see their plans come to fruition. A moratorium would be unfair for them. Imagine if you and Rob wanted to renovate. How would you feel having your plans held up?"

"Don't make this personal, Jeff," Louise said.

The waitress came with their orders, and they talked of other things. Julienne's body felt stiff with discomfort; she poured herself a second glass of wine and downed it.

As soon as she and Rob were in their car on the way home, she burst out, "I wish you could have backed me up in there."

He kept his eyes on the road. She stared at his profile, his strong nose, defined chin.

"I thought I was helping clarify your position," he finally said. "You came across—"

"What?"

"Maybe a little overreacting."

"Everyone else is under-reacting! Overdevelopment is sinking sharp teeth into this place, and it's going to bleed out in agonizing slowness, and no one is going to pay attention until it's too late."

"You know I basically agree with you." He paused.

"What is it? Out with it."

"Wholesale rejection of all development just isn't feasible. There have to be compromises. We have to be a bit more strategic."

"We're going to end up with a Disneyesque theme park!"

He had the temerity to laugh, and then, as if to make up for it, reached for her hand. She slapped it away.

"I don't mean to laugh. That was just a funny image. You have such an imagination."

They walked in silence into the house. Inside, she checked on Max while he drove the sitter home. She put on a long T-shirt and crawled into bed without waiting for him.

She was still awake when he returned but kept her back to him as he slipped in beside her. Tentatively he snuggled up and put his arm over hers.

"Jules?"

She didn't answer.

"I know you're awake. I'm sorry. You're right. I should have done more to back you up."

She let this sink in, then rolled over to face him. "You mean it?"

"I was a bit of a coward."

"I don't want you to agree with me if you really don't."

"Jules, I know what this place means to you. I've always known. From the first time I saw you cross-legged on a rock—do you remember? You were on that boulder completely oblivious that the tide was coming in around you, as if you were an extension of the sea. I understood in that moment you were as much a part of this place as the cliffs and the rocks and the sand. I understood you would never want to leave."

There was a throbbing in her throat. She forced herself to ask. "And is that okay?"

He stroked her cheek with a finger. "Yes. It will always be okay."

⊷⊶⊷

In the morning Julienne went down to the beach to paint, her brain alive with impulse. Rob had taunted her about her imagination. She would use her imagination then. Her mind circled back to the conversation in the restaurant.

She smooshed ultramarine violet and cobalt blue directly from the tube onto a canvas, then slashed her palette knife into the thick globs.

Years back, when some in town began to be alarmed about how things were changing, others said, "You have to have growth. You can't hold back time." If they had known what was to come, maybe they would have acted differently. They hadn't, perhaps, had enough imagination.

She was making a mess of her canvas, but it felt good. She moved the palette knife back and forth in a wave-like motion. If it was immutable that people would always choose an immediate interest over what would be best in the long term, there could be no hope. She slashed on thick bands of black. She chose to believe instead that there was something fundamental at fault in the system. Then it could be challenged and corrected, given the political will.

She feathered in tiny vertical strokes of white into the black. At the end of the dinner, as they were leaving the restaurant, Jeff had asked, "What if someone offered you five million for Bishops. Would you turn it down? When you have Max's future to consider?"

"Jeff, really!" Louise slapped his arm.

"It's a fair question, one I would hope they would ask themselves. It's why so many of the old families are cashing out. They love it here, but unless they want to destroy their own financial futures, they *have* to sell."

It *was* a fair question. Julienne didn't know what she and Rob would do if economic forces shifted to that point. There was something very wrong with a world that created such an equation and locked people into it. Julienne took a step back from her painting; she had really overdone it with the colors. The painting was so loud and chaotic, it screamed.

She propped it against the trunk of the little pitch pine and placed another blank canvas on her easel.

She worried all the time about what the future would be for Max. She worried not about money but about him losing access to the wild, to a place in balance with nature.

She put dollops of burnt sienna, burnt umber, iron oxide, and pure white onto her palette, then dipped her paintbrush into the colors and onto the canvas without mixing. She could never quite capture the color of wet sand. It always drove her crazy. She put down the paintbrush and walked to the water's edge, scooped up a tablespoon's worth of sand and smoothed the grains in her palm.

Sand was just tiny particles ground down, specks that could be traced back to the Ice Age, when massive glaciers retreated, leaving behind rocks, huge and small, in their wake. Up close, the particles were coral and blue and gray and white, yet all blended into beige to the eye. The sand came and went during the year, narrowing and then widening the beaches, disappearing in the fall and winter and building back up in the spring.

She let the sand sift from her fingers and stood watching the waves; a few scoters rested on the water just beyond the breakers. The air was so fresh she could taste the salt on her tongue; light formed diamonds on the surface of the water, crinkled like aluminum foil. She closed her eyes to the layers of sound, the boom as waves made contact, the hiss as they dissipated. When she opened her eyes, a woman was coming toward her in flowered tights and an oversized yellow T-shirt, her floppy hat bouncing with her exuberance.

She called out, "Isn't this a glorious day!"

Julienne felt a pang. Such innocent joy was lost to her forever.

Anger bubbled up. She refused to give into despair. She returned to her easel and squeezed out a bit more white. For the wet sand at the edge of the ocean, where it reflected the sky, she let the blues she'd layered below show through. What emerged as the shimmer of light on sand was the exact color she had been searching for. She stared at her canvas in amazement.

A vision emerged as she stared. She grabbed another canvas and blocked out a scene, then another, excitement mounting. This was going to work.

She would make her fears visible. She was going to wake people up.

 *Summer*

THE EARTH THROBS with the impact of the season, the hum of lawn mowers and car engines and loud, laughing voices. Colors are bright, primary. Boldly striped beach chairs and umbrellas pock-mock the sand; bare-shouldered women crowd the downtown. The dunes are bright with new growth, the glossy green leaves and pink-and-white blossoms of rosa rugosa. The locals can't keep up with their guests, their laundry, the sand tracked into their homes.

Tourists take boats out to look for whales, agents to look at houses. They climb to the top of the lighthouse and gaze across the ocean toward Europe, gaze down on the surfcasters and surfers in Turtle Cove. Nearby at Camp Hero, the old air force station, they explore World War II bunkers. At the dock, early risers get on line for the ferry to Block Island or the charter fishing boats. The stores do the brisk summer business that will sustain their owners for most of the year.

Everything is perfect, glorious, in the summer breeze. The ocean sparkles, the cocktails refresh. The earth's distress is camouflaged behind the stark and glossy beauty.

Yet the earth remembers when only the soft soles of native people traversed the terrain. Its memory is lodged in the streaks of dark red in its sands, garnet turned to powder, and in the clam and muscle shells along the bay. Its memory is lodged in the layers of clay and sediment in scarred and fluted cliffs, knobby and gnarled like the roots of a giant tree. Its memory resides in shad and dwarf pine, in old oak forest, in the blades of remaining prairie grass still shimmering in the last acres of moorlands.

CHAPTER 37: Theresa

Hot sun through the nylon sides of her tent woke Theresa. She sat up, took a swig of tepid water, and went outside to relieve herself. Once dressed, she settled on a large piece of driftwood with a smooth indentation that exactly accommodated her rear and watched washes of sunrise color spread across the sky, reflected in the water.

She'd been camping here for most of May and part of June while the trailer park had been off-limits because of the septic problems. She parked her truck at one of the trailheads and hiked in and out each day, showering at the state campground a few miles away before going to work, church, or town. Heading from her truck, she moved quietly, watchful through the woods, on edge and alert. But she never encountered anyone. She hadn't told anyone, not even Father Molina, what she was up to. She knew he would worry and want to find her shelter, and she preferred to be on her own.

She sipped from her thermos, the coffee still warm from the night before when she had filled it at the bar. The waves today were perfect, glossy. Each one swelled in the distance, gathered itself up and tipped over into the tube surfers lived for, in their wake leaving behind a necklace of green-and-brown seaweed studded with sea gems.

It had been a strange time; she felt both more in touch and more disconnected. Alone in her tent, she learned the way the wind sounded when it came from the south, and how it sounded when it came from the north. She could identify the precise time the waves shifted between low and high tide on the rocks in the cove. But away from her tent, she felt like a ghost, floating above the world, not really part of it, no longer anchored. She went to work, mixed drinks, and pulled drafts. She even let Cody kiss her the night before. It was as if nothing mattered, as if a part of her were already gone.

She didn't understand why, but since the day when she had walked with Clancy Frederics in the dunes, she had begun to think about her parents with less pain. Memories surfaced from her childhood and adolescence that she'd forgotten or had refused to let herself recall. Sometimes when she went to walk the labyrinth on the slope of Hither Woods, moving through the spiral of rocks, she'd fall into a reverie. Once she had the sense her mother was standing just behind her; she could feel her warmth and her love.

Each night before she went to sleep, she opened the square of green-velvet cloth and fingered the charms on her mother's bracelet—a tennis racket, a bluebird, a watering can. The tinkling sound brought back a memory of her mother's hand on her forehead, lifting her bangs to feel for fever. It was as if touching Clancy's scars, holding him, had cracked open a seam in her soul to let memories and feelings in. She was no longer frightened of them.

The septic issue was finally resolved, and now the biggest shock, one that no one had seen coming. Buyouts at the trailer park. Cash in exchange for moving. The town wasn't going to seize the land via eminent domain as had been rumored. Instead, the land closest to the beach would be freed up for a modest dune reconstruction if a number of residents equal to the number of trailers in the first row agreed to leave.

At first the TP exploded into acrimony, but in the end, enough residents were willing to take the buyout, and the reshuffle of homes from the first row into lots farther back began to take place. The last month had been like a Tetris game, with some trailers shifting places and others leaving altogether. The owner of Theresa's trailer had been one of the first to accept the deal. Theresa had two weeks to clear out.

In a small, zippered compartment of her backpack was the bank statement showing the Moorlands payout deposited into her bank account. She was rich beyond her wildest imaginings.

She drove into town for the early morning Spanish Mass. She needed prayer, and she needed Father Molina.

There were just a handful of congregants, spaced out among the first ten pews. She slid down to her knees, elbows on the back of the pew before her.

Father Molina emerged in his white garments, bowed before the altar, and began the Mass. She followed along, loving the lilt of the Spanish, letting its music wash over her. When she closed her eyes, the sounds—of the kneelers being pushed up and down, the whisper of garments, the occasional cough—were a calming backdrop. She sang the final hymn, then remained after everyone else filed out. Father Molina disappeared into the sacristy and then, once changed, motioned for her to join him in his office.

He smiled at her from behind his desk. "I'm glad you wanted to talk. It's been too long. I heard about the buyout. How will it affect you?"

"The owner of my trailer is taking the deal. I have to vacate."

"Oh no! Do you need a place to live?"

"Not exactly." The wood of the old desk gleamed. She ran her finger along the surface, catching the faint citrus scent of Murphy oil. She unfolded the sheet of paper from her shirt pocket and passed it over. "This is why I need your advice."

"The Moorlands payout? Congratulations!"

"I had no idea it would be so much. I'm not convinced I should have taken it."

"It would have been extremely foolish not to. I would go so far as to say it would have been uncharitable to refuse just to spite your father."

"You're saying it would have been a sin?"

"Only you can answer that."

"But so much money. Isn't this also a sin, Father?" She couldn't meet his eyes. The sleeve of her jean jacket was fraying badly; her fingers hovered over the cloth as she restrained the urge to pull out more threads. "I was angry. I was uncharitable. Unforgiving. So isn't it unethical to take his money? I did nothing to earn this."

Father Molina leaned forward. "Don't you think it might be God's way of helping you? You've worked hard and you have little to show for it; you didn't deserve to lose your home."

She swallowed, unable to form a response. Father Molina put his palms back together and rested his mouth on the tips of his fingers, his habitual gesture. Theresa was conscious of a soft ticking sound, though she'd never noticed a clock in the room. There was a slight rustling from outside, perhaps a cat or a squirrel rummaging in the bushes under the window, and then a car honk from far away. The silence settled between them, like dust.

"I can buy a house."

Father Molina threw back his head and laughed. "I'd say so."

She smoothed the edge of the dark-green blotter paper, pressing down the corner where it curled upward. "I don't know . . ."

"What is it?"

She wiped at her eyes. "I'm not worthy."

"Ah, dear girl!" He reached across the desk and touched her hand for a brief second. "None of us is worthy, except in the eyes of God. That's your faith, Theresa. To God even the worst sinner is worthy."

"Then why does it feel so wrong?"

"Perhaps you've gotten used to fending for yourself, so this bounty is in a way a threat to your sense of self, your identity?"

She let the idea register a moment. "Maybe."

"You can always do good with the money. If it really is more than you need, you can donate to a charity you believe in. There are many worthy causes."

She could donate to the church, she realized, with a lift of her spirits. She would say nothing to Father Molina and surprise him.

"What's to become of the parcel of land, now that you've withdrawn your suit?" he asked. "I wasn't able to attend the public hearing."

"The executor hasn't decided yet. He actually asked me for advice, what I thought my father would have wanted."

"What did you tell him?"

"That I had no idea."

"You don't have an opinion?"

"My own opinion?" Theresa gave into the urge to pluck at her jacket. She'd been so intent on her anger, and with stymieing Clancy, that she'd barely thought of how she would vote if she had the right. "I guess I could tell him I think the land should be used for housing that's affordable. Housing for people like me." She gave a little laugh. "Like me, before this." She waved the bank statement.

"Can you try and be a little excited?" Father Molina smiled. "Imagine! A house!"

White walls, hammock swing, a smoky-gray cat with white paws.

<hr>

"Can you tell me what doesn't seem to suit you?" the realtor's voice was beginning to sound strained.

"I'm not sure."

The agent drove to the final house on that day's list, along Second House Road and past the school. As they headed up a street with an abundance of trees, Theresa relaxed a little. They turned into a driveway and a small house came into view, a two-story boxlike building with gray siding. "I know it seems a bit boring, but it's quite nice inside." The agent's words came faster as she talked, as if to compensate for Theresa's silence.

Theresa followed the agent through the living room and dining room, fighting boredom, and then up the stairs to the bedrooms. Outside were the cries of children, the splash of a swimming pool. That was the problem: This house wanted a family.

"Is it more privacy you want?" the agent frowned.

Theresa bit her lip. "Something smaller? Woods?"

"Is it less about the house and more about the landscape? More nature?"

"Yeah, you're right. Sorry. I should have figured that out from the get-go."

"It often takes people a while to know what they are looking for. A million dollars sounds like a lot of money and being able to do this as an all-cash deal makes a huge difference. But if it's serious acreage you want, you won't find it even at this price range. Look, if you're not ready, you could rent a condo and take your time. I can put some options together for you, if you like."

"I'll think about it and let you know." Theresa was brain weary. She and the agent had driven through all the parts of town she knew so well, but the houses seemed different once she was inside and imagining what living there would feel like.

As she pulled into the trailer park, the pressure in her chest eased. This place, bordering the forest, close to the tip of the island—this was home. This was where she needed to be.

She wandered up and down the rows of mobile homes. The newly opened-up area of flattened sand, where the first row of trailers had been, took a little getting used to. Now that she had the money to buy a trailer, not a single one was available for purchase. The people who had chosen to stay were as tenacious as limpets on a rock. Unless she wanted to hook up with one of the single men—Tretorn or Beach Bum Barry—this was the one place she could no longer live.

She ran her fingers along the silky inside of a mussel shell. If she couldn't stay here, exactly here, she wasn't sure she belonged in Montauk at all.

CHAPTER 38: Molly

At the new house, the sounds were different. No longer did Molly awake to water gently lapping along the shore. Here she awoke to distant children's voices, the low hum of a lawnmower. There were different birds here, too. She had never seen so many starlings. The week after they moved in, the starlings had descended all at once, as if they'd all received a summons, tree branches bobbing with their weight.

They got Jonah a puppy from the Animal Rescue Center, a little black mutt he named Licorice, and on weekends they went for walks along the ocean or in the woods. The last few weeks, it had been hot enough to swim after work in the quiet waters at Gin Beach and to have a picnic dinner. But it wasn't the same, though none of them would say it out loud. As if they had made a solemn oath, they never talked about the storm or about their old house.

If it wasn't raining, Molly walked to work through the residential area, noticing the magnolias coming into bloom and the new, lighter growth on the edges of the pine tree branches, reminding her of her friend Rachel's French-tipped nails. Her anticipation built as she emerged to the sight of marinas and boatyards, to men with shaggy hair wearing coveralls and rubber boots, the reflections of boat masts like ribbons on the water.

The fish market was once again open six days a week. By midday, when she went outside to eat her lunch and get some air, the dock area was teeming: Lines spilled out the door of the clam shack; the souvenir and fashionable clothing shops were mobbed; and men, loaded with gear and cases of beer, boarded party boats for a half or full day of fishing.

Molly munched her sandwich and watched kids racing around the large metal whale mounted on a slab of concrete near the pavilion, reminding her of the dead whale she and Julienne and the boys had seen beached the past spring. This facsimile, with its cute face and flippy tail, didn't begin to capture the majesty of the real one. The tourist season did that to the town—transformed it into a carnival pop-up version of itself.

She balled up her napkin with her sandwich wrapper and wedged it into a trash bin, then strolled alongside the channel, a breeze lifting sweat-stuck strands of hair from her forehead. A gleaming yacht moved slowly by, crammed with people lounging on deck in bathing suits. Luxury boats filled the marinas alongside the fishing boats these days, and in June, for the Blessing of the Fleet, all manner of water-craft—kayaks and draggers and sport-fishing boats—were blessed by the priest and minister and rabbi as they passed the jetty and went out into the harbor.

"You!" Vince said, when she returned from her lunch break, pointing a finger as she came through the shop door, "Get out."

"What?" She blanched.

"A little birdie told me it's your birthday. You have the rest of the day off."

"Oh," Molly laughed, relieved.

"Get on home. I think there's a surprise afoot."

Molly walked back from the docks, crossing to the house from the backyard. She stood for a moment on the deck, savoring the unexpected free afternoon. This had been the best year of her life with finding Billy and Jonah, but also one of the hardest. She had expected that the first flush of love would ease into something solid and comfortable, like Billy's sturdy old bureau, with its lovely cedar scent and drawers that opened on smooth runners. She hadn't quite expected how complicated the adjustments of love could be.

The screen door slapped, and Jonah barreled into her. "Happy Birthday!" he clasped her around the waist. "Are you excited? Do you want to know what we're going to do today?"

"I *am* really excited. But don't tell me. I want to be surprised."

As Billy opened the back door to join them, the puppy streaked past. Jonah leapt up in pursuit.

"Keep him out of the garden!" she shouted.

"Getting Licorice was a smart move," Billy said, as boy and dog raced around the yard, Jonah tripping over himself. The dog slept with Jonah, and he had stopped waking up in the middle of the night with nightmares.

Billy had found a job with a landscaping company and brought home bags and bags of manure. They'd dug up part of the yard and planted all sorts of vegetables and herbs. Every evening, Molly plucked a few sprigs of oregano or mint—and now lettuce and cucumbers—to incorporate into their meal. It was the one thing she loved about their new home.

"Let's give Molly her present!" Billy called to Jonah.

He raced back, the puppy at his heels. Billy tied a bandanna around her head, covering her eyes. Each taking a hand, Billy and Jonah led her around the yard until she was dizzy.

"Okay. Open!"

She untied the scarf and shrieked. Leaning against the shed was a surf rod.

"Go ahead. Touch it."

She hoisted the rod slowly; it was heavier than she'd expected. She moved it back and forth tentatively, like a magic wand.

"Do you like it?" Jonah asked.

"It's gorgeous!"

"We had Sonny Williams make it," Billy said.

"Handmade rods cost a fortune!"

"We have the money now," Billy said proudly. "Check out the pattern."

The pole was wrapped tightly with red twine separating the blues and grays into diamonds.

"We're going fishing!" Jonah hopped up and down on the balls of his feet.

"I'll teach you how to cast off the beach," Billy said.

She understood. He wanted to give her a taste of fishing, if not an experience of being out on the ocean. Now that they no longer lived by the water, Molly had had to drop the idea of oyster farming. This was a magnificent gesture on Billy's part.

Tears filled her eyes. "I'm so touched."

They put Licorice in his doggy crate, pulled on bathing suits, tied the rod to the roof of Billy's truck, and headed to the town beach.

It was crowded in front of the lifeguard stand, so they trooped farther down the beach, passing chairs, umbrellas, and shrieking children until they found an empty stretch.

At the water's edge, Billy showed her how the spinner worked and how to play out the line to about four feet, place a finger on the line, and move the bale to the "go" position. She stood with her feet shoulder-width apart and followed his instructions to bring the rod up and over her head as she released her hold and to sweep the rod forward to whip the line out beyond the waves.

On her first attempt she didn't bring the rod up high enough and the hook fell too close to shore. On her second try, she released the line too late. By the fifth time, she made a perfect cast, and Jonah and Billy clapped.

She didn't get so much as a bite. After an hour, they were hot and prickly with sweat and lotion. She put her rod into the holder near their blanket.

"Let's race!" She dashed to the water, Jonah quickly overtaking her.

The waves were gentle, so Molly flopped onto her back and relaxed into the rocking up-and-down motion. She couldn't remember the last time she'd felt so at peace.

Back at the blanket after their swim, Jonah unwrapped the peanut butter and jelly sandwiches he'd made. They watched a steady stream of walkers up and down the beach as they ate, to the blended sounds of distant radios and children's squeals, the incessant thrum of the ocean muting everything.

"Walk?" Billy asked. She nodded, and he reached out a hand to pull her from her chair. Jonah was digging in the sand, creating a deep pit and a long descending roadway.

"Jonah, Molly and I are going for a walk. Please stay out of the water—all the way out—until we come back."

Jonah stopped mid-motion, startled out of his concentration. Molly was surprised he didn't give Billy an argument. A tiny grin flashed across his face. "Sure."

Billy swung her hand as they walked east; with each curve in the shore a different view unfolded. Low cliffs began to form, and around one bend several staircases dangled down from the houses above, the sand eroded out from under them.

They settled on a driftwood log to watch the water. The waves hissed and clacked among the pebbles. Molly pulled her cap lower over her eyes and licked her dry lips. They tasted of peanut butter and salt.

"Molly." Billy drew a glittery box from his bathing suit pocket.

"Another present? You've given me enough!"

"It's recycled. A hand-me-down."

"Now I'm really curious!" She took her time unwrapping the gift, trying not to rip the glossy striped paper. It was a black velvet jewelry case, and her face heated in a blush as she opened it. Inside was a ring with a small diamond in a slightly raised, antique-looking setting.

"It was my grandmother's and then my mother's. Do you like it?"

"Oh my god, Billy," she breathed. She held the ring to the sun so the light was caught in its facets. "It's so beautiful. And to think it's been in your family!"

"Yes, that's why I thought you'd especially like it. So, will you?"

"Will I what?"

Billy closed his eyes, as if steeling himself. "Molly, come on! Will you marry me?"

"Of course I will!" No wonder Jonah had smirked when Billy asked her on the walk.

Billy slipped to the sand in front of her on both knees, and pressed his head into her lap. "I knew you were the one for me the minute I saw you. I'll make you happy, I promise. You won't regret it."

"You already make me happier than I've ever been, Billy." She put her hands on either side of his face. "I need to say something first."

He lifted his gaze. "What?"

"Stu told me how your parents died. You never talk about them. I think you need to. We can't get married if there are things you can't talk to me about."

He flushed and glanced away. "It's hard."

"I know, but you need to." She waited. He studied the sand. "You know I'm right, don't you?"

He pursed his lips, then grinned. "You're always right, aren't you?"

"Probably."

Still, he said nothing.

"I mean now, Billy. Tell me about your parents now."

He bit his lip, stared out at the ocean. "I never was afraid, you know," he gestured at the water. "It was just part of my life. I felt total trust when we were in boats, totally secure. It never occurred to me . . . Not even when there were storms or accidents." He shuddered. "Ironic, isn't it? I mean, neither of them died at sea, technically." He straightened, and his tone grew more matter of fact. "So, Stu told you my mother died from pneumonia? It was so quick I couldn't absorb that she was gone. And then my father . . . he just went nuts. Completely derailed." Billy ran his hand over his face; there was a glisten of sweat. "I didn't know what to do for him. I was too out of it myself. And then, the night he didn't come back. It took a day before he was found. A gash on the back of his head. On the jetty." Billy shuddered again. "They wouldn't let me see him. I didn't identify the body. Maybe it would have been better if I had."

Molly gathered Billy to her. "It's a terrible tragedy, a terrible trauma you've faced." She rubbed his back. "I respect that you're afraid for me and Jonah." She felt his nod against her chest. "We can talk about it more, but I promised Jonah that once the whales were migrating, we'd go on a whale watching boat. I want you to come, too."

He stiffened.

"We learned about phobias in my psych courses. I think if we all go together, it will help."

"OK," he mumbled.

Holding him, she stroked his hair and watched the waves lift and build. Any lingering hesitation about giving herself over so completely to him and Jonah sifted away. She felt herself swell like a sponge to near bursting. Overcome. Overcome not just with love for them but for this place. Brimming over.

Her friend Rachel used to call her a Pollyanna. She tried to explain that she found it pleasing to please others. Rachel would lecture her not to be so agreeable, to be more of a feminist and assert herself. Molly understood the point Rachel was making. She knew she blended in, like monkfish in a stew. Sometimes she thought she had no distinct taste of her own and simply absorbed others' flavors. Other times she thought she was like salt and enhanced whatever she joined.

Maybe she had been granted an overabundance of love, and love needed to be dispensed. She had more to give, so she would go on giving more.

The next morning before work, Molly drove through the woods to the bay. The leaf pattern on the roadway in the bright summer sun was as sharply etched as a stencil. She lowered the car windows and the air rushed in. It smelled of damp soil, reminding her of the early mornings the previous fall, when she would go outside in her pajamas with her coffee cup, the ceramic warm against her hands, the grass cool against her bare feet.

Now, as she rounded the bend to the clearing, an enormous house blocked the view. A berm had been created fronting the shore, and the ground was covered with bright-white crushed rock. Trees had been cleared, and there were two other houses already framed. She did a quick U-turn and drove away.

In the fish house, she stood a moment inhaling the odor of ice and chill, then slipped her apron over her head. Fish were waiting, ready for packing. Their scales were glistening, their eyes searching for home.

CHAPTER 39: Clancy

It was the fourth scorcher in a row. Clancy wore his new gardening pants and an old T-shirt and headed out into the morning, grabbing a three-pronged trowel and silly straw hat. The soil looked dry again. He knelt at one end of the garden. The heavy air, alive with insect and bird sound, settled on him like a shawl; he was sweating within minutes.

Weeds came up so fast. *How tough these skinny little things are.* He loosened the soil with the trowel and then tugged at the weeds with his fingers. Weeding was surprisingly satisfying; he loved the smell of the exposed earth, the darker color underneath, the tidy look he left behind.

He did a different section every day, and by the time he'd finished the entire garden, it was time to start over again. He would miss all this when he went back to work. His leave of absence was up at the end of the week.

Today he was in the carrots. He fingered the curious leaves and lifted one to sniff. It smelled carroty! Fresh and sweet, like newness itself. Peter Rabbit came to mind. He recalled the books from childhood, but not where he had read them. A library? School? One of the foster homes? He remembered feeling stirred by the airy drawings and pastel coloring, the allure of the garden patch, the foliage—odd that he had forgotten the books until this minute. He couldn't remember much of the story, except that Peter was very naughty. He had known he, Clancy, would never misbehave that way.

The heat had become too oppressive to bear. As he took off his shirt, he shivered at the recollection of Theresa's finger, cold and wet, tracing a scar down his back, and the warmth of her embrace as she held him. He felt the emotion of it blooming again now, but although it had been a long time since he'd been with a woman, the feeling wasn't sexual, exactly. He had cried, just as she had cried in his arms in his car.

He hadn't seen her since, but he'd kept up with the news about the trailer park buyback plan and was glad he'd managed to get her the payout.

With Theresa's situation settled, he felt free of any obligation to consider Pete Walker's plan. The public hearing had revealed only that the townspeople were as divided as the partners on what they thought the best use of the land should be. In a few hours, he was to meet with the other men, and still he wasn't ready. He moved on to the squash.

In the last few days, an idea had begun to sprout, winding around like a vine in his thoughts. He considered proposing a melding of the different ideas, a mix just like the garden, the various vegetables and flowers coexisting happily in the same soil. He would propose a combination of affordable housing and open space, including a community garden. He had played around with Otto's diagram, apportioning the circles and squares and hashtags to these various elements. He assigned the circles to open space, rectangles for the houses, and the hashtags representing small garden areas, a synthesis of different elements in balance.

It was the best he could do. He moved on to the kale.

* * *

He was toweling off after a shower when he heard his phone.

"Clancy, I thought of something," Theresa said without preamble. "You know about the buyout plan at the trailer park? Moving back from the shore? Rising sea levels means it's smart to move away from the coast. It's called coastal retreat."

"Okay," he said slowly. "I hear you. But how would that relate to Moorlands? It's not on the water."

"No idea. But you were looking for a grand idea."

Clancy went into the kitchen, where he'd left Otto's drawing. Clancy suddenly recalled the overheard conversations at the fundraising party, and the motel owner who'd knocked the glass out of the town supervisor's hands. Everything came together in his mind, and the drawing seemed to shift before his eyes. Now he realized that the arrows showed the movement of the rectangles from the bottom area of the drawing and into the large circle on the top.

Otto was moving the downtown motels into the Moorlands parcel.

———•◦•◦•———

The men looked up, expressions somewhere between expectant and wary. They were sitting around a picnic table on the deck of the Lobster Crate, a stiff breeze fluttering the napkins weighted down with bright-blue beach pails filled with pebbles. The menu—paper, with little boxes to tick off selections—were in the middle of the table with stubby pencils attached to clipboards.

Pete shoved one at Clancy without a word. He quickly marked, "Lobster roll: Classic with mayo and celery" and asked for an iced tea when the waiter gathered their clipboards.

He leaned forward. Even with sunglasses, the rays were too strong and he pulled his cap lower. "I've thought of a way to combine most of your ideas into one plan."

"That's impossible," Pete said bluntly.

There was an abrupt cry from the water and a splash as someone fell off a paddleboard, momentarily diverting everyone's attention.

Clancy waited until the paddle boarder righted himself before continuing. "Hear me out, and if you don't like it, I'm prepared to flip a coin."

Pete folded his arms over his chest and tilted his chair back. Clancy had the momentary hope he'd fall into the water, too.

"This idea allows some open space and even some development. And there's a way it could help with workforce or affordable housing."

"Impossible," Pete said again.

Clancy ignored him. "You know about the town buyback program at the trailer park? What I'm proposing is something similar. I propose that we offer the Moorlands parcel to the town for them to relocate the downtown motels that are perched along the dune line."

"This is off-the-charts crazy on so many levels," Pete said. "The motels will never agree to relocate. They're in a prime location."

"That stretch of beach, even with the artificial sand dune, is going to disappear in time. Long term, the motels aren't going to make it, and they know it. They'll have no other option but to be bought out or moved, or nature will take its course. And we can create an added incentive." Otto had drawn rectangles within the large circle with smaller squares on top. Clancy decided these indicated second stories. "The motels won't actually move. They'll be torn down and rebuilt on the Moorlands parcel. The incentive will be to allow them to build a second story for workforce apartments for local families. Under the current zoning, the motels aren't allowed to expand, so this will be a win for them. They'll gain year-round revenue from the apartments."

"For once I agree with Pete," Tim said slowly. "This is pretty far-fetched. And you mentioned open space. Even assuming this could fly, where's the open space in this scheme?"

"The oceanfront. With the motels gone, there will be more primary natural dune. It will build up and be even more beautiful. Tim, you've said yourself that the Moorland parcel has no special features. Why not swap it, in essence, for the beach and dunes? And the parcel is large enough for areas of garden or meadow, too." In his conception of Otto's design, this was what Clancy ascribed to the hashtags. "Gaspar, I know this doesn't give you what you were angling for, but hey, you should like something this visionary. It also won't give Pete quite the payout he wants, but the returns will be decent. And I suggest there could be a walking path along the perimeter dedicated to the memory of Pete Walker Sr."

Theresa had mentioned that Pete Walker Jr. idolized his father. Pete's eyes widened; he took large swallow of his beer.

"This is awfully complicated," Harve said.

"I had a conversation this morning with the town supervisor." Clancy had called Julienne, who had called Grace Morgan, who had made the conversation happen. "It will depend on the town to carry it through, but the supervisor was pretty excited by the idea."

Clancy sat back. He itched to tighten his tie but wasn't wearing one, and he was trying to break that habit, anyway. The waiter arrived with their food, but nobody moved to pick up their lobster rolls.

"I'm kind of flabbergasted," Harve said.

"I think it's fantastic," Gaspar said.

Clancy shot him a grateful look, and Gaspar saluted him back with his fork.

"I guess I'm on board," Tim said. "If I have this right, we sell to the town, with various caveats as to use. After that, the details are on them to work out?"

Clancy nodded.

Pete still hadn't spoken. His eyes bore into Clancy's with such intensity, it took effort not to look away. He picked up his roll and took a large, audible bite. They all waited while he chewed. His eyes watered as he swallowed.

"I know when I'm beat," he said. He patted his mouth with his napkin. Then, when no one spoke, he added, "Best damn lobster roll I've ever had."

So it was done. They had the basis of an agreement. It would be over to the lawyers to negotiate the purchase with the town, and many more details to follow, but for now, Clancy's work was over, his obligation to Otto completed.

Clancy's body buzzed with adrenalin and jubilation. After lunch he watched the others get into their cars and drive away, but he was too wired to get behind a wheel just yet. He decided to explore along the shore of Fort Pond Bay and up Tuthill Road. Stretching his legs felt good, and he quickly came to a high point of land that looked over the Sound. There were a few boats on the water, leaving tiny white waves in their wake, and in the distance, the curve of Hither Woods and the pier were visible. He continued walking until he came to the V of Kettlehole and Falcon and decided he should turn back before he got himself lost. As he came down the hill, the landscape spread out before him; it occurred to him that he had not left the East End in months. It was strange to him that it was possible to make a full life, complete with drama and excitement and challenges, within such a small geographical area.

He leaned on the railing of a deck that jutted out above the water. He had not felt a lack; he had not pined for his apartment or his neighborhood or trips into the city. While he had accepted the gift of Otto's house and its terms that he live in Montauk part-time, he had not once considered if he might want to move here year round.

He watched a sailboat as it headed out into the Atlantic. He had no interest in being on the water, especially after getting seasick all those years ago when Otto had taken him fishing, but watching boats was something else. His chest opened up, filled with air like a balloon about to fly, and he felt as if he might lift off over the water. He became more expansive out here, as if the more connected he was to the elements and nature, the larger he became. Perhaps nature did have the power to change a person, as Julienne had argued. Perhaps nature was more essential to human beings than he'd ever imagined. It came to him that he felt more fully alive than he ever had before.

He continued on down the hill. What if he made this permanent? He could work his job remotely or find another job in his field easily enough. Even in the questioning, he realized the decision was already made. Some part of him had known. Some part of him must have wanted to escape the safe familiarity of his old life and plunge into this world, a world with a house and garden to care for, a project he could watch develop, people with whom he'd begun to forge ties. He felt a pulse of excitement.

He could never be sure if the way he interpreted Otto's diagram was correct, but it struck him that it was only once he had a home that he was able to imagine an answer to the puzzle Otto had left him. His solution occurred only once he had begun to allow an opening into something new in himself.

He plucked out a small weed with a purple flower poking up between the joins of the wooden platform and fingered its feathery petals. Yes, he would stay. He would do for others what Otto had done for him. He would create a foundation and bring foster kids from the city to hike and garden and walk on the beach. He fully accepted all that Julienne had made him aware of—how much was being lost, how much was at stake—and he would join the work to do what was possible to save it. He'd hire teachers to teach the kids about nature and climate change. He'd ask Julienne if she would give workshops on painting from nature. The idea bloomed in his chest, quickening his heart.

He recalled something quoted in one of Otto's note-books that had struck him: "For some it is the mountains, for some the wide flat prairie, for some the undulating curves of the desert, for some the city's chiaroscuro. And for some, the place that is home to the soul, is a place by the sea."

CHAPTER 40: Julienne

Every year it caught her by surprise. She would emerge from the passageway through the dunes to find the beach, empty most of the year, dotted with near-naked bodies arrayed on beach towels.

This summer brought new changes. The owners of the Black Box spent only a few weeks in their home before turning it over to a steady parade of renters. The renters took their coffee on the deck that caught the morning sun, lounged by the pool in the afternoon, and then sipped cocktails on a different deck in the evening, music blaring just below the legal threshold. The renters' laughter followed Julienne into the cottages as she made up the beds. She was often distracted by the women's outfits—long caftans and high-heeled sandals, lacy cover-ups and oversized sunglasses—as if this were the Riviera or Capri.

When she and Rob intersected on the lawn as they went about their tasks, one of them would whisper to the other, "Did you get a load of *that?*"

She made a point to wrap her arms around him and rest her head against his chest for a moment. She was trying.

Rob called a broker friend to find out what the neighbors were charging. At the number, Julienne felt as if her hair had been lit by a match.

"It should be illegal."

"The capitalist way," he laughed. "At least you should feel better about *our* prices." They would stay below market no matter what, they agreed, as affordable as possible. The rich shouldn't be the only ones who got to enjoy the area.

Their own guests were thrilled to be back, to have a week or two of sun and surf. The children ran around the grounds as always, and Max couldn't contain his joy. Everyone commented on the showpiece house next door, but it didn't seem to faze them. One or two asked if perhaps the beach had gotten a little narrower, and she explained about the storm, and how the sand would soon replenish, though she knew that might not prove to be true.

In town, there were the usual summer complaints about lines at restaurants, crowded bars and beaches, but with the positive resolution of the Moorlands parcel, SOS took a break from activity. Still, a kind of foreboding anxiety settled over her like a clammy sea breeze. She took that anxiety to the studio, late at night and very early in the mornings, squeezing in work when she could.

Her new paintings were in sets of three, like triptychs. The first set was of their motel: one painting as it had been in the past, surrounded by trees and open space; one as it was in the present, with the Black Box looming near; and the final one showing the motel as it might be one day, overwhelmed on all sides by towering homes. She chose several other locations in town and gave them the same approach: a historical view, a current iteration, and a prophetic vision, with the town morphed into an overcrowded suburb.

When she had completed five sets, she asked Rob to come to the studio. This work was so different from anything she'd done before that she was eager for a reaction. If there was one thing she could count on with Rob, it was his honesty. He'd be honest even if he knew it would hurt.

Julienne moved off to the side where she could watch his expression.

Rob studied the first painting of their motel and started to say something, but she put a finger to her mouth. He nodded and then took his time going down the row.

He faced her, his eyes serious. "These are remarkable, Jules. I mean that."

"You like the concept?"

"Oh my god, yes. Your colors are wonderful, too. I like that they're more muted in the last ones of each set, as if the changes you depict have a dulling effect. These are so very different from your usual work. Even your brush strokes are different."

"I'm glad you're picking up on that. I don't really know why that's happened."

"You've really hit on a way to say what you've been feeling."

In the past, she'd only wanted to convey her deep love for this place; there hadn't been more she'd needed to say. "You don't think there's too much of an agenda? Too polemical?"

He glanced back at the paintings. "No, they just draw you in. They're really striking."

She dropped into her overstuffed armchair. "I didn't realize until this moment how much this series matters to me."

He sat on the edge of the chair's thickly padded arm. "I know sometimes I've tried to get you to let up." He tucked a curl behind her ear. "But I admire—no, love—your passion."

She began to get choked up.

"What is it? What's the matter, sweetheart?"

"I'm afraid I'm only paying tribute to what's already lost."

"I think what you're saying is it's not yet too late."

"I'm not sure I know what I really think anymore."

"It's a warning. That's what this is. A wake-up call for those who can see it."

Julienne slept badly and awoke while it was still dark, knowing she'd sleep no further. She slipped out of bed and went to her studio, and her painting took a direction she didn't expect; the beached whale she had seen on the beach with Molly and the boys during the spring appeared on her canvas. She had been shocked by the whale's massive size and the rawness of its injuries and tried to shield the boys from the sight. Now she found herself painting the bloody gash in its side, its festering wound.

It was a darker vision than she wanted to own. She realized Rob was partly wrong; she wasn't just painting the hope that it wasn't too late, she was painting her despair and her intent to fight despite that despair. Because she felt—in her bones, her blood, her soul—a oneness, as if she was an extension, on a cellular level, with this place. These trees, this earth, these rocks, this ocean. To not fight would be like failing to try and prevent her own death.

Light penetrated the studio; outside the dawn was breaking. She walked away from her painting and headed to the beach.

A bank of low, dark clouds lay along the horizon and a light mist was coming off the water. The sand was still in shadow, cold on her bare soles. She began a slow jog, letting her head fill with the thrum of the ocean. She had read that humans feel an affinity with the ocean because blood is saline, like seawater, and that bodily fluids are subject to the same moon-sun gravitational forces affecting the ocean. As she ran down the beach, she felt as if the boundary of her physical self dissolved and the landscape flowed in. The light shifted second by second as clouds swept across the sky, creating a pool of gold far out on the horizon, then extinguishing it. She reversed direction and jogged back, face into the sun. The ocean provided half of all the oxygen used by human beings. Every second breath. She bent over to catch her own breath and came up with her palms together.

As she straightened, the sky seemed to explode. Along the horizon tall vertical wisps rose like spires. Above them, the sun stabbed through the mass of dark clouds, rays spearing one spot on the water just beneath the ghostly flames, an electrifying clash of opposites, a vision unlike anything she had ever seen.

A feeling of power filled her. She watched until the sun shifted out of daybreak, and then raced home to paint.

CHAPTER 41: Theresa

It was the time of day when the light became intensely golden, so vibrant it was as if the air was singing, its beauty hard to bear. The light softened the weathered wood of the funky little bar, sparkled the windows: Primary colors juxtaposed brilliantly, like those of a stained glass window. The green canopy over the door sighed in the wind, brushing vivid black shadows onto the sidewalk. Theresa put her key in the door and entered, feeling as if she was stepping out of Candyland and into a warm cocoon.

The chairs were upside down on the tables; the top of the bar glowed in the weak light that made its way in. She hung her jean jacket on the peg outside the kitchen and turned on the A/C and lights. She stood for a moment, listening. The hum of the refrigerator. A drip every five seconds from the faucet. She tightened the faucet and reduced the drip, but not completely. She wondered how many hours she had spent in this place, what percentage of her life had been lived within these walls.

There was a sound, and then, "Hello?" Kathy called out from the front.

"You? Early?" Theresa came out of the kitchen.

"Gordon dropped me. All he does is bitch about the day-trippers. With the town so crowded, he has to build in extra time to get to his job sites."

Theresa deployed a can of Pledge, filling the air with lemon scent, and wiped the surface of the bar.

Kathy chattered away about her weekend and the sale at the nearby boutique. Together, they began taking the chairs off the tables. They were beat-up wooden dining-table style, with seats so worn they had a satin-like feel.

"I wonder how old these are," Kathy said.

"I'm guessing from when Marty opened this place."

"What are you saying about me?" Marty came in from the back parking lot.

"We were saying you could maybe use some new chairs," Kathy said.

"Are you crazy? Ruin the vibe that everyone comes here for?" He wore a white T-shirt that showed off the swordfish tattoo on his left inner forearm. He leaned back against the bar. "How you girls doing?"

"Women," Theresa said, reflexively. She hated being called a girl, as if she was still in pigtails.

"So how are you *women* doing?"

"I'm good, Marty," Kathy said sweetly. "How was your day off?"

He pushed off from the bar. "Fabulous. Went sailing!"

"I didn't know you sailed," Theresa said.

"First time. This guy who comes in here, Theodore Miloxi? He took me."

"That developer? What were you doing with him?"

"He's trying to wine and dine me. I think he thinks I don't realize he's got ideas."

"Wait, you don't mean he's looking to buy this place?"

"Probably. He's already in the middle of developing over by Hither Woods. He represents some consortium or whatnot. Why so interested?"

"He's the one was pressuring Molly and Billy to sell."

"Holy fuck." Marty looked taken aback. "I didn't know

that. Well, don't worry, my lovelies. Marty isn't selling. Your livelihoods are safe. Nobody pushes me around."

"I know who you're talking about," Kathy's eyes widened. "He's got this really powerful vibe, like scary? With these piercing eyes? Kind of like a fox?"

"Well he won't outfox me."

"Can't outfox a fox," Theresa said. Marty narrowed his eyes, as if trying to decide if she was mocking him or not.

"Get to work you two."

Theresa slid cherries from a jar into a dish, popping one in her mouth, savoring the sweetness, then washed her hands and prepped the rest of her set up. She filled the pretzel and goldfish bowls and placed them at regular intervals along the bar. Lots of bars no longer provided snacks, but Marty, for everything else she could say about him, was a generous man.

A burst of radio static shattered the quiet, then the volume was turned down and the screen showed the mellow classic rock station on Pandora Marty favored. The delicate finger-picked opening of "The Boxer" began to play, with its lyrics about looking for home. Her breath caught and her eyes filmed over. She turned abruptly to the wall.

Outside, her truck was already packed with most of her possessions. In the morning, she had to relinquish her trailer. She would take her things and leave the trailer park. First, she would drop in on Tretorn to wish him well. And even before that, she would plant a silver bracelet under the sand just so BB would find it.

Beyond that, she wasn't yet sure. She didn't know if she would be able to bear not waking up to the sound of the wind whistling through the cracks in her trailer. She didn't know if she could bear not walking along the shore to see how the morning light struck the cliffs, creating dark crevices and sparkling off embedded mica, or not feeling the way the pebbles shifted underfoot, and the sound of the ocean cracking and hissing among the rocks. If she left, she would no longer be assaulted by the smells of dried seaweed, pungent and dank, or hear the piercing, agonized cry of the gulls as they dove and swooped, forever restless and searching, forever unsatisfied.

"You coming to the party tomorrow night?"

Theresa blinked back tears before turning to Kathy. "Huh?"

"The one Marty's hosting for the roofer who fell and doesn't have insurance?"

"Oh, of course," she said, although she didn't know where she would be. She would let the decision gather itself inside her, as if it could be made on a cellular rather than a conscious level. She hadn't discussed what she would do, where she would go after leaving the trailer park, not with Molly, not even with Father Molina. She imagined Father's face when he opened her card and saw the check inside. She wondered if he would like her idea of setting up a legal fund for the Latino community.

Kathy flipped the sign from CLOSED to OPEN, and the waiting crowd poured in: tourists, dressed in beach wear, locals in jeans and Ts, and the gang of regulars who headed for the back room as if it were reserved for them.

"Sky! Stu! Will!" Theresa pulled beers. "On me!"

"Wow, what's the occasion?"

"Just showing my love." Theresa let herself be grabbed and kissed. People kept coming. She didn't even try to remember people's drinks; there were too many of them. The summer-help bartender was scrambling to keep up, and Theresa flew from one end of the bar to the other, swept up in the work, closing her mind to anything else, going through rags to keep up with the spills, her neck and shoulders beginning to ache.

At 11:00 p.m., she told Marty she needed to take a break. She went out the back and through the short alleyway behind the stores to the edge of the dock. Sturdy fishing boats were tied up along this stretch, swaying almost imperceptibly. In the light of the quarter moon, the water was as black as motor oil, shimmying with the wavy reflections of the dock lights. She leaned her cheek against one of the rough wooden pillars and closed her eyes.

She couldn't remember much about the place she lived before her family moved to Montauk, the small house in Floral Park. There had been a tiny cement backyard, stores nearby—a laundromat, corner grocery, pizza parlor. There had been big boys who scared her when she walked alone to school. She had had a friend, Janet, whom she loved with a passion, but Janet's family had moved away in second grade. When Theresa's parents said they were moving, too, she thought that meant she would live where Janet had gone. Instead, they'd driven to Montauk to the house in Hither Hills. It was as if she'd left Earth and gone to a different planet entirely.

She stretched, arched her back, and touched her toes. She felt lightheaded; the ground seemed far away. It was hard to take a deep-enough breath.

"You feeling okay?" Marty said as she slipped back behind the bar. "You don't look so hot."

"I just need some water. I think I'm a little dehydrated."

"Let me know if you need to leave."

"Thanks. I should be all right."

A customer asked for a celery margarita. Every summer there were new trends to keep up with, lately vegetables and fermentation. CBD oil was hot, though Marty said, "No dice." He was conservative that way.

A couple was leaving and held the door for someone. Her heart sank. It was Cody. He headed for the bar, where there was an empty seat for the first time in hours.

His beard was trimmed, and he wore a lightweight Irish sweater, a blue shade that brought out the blue of his eyes and his summer tan. She felt a sharp sizzle of regret.

They looked at each other, the kiss the other night in the air between them. She poured his usual and slapped away the money he was pulling out of his wallet.

"It's on me."

"I'm honored."

"Well, I hate to burst your bubble, but it's for all my regulars tonight."

"What's the occasion?"

"Just a whim. So, how's the crop?"

"Way too soon to tell. I hope we'll get lucky with this batch. We're hoping there's enough time for them to settle in before the weather gets unpredictable."

"Good, that's really good. I hope it works."

"You said you'd come to the hatchery."

"Sure, one of these days."

"You are so unconvincing when you lie," he laughed. "Is it me, or do you just not like tanks of water with squirmy things?"

"Exactly."

"Which?"

"For me to know and you to find out."

"You're a hard woman, Theresa."

"So I've been told." She smiled to soften the words.

He took a sip of his beer, regarding her over his glass. He began to say something, but she put a finger over his lips and whispered, "Not now." She gathered up glasses that had been left on the bar and headed to the kitchen. She glanced back over her shoulder and caught a look of confusion cross his face. If she left, he would understand soon enough.

As the evening wore on, she kept needing glasses of water, and she felt breathless, as if the bar were full of smoke. She kept losing the thread of conversations, of who was drinking what. Marty asked if she wanted him to close, but again she said no, so he said, "your funeral," and headed home.

Little by little, the place emptied. At one point, as she was returning from the ladies' room, Cody gestured for her to come outside with him, but she shook her head. He frowned and when she didn't budge, barged out. It was better this way. Better that he be angry with her. She looked around. Stu and Sky were in a final darts game, and Will was putting on his jacket. She waited five minutes and dimmed the lights for last call.

"Night Theresa, thanks for the drinks."

"Safe home, drive safe!" everyone called.

She and Kathy stacked the chairs, and then Theresa gave her an impromptu hug.

"Ahhhhhhh," Kathy giggled. "Love you, too."

Theresa started to put on her jean jacket, then left it hanging on the peg. If she didn't leave, it would be waiting for her tomorrow. If she did leave, it would be for them to remember her by.

———◆•×•◆———

Above all, Theresa needs to walk. She needs to feel her soles on the soft, resistant sand one last time. She wants to own it just a little longer. She passes the garish pink of Tretorn's trailer, stops to admire the artful arrangement of potted cacti in another yard. Beach Bum Barry's ramshackle trailer is festooned with metallic beach finds. She leaves her red wagon outside for him with her chimes and solar lanterns. She's been pretending that she doesn't know she may never return, but there's a fish hook tearing at her heart.

At the water's edge, a gull lifts off with what can only be described as an affronted look, and she laughs through her tears. She knows this particular gull from his deformed right foot; he often pecks at her trailer door for scraps. Perhaps these images, these sensations, will fade and become indistinct over time as they are superimposed by new ones. But right now, the feel of the stones underfoot and the way she must balance on the rocks is so familiar that she can walk with her eyes closed, absorbing the warm air against her skin, praying to the wisdom of the waves.

She doesn't quite know why she must leave, only that she must. And she doesn't know where she will end up, except that she'll head north. She puts a final tray of grass seedlings in her car to plant along the beach on her way, and then she'll drive to Maine, her big check in her pocket. If she can't find what she needs, she'll drive on into Canada. She'll drive and drive, as far as is necessary.

Somewhere, waiting for her, there must be wildness.

CHAPTER 42: Clancy

Within a day of being in Astoria, Clancy is packing up to leave for good. Astoria has become a foreign country whose language he no longer knows. It's as if he's lost the ability to tune out the noise, to know how to navigate with people rushing past him. He is newly sensitive to the heat-baked stench of garbage, the pothole-tar scent of summer. He misses the sound of the wind and the light on the waves. He misses walking out on the stone patio in the morning in his bare feet. He feels vertigo on his balcony, imprisoned behind the high railing. He keeps turning on lights against the gray dimness of his north-facing windows. An alchemy has occurred; he no longer belongs to this place.

When he locks himself out of the apartment, he laughs. Clearly this is a sign that he must leave—except he no longer needs signs from the universe.

On his drive back to Montauk, he pulls over at the overlook near the campground where he almost drowned. He takes in the expanse of Napeague Harbor and the isthmus, the green and beige of the dunes and the soft grays of the ocean in the distance. He feels as if he is coming awake, as if he has forgotten how sharp and clear everything can be. Driving the last few miles through the woods and to the beginning of town, it's as if he passes through his own *Looking Glass*. The rest of the world drops away.

Back at the house, Clancy unloads his groceries and opens the slider to let in the fresh air. The afternoon sun is waning, casting a golden glow over the meadow. He pours himself a glass of pinot and steps outside. The wine puckers his mouth; the flagstones are warm under his bare feet. Above his head, the birdfeeder in the tree on the side of the house rocks back and forth with the comings and goings of red-winged blackbirds, chickadees, cardinals. He mimics their songs back to them.

He wanders to the garden. The last of the tomatoes are ripening, surrounded by the surprise of zinnias in an explosion of color. Clancy recalls how Otto dropped to his knees to scoop up a handful of soil and placed it in his palm, the softness of it. He didn't know then that this soil, soft and fragrant, would come to mean home. He hadn't known how dirt has the power to heal.

He breaks off a marigold, holds it to his nose, and surrenders to its intense, spicy, scent.

Book Club Discussion Guide

1. Nature itself plays a big role in this novel. How did you see the forces of nature play out in the various storylines and in what happens with the characters?

2. *The Stark Beauty of Last Things* opens with a map of the hamlet of Montauk. In what ways can the setting be said to be a character in the novel?

3. In *The Stark Beauty of Last Things*, the main female characters—Julienne, Theresa, and Molly—are each trying to save their homes, whether the threat is environmental, economic, or both. To what degree did you feel sympathy for all three women? Did one story resonate most for you? Why?

4. In an argument with Rob, Julienne says that something is wrong with an economic system in which housing prices can escalate to the point where people are, in essence, forced to cash out. "There was something very wrong with a world that created such an equation and locked people into it," she thinks. Do you agree? Why or why not?

5. Did you feel that Molly and Billy made the right decisions regarding their house? How would you react in their situation?

6. How did you feel about Theresa and her decision at the end of the novel? Did you expect it? Why or why not?

7. How did you feel about the character of Clancy and how he handled the legacy he received from Otto? Did Clancy go about finding a solution to the Moorlands parcel the way you would have? Were you satisfied by the solution he came up with? How did you feel about his decision regarding keeping the house?

8. What themes did you identify in the book? Which resonated most for you?

9. Class is a theme in *The Stark Beauty of Last Things*. In which characters' lives did you feel it was especially potent?

10. What symbolism did you notice in the novel? Did you think the weather was used in a symbolic way?

11. How does the author use metaphor to describe the way Julienne and Clancy each view the other? What was the basis of Clancy's attraction to Julienne? Did you expect Clancy and Julienne to have a romantic relationship?

12. Over the course of the novel, Clancy goes from intense dislike of Theresa to feeling sympathy for her. What do you think is the reason for his change of heart? Did you expect Clancy and Theresa to have a romantic relationship?

13. Who among the main characters are most memorable to you? Why?

14. How would you describe the tone of the book and how it ties in to what you think the author is trying to convey?

15. Are there places that are special to you in the way Montauk is special to the characters in *The Stark Beauty of Last Things?* What makes these places special?

Acknowledgments

This novel has been in the gestation phase for so long I fear I'll overlook some of the many people who deserve my thanks. I'm so appreciative of the communities of which I am a part and for the friends and family who have always been so supportive of my writing.

Thank you to Ed Johann, Bill Akin, and Margueritte Wolfson for reading and fact checking details of Montauk's flora and fauna, fishing industry and town zoning and planning. Thanks as well to detectives Rich Mamay and Mike Mahoney for providing information about policing, arson, and suspicious deaths.

Much appreciation to the Montauk Writers' Group for your support, comradery, and creative zest: Miriam Bloomfield, Ed Johann, Miranda Johann, Maureen Julien, Patti Lieber, Stephanie Krusa, Loretta Kuhland, Genevieve Monks, Vida Penezic, Ken Quinn, Renee Terry, and Joe Totten.

Thanks so much to writer friends for insights, support, and encouragement: Marilyn Berkman, Pamela Bicket, Annette Chandler, Jessica James, Sheila Lewis, Sue Mell, Greg Phelan, Nahid Rachlin, and Robert Rosenberg. A very special thanks to Jane Bosveld for her smart ideas (including that of a map—with a whale!) and Jody Winer for her sharp eye and chocolate treats.

I owe a huge debt of gratitude for scholarships and fellowships to Vermont Studio Center, BookEnds (Stony Brook Southampton), the MacDowell Colony, and the Tucson Festival of Books.

Heartfelt thanks to She Writes Press, especially Publisher Brook Warner and Project Manager Lauren Wise, and to the amazing community of writers they've fostered.

Much thanks to publicist Caitlin Hamilton Summie for her creativity and optimism.

Thank you from the bottom of my heart to those writers who were so generous with endorsements: Mia Certic, Tom Clavin, Alice Elliott Dark, Edward J. Delaney, Robert Eversz, Ellen Meeropol, Suzanne Simonetti, and Hilma Wolitzer.

Thank you to my family, especially my sister Merren Keating—you are my first and best reader, every time.

And of course I must thank my husband, Mark Levy, for his encouragement, nagging, and most especially for observing the "cone of silence" when we have to share our workspace.

About the Author

Céline Keating is an award-winning writer living in Bristol, Rhode Island. She is the author of two novels: *Layla* (2011), a Huffington Post featured title, and *Play for Me* (2015), a finalist in the International Book Awards, the Indie Excellence Awards, and the USA Book Awards. Her short fiction and articles have been published in many literary journals and magazines. For many years a part-time resident of New York City and Montauk, NY, Céline continues to serve on the board of environmental organization Concerned Citizens of Montauk. She is the coeditor of the anthology *On Montauk: A Literary Celebration*.

Author photo ©Alexa Brandenberg

SELECTED TITLES FROM SHE WRITES PRESS

She Writes Press is an independent publishing
company founded to serve women writers everywhere.
Visit us at www.shewritespress.com.

Play for Me by Céline Keating. $16.95, 978-1-63152-972-6. Middle-aged Lily impulsively joins a touring folk-rock band, leaving her job and marriage behind in an attempt to find a second chance at life, passion, and art.

The Best Part of Us by Sally Cole-Misch. $16.95, 978-1-63152-741-8. Beth cherished her childhood summers on her family's beautiful northern Canadian island—until their ownership was questioned and a horrible storm forced them to leave. Fourteen years later, after she's created a new life in urban Chicago, far from the natural world, her grandfather asks her to return to the island to see if what was lost still remains.

Ferry to Cooperation Island by Carol Newman Cronin. $16.95, 978-1-63152-864-4. Former ferry captain James Malloy is a loner—but in order to save his New England island home from developers, he'll have to join forces with the woman who stole his job.

A Drop in the Ocean: A Novel by Jenni Ogden. $16.95, 978-1-63152-026-6. When middle-aged Anna Fergusson's research lab is abruptly closed, she flees Boston to an island on Australia's Great Barrier Reef—where, amongst the seabirds, nesting turtles, and eccentric islanders, she finds a family and learns some bittersweet lessons about love.

The Moon Always Rising by Alice C. Early. $16.95, 978-1-63152-683-1. When Eleanor "Els" Gordon's life cracks apart, she exiles herself to a derelict plantation house on the Caribbean island of Nevis—and discovers, with the help of her resident ghost, that only through love and forgiveness can she untangle years-old family secrets and set herself free to love again.

Bridge of the Gods by Diane Rios. $16.95, 978-1-63152-244-4. When twelve year-old Chloe Ashton is abducted and sold to vagabonds, she is taken deep into the Oregon woods, where she learns that the old legends are true: animals can talk, mountains do think, and deep in the forests, the trees still practice their old ways.